Praise for Larry Beinhart

American Hero:

"Funny, ingenious and outrageous."
—Richard Eder, *Los Angeles Times*

"Incomparably funny, clever, and inspired—the most
absorbing story I've read in some time."
—Katherine A. Powers, *The Boston Globe*

"An absolutely marvelous time . . . a Hollywood superbly
imagined."—Carolyn See, *The Washington Post*

Foreign Exchange:

A *New York Times* Notable Book of the Year, 1992

"Larry Beinhart writes well, the way that Elmore Leonard
and Douglas Adams write well."—UPI

"Sparkling international escapade . . .
a witty, near-perfect caper." —*Publishers Weekly*

"A witty, stylish thriller."
—*Times Literary Supplement* (London)

"A slick, well-crafted thriller."—*Sunday Telegraph* (London)

"A delicious and devious thriller."—*Daily News*

"A cynical, at times hilarious book, by an elegant writer."
—*The New York Times*

The
LIBRARIAN

by Larry Beinhart

NATION
BOOKS

NEW YORK

To Gillian Farrell
Muse
and for Larry Berk
Librarian
Keeper of the Flame

The LIBRARIAN

Chapter ONE

"WHEN MEN PLOT to rule the world," the old man said, "they do it in plain sight."

He said this outdoors, in the bright sunshine, on a splendid day in early autumn, one of those days when the light is pure and the breeze is kind rather than cutting and the air is full of nature's scents. Horses ran in the distance, beautiful things.

What was left of his hair was white and thin. He wore a tweed cap and a quilted parka.

The other old man was twenty years younger. He had gray hair and he wore a cashmere coat over his suit but he had cross-trainers on his feet for comfort. He said, "No enterprise is more likely to succeed than one concealed from the enemy until it is ripe for execution." He mumbled and it was only because the man in the cap was already familiar with Machiavelli that he caught it.

"Tactics," the older man said, "you keep your tactics secret, but you can't hide that you're at war."

"What about Pearl Harbor?"

"Pah," the older man said. "We knew, or should have known, that we were on a collision course with Japan. They were trying to conquer all of Asia and we were denying them oil. Oil. What else were they going to do?"

"And the terrorists?"

"Al-Qaeda and Hizbollah and all the others, there's no secret, never was any secret about what they want to do. They preach it in the mosques, on the street corners. It has to be in plain sight, to convince, to recruit."

The other man shook his head as if unconvinced. He was here to pick up a check, a bundle of checks, to keep the money flowing that kept his man in office. He didn't mind listening, he just wasn't buying.

"We're this close to it," the old man said, holding his thumb and forefinger less than an inch apart, "to ruling the world. And we have done it in plain sight. From Manifest Destiny to preemptive war. Of course we say we do it for the world's own good, but that doesn't make it a secret."

The sun felt good and both men kept their faces turned toward it for the warmth that old men crave. They didn't really look at each other but they understood each other and the younger of the pair murmured sounds of agreement, satisfied sounds.

"The only thing that could ruin it," the first man said, "would be if he loses this election. Set us back . . ." He gestured to indicate some length of time that was not forever, but was certainly too long.

"We won't," his friend said, thinking about the check and the many like it and the hundreds of millions of dollars they had for the campaign. If you counted all the PACS and the interest groups and the state party organizations and the church groups, they might well be rolling up on a billion. The thought made him feel warmer and cozier than the sun.

"Just in case," the old man said.

"What?"

"I have a plan."

"Well," the younger man said, indicating he would listen out of respect and because of the money but also implying that he didn't think they needed any special plan.

"You'll like this," the old man said, peering out from under his cap, cunning and pleased with himself for being so cunning.

The man in the cashmere overcoat leaned closer, intrigued, because he knew how smart the old man was. He didn't expect it to be anything that they would ever do, but he was curious to hear it.

"This is not grand strategy," the old man said. "This is tactics. So you will want to keep this secret. Very secret."

Chapter

Two

ELAINA WHISTHOVEN LOVED books and presumed they would love her back and she wanted to serve humanity, so she became a librarian. She wore large glasses and had large curls that were always clean and always brushed and never styled. She lived like a nun on her meager starting salary in a room she rented from a retired professor and his elderly wife, empty because their own children had grown up and gone west.

When I fired her, her mouth opened but she couldn't speak. I thought she wavered where she stood. She was slender and probably had an attractive body under her dowdy clothes, but to imagine undressing her, even mentally, would have made me feel like I was the Marquis de Sade disrobing Justine as the prelude to sordid and perverse desecrations.

When I fired her I felt like I'd broken some delicate flower, snapped its stalk, and crushed its petals.

She had done nothing wrong. Nothing at all. I told her that.

Her mouth moved, I couldn't hear the words, but I knew she'd said, "I must have."

"No, no, your work was very good," I said, trying to repair the damage that I was watching myself do. She stood there and I could see that my words had no effect and the tearing apart was continuing, down from her eyes, through her slender, quivering neck to her chest. I was frantic to explain, and I said, "The national budget, you see, it was designed to destroy government services." I didn't know if she disagreed with that as an unacceptable allegation or she was just stuck like a fawn who had wandered out on the highway. "And that has had its effect on our state, as with so many others." I thought she shook her head slightly. "I know our president said he was the education president and it's hard to imagine that he's deliberately set out to destroy public education, but he has and it has hit our school along with all the rest. The chancellor of the university has a privately funded study that he received from the Heritage Institute, on libraries, both public libraries and academic libraries, and it says that there are far too many physical volumes. That all of this can be replaced, except for some rare volumes of historic value, perhaps, by a great cyber-library, one library for all, accessed from our home and office PCs. That would cut down on the need for almost all librarians, except for the cyber ones and it would make all this space available." I gestured to the reading rooms and stacks outside my office, both on this floor and down below four levels and one up above. "That would create additional savings by cutting the need for capital construction. This could be turned into classrooms, or dorm rooms, which actually earn money."

"Personally," I said, "I like books," and I thought

she might cry and I might, too. She, for her crushed sense of self, and myself, from guilt and love of books, poetry even, "and," I said, emphatically, "I don't like reading anything serious on a screen and I feel, though I don't have the funding to prove it, that my feelings are more than a personal prejudice. I've noticed and I'm sure you have, that when students work at computer stations they tend to multitask. While they're supposedly reading they're downloading music and playing games and having instant messenger conversations and looking at . . ." I stopped myself from saying porn but couldn't quite cut off the train of thought and made it, ". . . erotic materials," and still I felt like I'd made an inappropriate remark. It was too much for her and she began to cry and turned and ran out, even as I was saying, "So you see, it's budget cuts, budget cuts, not you."

I didn't think she heard that.

After all that, I didn't think she would ever speak to me again, but some six months later, on a fine day in early autumn, at the beginning of the new semester, she showed up at the library and asked to see me. She looked stressed but determined and I remember that she wore a blue dress with a floral design on it. And sensible shoes. "I have a job," she said.

Rarely have I felt such relief. "That's wonderful," I said.

"I work, I have a job," she said, sort of a stutter, "in a private library sort of situation."

"That's good," I said.

"You've heard of Alan Carston Stowe," she said. It was not a question. But I nodded yes, I'd heard of him. I didn't know his age offhand, but he was quite old. He lived on a great estate not too far away. He had inherited significant tracts of land in Virginia and realized that he could subdivide, build, and sell, and make a profit. Not a startling revelation perhaps, but he took to it with rare will and enthusiasm and went into the business of buying more land, subdividing, building, and selling. Then he added malls and industrial parks and was one of our national leaders in the creation of sprawl. He probably wasn't the first or the only one, but he got a lot of credit for introducing McMansions, the SUVs of the new home market.

"It's only part-time," she said. "Two or three hours, in the evening."

"Well, still," I said.

"I, I lied . . . no, no, I didn't lie, Mr. Hauser . . ." that was the retired professor she rented a room from, ". . . it was when I still, during the severance period, when I was still receiving my severance that I applied for the job, Mr. Hauser made me say that I was still working because that would give me a better chance at the job and then he said if I weren't making any money at all he would have to kick me out and I would be homeless and I would not be very good at being a homeless person."

"It's OK," I said. "Technically it wasn't a lie, it was OK. You're a good person, Elaina."

"I need your help," she said.

"What can I do?" I asked her.

"I need . . . I have some stress," she said. "I need to not go to work for a few days."

"What?" I mumbled, asking what it had to do with me.

"I'm very afraid of losing the job, so I thought perhaps if I could get someone to cover for me, it would be all right and I wouldn't get fired for not coming in."

"Why not just call in sick?"

She shook her head, full of terror. She was such a nervous mouse. I pulled out my staff list, wondering who would appreciate a few extra hours a week. Or I should say, who would appreciate it most, as we all needed it? I mentioned a few names and realized she was moving her head in a way that meant no, nothing so emphatic as a shake, but it was clear that I had gotten the wrong message.

"What is it, Elaina?"

"Would you do it?" she blurted.

"I don't know," I said. "There are several . . ."

"I'm really afraid of losing this job. I asked Mr. Stowe and he asked who there was and I mentioned Inga, Ms. Lokisborg, and he said that would be all right, after all she's the head librarian, but . . . but . . ."

"What is it?"

"She refused. She got angry with me."

"I'm sorry."

"So I thought, perhaps, you're head of library services, actually . . ." rather than say that I was higher than Inga, she made a gesture, ". . . and I know you would do the best job and so if you went, they wouldn't be disappointed. Please," she said.

In the ordinary course of things, I'm sure I would have said no, but when the petals that you've crushed drag themselves up from their crumpled place in the mud, and ask you to rescue them, what can you say?

That evening, promptly at 6:30, I arrived at Stowe Stud Farm, which was where old man Stowe lived. It had not been subdivided. It was 230 acres of prime real estate. If you've ever gone to England and done a tour of the stately homes with ponds dug out and hills raised up to create the bucolic fantasies of landscape architects like Capability Brown, sheep-cropped lawns and fences stacked from flinty native stone and ancient trees standing noble and alone with nothing but well-groomed grass at their feet, then you've some idea of the place.

I had made Elaina call ahead, so at least I was expected.

It was a working horse farm. I only saw the horses from the window of my fourteen-year-old Saab, but from what I did see, they looked to be as groomed, glossy, and costly as the land itself.

A man in a sort of uniform answered the door and it came to my mind that he must be the butler, but I'd never been to a home with a butler before, so I didn't know and I didn't ask, in case he was the son and just dressed in a peculiar way. When I introduced myself he led me into the house. What filet mignon is to a Big Mac, this house was to Stowe's McMansions. It was the dream that they were the ticky-tacky imitation of and a blow-by-blow and detail-by-detail description of the wood and the paintings and the polish and the carpets and the furniture will not alter that simple essence in any useful way.

The library was wonderful, the literary portion of the dream that was the house. While we were closing earlier and earlier and cutting Sundays and holidays and our walls were blank and barren and the steel shelves were unadorned and it all flickered under that shuttering light that fluorescents put out, this had mahogany shelves and tungsten lighting and fine comfortable furniture.

Stowe was old and had the look of a crank about him. "Where's Miss Lokisborg?" he said.

"She wasn't available," I said. "Actually I'm head of library services and Ms. Whisthoven hoped you would find my qualifications satisfactory."

"Well, well, you tell Miss Lokisborg what she's missing. You'll do, I suppose. You know the assignment, do you?"

"Well, somewhat," I said, "but you can tell me if you like."

"Shouldn't have to tell you. Workers should know their job. All my people know their jobs, or they're out on their cans. You will be, too, if you get it wrong."

Libraries are free places. They are clean, dry places in a stormy world. They are full of ideas and information. With all of that together, they tend to collect kooks and wackos and people who bring shopping carts with them, filled with conspiracy theories. Even a university library with restrictions on access and with campus security. There are, after all, quite a few members of the faculty and student body who have wandered off the deep end of the pier. Over the years I've grown accustomed to them and learned to think of them as harmless and I'm never offended by them and I've learned that the best way to handle them, if there's no incidence of a physical violation, is on their own terms. Stowe seemed like one of them, so I treated him like one of them and nodded along, neither offended nor patronizing.

"There are secrets here," he said, "great secrets."

"I'm sure," I said.

"Sign," he said, and slid a set of papers toward me across the reading table at which he sat. I looked down and the wood on which the black-and-white page rested was so deeply polished that the ceiling and the lights and old man Stowe and my hand and arm were all reflected in it and we looked like the distorted dwarves who live in the mud world at the bottom of the river.

The pages themselves were a confidentiality agreement. It was boilerplate, the basic statement that a corporation or a rich man makes to a poor man, that if you tell my business, I am entitled to ruin you, strip the shirt from your back, remove the shelter from over your head, take the wheels from your ride as well as whatever monies you have put aside as comfort in your old age. Of course, I signed, assuming that he would not have anything that I would have any need, or desire, to disclose. After all, I was only going to be there two days while Elaina rested or went to the doctor or whatever she was doing.

"Do you like poetry?" he asked, while I patted my pockets for a pen.

"Yes, I do, very much," I said.

"I mean the real kind, with rhymes!" he said. "And something to say!"

"Like, 'You may talk o' gin an' beer when you're quartered safe out 'ere,'" I said, reciting "Gunga Din." I suppose I was subconsciously prompted by the twenty-six bound-in-red-leather complete works of Rudyard Kipling on the shelves.

It is the story of an Indian water boy serving the British Army, who is so loyal to his masters that he takes a bullet for the British soldier who is the narrator. It is a paean to Imperialism and full of casual racism—'for all 'is dirty 'ide, 'e was white, clear white inside . . .' Nonetheless, Kipling had great gifts, almost unequaled gifts, powerful narratives, comfortable colloquialisms, his poems are full of humanity and they march along in perfect step like the tramp of well-trained infantry, they never strain for rhymes, indeed, the rhymes are often so strong that they feel as if the things they say could never have been said any other way:

> *I shan't forgit the night*
> *When I dropped be'ind the fight*
> *With a bullet where my belt-plate should 'a' been.*
> *I was chokin' mad with thirst,*
> *An' the man that spied me first*
> *Was our good old grinnin', gruntin' Gunga Din.*

> *'E lifted up my 'ead,*
> *An' 'e plugged me where I bled,*
> *An' 'e guv me 'arf-a-pint o' water—green;*
> *It was crawlin' an' it stunk,*
> *But of all the drinks I've drunk,*
> *I'm gratefullest to the one from Gunga Din.*

He's the poet of boys' adventures, as well as imperialism, and I did love him, memorized him, obviously, when I was ten, maybe eleven years old. There's something noble, you know, in boys that age, that innocently aspires to be rootin', tootin', gun-totin' cowboys and Indian scouts and explorers, members of the King's own Musketeers and, yes, soldiers of the Queen.

Stowe had been a ten-year-old boy, too, once upon a time, and he learned those poems back then and now he mumbled along and urged me on, to the rousing, sentimental finale:

> *An' just before 'e died,*
> *"I 'ope you liked your drink," sez Gunga Din.*

So I'll meet 'im later on
At the place where 'e is gone—
Where it's always double drill and no canteen;
'E'll be squattin' on the coals
Givin' drink to poor damned souls,
An' I'll get a swig in Hell from Gunga Din!

Yes, Din! Din! Din!
You Lazarushian-leather Gunga Din!
Tho' I've belted you an' flayed you,
By the livin' Gawd that made you,
You're a better man than I am, Gunga Din!

He rang a hand bell and the maid came in within seconds and he said, "Rita, get me a drink," and he didn't have to explain to Rita what he wanted a drink of, or how it was to be made, "and give the librarian one, too."

It was some sort of expensive bourbon, but I had no way of knowing which because it was in a decanter. I sipped appreciatively, as did he, though he drank faster and deeper than I did. "When I was a boy," he said, "the map was red. I don't mean the Communists," he added with a snap.

"I understand what you mean," I said. I remembered those world maps, still in common use up through the mid-fifties, in which tiny England and the British Empire—or the Commonwealth—were always marked in red and the territories were vast, Canada and India and Australia and much of Africa and the protectorates of the Mideast and the outposts on the Asian side of the Pacific and if you spun a globe you could see that it was literally true that the sun never set on the British Empire.

"It was Kipling," he said, "who told the Americans that it was up to us to pick up the torch."

"Right," I said. More specifically what Kipling had said was that we were to pick up the "white man's burden," in a poem of that title, published in *McClure's* magazine in 1899.

"And we have, son, we have."

"Um," I said.

"This is my life," he said, and he pointed, vaguely, with a waggling finger, at the corner of the room where the lower shelves where filled with papers and there were, as well, plastic storage boxes with snap-top lids stacked two deep, in front of those lower shelves, "and lots more, warehouses full. To work, to work!"

The work itself seemed uncomplicated and easy enough. Most of his papers and memories seemed to be about land he had despoiled and turned into money. My egalitarian instincts notwithstanding, once I accepted that the staff was there to be used, I mostly found the business of having a staff to be quite pleasant. Rita, the maid, was the person to ask for coffee, or any other refreshments. I was to tell Bill, the butler, when I was ready to leave and he would have my car brought round. They both called me sir. I said I was an employee like themselves and sir didn't seem appropriate and Bill said, "Yes, sir." And Rita said, "Of course, sir."

I was at home the third day and Bill called and asked where I was. I said, "I'm just substituting, I was just substituting for Elaina. For two days, she said. I thought she'd be back."

"Oh, dear," Bill said. "She's not here and Mr.

Stowe is upset. He was looking forward to the work, you see."

"I don't know," I said. "It's been a long day."

"If it would help," Bill said, "I could send the car for you. I know driving is stressful for so many of us."

I had never had "the car" sent for me, in my whole life. So I said yes.

It was a large BMW, very large. The driver was named Raymond. He was polite but had a fearsome mien.

The next day, Bill called me at the college. He had not been able to reach Elaina and rather than have her not show up and then have to scramble, could he ask that I come once again? If I liked, Raymond would pick me up directly from the school and the cook would prepare a light repast for me, too, if that would help, the old man liked his project, you see. When Elaina continued not to show up, I continued to take her place and became Mr. Stowe's librarian.

I saw, in his account books, that cutting the fields and forests and hills into half-acre plots had been profitable. He had turned a mere few millions into one point eight billion. "I do want to make it two before I die," he said. Then one day he said, "They would have stopped me, you know."

"Oh, really," I said.

"That prick Roosevelt," he said. "Wanted to make this a socialist country."

I made one of those mumbling assents that you make to the ramblings of a loon.

"Well, well, we're rolling him back. That's why," he said, his voice and volume rising with enthusiasm, "this is the goddamn *Second* American Century. That's

why we didn't stop with just one." Then, in a softer
voice, almost an aside, he said, "Took a lot of money. I
myself delivered cash to three different presidents. The
notes are in there somewhere."

Chapter

THREE

JACK MORGAN STOOD very straight and looked the older man square in the eye.

They were gray eyes, and he had gray hair and his face had a gray pallor that made him look like he should have died a while ago, or if not then, sometime very soon. But it was because he seemed to pull at the world with invisible strings and was in touch with subterranean forces that Morgan, like many others, thought of him as the Gray Man.

The Gray Man was in no sort of shape at all, his muscle tone was bad and he moved awkwardly, and there was a flabbiness around his mouth, but those eyes were as hard and opaque as the hull of the battleship *Missouri*. He seemed completely unaware that he was physically unprepossessing, indeed, quite the opposite—he cloaked himself in wealth and power and his connections to more wealth and power, and he dominated the room.

"The old fool has another librarian. How did that happen?" the Gray Man asked.

Meaning, How did it happen without anybody knowing for so long? How had this librarian fellow slipped in under the radar? How did *Morgan* let it happen?

"I take responsibility, sir," Jack said, smartly, militarily; a leader takes the weight. He may kick ass when he gets back to battalion—that being a metaphoric generality, there was no battalion, but he did have subordinates—but in front of his superiors, he takes the weight. The Gray Man had a gaze so bleak that he didn't even have to say, "Fuck that," and Morgan heard him loud and clear, and said, "I'll clean it up. You can count on me."

"Don't do more than is necessary, but do what is necessary."

The Gray Man often spoke that way, homely versions of martial arts koans. Ostensibly it gave his subordinates "guidance," but what it really did was set things up so that if things went well the Gray Man got the credit and if things went badly the subordinate took the blame. It was a method that had served him well in his rise to power, first in the corporate world and then in the political world, and continued to do so. A method to be admired and emulated, but it wasn't something Jack could do, it was too political, too conniving, and Jack believed in the military virtues, which had limited his rise in the military as well.

"The problem," Jack said, "is that we can't do surveillance at the Stowe place. He has his own security people sweep it daily. They are, of course, the best."

"There's no cooperation?"

"We tried," by God, how Jack hated saying *tried*. Never say *try*—Do! "And the household staff is very,

very loyal. Generally speaking, it's not a problem because we're all on the same side. I mean, who more than Alan Stowe is on the right side?"

"For his own good," the Gray Man murmured. "Age takes its toll."

"I'll drop in," Jack said. The last librarian had been easy, even too easy. He would handle this one. "I'll take care of it personally." Then Jack had a stroke of genius. "Since Stowe seems set on this project, I'll just suggest that we help him find someone secure, truly secure, and we can slip our own man in."

The Gray Man gave him that rictus grimace, lips tight, turned down, that those who knew him knew to be a smile. That was the sort of thinking he liked. He even murmured, "The backside of a problem is an opportunity."

Jack swelled with pride and pleasure, but kept his cool and simply nodded and said, "Yes, sir."

Chapter

Four

"YOU MUST NOT work for that man," Inga Lokisborg said.

Forty-seven years in this country and still with an accent thick as hand-cut bread.

As head librarian, Inga is in charge of the room that's called the library and the physical volumes and the stacks in back and below and the staff that works there. She's a crone, judgmental, and, by librarian standards, fierce. The lines in her face are like the fissures in layered shale, her eyes, overall, are the color of slate, but there are chips in them the color of bluestone, which is what the sidewalks of New York were once upon a time made of, back when the streets were paved with cobblestones.

"He is an evil person," she pronounced. Her fist shook like she was rattling the runes and was about to cast them, just for verification, because she knew already that this was an ill-fated voyage.

"He despoils the land," she said. Which was true. If

you're one of those people who believes that sprawl and malls and straight-line, eight-lane motorways where forests and meadows used to be, and still could be, are bad things.

"He's an old man," I said. "I won't say he's harmless, but he's starting to slide away."

"He corrupts people," she said, that fist moving, and I thought I could hear the clicking of the stones. *Throw them already,* I wanted to say, though they weren't there, *and pronounce whatever curses you imagine, and get them done with.* "He takes people and tempts them and destroys them."

I vaguely recalled that there had been some incident. Long ago. Her husband had entered into a real estate deal and thought he would get rich, but instead he lost a lot of money and accumulated a lot of bitterness from people he had brought into the deal with him and there was a Wal-Mart and Sam's Club and a Burger King and a Toys "R" Us and around those big players, there were sets of strip malls, and three old-fashioned, regular small towns had slowly folded, store by store, and then collapsed inward into peeling public assistance zones.

Her husband had been a well-known teacher of the classics, with some family inheritance to elevate his lifestyle, a very genteel sort of life. He'd had a first wife. Once Inga had been young, that gray hair, brittle and stiff, had been sunshine braided down her back and the breasts she now hid in shapeless sweaters had been succulent and proud and when her skin caught the sun it turned honey brown and the blue in her eyes were hints of sunlit seas, a Viking girl, you could get drunk on her juices like they were mead and run riot—or so

I imagined it—perhaps I was wrong, but whoever she'd been then, this professor of classics, yes, Latin and Greek, was indeed intoxicated by her, his student, and lit up the campus with scandal, and he left that other wife of seventeen years, whom I've never known, it was long ago, leaving her behind for this exchange student from Norway.

Left the one, married the other, then had varieties of happiness and misery. I was not intimate with either the details or with the husband or with Inga herself, in spite of our long working association, and he died before her and she remained a widow. She had a pension from him and they owned the small home they'd moved into after he'd lost the big house, so she lived all right on her librarian's pay. With the lines and the gray, being nobody's passion, she was still vibrant and fierce and into business that was none of her business.

"The summer's been tough," I said. The university tries, quite valiantly, to stay in business through the summer. Every financial officer we've had these last twenty years, and every outside consultant, has declaimed that we must treat the college more like a business! Closing the plant, in any business, three months a year, is a huge waste of overhead and a terrible failure to maximize return on capital investment. So we try to keep the factory in use through all those summer months and we host seminars and conferences and we rent out dorm rooms. We've tried sport camps and three years ago we had a invasion of Little Leaguers but the organizers underestimated the amount of supervision modern ten-to-twelve-year-olds require and the drug, sex, alcohol, vandalism, and hazing incidents put an end to that. We now have a convention manager and she's gotten a few takers, the Tri-State Health Food Distributors Conference, a Philosophy and Art History Majors Job Fair, and a Hyundai course on service and warrantees for salesmen and dealer service managers.

Unfortunately, none of these activities requires library services, so in the interest of rational economics, library hours are cut way back during the summer months and so is my salary. "I could use the money."

"And whose fault is it that you need an extra job? That all of our wages are lower than they used to be, in real dollars? Whose fault is that? Whose fault is it that the university is cutting back and back, on teachers and on libraries? What is a university if it is not teaching and scholarship? It is a disgrace!"

"Look, Inga . . ."

"And," she declaimed, "he's one of those elephants, one of those rampaging elephants!"

"What are you talking about?"

"You know what I'm talking about!"

"You mean one of the Golden Elephants?" Actually Stowe was a charter member of the Elephant Society, made up of big contributors to the Republican Party. The Golden Elephants were individuals who brought in at least one hundred other men who each then contributed the full two-thousand-dollar contribution to the candidate allowed by law, each Golden Elephant being two hundred thousand dollars lumbering around the center ring of the circus of American politics. I was brand-new at Stowe Stud and I'd already heard Stowe on the phone, two or three times raising those funds. *Politics,* he told potential donors, *is one of the businesses of business. Put the right people in and your giving will return to you tenfold.* Then he'd launch into some specific anecdote, like how big coal gave and gave to President Scott's first campaign and in return they got their own guy, *their own lobbyist,* appointed as undersecretary of the Interior.

"You see," Inga said. "You know exactly what I'm talking about!"

"It's not like it's any of your business," I said.

"It's everyone's business," she said passionately. "Money is ruling this country like it never has before and every single one of us has to stand up and do something. For the first time we have a truly wonderful candidate for president, somebody who is a decent human being, who is for libraries, free libraries, and doesn't get all her money from the corporations, and that man is spending millions against her. He wants to pound her to her death with moneybags."

Inga was a big fan of the Democratic candidate, Anne Lynn Murphy. Informed opinion had it that Ms. Murphy's campaign was a lost cause, her election an impossibility.

"Listen to me," I said. "A librarian's job is to preserve and disseminate information."

"Not for those people."

"What about the Nixon library? And the Johnson library? And the things we know from them?" It didn't faze her. She kept that sour, dour look, but she wasn't the only one who could rant, "And the Nazis!" I said, "It is because of, it is only because of the meticulous record-keeping of the Nazis that we know the full dimensions of the Holocaust. So even if you want to say that Stowe is Hitler, which he is not, he's an old man, on lots of medications." In fact he kept one of those plastic containers nearby at all times, ten inches long, three inches deep, divided into twelve compartments, different pills in each mini-section, and with a note to say how many to take and when to take them. Really, there were far too many to remember even for a man in full possession of his accounting principals.

At least a third of them were clearly there to handle the side effects of the first third and those two thirds intersected and interacted in ways that nobody could determine or assess, and their combination, I am certain, with my nonmedical expertise, caused the symptoms that caused the doctors to prescribe the third wave of medications. In fact, I suspected that the medication was the source of much of the mental deterioration that I witnessed and he would have been happier and healthier taking nothing but water. But perhaps not. "This monster of yours," I said, "likes story poems with people galloping and carrying pistols, and there were tears in his eyes at a recitation of "The Death of the Hired Man" and "Anathea", too."

"Monsters are always sentimental."

"He wanted me to tell you what you're missing."

"Everything that man touches comes to a bad end. You should stay away."

"Never mind," I said, and I started to walk away.

"Just tell me," she said. "How can you do it?"

"Listen, I didn't go looking for the job. Elaina asked me to cover for her for a couple of days. She asked you first, but you didn't want to do it. Then she didn't show up. So they asked me to keep covering. Which I've been doing. Now, she's disappeared and they need a librarian. Even with the new semester, they want me, evenings, weekends, whatever I can do. Case closed, not your business."

"You don't find anything sinister in that?"

"In what?"

"Elaina disappearing."

"No. She's that kind of person, who has trouble dealing with the real world and probably just took off."

"Hah!"

Chapter
Five

ANNE LYNN MURPHY was used to lost causes and impossible objectives.

The first time she'd really taken up a lost cause had been her first day in Vietnam. She'd gone to nursing school in St. Louis and when the army recruiters came around she signed up because they told her that was where she was needed the most. What they didn't tell her was that she'd get off the plane, into a jeep, and be rushed to a field hospital. They didn't tell her that she'd be administering morphine to screaming dying boys her own age. Sometimes younger. Sometimes a bit older. That she'd hold them down while doctors, fresh from med school, cut shattered bones off neatly, just above the knee, using saws, and then they would flush the raw flesh as the blood oozed, flowed, spurted, splashed, drooled, pumped out, they would sew and cauterize and splash Bactine over it all and flap the flesh around the stump and sew it up tight. Didn't tell her that after doing that all day, the first day, and on into the night, that as darkness fell, they themselves would come under attack and to make it to the latrine; if she didn't want to die, she had to slither doubled over in a double-time walk. Didn't mention any of that.

That first night they'd brought in a boy name of Kenny. PFC Kenneth Michael Sandusky. Lost his legs, lost his genitals, lost one arm. One good eye, one eye iffy. Shrapnel or whatever it was, bits of metal of something that exploded up into his chest, too. The surgeons had chopped off the raggedy skin and the shattered bones and slapped it back together. A major, a surgeon, she remembered his name, it was Konigsberg, Major Konigsberg told her, told her softly, told her gently, his voice tired and sad, but trying, really, to help her, he said, "Give him lots of morphine and let him die."

"No," she'd blurted in that young nurse, naive, idealistic way. Young nurses didn't do that. No nurse she'd ever heard of, then, would do that. Later on, of course, well, later on . . . she'd seen it happen more than once and later on she thought, sometimes when it was very bad and she was very tired, tired as Konigsberg was that night, that it was the Lord's own mercy and it was for the best.

But that first night, she cried out, "No."

"The weather's bad," he said. Which was true, it was raining hard, coming down, a thousand million miniature drums on the canvas tents, and she always thought that some military musician should write a song of violent military death with that sound in it. "The medevac can't come." The choppers couldn't get the boy out to a real hospital and they weren't equipped here, in the tents, to handle that much damage, they were sort of a halfway house between the medics who ran to the wounded under fire and the full-fledged care the kid needed.

· "No," she said, again, anyway.

She stayed up beside Kenny's cot and when he woke, moaning and crying, she tended to him, mopped the sweat, gave him some more morphine, but not so much he could drift off and die.

When PFC Kenneth Sandusky came awake enough to realize what fate and friendly fire or somebody's land mine caused, he never really was sure what had happened, just noise and pain and waking in the hospital with this young nurse and then this horror, this utter horror, the worst dread a young man could have, worse than fear of cowardice, worse than fear of death, to be a helpless, sexless, useless thing who would need care the rest of his pathetic, joyless life. He woke to that and this nurse. This stupid fucking, fucking bitch who would not let him die. Who said stupid fucking things like if God wants you to die, He'll take you, if He wants you to live you better do it, you'll find joy or duty in it or something.

When he could talk he begged everyone he could talk to for a mercy killing. One extra shot baby, one extra shot. Lemme float off to wherever we go to. Help me baby, somebody help me, please help me die.

And this stubborn young nurse who had just landed in this hellhole of duty and death and murder and burning flesh, kept saying no, and sitting with him and holding his good hand and kissed him sometimes, too.

The weather broke for a few hours and Sandusky was still alive after three days and they took him to Saigon and kept him there a week, two weeks, three weeks, then flew him to Hawaii and into a VA hospital.

Some fifteen years later Kenny was watching TV and he was watching this medical show and the host was a woman doctor from some Podunk town in Idaho. It had been picked up and it was syndicated and Kenny was feeling miserable in a fucking VA hospital, which was how he was spending his miserable life, though he'd come to like drawing and painting with his one good hand. He could see and liked making something out of that and sharing it, though he didn't get many people who really, really looked and saw what he was doing.

He thought he recognized that woman from those few drug- and pain- and horror-induced hallucinatory days and he badgered a VA orderly to track the show down and get him to the phone and he called the show up and when he said he was calling from a VA hospital they put him right through because the woman on the show had given standing orders to put anybody calling from a VA hospital right through to her, no matter who, no matter what, no matter when, and he asked her if she had been that nurse.

She said she had been a nurse in Vietnam and gone back to medical school after and she asked his name and when he told her, she said, "Oh, Kenny, I remember you. How are you?"

"Not so good," he said. "Pretty miserable, in fact."

"I'm sorry," she said. And then asked him about his life and when he told her about the drawing she asked if she could see some and he said sure, he would send some, and he did. Then there came a call and she asked him if he would like to do the graphics for her show. She said she'd liked what he was saying with his good hand, there was something about it, she said.

"I don't need your fucking pity," he said, "or are

you trying to make yourself feel better for making the mistake of saving me when you should have let me go."

"I showed your work to my producer," she said. "He likes it, too. You want to do it or not?"

"Sure," he said. "Why the fuck not?"

So Kenneth Sandusky redesigned their logo. Then did a series of illustrations that they also used. Two years later he moved out of the VA hospital and up to Idaho and between his veteran's benefits and the money he made off the show he got an apartment with homecare assistance.

Bodies don't like to function with that much missing and they're liable to infections and diseases and dysfunctions of a thousand different kinds. Kenny got another five years out of his life. He got to see Anne Lynn run for Congress the first time. He did the graphics for her campaign. He cheered her on and told her the world needed people like her and before he died, he got to say I'm glad I got these extra years, I didn't think so for a long time, but life is life and better some small piece of it than none at all.

So when they told Anne Lynn Murphy that running for president was a lost cause and that she could never win, short of a miracle, and they weren't making many miracles anymore, it didn't bother her. At least not so much that it would make her stop.

Chapter
Six

TWO, THREE, FOUR in the morning. The night is deep. Sleep is thick and woven in layers. The phone rings. My eyes open, but the room is darker than my dreams and I blink. The sound keeps ripping at my rest and I wish it would stop so I grab at it, grab at the sound. Is this a dream? My hand hits the phone and knocks it off the nightstand and it clatters to the floor, the handset coming off the base, and I reach for it, but I have to get out of bed to get it. A tiny, tinny voice comes out of it, calling my name. In the dark, swearing to myself, I fumble around for it and grab and the voice is still calling my name.

"David? David?"

"Yeah, what?"

"You're all right?"

"Yeah, yeah, who is this?"

"Are you still working for Mister Stowe?"

"Wha'? Yeah. Is this . . ."

"I'm sorry."

"Elaina?"

"Have you seen anything?"

"What are you talking about?"

The phone goes dead.

At that point I was awake or I woke up or I had been awake and I was, without doubt, on the floor with the phone in my hand, but I wasn't entirely sure if the call had been a dream or real. If it was real, what was it about?

Chapter SEVEN

THE CLASSICAL WAY to have approached the job at Stowe's would have been to read the material so as to create subject headings that fit into standard library subject systems and, more or less at the same time, to identify and organize sets of subheadings and appropriate cross-references. It would have been very scholarly and very slow.

With the advent of computers we are moving to key word systems because that's how computers work best. It has its advantages and disadvantages. Basically, what I did was set up a system of scanners and a dedicated computer and I began by feeding the material, in its raw state, onto the hard drive and, of course, backing it up. I hardly read it at all. Just a glance to see if the pieces were dated in some way. If they weren't I'd have to find some way to place them in time, either by internal references or by asking Stowe. The older the material, of course, the more likely he was to be able to recall when it was and what it was related to.

The biggest problems were physical. Loose sheets could be fed in mechanically, like running them through a copy machine. Notebooks, appointment books, and date books had to be handled by hand, a page at a time.

It was only after the material had been entered that I began to try to make good old-fashioned subject-heading sense out of it.

After Elaina's phone call, or after my dream of Elaina's phone call, I began to look for something, anything, that might be of some significance, so significant as to be dangerous to know, though in America today, I couldn't think of that much that would be. Stowe Stud was not a suburb of the Sopranos. I didn't get the sense that Raymond the chauffeur doubled as Ramon the hitman.

That first day, Stowe had said something about conveying money to presidents. That was the closest thing to a clue that I had. I punched in several presidential names. There was no entry for "Nixon, Richard" that was followed by "delivered $100K cash Rebozo house, Key Biscayne." I tried initials and stuff began to turn up, but not something so incriminating that it would be dangerous for me to know.

Stowe was having one of his slightly daffy interludes. Like that first day. I noticed they seem to come about forty minutes after the four o'clock round of pharmaceuticals. He'd begun to mumble a rhyme. His voice was soft and wobbling, full of sentiment, even suggesting tears. I leaned toward him to catch what he was saying.

When the judge he saw Reilly's daughter
His old eyes deepened in his head,

Sayin', "Gold will never free your father,
The price, my dear, is you instead."

"Oh I'm as good as dead," cried Reilly,
"It's only you that he does crave
And my skin will surely crawl if he touches you at all.
Get on your horse and ride away."

She stays and sleeps with the judge, but the judge lets her father hang anyway. It sounds so exactly traditional that you'd think it had to come from the Childe Ballads or from Bobbie Burns's collections, but it's a Dylan song, "Seven Curses," from 1963, and I would never have associated Alan Stowe with Bob Dylan.

Not only that, he also knew "Anathea," written by Neil Roth and Lydia Wood in the same year, and sung by Judy Collins, which tells almost exactly the same story. In "Seven Curses," Reilly stole a stallion, in the Roth/Wood song Lazlo Feher stole a stallion, and they both were bound in iron. In both songs the women offer gold, Reilly's daughter to free her father, Anathea to free her brother, both women give their virtue, both judges break their deals, both women put curses on them.

"Do you know the curses?" he said, sounding plaintive.

I tried to recall. "Something about doctors not being able to heal him."

"Do you think there is such a thing? Such a thing as curses?"

Right then there was a knock on the door and then it swung open. Two people walked in. The most striking thing about the man was his military bearing and as he

said, "Good afternoon, sir," his back got even straighter
and his voice had so many years of military in it that it
seemed as if he had restrain himself from snapping his
hand to his forehead. He had cool blue eyes and hair the
color of sand. He was clearly fit and his suit fit, too. His
shoes were shined. There were Marine Corps emblems
in the pattern on his tie. The knot was neatly tied and
drawn all the way up to his buttoned collar.

I was more interested in the woman who came in
with him. She had fair skin, blue eyes, a deeper blue than
his, an ocean blue, and jet black hair. She had high
cheekbones and a shape to her eyes that suggested
American Indian. But to describe her physical appearance was no more important than listing the paintings
on Stowe's walls or the estimated prices of his furniture.
There was a life there. There was vitality, intelligence,
and mystery.

Though he addressed himself to Stowe and she
smiled at the old man, both of them looked at me. I
drank her in and wondered about him and how it could
be that these two seemed to have so much to do with me.
Or if that was some self-centered illusion.

Remarkably, Stowe pulled himself back into his
adult, billionaire persona. It took about a breath and a
half. It was like some superhero in a comic book
changing forms. "Jack," he said, acknowledging this
loyal lieutenant—his tone of voice made both roles completely clear. "And my dear Niobe," he added.

I heard myself repeat the phrase in my head, *My
dear Niobe*. She looked at me and whatever she thought
about what she saw, she gave nothing away. Less so, Jack.
He looked me over and saw slightly shabby clothes, that
I wasn't marine fit! and that my hair was not cropped

close, it probably had never been buzz cut and it curled, it was curly black hair, and that my eyes are brown.

"This is David," Stowe said.

"Colonel Morgan," Jack said, stepping up to me, sticking out his hand. I knew his handshake would be firm, and braced myself for a macho crunch, which came, as he gave me a stare that sized me up. "David . . . ?" with a silent, what's your last name?

"Goldberg," I said.

"Ah," he said, "Goldberg."

I wanted to say, you anti-Semitic sonofabitch, but the signals were slight and the signs were subtle and they weren't about driving my people into the sea or consigning them to camps with ovens, it was more about consigning me to a set of categories and assumptions and limitations. If I said anything I would have been accused of overreacting. Rightly so. Also, of course, if we went at it, I figured he'd take me down faster than I could see it happen, I'd just find myself on the floor, wondering why it was so damn hard down there. I just said, "Colonel?" with a question mark on it.

"Retired," he said. Though he seemed young, indeed, to have retired.

"Hero of the Second Gulf War," our host volunteered. "Jack was the one who brought out the video footage of the rescue of Jessica Lynch."

"And now?" I asked.

"I'm with Homeland Security," he said, with a tone that said: ask no more, I can say no more.

"Ah," I said. I looked over his shoulder at Niobe. I wanted to write poems about her. Unfortunately I'm not really a good poet and I didn't want to write doggerel about her.

"What's David do?" Jack said to Stowe.

"He's my new librarian . . ." Stowe said, and as I looked back at Jack, I watched my image in his eyes fall farther, I was now one of the spinster women. I panicked a little and looked back to Niobe. She seemed a lot less judgmental than he did. Her eyes seemed to be made of layers of transparencies and secrets and as with one of the good actresses she made you want to rush up to her and ask her what those thoughts were, and then, before she spoke and shattered your hopes, you'd say, wait, don't talk, you'd touch her lips gently and just gaze into her eyes so you could believe she thought the thoughts that you yourself made up for her to be thinking.

All that in the gap, in the comma between phrases, and then Stowe said, ". . . helping me file my papers," and a whole new chain of events began.

"Oh," Jack said. That's all he said. I knew that some strange flares had been lit where secretive sentries hid, and some small action was to be taken, just to be on the safe side, and that action was going to be that he was about to try to get me fired.

Then how would I ever run into this woman, this Niobe, again?

I got the sick, falling feeling, of things about to happen to me that I was powerless to halt or change.

"Do you mind?" Jack said to me. "I need a private moment with Mr. Stowe."

Chapter

EIGHT

NIOBE AND I stepped out of the library and into the hall. My mind was still back in the library, being nervous. There was this woman standing there, looking at me, like she expected something from me. And that was making me nervous, too. I said, "Uh, uh, uh," that was really smooth, then came up with, "I can ring for Rita . . . uh, uh, uh . . . if you want something to drink or eat."

"Thank you, no," she said.

Now what? I said, "I can show you around the grounds . . . uh . . . if you haven't seen them. They're beautiful."

"Yes, they are," she said. "I have seen them."

Well, that wasn't a happening thing. "Well then, I could recite you a poem as I sometimes do for Mr. Stowe."

With that she smiled and laughed and her teeth were white and mostly even, but not entirely, and her laughter was that sound that comes from girls and when it's sweet, it makes the hearts of males goggle with wonder and when it's mean, men know they are defenseless except through violence.

"So, uh," there was that uh again, "I'm David." I put out my hand for a handshake. Oh God, I thought, she already knows that. But, by reflex, she would take my hand in hers and that was good because I got to touch her.

"Niobe," she said, and then the laugh again, but not laughing at me, I was grateful for that, just enjoying herself, "but didn't we know that."

"Yes," I said, still holding her hand, and her not withdrawing it, and I was relaxing a little bit and the chaos in my mind was calming down and I could hear the thoughts I was having about her. "But now we know it . . . differently."

"Oh," she said, and I felt like now that I could read my mind, she could read it, too. Would she be offended by it? No, she didn't seem to be, not that she was going along with it or agreeing to anything, but she wasn't bothered by it.

"And what do you do?" I asked her. I could not, in decency, hold her hand any longer. I let go, reluctantly. But I was pleased to find that she did not whip it away; she let it linger for a heartbeat.

"I'm a statistician," she said.

"I'm impressed," I said. God, I like smart women and don't know how to get along with dumb ones any better than with dull men.

"I have a flare for math," she said, in a self-deprecating way. "Like Dr. Doolittle can talk to the animals, I can talk to the numbers."

"Where do you work?" I asked her.

"The Octavian Institute," she said.

"Ah," I said, or some such sound, some neutral sound, and she asked if I knew it. "Yes, of course," I said. It was one of those conservative think tanks funded by the right. "Named for Octavius Caesar, to study how our Pax Americana should function. What is the proper way for us to rule the world." Then I added, "It's funded primarily by Alan Carston Stowe, so we have the same employer."

Then she said, "You're a librarian," which was something she already knew, so she was fumbling like I was, which I was very pleased to see.

"Keeper of the flame," I said. "I wish, sometimes, that I was the fire, but most of the time, it seems, I'm not, so I'm keeper of the flame. It's a noble profession, in its own modest way."

"Is that why you do it?"

"I stumbled into it, I guess," I said. I noticed the wedding ring on her hand and suddenly Charlton Heston appeared to me, not fronting for the NRA, but bearded and wearing sandals, with lightning and wind and holding the twin tablets, and even though that all happened quick as thoughts can go, it was impossible not to notice Commandment X, "Thou shalt not covet thy neighbor's wife." So I asked her, "Where do you live?'

She said, "We have a condo in Bethesda."

I said, "Oh, we're not neighbors at all."

She smiled and almost laughed, and shook her head slightly, no, but the fact that she got it and found it funny was better than a yes with no understanding at all. But, unfortunately, so long as we were on the subject— if only in our minds—she was reading dear old Number VI, "Thou shalt not commit adultery," and she made it clear, elliptically clear, but clear nonetheless. She said, "That's my husband," referring to the man with military bearing in the next room trying to get me fired, "Jack."

That's all we had. As if on cue, the door swung open and my cartoon balloon was punctured as Jack summoned us back.

Mr. Stowe looked sad as if he didn't want to lose me and was being coerced into it. "David," he said, a little reticent, which surprised me, since he'd decimated small towns all across America and shut down entire industries. Maybe this was part of the secret of his success, the demeanor of reluctance.

"David," he said again.

There was a clattering and a to-do in the hall, and the door came open behind us. We all turned, except Alan, who was looking that way. Senator Bransom strode in. "Alan," he said, with that great, wide, white, capped-tooth smile. It served him well when he was selling cars and it serves him well in Washington. Then he saw Niobe and said, "My dear Niobe, lovely as always, and your husband, the noble colonel." He came to attention and gave Jack a salute, and then he said to me, "David, what a delight to see you here." And all of the other three looked positively astounded that the great Bransom knew the lowly librarian.

The inspiration had come from another librarian, Larry Berk, a wonderful man whom God has mistaken for Job. Larry created an artist in residence program at Ulster County Community College in upstate New York. Community colleges are generally regarded as halfway houses for the not quite good enoughs. Nobody has ever run an artist in residence program in a community college.

Berk believed in poetry and the civilizing power of art and he had the imagination to see that artists were hanging about the Hudson Valley as ripe for the picking as apples in October. For little more than adjunct pay—and no benefits—he was able to bring in world-class writers, actors, dancers, and musicians.

Down here, no matter what the D.C. and Virginia chambers of commerce and tourism tell you, we do not have an oversupply of great, but underutilized, artists. What we do have, like Iowa has soybeans, are politicians. Also aides, consultants, administrators, facilitators, lobbyists, regulators, counselors, bureaucrats, cabinet officers, chiefs of staff, and endless staffers. I started a *politician in residence* program.

Senator Robert Bransom was my third politician in residence. He was, and is, pro-gun, anti-abortion, for making money, against snail darters, for the death penalty, against environmental regulations, he used to be against deficit spending, but now that deficits come from President Scott he thinks deficits are just dandy; he was, and is, for any war, anywhere, any time and if it takes nukes to win it, that's fine, too, provided they're ours.

He could quote Plato in support of his belief that wealth and property need to have more clout than the rabble so as to protect the state. He believed that the Founding Fathers believed that, too, and had put buffers in place to protect the nation from excessive democracy. They were that only white males with property could vote, that senators were to be elected by state legislatures, and that the president and vice president should be elected by electors. The first two have disappeared and the third remains only as a vestigial technicality. We needed, he believed, a new buffer to replace them. It was, therefore, a good thing that political campaigns cost millions of dollars, because it kept the riffraff out.

He was Alan Stowe's kind of guy.

It was my program and I wanted it to be a success, so I recruited every conservative group on campus and every gun-loving, homophobic, sexaphobic, America-firster in the community, and got them to turn up for his reception and then for his lectures. I got some liberals, too, so that there would be "lively discourses." Bransom was thrilled and decided that when he had lived longer than Strom Thurmond and served in the Senate longer, too, he would retire to a position of academic dignity just like the one he experienced here. He made me call him Bob and thought I was the best thing to come down the pike since bundling campaign contributions.

And here Bob Bransom was, all smiles, gleaming veneers and shining caps a little farther back in his mouth, and he put his left arm around me and took my right hand in his right hand, calloused from shaking a million other palms, and said, "What are you doing here, Dave?"

"Moonlighting," I said, "as Mr. Stowe's librarian."

"Well, good for Mr. Stowe," he said, and turned to my employer to add, "You have a good man here. None better."

Jack tried very hard to keep his expression cool and unperturbed, but he looked at me with that look that President Scott has when some country whose ass we've already thoroughly kicked doesn't stay quite as kicked as it ought to and some GIs are shot and a pipeline is bombed.

I, too, tried very hard to keep my face expression-less. I didn't want my relief to show them how much I now wanted this job.

Niobe looked to her husband and then to me, and finally, to herself, mirrored in my eyes.

Chapter
NINE

AUGUSTUS WINTHROP SCOTT found himself when he was ten years old.

He was in Little League. There were six teams in his league, all named after big-league teams. He was on the Yankees. Unlike their namesake, these Yankees sucked. They ended the season two and seven, dead last. Young Augustus threw a fit. His coach said, "Everybody loses sometimes. It's part of the game." Augustus had been born with a silver spoon in his mouth and free passes to Exeter and to Princeton clutched in his chubby little fists. Such a thought had never occurred to him. He reacted the way some children react when they discover mortality, when a prized puppy or a loved grandparent or their mother dies. The fit became a three-day tantrum. Crying, screaming, breaking things, hitting (Chuck Fleagle, the shortstop who made fun of him), and biting (Carlton Tusk, their gardener, a very patient, colored man).

Late in the second day, his mother informed his

father, who came home the following day, the third day of the fit, from work or business or whatever it was he did when he disappeared from home. He hit his son once or twice. That put a temporary halt to the hysteria, a sort of breathing space that lasted long enough for his father to question him.

There was a lot of spluttering and a lot of details about batting orders and a second baseman who couldn't turn a double play and a shortstop who was a crybaby and a pitcher who was wild and a left fielder who didn't seem to know what the word *backup* meant and a third baseman who should've been in right field but he was the coach's son and a detailed history of their losses, but what it came down to was losing, per se, and the statement that the coach had made "everybody loses sometimes." His father, Andrew, could see by the panic in young Augustus's eyes and the twitching of his limbs and the quiver of his lip that he was about to launch himself into wa-wa land again, which Andrew considered the province entirely of women, his wife, the boy's mother, in particular, and not something that men, or boys who intended to become men, should indulge in. So Andrew grabbed Augustus by the ears to get his attention and said, "That's not true."

"It's not?" Augustus said.

"No," his father said. "Some people never lose," he said with calm certainty. He paused a moment and said, "Of course, everybody dies. But that's different."

"Yes," Augustus said, understanding.

His father then proceeded to use his money, influence, and skills—which were significant—to get a new coach, introduce player trades, and create an off-season training program for the rebuilt team. The next season the Yankees tied for first place with the Angels. At the play-off game, Byron Tompkins, a big lug of a kid and the worst player on the Yankees, got in a shoving match with their opponent's star pitcher. Both players were ejected. Byron was no loss to the Yankees, but the loss of their pitcher virtually guaranteed that the Angels would lose.

Byron Tompkins grew up to be President Scott's director of Homeland Security.

Chapter
TEN

HOMELAND SECURITY WAS new, confused, and confusing. It was huge, diffuse, and diverse. There was a rich array of talent spread thither and hither throughout and nobody to really keep track of it and that made it possible for someone like Jack Morgan, who had drive, a mission, and a calling, to create his own organization within the organization, to have his own special teams that belonged to other people on paper but that answered to him in practice.

Morgan didn't like being thwarted. Morgan hated going back to someone like the Gray Man and reporting that the mission had not gone as planned, that he had not accomplished what he had promised to accomplish.

Now he assembled his favorite crew. The kind of crew, he thought proudly, that civilians only saw in the movies: Mark Ryan, Joseph Spinnelli, Randall Parks, and Dan Whittaker, each one ex-military, each one with special talents and training. They met in a conference room assigned to the technology research division. Their

time was billed to the personnel and training depart-
ments of port security. Morgan briefed them on the
librarian.

Ryan smiled. He was, by a large margin, the oldest
of the group, so old that he'd done two tours of duty in
Vietnam as a navy SEAL. He'd collected ears and strung
them on a necklace and he mourned the loss of the wild
and wooly days. "I'll put the fear of God in him," he said.

"No," Jack said. He could be pretty straight with
these guys. They were the kind you could really trust.
"The girl was one thing. Say boo and she twittered
and flew."

"Yeah, that's right," Ryan said, laughing at the
memory and pleasure it brought him.

"This guy's different," Morgan said.

"Thinks he's a tough guy?" Randall Parks said.

Parks was a genuinely tough guy. He'd been an
MP. He'd spent fifteen years answering calls when some
DI came home and caught his wife and started
pounding on her and her boyfriend. Fifteen years going
down to the strip when the boots, fresh out of training,
tougher than leather, full of juice, tanked on crank, full
of themselves, in gangs of maniacal friends just like
themselves, started to mix it up with the jarheads. Parks
was the guy they called when the tough guys needed
some stomping.

After Parks came over to HS he'd had a few problems over detained aliens. He'd been accused of name-
calling some Arabs and using his nightstick to point out
the virtues of telling interrogators whatever their interrogators needed to know. The security of Americans
was at stake. Morgan had pulled Parks out of that mess.
Parks understood loyalty.

"No," Morgan said. "Not a tough guy, a complainer, I figure. Lean on him, he calls the cops. Lean on him *and* tell him not to work for Stowe, he goes directly to old man Stowe. Right now, because of Senator Bransom, this librarian is Stowe's flavor of the month and if Stowe feels we interfered with one of his people improperly, we'll all be doing border patrol in Kafiristan. Before we do anything, we need a reason. I need something on the guy."

"Surveil him," Spinnelli said, as a statement, not a question. Spinnelli was another navy guy, though much younger than Ryan. His tour had been Gulf War One. His field was electronics. He'd left the navy, in fury, when all the high-end stuff, the fun stuff, was privatized out to civilian contractors.

"What's he got, an apartment? House?" Whittaker asked. Whatever it was, Whittaker would get in. He was, by nature, a sneak, a cheat, a blackmailer, a bully, and loved looking down the barrel of a gun at some mope pissing his pants and begging for mercy. In some earlier day, maybe in the twenties or thirties, the period celebrated in Cagney and Bogart and Edward G. Robinson movies, Whittaker would have happily turned to a life of crime. But by the time he was coming up through the juvie justice system he perceived that crime had turned into an African-American franchise and he was getting called a nigger and treated as a nigger and was going to have to join the niggers, and so he joined the army instead. Hooking and crooking and keeping his pants pressed and his salutes sharp and always barking "Yes, sir!" and "No, sir!" he'd made himself useful and survived twenty years. He felt incredibly at home in Homeland Security.

"I don't want any noise, I don't want any blow-back," Morgan said. Then he turned to Parks and said, "Stay on top of it." Then he said, because sometimes understanding helps, "The ultimate goal of this operation is to protect President Scott. So we're protecting Alan Stowe from himself. Over the years Stowe has been involved in a lot of financial transactions. I don't know the details. I don't want to know the details. And most of all I don't want CNN to know the details. This librarian may find information he should not find and do the wrong things with it. That's what we want to prevent.

"However, if we create an incident, some strange small scandal—librarian for major Republican donor killed, murder linked to Homeland Security operative, operative linked to Scott campaign—then the solution is worse than the original problem, like the break-in at the Watergate.

"I want to make sure we're on the same page with this. Right now, Scott is the front-runner. It looks like he'll remain the front-runner, so, all things being equal, maintain the status quo."

"So what's the game plan?" Whittaker asked.

"Keep him under surveillance and check him out from his phone bills to his rectum. If we find something, fine. If he's clean, we wait and watch, very closely, everything wired, and if he makes a wrong move, same thing, we move on him. If he's clean and minds his manners, we wait."

"Speaking of rectums," Parks said, "which way does his wind blow?"

"Hetero," Morgan said.

"You sure?" Parks asked. "He sure? I mean, he's Marion the Librarian."

Whittaker and Spinnelli laughed. Whittaker heartily, Spinnelli uncomfortably, and Parks joined in. He had a dirty laugh. During long boring nights in military lockups his sexuality had become opportunistic. It would be wrong to call him bisexual. Opportunistic was the right word. And predatory.

"If he's bent, maybe we can use it on him," Parks said with a shrug.

"Where you been living," Ryan said. "Not in America. You expose him as gay, what's he gonna get? His own TV show?"

"Hey, you never know what people want to keep kept in the closet."

"Right, whatever," Morgan said. "Find out. It can't hurt to know." But Morgan was certain that the librarian was heterosexual. Niobe had told him so. Niobe was not a metaphor for a litmus test, she was a litmus test. Straight men turned colors in her presence.

It was a plan. It was, given the circumstances, a reasonable, sensible plan. And when he reported to the Gray Man, the Gray Man would understand that this wasn't really a failure, it was discovering that Plan A wouldn't work and then moving immediately into Plan B, and that demonstrated flexibility, responsiveness, and initiative, all things Morgan had always scored high marks on in his fitness reports. The Gray Man would see that. Yet Morgan was uncomfortable and dissatisfied.

"You figure," Parks asked, "that this guy is just some numb nut stumbling around or he's some actual secret agent?"

"Good question," Morgan said, slowly. That was, precisely, the flaw in his thinking. He assumed, just looking at the guy, and from the way it had all come about, that this was a sheer accident and the only real danger was that of dealing with an amateur who might feel the need to turn himself into a public event. But if this Goldberg was a pro, some deep cover, Democratic Party operative, or some Arab terrorist, or spying for Israel, or some other as yet unknown enemy of America, then he would take more than routine steps to avoid routine detection and he might well be successful.

If that was the case, then what was there to do?

The strengths of the secret agent are his weaknesses. The fact that he knows better than to talk on his telephones or even in his home, that he knows not to talk to anyone about his mission, means that he is prey to loneliness and a kind of grinding solitude. He would have been instructed to clam up when questioned and toughen up in the face of threats. Come at him hard and he'd tuck in like a turtle. That was the classic analysis. You didn't even want to play good cop/bad cop with a spy, that would only alert him. Besides, for a spy, the whole world was one constant bad cop, watching him and waiting for him to make a false move, the way to make a spy come unraveled was to offer him understanding, a safe haven, even love.

Morgan knew where his own thoughts were taking him. He felt the shiver, an ugly chill on both sides of his spine, just above his pelvic bone. He hid it and didn't let it show. He needed to be rational about this one. Rationality said that to cover every base he needed someone to get close to Goldberg. Someone smart and subtle.

Morgan didn't have anyone at Stowe Stud. But he did have an agent in place at Stowe's Octavian Institute who already knew the subject. Indeed, his agent reported that the spark was already there. Run with it. Let Niobe get close to the librarian, sympathize, admire, flatter, flirt a little. Lead him on. The steady pumping of Morgan's heart dropped a beat, then stuttered; then he focused, as he did in the dojo, and it all steadied. Modern days, modern ways, in today's armed forces women go into combat, ancient days, ancient ways, there have always been warrior women, and he had chosen one, should he let her do her duty? Duty. For the cause. So, admiration, sympathy, flattery, flirtation, and the librarian would open up.

Chapter
ELEVEN

LUCK. IT SEEMED as if luck had played a big part in this campaign. More than in most. Anne Lynn Murphy had to count herself lucky, very lucky, to be the Democratic nominee.

After she came home from Vietnam she was restless and unsettled. A lot of her friends were drinking a lot and smoking a lot of reefer. It was worse among the combat vets, but it was happening with the nurses, too. Nobody was understanding it too well or even acknowledging, in those days, that there was a special problem.

She needed something to get involved in, something to hang on to, that would keep her from going there with them. She applied to medical school and was accepted and once she was in she realized that she could get lost in the work, she *had* to get lost in the work, and that she liked that. It was her way out. Once she graduated she liked the insane hours of her internship. By then it had become clear that there was something going on, generally, with Vietnam vets and what used to be called shell shock in one war and combat fatigue in another was now renamed PTSD, post-traumatic stress disorder, and that gave her a name to go with the symptoms scattered like shrapnel through the veterans. A name helped because it allowed her to put it in a category and make a categorical decision. She could either continue to hide in a frantic work schedule or she could find some quiet time to face herself. She became a country doctor, up in Idaho.

A TV producer in Boise decided it would be nice to have a once-a-week medical advice segment on the local news. He knew Dr. Murphy, liked her, and asked her to do it. He later asked her to marry him and she did that, too.

But before their personal life had gone that far, the segment had become quite popular. Popular enough that the station gave her a half-hour show on Sunday, stuck between God and football, which turned out to be a pretty good place to be. She became a local celebrity. The show got syndicated and she became known nationally, in a relatively very minor way. More important, she developed the TV manner, the Oprah, Donohue, Reagan, Clinton thing: conversational, personable, caring, unflappable, able to take direction and yet able to improvise, very sincere with a mild, mainstream sense of humor that never gave offense.

Local Democrats recruited her to run for Congress. Even the survivalists liked her because her medical advice stressed self-reliance and she explained how to take care of wounds if you were alone in the wilderness. Her opponent helped her out by accosting a ranger in a men's room at a state park. Idaho is not Massachusetts and it did not go down well.

Then a Senate seat opened up and she won that,

too, with relative ease. Being one of the few women in the Senate got her more attention than she might have received otherwise, plus she continued with her TV show, sometimes from DC, sometimes from back home, framed by high mountains and tall trees.

She saw a shot at running for the presidency. She managed to make it seem as if a groundswell of public opinion—her viewers, her fans, the women of America—had all talked her into it and sent her money unsolicited. There was some truth in that. Indeed, she inspired a devotion that was close to worship.

But a woman who lifts herself out of the ranks of nursing and puts herself through med school and turns herself into a national celebrity and turns that celebrity into election to the United States Senate is not some passive cork bobbing in the sea and carried along by a mystery tide. Underneath all that good-natured, easygoing, TV chatty persona, there was a ferocious ambition. Hidden, like Eisenhower had hidden his, so you didn't feel the greed and the grab and the vainglory coming off him, yet every time you turned around there was that moonfaced man holding the prize.

So she ran.

There were eight contenders for the Democratic nomination. Murphy came in a close third in New Hampshire. Senator Neil Swenson was second.

On February 3, Swenson won Arizona, Delaware, New Mexico, and Oklahoma, as well as running a close second to the favorite son in South Carolina, to become the front-runner.

Murphy didn't do badly. She won North Dakota and came in second in the southwest, Arizona and New Mexico.

Win Davidson, the governor of Michigan, picked up scattered support, in addition to winning Missouri.

Four days later, Davidson won his home state and Swenson won in the state of Washington.

It was a horse race until March 2, Super Tuesday, when Swenson won California, Connecticut, Maryland, New York, Ohio, and Rhode Island. That put him 428 delegates short of the magic number, 2,161, which would clinch the nomination.

After that, the money dried up for everybody but Swenson. Only Davidson and Murphy stayed in against him.

The media, which tends to sing together like a choir, said Davidson was a fool to keep going and divisive to his party, but Murphy, although she could not win, showed lots of "grit."

Swenson was already thinking past the convention to the campaign against Scott and now he wanted to "build bridges, unite, and fight the common enemy." In April, after the Pennsylvania primary put him within twenty votes of the nomination, he made the extraordinary gesture of inviting the other two to travel on his campaign plane with him to the next two sets of primaries, Indiana and North Carolina, followed by Nebraska and North Carolina. Some pundits said this was a sort of audition for Murphy and Davidson: let's see who can play nice and I might make that one my candidate for vice president.

Tired and broke, Murphy accepted. But then Oprah herself invited her onto the show and of course she had to say yes to that, so she went to Chicago instead, on a commercial flight.

Neil Swenson's plane went down, with Swenson and Davidson on board. There were no survivors.

The last man standing was a woman. Anne Lynn Murphy.

Gus Scott thought about luck differently than most people.

Born rich into an influential family, a lot of people would have said that he was born lucky. But, in point of fact, most of the people he knew and that he grew up with had been born rich, too. What had become of them? Some took the well-worn route to Wall Street and collected more and more, some became junkies and lived just to score, some felt guilty about their goodies and became social workers to do good deeds, some became drunken monkeys and went swinging in the trees.

But Augustus had gifts, in addition to his luck, and it was those gifts that made the luck worth having.

First of all, he had the gift of being comfortable with all his good luck. That was more unusual than it seemed. A lot of kids, for example, would *not* have felt that they were really, really winners after their dad put the fix in. Even if they were happy with it as ten-year-olds, normally, when they got to be thirty or forty, and looked back, they would feel, somewhere inside, that the achievement was diminished by the knowledge that it was not earned. Not Gus. He thought of it, to this day, as a great, great season and he kept the trophy in the Oval Office and he pointed it out to people and used it as a starting point for any number of talks about the virtues of old-fashioned America and self-help and how sports promoted teamwork and character building and we needed more of that kind of private volunteerism and less welfare.

Second was that other people took care of things for him. His father first. Then strangers like Byron Tompkins. And the fellows who got him into the National Guard, instead of going to war. After that, the men he went into business with who saw to it that he made money even when the companies he was involved with went bankrupt (a vacation time-share company, a soybean futures syndicate, and a Yugo dealership). Then, when he went into politics, more people threw money at him.

A peculiarity of the bellicose Scott administration, with its three wars, was that virtually all of the key players, who had been of age to go and fight in Vietnam, had avoided Vietnam. The vice president had used college, marriage, and teaching deferments. The House majority leader had used college and then grad school. The majority whip, that pugnacious pest exterminator Rodney Lumpike, used a college deferment. Then the draft lottery came along and he got a good number, so he dropped out and went into business. When he went into politics and he was asked about his military service, he explained that he'd wanted to go to Vietnam but minorities had all rushed in and taken all the spots and there'd been none left for him.

Like them, Gus wasn't the type to run off to Canada or apply for conscientious objector status or to go to his induction in drag. But if you were a rich kid, and you ran out of deferments, there was one other really great place to hide out from the war. The National Guard.

Nowadays, with a volunteer army, the Guard does get called up. But in those days, with the draft, it was the best-kept secret in war evasion. They never got called into combat, the duty was light—two weeks during the summer, one weekend a month the rest of the year—and the discipline even lighter, so light that if you didn't show up, it didn't matter all that much and you could get on with your life, get a job, party, start a business, go into politics.

Because of that, there were one- and two-year waiting lists. You needed pull to get in before your draft board snatched you up and tossed you into General Westmoreland's meat grinder. Of course, Scott had that kind of pull, like Dan Quayle and Don Nickles, who both went on to the Senate, and the Futter boy who was now governor of Ohio.

The really strange thing about this is that it was one of the Fog Facts.

That is, it was not a secret. It was known. But it was not known. That is, if you asked a knowledgeable journalist, or political analyst, or a historian, they knew about it. If you yourself went and checked the record, you could find it out. But if you asked the man in the street if President Scott, who loved to have his picture taken among the troops and driving armored vehicles and aboard naval vessels, if you asked if Scott had found a way to evade service in Vietnam, they wouldn't have a clue, and, unless they were anti-Scott already, they wouldn't believe it.

In the information age there is so much information that sorting and focus and giving the appropriate weight to anything have become incredibly difficult. Then some fact, or event, or factoid mysteriously captures the world's attention and there's a media frenzy. Like Clinton and Lewinsky. Like O. J. Simpson. And everybody in the world knows everything about it. On the flip side are the Fog Facts, important things that nobody seems able to focus on any more than they can focus on a single droplet in the mist. They are known, but not known.

There Scott was, running for reelection and the polls said it was going to be tough, very tough. Before there was an official opposition candidate and the Democrats were still beating up on one another in the primaries, the polls put him dead even with Swenson. And the computer simulations said that Swenson would get a bounce after the convention, three or four points, maybe as much as six points, and then it would be up to the president to claw his way back into the lead.

Well, the famous Scott luck held. If you wanted to look at it that way. Fifteen people had died. Including some secret service guys. Scott felt particularly bad about them. He liked the secret service guys. They were always good for some touch football.

Of course, there had been a flurry of speculation and all sorts of far-out conspiracy theories. Which is why Scott had put the full resources of the government into an intensive, rush investigation of the crash. Rather than have just the FAA look into it, which would have taken months and would not have covered the terrorism angle, he had called on the office of Homeland Security, which could bring to bear the resources of the CIA and the FBI and local police in addition to the FAA.

Byron Tompkins, the director of Homeland Security himself, had taken personal, hands-on charge of the investigation.

The Democrats took huge advantage of the

tragedy and turned their convention into a giant tear-jerking memorial service. Coming into that convention, Anne Lynn Murphy had been twenty-two points back. But as the convention went on she rose steadily and once she was nominated, she got the usual bounce.

Two hours after her nomination, Byron Tompkins was able to announce the result of the investigation into the Swenson plane crash: a combination of bad weather and radar malfunction had caused the crash. In short, an act of God, not of man. The news swept the headlines and airwaves.

Murphy disappeared from the media for two full days. Her rise in the polls stalled. She'd come within seven points of President Scott, but that was it and she hadn't moved a point closer since.

Gus couldn't help it if he was lucky.

Chapter

Twelve

DEXTER HUDLEY, PRESIDENT of the college, was in the library to get some historical material for a presentation at an alumni fund-raiser. The staff alerted me that he was in, so I went to greet him and welcome him and, in general, put butter on the bread. He was genial and cordial and said he'd heard what a fine job I'd been doing in the face of financial adversity and went out of his way to speak highly of the politician in residence program and even suggested a couple of people we might try to recruit for it. I dutifully wrote the names down in my Palm Pilot. I said I would contact them immediately, what great suggestions, though we were already set for the next five years. Unless, I said, he would like to come up with more funding for a second program, there was enough interest to run two at once.

"You, you, you," he said, wagging his finger at me. Dexter likes to do imitations, this one was Robert De Niro in *Analyze This,* or *That,* or both, with Billy Crystal, "You, you, you, you're good." Then he dropped the De Niro and said, "You know we don't have any extra money. Sorry. Hey, but hey, you know what I have." He started patting his pockets. "Ahh." He pulled a small envelope out of his pocket. "I got sent a ticket for Kennedy Center, the benefit? The big get-out-the-vote thing? You know about it?"

I did. A new foundation, Everybody Vote, was sponsoring a nonpartisan concert with a wide variety of stars, to be broadcast live. It was a response to the polls that said that almost nobody was going to vote. Gus Scott was running as the hero of his three wars, Afghanistan, Kafiristan, and Iraq. The missions had been as swift as service at Burger King but the afterward had become a slow torture of indigestion. Still, the flag wavers loved him the way the NRA loves its guns. But the economy had been stumbling and bumbling since he'd come into office and Joe Public was sort of scratching his head and saying, What did I get out of this?

Lots of people simply adored Anne Lynn Murphy, but she was a she and he had all the money and nobody believed she could win, which left Joe and even Jane Public scratching their heads and saying what's the point?

So a get-out-the-vote rally sounded great. And lots of big stars jumped on board.

Then some ambitious kid reporter in Heidelberg, South Carolina, where Everybody Vote was located, tracked down a list of the backers and they were all, each and every one of them, also Golden Elephants. Alan Carston Stowe among them.

So it became controversial for a day or two and a couple of stars pulled out and then Everybody Vote spent a lot of money on PR and advertising and stirred the waters until they were muddied again and the fact that the whole thing was backed by Scott's people became a Fog Fact, known, but not known, and most of the performers stayed with the show and it was going to be quite an extravaganza.

"I can't go," Dexter said. "One ticket, I have a wife. You don't have a wife, right?"

"You're right."

"There you go. So, you want it?"

"Well, sure," I said.

"Great," he said. "Always hate for those things to go to waste."

It was a five-hundred-dollar ticket. I wore a jacket and tie and fresh pressed jeans and thought I was dressed well. There were hordes of men in black tie and five women in black tie and lots of women in gowns with rhinestones and zircons and real stones, standing tall in trophy-wife heels. I made up poems about them in my head. They look so perfect and in control, they own the world and their world is whole, twitter and glitter and don't be bitter, later tonight daddy hits on the babysitter. That sort of thing. Doggerel and defensive as well. At the break I went out for air. Of course the air was fresher indoors than out because America's thirty-seven remaining smokers, three of them with cigars, had all rushed through the doors and lit up and left a cloud bank around the entrance, so it was a bit like trying to escape Los Angeles on foot because you'd heard that if you got through, somewhere on the other side the air was clear and the sun shone bright and there were even mountains, or something scenic, so I did it, I went out past them, and there, on the other side, there was no sunshine, but the night air was clear and there was a streetlamp, and standing underneath it was Niobe. I remember especially that her hair was up and back and she had earrings, small ones, with prismatic facets that diffracted the light into small sparks of color and I expected that if we could get off someplace really dark, beyond light pollution, and look up and see the sky, those were the colors we would catch coming off the stars.

She smiled when she saw me. Of course I went up to her. One familiar face in that bobbing supercilious sea of hideously camera-ready heads.

The last performer had been Billie George Cornhoe, the number three best-selling country music singer and winner of this year's Grammy for Best Patriotic Song and he'd just sung it for us: "My heart beats faster when that eagle screams, our enemies have come to know what it means, it means choppers and jets and fighting marines, better step back when that eagle screams! Yeah! . . . Let's hear some screams . . . yeah!" And the audience had screamed.

"So," she said.

"So it's good to see you," I said.

"What did you think?"

"Well," I said.

"Don't like country music?" she asked.

"I love country music," I said, "when Willie Nelson sings."

"Do you want to see the rest of the concert?" she asked me.

I hesitated.

She said, "There's Buht Bohng coming up and Turkey Talking."

"I could pass on Buht Bohng, unless you . . ."

"Not especially and it's a bit much, everybody dressed in their power clothes."

"Let's go for a walk," I said.

She looked at me and said, "Let's go for a walk," and there was a rush of memories and a flood of hormones bumping up out of my past, decade by decade, and I was ready to make as much a fool of myself as I thought might possibly work. I offered her my arm and she took it.

The official parts of Washington are beautiful places. The city has its ghettos and poverty and blocks and blocks of dreary doper despair, but the official city is a beautiful place. There is little or no need for me to describe it. You've seen it in your high school textbooks, on postcards, and in the movies just before the aliens blow it all up. At night, with parks and the classical architecture and the river and a cool breeze gifted from early autumn, it is a wonderful, romantic place.

She asked me, with her arm tucked in mine and a constant flow of casual, intermittent, consequential touches along our flanks, what I thought of working for Alan Stowe. I told her it was fascinating, like being at the court of some king, not quite Louis Quatorze, but some minor king, Little Louie, Little Old Louie. All that wealth turned everyone who entered into a courtier and it was an invitation to corruption, a continuous seduction into self-corruption, everyone who entered automatically scrapped and bowed and sat on their haunches like dogs at dinner so they could be there to be handed a treat or scarf up any crumbs that fell to the floor.

"You are a poet," she said.

"You flatter me."

"Is that a flattering thing to say?"

"To me? Yes. That's what I would've, if I could've. Though poetry today is more an activity you do for yourself, the way some people go to the gym and work on their biceps. There was a magazine, poetry magazine, somebody gave them a grant, and it turned out they had four or five hundred subscribers but they got some fifty, sixty thousand submissions every year. So, the facts are, that people write poetry and nobody reads poetry, so stop fighting the facts, stop pretending, do it for yourself or not at all. Or write country music lyrics and hope you get hot."

"Yeah," she said, like the audience did, then sang, to Billie George Cornhoe's tune, "I'm a mean, mean, mean, mean marine, my heart beats faster when that eagle screams, and I know what that means, it means there's a pigeon on the scene."

"That's good," I said.

"Thank you."

"Was that an instant, impromptu parody or was that something that's known, just not to me."

"Well, I thought it up when he was singing."

"Very good," I said. "You could be a star."

"Yes, yes, I know," she said, teasing at it all.

Then no more words seemed to come, to either of us, and we just walked and I tried to be comfortable in it and not nervous, just feeling the electricity, not electricity as a metaphor, but the actual electricity generated by our bodies and nervous systems. Then she said, "So, David, you're a librarian," playing off the conversation we'd had outside the library, playing off the moment of silence, and I took that to mean that we already had a past and also that we had a present. Then she said, more conversationally, more conventionally, "Tell me about being a librarian."

I said, "It's the opposite of all that Stowe is, if you

think about it, and nowadays I do. It's a sort of commu-
nism, without ideology or Marx or any of that bullshit.
We're in the business of giving away knowledge. For
free. Come in, please come in, and take some knowledge
for free, no, no limit, keep going, gorge on it if you want,
no, it's not a trick, a come on, a free sample and then
we'll bill you later, or we'll paper your head with ban-
ners and pop-ups. Librarians don't have a lot of status
and we don't make a lot of money, more than poets, but
not so much, say, as your more successful panhandlers,
so our ideals are important to us and the love of books
and the love of knowledge and the love of truth and free
information and letting people discover things for themselves and let them, oh, read romance novels or detective
novels, whatever they want, and giving poor people
Internet access."

"You're a good man," she said, softly.

"Thanks," I said.

"So what are Alan Stowe's papers all about? Real
estate deals? His romantic life?"

I laughed. Though I suppose he'd had one and
might have still, especially if it was financially facilitated.

"So?"

"I'm sworn to secrecy," I said.

"Sure," she said.

"Really," I said. "I signed a nondisclosure on pain
of death and dishonor and destitution for me and my
descendants, now on into eternity on earth and
throughout the universe."

"Did you really?"

"Yeah, and you could be a spy, sent to test me, test
my resolve."

"How is your resolve?"

"Against you?"

"Yes."

I laughed and I said, "It's all about deals. Lots of real estate deals."

"Politics?"

"Mostly local things. Development is zoning and zoning is local. As I'm moving up into the eighties, there are some federal things, environmental issues, wetlands, parks, and so on. Is that what you want me for, to find out about the inner workings of old man Stowe?"

We were near the river and she slipped her arm out from mine and walked down to the edge so she could look at the water and so that we were not in physical contact. I looked at her; she looked out, facing ninety degrees away.

There was silence, I mean between us, there's always noise in a city, car noise, truck noise, sirens, distant voices, nearby voices, planes overhead, and the sound of wind and dust and the heaviness of several million people, all breathing. I kept looking at her and she kept looking out. Finally I said, "You know, I'm thinking of a couple of movie scenes."

"Oh, what movie are we in?"

"Well, there's *Annie Hall.*"

"I don't know it."

"It's with Woody Allen."

"Oh, that New York person who ran off with his own daughter."

"OhmiGod," I said, "I'm in a Woody Allen movie."

"What's that mean?"

"Well, people like me know all of Woody Allen."

"People like you?"

"Jews. Intellectuals. City types."

"Humph," she said.

"Anyway, there's this scene, and he's with a woman, Diane Keaton, and they're on a balcony, looking out over a view. We hear what they're saying to each other, but we also get to hear what they're thinking, which is totally the opposite of what they're saying. It's a very funny scene. I'll take you to see it."

"You will, huh?"

"Yeah, I will. It'll be . . ." I was about to say first date, but that was off the list of things I was allowed to say to her.

There was a long pause and then she said, still not looking at me, "What's the other movie?"

"*Tootsie,*" I said. "When Dustin Hoffman is in drag, the girl he's in love with thinks he's actually another woman and they're having girl talk, woman to woman, and she tells him that she'd love to have a man just come up to her and be honest, just say, hey, I think you're attractive and I want to make love to you. So when Hoffman's dressed as a man, the next time he sees her, he tries it and of course she slaps his face."

Niobe turned and looked at me. Then she slapped my face.

"What?"

"To save you the trouble. Of saying it. I'm married. I don't sleep around. That's important to me."

"Why's it so important?"

" 'Cause it's right."

"It could be right and you could just do it. You don't have to slap my face."

"I'm sorry," she said. And turned back away.

I reached out for her and touched her face and

tried to turn her back to me. She resisted. I kept my hand there and pushed a little bit harder, which was not hard at all, but still, a little more force and she turned to me, breathing like we were fighting or were going to kiss.

"We already talked about the Commandments," she said.

"We didn't talk about them. We thought them," I said, "and we read each other's minds."

"You think you know my mind. You don't. You don't know what you're getting into here."

"I do think I do."

"No, no, you really . . . I'm warning you, David. You don't have a clue what you're getting into."

"You can read *my* mind," I said, "can't you?"

"I don't know. Maybe, I don't know."

"You already slapped my face. So I'll tell you what I'm thinking."

"What?" and in a girl sarcastic "how hard is it to guess?" tone, she said, "You find me attractive and want to take me to bed, and to hell with my marriage vows."

"I want to tell you that I'm in love with you."

"That's ridiculous. You don't know me."

"People don't fall in love from knowing, they fall in love from . . ." I didn't know how to finish the sentence, I don't know what people fall in love from and neither does anyone else.

". . . poems," she said, finishing the sentence, saying it romantically and derisively both.

"I'm not going to bother you if you don't want me to. I'm not going to turn into a stalker," I said. I reached up my hand to touch her again and she stood frozen while I did, and my fingertips traced her cheeks, in the disbelief that she was real and the wonder that I was lucky enough to touch her, even in this small way, though in a way so much more profoundly and disturbingly intimate than shaking her hand or having her hand on my arm.

With a small noise, she pushed my hand away.

We stared at each other and in our gazes we came off of my yearning and her fear into some drifting place, a soft cloudy place, and she grew soft, her mouth grew soft and her lips parted. She kissed me. She came forward into my arms and she kissed me, full of hunger and exploration and tenderness and lust and fully half of all the things that my love dreams of her wanted.

She abruptly pushed away and turned and ran. She had heels on. She stopped, bent down, took them off, she looked over her shoulder, and saw me coming toward her. "Leave me alone," she said, then with her shoes in her hand, walked away.

Wow. I really was in a Woody Allen movie.

Chapter
THIRTEEN

WHERE RICHARD NIXON had so ignominiously failed, the Gray Man and Homeland Security and Jack Morgan had succeeded. They had bugged Democratic Party headquarters. And, while they were at it, the campaign offices of the Democratic candidate for president, her campaign cell phones, her personal office, and her home.

No Plumbers, no break-in, no fuss, no muss, no bother, and they walked away clean.

It was easy because the equation had been changed by the Uniting and Strengthening America by Providing Appropriate Tools Required to Intercept and Obstruct Terrorism Act II, usually known by its acronym, the USA PATRIOT Act II. Among the "appropriate tools" provided to various agencies was the ability to wiretap anyone for fifteen days without a warrant or judicial notification.

All the campaign's phones, and even Murphy's personal phone, had multiple users. The Homeland Security operatives simply rotated the names. Six names gave them ninety days, three months, from the first Tuesday in August all the way through the election, on the first Tuesday in November.

They did file memos. Just in case. Just in the far-fetched case that it ever came out. These memos showed that the surveillance was justified.

It would seem, on the face of things, a stretch to claim that a major party candidate for the presidency was a terrorist threat. But that was not the claim. The assertion was that Murphy was the *target* of a terrorist threat and the terrorists, and/or their associates, could be calling the campaign, or trying to infiltrate the campaign, to determine such information as the candidate's schedule, or to contact and subvert a staff member. The file included a three-CD set of the television show *24,* in which terrorists had done those very things in their attempt to assassinate *a Democratic candidate for the presidency!*

"What do you make of this?" the Gray Man said. He had telephone transcripts from Murphy's chief campaign strategist, Calvin Hagopian. Fluorescent yellow highlighter glowed over the words, OCTOBER SURPRISE, Surveillance had picked up the phrase eleven times, nine from Hagopian, twice from an unknown party. The unrecognized voice had been a woman's voice, but that didn't help much. A pin register had tracked that phone call back to a pay phone in Virginia, the call had been paid for with a calling card, and the card had been paid for with cash at a convenience store that did not have video surveillance.

Echoes from the past. But what, what could they possibly mean?

Way back in the day, on November 4, 1979, to be precise, exactly a year before the 1980 Reagan-Carter presidential election, Iranian students, backed by their new Islamic government, stormed the U.S. embassy in Tehran and took fifty-two Americans captive.

Every day, in every newspaper around the country and on every news show, there were banner headlines tracking the number of days that they were still in captivity, hammering home how helpless America was under the hapless helm of President Jimmy Carter.

Carter was in negotiations with the Iranians. If he could somehow manage to get them back, especially if he got them in October, just before the election, he would almost certainly jump ahead of Reagan and win reelection. The Republicans were determined not to be derailed by that "October Surprise," so they entered their own private negotiations with Iran and promised them the arms that Carter would not give them if they would hold the hostages until at least after the election. The Iranians withdrew from the official negotiations and then, as if they had been informed that Carter was ready to launch a second rescue attempt, they abruptly scattered the hostages so that they could not be rescued.

Reagan became president. The Iranians sent the hostages back on the day Reagan was inaugurated.

Now the situation was very different. The Republicans were in office; they were ahead, comfortably ahead. What the hell could Hagopian be talking about?

"October Surprise?" the Gray Man asked.

Jack Morgan could only say, "There is nothing that we know of, sir."

"What is it?" the Gray Man asked, in a brooding monotone. When Jack didn't answer, he said, "What do they have?"

"I don't know, sir."

The Gray Man's finger tapped on the manuscript, his finger like a raven's beak, from phrase to phrase: *Their strength is their weakness,* tap-tap, *Don't worry, don't worry. Their success will be their failure,* tap-tap, *We'll channel their power and use it against them,* tap-tap, *rope-a-dope.*

"Does he know we're listening? Is he just fucking with us, Morgan?"

Hagopian was into McLuhan, fuzzy logic, aikido, and Zen. He'd started in advertising and gone from advertising into reality TV. He'd said that American politics was just a TV show. That every election since Kennedy had been decided as a TV show. That his real first choice of a candidate had been Oprah Winfrey. But that Anne Lynn Murphy would do, as she was a Democratic Ronald Reagan in drag. He also liked to say, "Reality is viction," a contraction of video fiction, "viction is reality." Was it possible that Hagopian was just fucking with them?

"Yes sir," Jack said, "it's definitely possible."

"Do they have a man inside?"

"Inside?"

"Yes. Does Hagopian have a spy inside Scott's campaign?"

Chapter

FOURTEEN

WHEN ALAN STOWE was sharp he was very sharp, when he wandered, you'd never know where he'd go. He liked Vachel Lindsey's "The Congo," "Then I saw the Congo, creeping through the black, creeping through the jungle, with a golden track." And "General Booth Enters into Heaven," "Are you washed in the blood of the Lamb?" He told me he had no children and no one to leave his money to and wondered if that made it pointless. He wondered if he would be mourned when he died and how soon after he died he would be forgotten. He didn't ever dwell on these things; he would just mention them as if they had floated through his mind like the wreckage of some other sailing vessel suddenly carried by its own on an invisible current. If I tried to reply, or to engage, he generally ignored it. He asked me if I believed in curses. When I said no, he asked if I believed in blessings. I said no to that, too, and he humphed and I asked him what's humph and he said that most people said yes about the blessings, and then he would say if you believe in the second, how can you not believe in the first, in curses.

He also asked if I thought a library would help him to be remembered.

It is impossible to be near that much money and not have dreams. I tried to keep my greed idealistic, but I did see myself guiding him to follow in the footsteps of Andrew Carnegie, who endowed over two thousand libraries in America alone, and myself administering his bequests. So now that he asked, I spoke of how libraries virtually guaranteed eternal memory and affection and gratitude. Who remembers that the Astors started their fortune in furs, but lots of people know that they spent at least some of it building public libraries.

He changed the subject as if his attention was wandering.

Then one fine autumn evening, cool and sweet, it was October 18, Stowe said to me, "David, have you ever seen a really big cock in action?"

What does one say to such a question? Besides, I thought it was another of those random remarks.

Stowe cackled at my embarrassment. "The twenty-eighth," he said. "Angela's Star is being covered . . ." ahh, we were talking horse cock. ". . . by Glorious Morning," which I thought was a funny name for a stud, unless it was some sort of an in joke about a stud muffin, but he'd been a famous horse when he was racing, won the Preakness, placed at Churchill Downs, and quite a few of his progeny had been running in the money, so this was a seventy-five-thousand-dollar event, and yes, it would be a large penis in action. Real action. "It's something to see, if you've never seen it," Stowe said with one of his stranger smiles.

I knew that Stowe used these matings as featured entertainments for his social events and to be invited to one meant that I was being moved up in status from employee to something else. I would hesitate to say *friend*. *Acquaintance* is a meaningless term in this context. Not a business associate, not a connection in the web of power that he was part of, but something more than a servant.

"We'll make an afternoon and evening of it," he said. "It's the final presidential debate. Last nail in Murphy's coffin, then five days to the election. Appropriate, eh?" I got it, but he needed to wallow in it. "First we'll watch Glorious Morning put it to Angela's Star, then we'll watch The Man put it to Anne Lynn Murphy. Hah!" So this was the Republican version of an orgy. I didn't know if I could handle it. In between the two screwings they would no doubt talk about golf. "We're havin' twenty, thirty people over, includin' that gal you like, Niobe. Don't blame you. But watch yourself, son. Jack Morgan is one tough marine. He'll slice you and dice you if he catches you climbing out the rear window." Stowe cackled.

"Sure," I said. "Thanks for the invitation."

Chapter

FIFTEEN

I CHANGED MY shirt three times. I showered, shaved, put on aftershave, then couldn't stand the smell of it, which I found sickly and dishonest, and climbed back in the shower and tried to scrub it away.

Bill, the butler, who organized these domestic affairs, had hired extra help, including parking valets. After my car was taken and whisked away, I was directed toward the mating barn, on foot if I was capable, offered a golf cart if I was not.

I didn't see Niobe, nor anybody else whom I knew, not on the walk, not in the barn, except the associate justice of the Supreme Court of the United States, Andrew McClellan, to whom I'd been introduced twice already at Stowe's. He was tweedy for the occasion and wearing Wellingtons for the mud and the manure, though every time there was mud, a crew came and fixed the drainage and every time there was manure someone appeared with a shovel.

I said hello, not really expecting him to engage me in conversation, but he did. He introduced me to the woman who was with him, Juliet. She was African-American, certainly out of her teens, but just as certainly not yet in her third decade. He said she was a secretary at the law firm where he used to work. I called him "Your Honor." He insisted I call him Andy. He insisted three times and then I did. I was impressed. I was still looking around for Niobe.

Two grooms brought in the mare. There were eight or nine of us voyeurs there and we all admired her for her lines and her glossy coat and size and for how much she cost and how much she might be sold for if she was resold and what the foal might be worth.

One groom hung onto Angela's Star's halter. The other attached her right foreleg to a rig that kept it up in the air, so that if she didn't like what was about to occur to her, she would be too off balance to do much about it.

"That's the vet," Andy said, and he pointed to a pinched faced woman with a happy smile and a large thermometer in her hand. "There's a lot of money on the line here, so you don't do it unless you're sure she's ready for it." I was looking at Andy, or really over his shoulder, at the door, and Niobe came in. My breath caught. Jack was with her. He was almost invisible to me, an out-of-focus, shrouded specter. But then he saw me and in that moment the specter grew eyes, visible through the dim parts of the barn, even at that distance, blue, of course, good solid blue, to go with that blond combat-ready crew cut. He put his hand out and placed it on Niobe, around her waist, but low, so it rested on the top of the curve of her buttocks. He looked at me.

At that moment there was a new sound of horse-shoes stepping impatiently on the woodchips that covered the stone floor. We all turned to the sound. Angela's Star whinnied and snorted and stomped her feet.

A groom was leading a horse in. An excited horse, his extended penis sticking out and hanging down, huge and weighty. His nostrils were quivering and he was trying to yank his head up to get more of the mare's smell. The groom held on tight. He was a good-sized horse, and handsome, I guess, but he didn't have that skinny-legged, intense, neurotic ballerina aura you expect from a champion thoroughbred.

"Is that Glorious Morning?"

"No," Andy, the associate justice, said. "That's the warm-up stallion. His name happens to be Tommy. Everyone calls him Poor Tommy, 'cause his job is to get excited and emit pheromones that tell the mare what's coming up, and then when she's ready, they take poor Tommy away and the real stud comes in and does the job."

During this I kept looking over Andy's shoulder, glancing at Jack and Niobe. Niobe serenely ignored me. She didn't look away, she simply kept her focus wide, as if seeing the vista, never focusing on a single detail. But Jack looked at me.

"And he doesn't . . . ," I couldn't help but ask. "I mean Tommy doesn't . . ."

"Right. He does not."

"Poor Tommy," I said.

"See," the associate justice of the Supreme Court said. "Though I'm told that sometimes the vet or one of the grooms takes pity on him and gives him some relief."

I looked at him with the obvious question.

"Manually," he said.

"Really," I said.

"A most copious emission," the judge said, judiciously, and conveyed by the certainty of his tone that he had witnessed such. Andy took a flask from his pocket, a flat, silver thing, made to hide moonshine and make moonbeams on Prohibition nights. He offered it to me. I took a drink. It was smooth and fiery. I'm not much of drinker so I can only assume it was brandy or something more exotic that's just like brandy, cognac, or armagnac.

The mare was excited now and Tommy was excited. She was lifting her tail and arching her back and presenting. He was trying to lunge forward. The vet stepped up and stuck her thermometer in the mare. She held it there, all of us breathing in unison, heavily, everyone still and poised and waiting, except the horses who were struggling, and Jack and Niobe, still coming in, coming closer. Jack's eyes were intense, not looking at me now, looking at the horses. Niobe still looked cool, cool and indifferent. I wanted her to look some other way, to have some expression that had something to do with me.

The pinch-faced vet looked at her thermometer, and she nodded, and the groom yanked on poor Tommy's bridle and started leading him away, his erection lurching beneath him.

Now they brought in the star of the show, Glorious Morning, the stud. You could tell, at a glance, that this was a thoroughbred, a top thoroughbred, and that he knew it, too. His testosterone was flowing, his erection was out of its sheath, his nostrils were snorting, and he was ready to do his job.

Jack looked at Glorious Morning. He stood straighter. He swelled his chest. He clutched at Niobe. He identified with the animal.

Then he looked over, disdainfully, in my direction. Just for a moment. He had a very satisfied expression. I had a sick feeling and a sick thought. Was I part of some strange game that Niobe and Jack played? Was I some poor Tommy whose job it was to help them arouse themselves?

Then Jack's gaze returned to the animal porn show. As did the other voyeurs'. Though I, mostly, kept an eye on Niobe. She let Jack pull up against her, but she didn't seem to respond, she didn't thrust out her buttocks in a gesture mimetic of the mare's, nor did her breathing change. On the other hand, she didn't seem resentful or embarrassed, that is, she didn't seem to care for my feelings. Not that she ought to have, only that I wanted her to.

There must be some sense of awe or propriety left in me, because I was somewhat shocked, quite shocked, to notice that Associate Justice of the Supreme Court Andrew McClellan had stepped back so he could gaze from the mare's rump to the also very round and prominent rump of Juliet. I wasn't sure, but it seemed to me that she was aware of it, too, and was playing to his interest, arching her back more than it had been arched when we were introduced.

There was a lot of heavy breathing. From the audience as well as the horses, though among the people there was no outright stomping of feet, snorting nostrils, or grabbing at one another with their teeth. Glorious Morning lifted his forelegs and sort of climbed up and crabbed forward with a lurching motion along Angela's Star's back. There was a special groom who stepped forward to help Glorious Morning with his aim. If it had been a movie I suppose his title on the credit roll would have been cock wrangler. Properly pointed, and the situation well primed by Tommy, Poor Tommy, Glorious Morning's huge penis slid in.

I saw Jack lean into Niobe and say something to her. Excitement rippled through everybody. The handlers, because it meant that they'd accomplished what they were there for, the voyeurs because this was it, the moment, and because it was a gigantic, muscular, mythic, almost apocryphal, act of sex.

Then it was over.

It was sort of the ultimate wham-bam-got-you-pregnant-m'am sex act.

We all went up to the big house for the big event, that final debate, between Gus Scott and Anne Lynn Murphy.

The media commentary was interesting in that there was no reference whatsoever to the issues. There was a lot of talk about the date; it was the latest debate *ever!*

"On my, is that true, George?" said Lena the coanchor.

"Yes, Lena," George said. "By a full seven days!"

"Oh my, that's a lot, seven days. And what was the latest date for a debate before this one, George?"

"Interestingly enough, the previous record was set by the first set of television debates, the Kennedy-Nixon debates, the final one of those was held on October twenty-second."

"Wow, and this is the twenty-ninth."

"That's right, Lena, a full seven days later."

"What does that mean to us?"

"Well, Lena, this is Thursday. And elections are held, by the rules set down in the Constitution itself, on the Tuesday after the first Monday in November. So that's just five days away!"

"You're right, George. Looking at our special

election calendar, we can see that after today, Thursday, we just have Friday, Saturday, Sunday, Monday, that's four days, and then Tuesday, that's Election Day. So would you say that's four days away or five days away?"

"Definitely five days away, Lena, with four days in between."

"What does that mean to the campaign?"

"Well, there are two ways to look at it. Scott is seven points ahead. He's been seven points ahead for quite awhile now. That seven points is Scott's Rock of Gibraltar. Murphy hasn't been able to even chip away at it.

"So all Scott has to do is hold his own here. Then he should be able to coast right up to the election. He's got a whirlwind tour planned, four cities on Friday, five cities on Saturday, home for church on Sunday, and photo ops, of course, and he's going to the football game, then five more cities on Monday, and back home to go into the voting booth and vote just like any other ordinary American. So that's the picture."

"I agree, George," Kareem jumped in. Kareem was usually on the sports desk, but he'd been enlisted by the network to bring his expertise to bear on the campaign. "It's a lot like a title fight. The conventional wisdom is that if the champ and the challenger are even on points, the champ keeps his crown. Well, in this go-round, the president has the title, see what I mean, and the challenger is behind on points. So the way I'm calling this fight is, if Anne Lynn Murphy, the challenger, does not score a clean knockout here tonight, the champ keeps his title and we have another four years of Scott!"

"I'm glad you used that boxing comparison, Kareem. Because there's been a lot of talk from the

Murphy camp of rope-a-dope. Do you want to tell us what that means?"

"I'd really like to know that," Lena chimed in.

"Sure, Lena, I'm glad to tell you. Back in the day, when Muhammad Ali was making his comeback, he went up against George Foreman. The young George Foreman was a very powerful fighter, he'd destroyed Joe Frazier and Kenny Norton, both of whom had beaten Ali. Ali deliberately let Foreman get him up against the ropes and let Foreman pound away for eight rounds. It looked like he was beating the hell out of Ali. Until Foreman was exhausted, and in the eighth, Ali hit him with a sharp left-right combination and knocked Foreman out."

"So, Kareem, do you think Anne Lynn Murphy can do that to the champ, Scott, tonight?"

"I would love to see it, 'cause we all love an upset, but from this desk I have to say, No Way!"

"Lena, you have the odds from Las Vegas. What are they saying about tonight's fight, debate, this sort of final round, before the election just five days away?"

"The smart money says, fifteen to one on Scott."

Stowe had a big HDTV flat screen, four and a half feet wide by three feet high. He normally kept it in his media room but for this party he'd had it moved to his living room. When the cameras framed headshots, which is what they did most of the time, the heads were three feet high, like the busts of leaders of totalitarian countries.

The ratings of the television debates have fallen steadily through the years. That's because the politicians have learned how to act on television. They hire smart ex-journalists to figure out what the reporters will ask and they get their pollsters to help them shape answers to those questions and then they test those answers on focus groups and then adjust the answers and then video themselves practicing their delivery of those replies and show those tapes to more focus groups who are wired so as to get their biochemical responses, which are regarded as more genuine than their articulated evaluations.

The reporters ask exactly the questions that the candidates expect them to and the replies come back cooked and canned. The more this becomes true, the more the reporters act as if their part in the docudrama is riveting, vital, and urgent.

Harry Lee Taunton of Fox News gave Scott one of the setups he was looking for, the one about security and who would be better for the security of America. Scott launched into his set speech, the theme, really, of his whole campaign. He spoke of how when the terrorists struck, he struck back. That thanks to God and to America's fighting men and women, we had rid the world of terrorist regimes in Afghanistan, Kafiristan, and Iraq. He talked about the creation of Homeland Security and said that under his leadership the world was a safer place and, more important, America was a safer place.

Then he wrapped it up. "My opponent is a wonderful woman, great background as a nurse and a, a, a medical talk show hostess . . ."—the "a, a, a" stutter had been rehearsed and the word *hostess* had been focus-group tested—"as well as some time in public office. But what it comes down to is this, the crisis has not gone away forever. It's a question of who do you trust when the enemy strikes at America. Who do you, the voter,

want to have as commander in chief. Who has the character, the will, the courage, to stand up for America!"

The crowd at Stowe's applauded, they whistled
and hooted.

Then came the rebuttal.

"When this country was at war in Vietnam, I
volunteered . . ."

"As a nurse," the Man interjected.

The rules, of course, did not permit interruptions.

But what could Murphy do? If she ignored it and
let it go, she would appear ineffectual. Would she be just
as ineffectual when the terrorists next attacked? If she
complained to the moderator, then she was someone
who needed assistance, who needed to go to big daddy to
ask for help. If she attacked back she would, according
to the focus groups, come off as a bitch and, also
according to the focus groups, the voters did not like
bitches.

So it looked like Scott had boxed her in.

"I saw war firsthand," Murphy said, apparently
choosing to ignore the interruption, play "the gal with
grit" and struggle on. Then she paused and looked . . .
like a person, like a real person . . . and she just talked to
us. Right at us. Like she was in our home and she knew
each and every one of us and she talked like she was no
farther away than across the kitchen table and you had
to *like* her and you had to believe her. "I went to war.
While the rich kid over here got his father to hook him
up with the National Guard. I would have more respect
for him if he had gone to Canada or burned his draft
card, anything, but to hide out. . . ."

"How dare you," Scott said.

Anne Lynn ignored him. "All those things are on

the record. Of course, it's true that I was a nurse. I cared for American servicemen and women when they were wounded. Sometimes when they were dying. Something else, which you all know, but I'll mention it again, because of the context. I was attached to a field hospital. We came under attack; a mortar shell exploded in the hospital tent. Well, I picked up an M-16 and I went out into the night and I defended the perimeter. Nobody was going to shoot at *my* patients.

"I have been under fire. I have fired a gun in the heat of battle. Of the two of us, I am the warrior and he is . . . the rich kid who hid out . . ."

The camera showed Scott's face. He knew he wasn't supposed to speak. In all the campaign, she'd never come at him this way. Never. His staff had never prepared him for this. Never in any of the rehearsals had his Murphy stand-in done this. And how was this Murphy, the real Murphy, doing it without sounding like a bitch. His advisers had all agreed that if she came on too hard, it was bitch city, and baby would be sent back to the kennels.

The words were vicious, but the manner was so, *so conversational,* so like Oprah. She didn't sound mean. Scott thought, what the hell was he supposed to do? His stress became televisible.

"My opponent wants you to think he's some sort of war hero," Murphy said. "He keeps staging these video events of himself riding around in a tank, or eating chow with our real fighting men and women. I think it shows a certain contempt for all of us, that he thinks that we're so stupid that we'll see him on TV and think that he actually goes out and fights. Or that he's the kind of person who would go out and fight.

"But the truth is that he was a coward during Vietnam. He was a coward on September 11. He got in an airplane and flew away from the capital and hid out in Des Moines. He said afterward that his advisers told him to do it."

The crowd at Stowe's, there to cheer their hero amid martinis and canapés, was furious and insulted.

"Do we want a president who meekly does what his advisers tell him to do," Murphy continued, "or do we want a president who actually has the courage to stand up and tell his advisers, 'No, that's wrong, I have to do the right thing!' Harry Truman had a famous sign on his desk, *the buck stops here.* The sign on Gus Scott's desk reads, *'hey, I'll get somebody else to take the fall.'*

"It took him three days to get to ground zero in New York. Three days. I tell you this, if I am president, and the enemy attacks us, you have my pledge, I will stand tall. I will not run. If there is a disaster, I will be there, to see it firsthand, to be a visible symbol for all of us. I will stand there, just as I did in Vietnam, with bandages in one hand and a rifle in the other, if I have to, a visible symbol for all of us, that these colors do not run."

There was a shock of silence. Then the room I was in broke out in boos and hisses and the sounds and the faces were as ugly as the words and the words were as ugly as the birds that dine on carcasses in a swamp, bitch and dyke and how dare she, women should know their place, in the kitchen and on their knees. And I saw Niobe take that hatred and fear of women personally— some of the other women did not, some joined in—but she took it as if a hand was slapping her back and forth across her soul and she looked at Jack to speak up for her sex, to castigate Murphy, if he wanted to, but not to slander women and say that they should be sexually abused as a life-lesson. He didn't. She turned, and he didn't seem to notice, and she walked quietly and swiftly out of the room and out of the house.

I followed her.

Chapter
SIXTEEN

IT WAS THE old man, Alan Carton Stowe, who was the fastest to understand. He gathered his energy and his ferocious will and became twenty years younger, a mere seventy or so, and stood up, fully focused, gestured to McClellan, grabbed Morgan, and, with a glance to the Gray Man, led them to his office. The television was on in there, too. Immediately Stowe was on the phone to the campaign and getting the focus group feedback and the minute-by-minute polls.

The president had slipped an instant four points.

Scott gathered himself. The next question was about the economy. He said, "I'm glad you asked me that, Wendy, it's an important question, but I'm going to take part of my time to address my opponent's slanderous, downright slanderous, remarks. I joined the National Guard in the belief that it was a fighting outfit. That we would be called up. And once in, I did my duty. I served six years. I marched. I shot. I was ready. Now I was not General Westmoreland so I could not send myself into combat, but it was my wish to go and had I been sent I would have served."

He was climbing back out of it. Good control. Grace under pressure. Which may well be more of what the debates are about than any sort of substance. The American people want to see how a candidate can stand up to the worst that can be thrown at him.

Then Anne Lynn Murphy got to rebut the economic question. She said, "Well, just as my opponent didn't answer the question that you asked, I won't either." She was addressing a hypocrisy that all the participants in these debates were party to, which was that the candidates did not answer the questions, they used the questions as occasions to make the speeches they wanted to make, but she had the knack, and she was so calm and low-key about it, that she got a chuckle from the moderator and several of the "tough, hard-bitten" journalists as well. "The truth is that he rarely showed up for his National Guard duties. We have a stack of affidavits that he only showed up for two days of his entire last year of duty."

The president began to splutter. Of course all this was *known*, it had come up before, but it had remained a Fog Fact. Maybe because being in the Guard was not draft dodging, it was war evading, a little subtle and a little muddy. But, by framing it in a charge of cowardice and attaching it to his conduct as president, it had already, in that moment, emerged from the mist and was solid and whole and the lighting crews were already running cable to set up spotlights on it and every commentator and pundit in America would walk up to it and examine it and have their picture taken beside it.

Scott looked at his watch. Hoping, praying, for

Murphy's time to be up. The cameras caught that. Alan Stowe groaned. Scott dropped another point in the polls. Looking at his watch. Stupid.

"So, on August 7, when he was supposed to be on the base for maneuvers, Gus Scott was at a party at his parent's lake house. He got drunk. He thought his girl-friend was flirting with another young man. There was an argument, a lot of shouting, and he hit her.

"This was a young man who didn't have the courage to go to Vietnam, but he hit a woman."

According to the instant feedback, the president's numbers were in free fall. They were going down so fast that they weren't numbers, they were just a trajectory.

Scott turned white. Then red. Then pale again. But this one, this one he had prepared for. After the first campaign, when he squeaked to a narrow victory, at the victory party he blurted out to his running mate how lucky they'd been that the Democrats never did find out about the girl at the lake. This time, just in case, his handlers had crafted a response and Scott had rehearsed it, in secrecy, but he'd rehearsed it and he knew his lines.

"D . . . duh . . . darn it. It is true. I can't believe you would sink into these kinds of mudslinging and half-truths. It's a mark of desperation. However, yes, when I was very young I got too drunk at a party. And it got out of hand and I did hit her. We are, of course, speaking of thirty years ago. And thirty years ago, I said this must never happen again. I asked myself how I could have gone so wrong and I was lucky, very lucky. I got help. I accepted Jesus Christ as my personal savior. And, Ms. Murphy, do all the dirt digging you want, Ms. Murphy, all the mudslinging you want, but in these thirty years since then, you will not find one single incident like it."

It was, many pundits later said, the best recovery since Richard Nixon's famous Checkers speech. As soon as the man acknowledged that it had happened his numbers stopped plummeting, like they'd landed on a platform and then, when he seemed so genuinely sorry and so genuinely moved and so genuine in his coming to Jesus, they bounced back up, to nine points ahead of her.

He only held that lead for a few minutes, then he fell back down, but not that far down and the spread became three, three and a half, maybe four points, with Scott still in the lead.

Stowe breathed easier. Pretty good, pretty damn good. They still had the election. They were all breathing sighs of relief.

Then the debate was over. The candidates walked off. Backstage.

Stowe was on the phone, urging the pollsters to widen the base, make sure of the numbers.

The cameras followed Scott and Murphy, reality TV–style, MTV–style, backstage.

President Gus Scott was fuming as he approached his handlers. He nodded to them. He reached into his jacket and took off the mike and stayed silent while he did so. He was obviously thinking about a vice presidential candidate some years back who forgot to turn off the microphone and made a remark about kicking ass that went out live on national TV. Gus, mad as he was, didn't fall into that trap.

He had the microphone in his hand. He looked for an off button. He couldn't find it. Frustrated, he flung it away, way down to the end of the hall. The camera followed it and you could almost see it bounce along. Curiously, in terms of his popularity, that was his high point for the night. Everyone identified with his absolute desire to stop being observed and have the freedom to vent his frustrations.

Which the president began to do.

Stowe sucked his breath in. "Oh no," he said.

Gus had been good and remembered the lavaliere on his lapel, but he forgot about the change of format and that reality TV cameras were tracking everything backstage and the camera that had followed the mic down the hall swung back and caught up with him just in time to hear him say, "Jesus wept. I'm gonna stick it up her ass and break it off."

Chapter
SEVENTEEN

MOONLIGHT, MOONBEAMS, MOONSHINE. Soft grass, smooth lawns, a landscape groomed to be as smooth as painting on velvet. A large, round moon, cool and blue, bright enough to cast shadows and wander by. I saw her standing there by a solitary tree, swearing like a sailor who's just been told his burning case of clap is a new incurable kind. She turned and saw me coming and said, "Get away from me, you horny bastard. I hate men. I'm sick of men. Men and their dicks and their obsession with dicks. Their own dicks, other men's dicks, horses' dicks. The hell with the dicks."

"I didn't know you were an Anne Lynn Murphy fan," I said. "I thought you were for Scott, like the rest of the crowd."

"No," she said abruptly, urgently, "It's not about Murphy or Scott. It's about their attitude toward women. What if they started making Jew remarks? Huh? What if they said, 'What do you expect from a money-grubbing, hook-nosed Jew? You know you can't trust 'em, maybe Hitler was right.' What if they said that?"

"You don't hold back much, do you?"

"Oh, I hold back plenty. Believe me. And a good thing, too."

"What do you hold back?" I asked, speaking gently, speaking softly and calmly, approaching her, the way you approach an animal that might bite or bolt.

"None of your business."

"Whatever you hold back, do you hold it back from what's'isname, Jack?"

"My relationship is none of your business."

"You know, I like women."

"I know what you like about women."

"I do. I think it would be fine to have a woman as president."

"What are you doing, trying to butter me up?"

"No," I said, coming closer to her. "Just talking to you."

"Did you hear those bastards in there?"

"Yes," I said.

She stared at me, stared at me hard, and I looked in her eyes, and when I reached for her she came into my arms and when I kissed her, she kissed me back. I kissed her slowly and lightly. The whole world was still echoing with the roar of horses and our nostrils were filled with the scents of mammalian sex and my head was filled with the roaring of my blood, but I kissed her lightly and slowly. She pushed against me, breasts and pelvis, daring me to press back. There was anger in it and sarcasm and temptation, daring me to make a grab for her, daring me to jab at her with my dick, so I kissed her lightly and slowly and she grabbed my upper arm, the left, with her right, and she dug her nails into it. I was sure my bicep could not compete with Jack Morgan's pull-up and push-up and weight trained–up arms so I didn't try and then I felt her teeth on my lower lip, pressing hard there, too, and finally she began to kiss me back, lightly and slowly, and it was as good as a sentence by Hemingway, back when he was good.

Then she pushed me away, as I knew she would, hoped she wouldn't but knew she would. She turned away from me, turned her back to me, looked away into the night, her arms around herself, and then she turned back around and looked square at me. "I can't do this," she said.

"I don't want to talk you into anything or con you into anything, even if I could. But, if where you are isn't where you want to be, then, well, then I'd love to."

"Uh-huh. Well, I got that."

"Well, then," I said.

She put her hand in mine and we started walking. The grass was soft and smooth and the smells of the night were sweet and her hand in mine was schoolgirl right. "I'm trying to tell you," she said, after a while, "that you don't know what you're messing with."

"Jack is not a civilized chap?" I said. "He'll get all savage about this?"

She didn't like the joking tone. She stopped up short. She let go of my hand, let go of my life, dropped the moonlight, right there in the mud, and said, "I'm not going to commit adultery. You're not going to sweet-talk me into having sex with someone not my husband. I won't."

"Did I try?"

"Yes, you did."

"Well, I wasn't pushy about it."

"No, you weren't. You're sweet, but no."

"All right, I accept that."

"We better go back our separate ways. I'm going in the front door, you go in the back and in a window or something and act like you never went out."

"Come on," I said, "I love drama, I do, but . . ."

"I mean it," she said, seriously and severely. "I really mean it. Don't mess up my life. And yours."

Chapter

EIGHTEEN

STOWE'S PERSONAL INVESTMENT in the presidency of Augustus Winthrop Scott was two million four hundred and twenty eight thousand dollars.

As best he could calculate—Stowe could calculate very, very well, but the data was partial to say the least, fragmented, hidden, and deliberately disguised—still, by the best of his calculations, the general investment in the presidency of Augustus Winthrop Scott, by corporations and by wealthy individuals, was two billion four hundred thousand dollars. Maybe two billion eight hundred thousand, maybe more. Hell, he didn't know, it could be a lot more, but it was at least, the very least, over two billion dollars.

And it was an investment that had paid off. Big time. Scott had cut taxes for the rich and put it back on the middle and working classes. He'd done it smart, like they told him to, with tax cuts across the board, just much, much bigger for rich people. That, plus the war spending, plus the recession, had starved the federal government. That shifted the burden for police and schools and environmental protection and drinking water and all the rest to the state and local level, where the money came from real estate taxes and sales taxes, fees and fines. Which effectively shifted the tax burden off the rich and on to all those other people.

Scott and his people had put lobbyists and business representatives all through the executive branch and they'd cut back on the rules and rewritten the rules and pulled back on enforcement of the rules and made it easier to do business. That was supposed to have created jobs and lifted the whole economy. It hadn't done either. But everyone seemed to be nodding along and there were no riots in the streets and the cities were not in flames.

Stowe was in high gear. Clear and focused as he had not been for two years, at least. He knew his energy was limited. He could already feel his body fading underneath his consciousness. He was furious with his aging body and his doctors and the world for doing this to him. He wondered if he would live to see the fruits of his labors, this vision of the greatest empire the world had ever known, world domination by business, mostly American, backed by American military force. That was what the wars in Central Asia and the Middle East had really been for. To show the world, every crumb pot, little dictator and the big, bold countries, too, that they were overmatched, they were Little League teams up against the World Champion Yankees. And it had worked and it was working. There was no way Stowe and his friends were going to let that go.

So here they were and Stowe's beady, rheumy eyes focused on the three others.

Morgan was ready, by his nature and by his ambition, to the point of recklessness. He had to be held back. McClellan was a procrastinator, a prevaricator, a vain and too cautious fool—as Supreme Court justices go—who had to be calmed and coaxed and kept in line. Then there was the Gray Man, and he needed to believe that he was the one in control, that his was the hand on the wheel and his were the feet on the gas pedal and on the brakes. But that was one of Stowe's favorite tricks, to make other men think the deal was actually their own.

"One-one-three, get it ready to go," Stowe said, a command to Morgan, a warning to McClellan, and a look and a nod to the Gray Man to let him think that his permission was being asked.

The Gray Man said, "If all else fails." But Morgan didn't seem disappointed, Stowe didn't seem frustrated, and McClellan didn't seem relieved enough, so he knew that they had taken his words to be pro forma noise, a parental sound like "drive carefully." So he made it more emphatic, much more emphatic. "Not one overt action, not a single one, until I say go. One-one-three is a brilliant plan, if we need it. If we don't, it's reckless, foolish, and dangerous. If it is discovered that we even planned, even contemplated, even discussed such a thing, we are all disgraced and instead of saving this administration we will bring it down in ruins."

Stowe wasn't paying that much attention. He looked around, his eyes passed over the window, and just then he saw a face at the window. The librarian.

Morgan saw the motion of Stowe's eyes. He turned and he, too, saw, who it was, even as the librarian was pulling away, into the shadows, into the dark.

Stowe was aware of Morgan and that Morgan

knew and that Morgan would act. With that certainty and having done what he had to do, he let his concentration lapse, with a long, soft sigh, it had cost so much effort and so much of his dwindling energy. Then he got sad, so very sad, he thought he was going to cry, like . . . like when he was six and his family had moved and he'd lost all his friends . . . that was it, the librarian was like his friend, and now he was going to lose him.

Chapter
NINETEEN

THERE IS A poem by Kenneth Patchen, "Irkalla's White Caves," that begins:

> *I believe that a young woman*
> *Is standing in a circle of lions*
> *In the other side of the sky*

Which is what I was thinking of after I came back into the house. I rejoined the group in the living room. People were drinking, in short urgent swallows, eating with tight little bites, and buzzing. Drinking and eating and buzzing like flies. Obviously I'd missed something big, important. The television was still on. This is the world of instant replay, and, once a Fog Fact becomes a piece of Frenzy Food, its image is repeated often enough to sell it as an Egg McMuffin. So there it was, President Scott in a most unpresidential fury, in what was clearly meant to be a private moment, in what he thought was a private moment, tearing off the constraint of being recorded and the oppression of always being watched, and flinging it from him, then cursing his opponent, as we all do, in what the fool thought was after the event, in the privacy behind the stage, but the expansion of public space and public time tricked him and flopped a fool's cap atop his presidential crown.

Ken Starr, doing color commentary for Fox, was doing his best to defend Scott. He said, "What we have here is a very human reaction and the American people will see it as such. It clearly has nothing to do with policies or abilities. Once again, it demonstrates the bias of the liberal press; I mean the reaction we're getting to this. It is such a trivial, innocuous event. After all, it's not sex." It was a pleasure to see Starr panic. Starr wanted the Supreme Court and Scott had the tickets for the trip.

Looking through the window, I'd seen Alan Stowe with Associate Justice McClellan and Jack Morgan and another man with his back turned. I believed that I'd pulled back before they'd seen me. No alarms had gone off. Nobody had said anything.

They looked like they were plotting furiously. But what, I had no idea. Probably to spend more money, lots more money.

I admit it, it gave me pleasure to see all these smug, self-assured, rule the world, loot and pollute and put on your evening clothes afterward types, rasping and gasping as if actual Bolsheviks were at the gate and ready to storm the Winter Palace. I realized that my current indifference to politics was somewhat feigned. It was really resignation. A defense against a sense that all things liberal were failing and all the liberal spokesmen had tongues that rattled gibberish and the Limbaughs and Coulters were so high on their turn of the wheel that their gibberish was heard as eloquence. So I had not dared to hope for Murphy, as I had not dared, until I saw Niobe, to hope for love. It was, of course, absurd to have fallen for her, more absurd to have confessed the truth to her, and more absurd yet to hope that my love would be requited. If I had told someone about all this, and I had no one to tell it to, not really, they would have said it was absurd for me to listen to myself, that I was, at best, simply romanticizing lust, I might as well look at a picture on the Internet and moon over that.

The poem ends:

On the other side of the sky
A young woman is standing
In a circle of lions—
The young woman who is dream
And the lions which are death.

Niobe stuck her head in one door, the side door, caught my eyes, and gestured for me to come to her. But just then Jack came in the main door and began looking around and I was certain he was looking for me. I briefly considered getting down on all fours and creeping out the side door, between the legs of all these golf-playing Republicans, but I had a sense that things weren't particularly comic.

Instead, I went right at Jack, looked him in the eye, and said, "Wow," and pointed at the screen, "who would've expected? What do you think? Will this affect the election?"

He glared at me. He clearly had something on his mind. Like "stay the fuck away from my wife." Then his expression changed. To a sort of smile. Not a pleasant smile. And if I had to read the words therein, I would have read them to say, you're a dead man.

I went on past him, a tightness in my chest and my throat feeling dry. I stepped outside the living room door into the main hall and closed the door behind me, wishing I could lock it or jam a chair under it or some other silly trick that would slow pursuit. But here I was in this civilized mansion and nothing was actually wrong. I looked both ways. The side door, that Niobe had come from, opened to the library, which was now to the right of me. I also wished that she'd come from some other place. If someone were looking for me, coming after me, they'd head for the library.

But she'd summoned me; I had to respond. I moved quickly to my right, hoping to get there and disappear from the hall before anyone arrived to see me. I took four quick steps to the library door and plunged inside. The lights were off and no light was coming through the windows. I realized later that the drapes must be closed, but I could feel her presence and smell her aroma, a faint perfume, mingled with scents from the mating shed, sex and horses and hay and leather, also whatever it was that she washed her hair with and something else, that I couldn't quite place, something not so enticing, which, also later, I thought might be fear.

Her eyes were better adjusted and she came to me.

"What do you know?" she said, not whaddaya know, like how are you, a very specific question, *what* do you know.

"I don't know what you're talking about."

She reached around me and locked the door I had just come through.

"David, this is serious. Tell me what you know."

"About what? What are you talking about?"

"About what's going on here."

"I know what everyone knows."

She moved away from me. I could see her now, a shape of darkness in the darkness, her skin a shimmer, her hair every once in a while catching a glint of light. She went to the side door and locked that, too. Then she came back to me.

She said it again, "What do you know? What did you find out?"

"Nothing."

"Then why are they coming to kill you?"

Chapter
TWENTY

SPINNELLI WAS WITH his family when his cell phone rang. His own private work phone and he didn't let anyone else use it.

Spinnelli had a wife and three daughters, eight, twelve, and fifteen. The two older girls had the presidential debate as a homework assignment. They had their own TVs but they'd hogged the one in the living room, who knows why, so Spinnelli was watching it, too, which he wouldn't have otherwise. Actually, the older girl had a choice, watching or reading some magazine article on the history of presidential debates. That was a no-brainer, as was Vicky herself; the fifteen-year-old, she would choose watching TV over anything.

There was no voice when he answered the phone, just a text message from Colonel Morgan, a simple code that was an immediate summons, not so much for secrecy as efficiency, and an address.

"I gotta go," Joe said.

Nobody answered him and he got up like a ghost.

He was half sad and half glad. Sad that his home was not what homes were somehow supposed to be, glad to get the hell out of there. Even when they weren't actively conspiring against him, to rob him of his authority and to swallow up his money the way they hoovered up junk food, their combined femaleness over-whelmed him. They were gimme, gimme, gimme girls, and, if he tried to impose discipline, they'd simply said, "Fuck you, you asshole, no," even the eight-year-old. If he'd spoken that way to his old man, his father would have taken a strap to him and Joe would have felt that his father was right to do so. But if he, in this fucked-up generation, tried to spank one of these little witches, as they deserved and as they needed, his wife would be right there to hand the girls the phone so they could call 911 and report him.

He went to his computer, punched in the address he'd received, and Google spit back a map, door to door. It seemed to Spinnelli that such services should be reserved for military and police personnel; the fact that anybody could do that, seemed . . . wrong.

He looked at the route. He estimated an hour and a half, maybe an hour forty-five to the destination, Stowe Stud Farm. He had to hook up with Whittaker on the way. Once they did, Dan would drive and Joe would get in back and run the listening post. The van was a silver-gray Chevy Express LT, roomy and com-fortable with CompSys.Org painted on the sides. It was fast enough, but not much on corners and you wouldn't want to use it as some kind of chase vehicle. But Spin-nelli didn't chase. He listened. He tracked. He got into your every electron.

At the moment he had his electronic tentacles

snaked into the librarian's entire life, cell phone, hard-wire phone, and his computer; he had microphones in all three rooms of what was, in Spinnelli's opinion, a pathetic little apartment, a thirteen-inch TV and stacks and stacks and stacks of books. Shelves of books. Books open on tables and books by the bed. Oddly enough, when they'd gone in to plant the microphones, Spinnelli had actually had his hands on the collected works of Strindberg, the great nineteenth-century Scandinavian misogynist, and if he'd read them he might have seen the slow deadly wars of derision in his own home as a con-temporary Jerry Springer suburban redux, redux of the plays therein. But he put it back down when he was fin-ished placing the microphone, being careful to put it exactly as it had been; you never knew when the inhab-itant of a place saw order in the disorder.

Spinnelli figured the guy had no real life, living in books so much.

But now there was a call to action, so maybe there was more to the librarian than he thought. See, you never knew about that either.

He put on his CompSys.Org windbreaker, to match the sign on the van, and headed out into the night. He wondered if things were already going down, if the librarian already knew his life was about to change, utterly, forever, probably for the worse. He wondered if Parks would get his hands on the guy. Parks had been getting more and more brutal lately. And twisted, too. Spinnelli had to admit that, twisted.

Parks and Ryan sort of feeding off each other, pushing each other, like his daughters. The older one did Special K, the twelve-year-old did Special K, passed out, had to take her to the emergency room. Spinnelli

knew the eight-year-old hadn't started yet; he had all
their rooms wired. It was easier just listening in on
them. The eight-year-old wanted her navel pierced, like
her big sisters, and her tongue, and the things she knew
about studs in the tongue and what they were good for,
no eight-year-old should know.

No father should know about his daughters. But
Spinnelli knew; he couldn't stop listening.

Going out the door, he looked over his shoulder,
instant debate replay, instant recycle, instant video virus,
that bitch woman attacking President Scott. Goddamn,
Spinnelli was glad that he was working for Scott and
against Murphy. Bitch in the White House, no fucking
way. Bitches were already ruining the world.

He slammed the door hard as he went out.

He wondered if they even heard him, if they
would react. He would find out, of course, he'd play it
back, sound and picture, what they did when he was
gone, as he always did. He wished, in an odd way, that
he didn't have the ability to do that. But he had it, so he
had to use it.

He got in the van, backed out slowly, checking the
convex mirror on top of the metal post pressed into the
lawn at the edge of the driveway, so he could be sure that
it was safe to back out, that one of these stupid suburban
women wasn't driving and fixing the baby seat and
talking on her cell at the same time and come careening
into him.

He had loved his girls when they were baby girls.
Loved them. And known what his job was, to protect
them. But he didn't have a clue how to protect them
from their real subverters and enemies, one another,
their mother, and themselves. Out of a job. Cut out of

love. Bitches ruled his home. Now a bitch wanted to rule the whole *she*bang. No way, no how.

The woman from downstairs in 4B was sitting on Whittaker's couch. She'd kicked off her high-heeled sandals and tucked her feet up under her, showing lots of leg, smooth, tan, freshly shaved.

He'd put some Rophynol into her beer. He had some generic sildenafil citrate and he was on his way to the kitchen to swallow it without her saying, "What's that?" in a suspicious whine, when the phone rang and it was that wimp Spinnelli. A fucking job. He could tell Spinnelli was glad to be getting out of the house, but he sure as hell wasn't. The only good thing was he hadn't popped the Viagra-erectalike. He didn't want to be that ready out on the job, could lead to a conflict of interest, or parked, waiting and bored, looking over Spinnelli's shoulder when Spinnelli was checking up on his daughters. Whittaker, for the most part, had the good sense to stay away from twelve- and fifteen-year-olds, and looking that way at the children of a guy you worked with was asking for trouble. But the things those girls did when they thought they were unobserved would drive a man crazy. He couldn't understand how Spinnelli could look, but he could understand how Spinnelli couldn't look away.

Nonetheless, he was pissed and he hoped they'd get to fuck up the librarian some, as a relief to how irritated he felt.

Mark Ryan didn't want something flashy or unique that stood out, no Dirty Harry or James Bond guns. He favored a Glock these days. Simple, clean, reliable, virtually generic. He had two of them. One registered. One that had slipped out of military stores.

Now he brought out both of them, checked the clips, chambered a round in the unregistered piece, and put it in his shoulder holster. He put the legal gun down the small of his back. The way he figured it, if he had to rush, he probably needed the untraceable throwaway piece. If the operation was . . . formal . . . slow and formal . . . he'd have plenty of time to switch and go with the registered gun.

He recognized the address. Stowe Stud Farm. He'd been out there before. Nice country. About a two-hour drive.

On the way out the door, he tapped the cigar box on his desk, for luck. It had his two necklaces in there. One from Vietnam and one he had slowly put together since. It wasn't always possible, in fact it was rarely possible, to collect an ear from a dead man in peacetime in the West, but he did it when he could, and he was up to five.

Every time he got one of these calls, he was hopeful of adding one more.

Randall Parks didn't take a gun. He avoided them whenever he could. Disposing of bodies with gunshot wounds was always immensely complicated. Even if someone got shot and they lived, doctors and hospitals always wanted to report things.

There were other ways. He drove a black BMW M3 and he kept a kit in there, stun gun, Taser, and a set of nun-chuks. But more important, he had his hands and his feet and his skills. He'd met very few men he hadn't been able to take.

He was a little farther away than Spinnelli. But there was no rush that he knew of. He used cruise control and stayed about eight miles over the limit. With his HS ID and all, there wasn't much he couldn't talk his way out of, but why leave footprints of any kind. A big guy, sure, with that scar and the very light hair, so he worked at not drawing attention to himself, concentrated on being a shadow, until he came up on the people he was after. If they lived, they never forgot him. He left his mark on them for life.

Chapter
TWENTY-ONE

THIS WAS MORE melodrama than I could believe. I looked at her with deep skepticism, but it was probably too dark for her to read my features. I said her name, but meaning something like *come on,* or *sure they are.*

"David, this is real," she said.

She was so close that when she exhaled, I inhaled her CO_2, that was probably what was making me dizzy. There, in the darkened library, with Niobe clutching my lapel, and, as I said, feeling oxygen deprived, I reflected on how often I had fallen for women who appeared to be neurotic who later turned out to be psychotic. Not as bad as this. But it wasn't the first time.

"I'm sorry," I said, as gently as I could.

"I'm going to tell you some things. It's up to you if you listen. Jack just made some calls. He called four men who are going to come looking for you. I overheard the calls. One of them, Spinnelli, you will probably never actually see, but he will see, hear, and track you. From a van, he works out of a van, a gray Chevy, last year's. There's Whittaker. Skinny, crew cut . . ."

"What are you telling me all this for, Whittaker and spaghetti, or whatever it was?"

"There are two more," she said urgently, "Ryan and Parks. Mark Ryan and Randall Parks. Ryan will just kill you."

"Stop it, Niobe."

"Ryan is about six feet. He's heavy, he's almost sixty now and he looks it. His hair used to be curly, there's not much left, he's mostly bald, and he keeps it pretty short. He drinks a lot and you can see it in his eyes, bloodshot, you know."

"Why are you telling me this?"

"I'm telling you this because you're acting like you don't believe me."

"Should I believe you?"

"It depends, it depends on who you are and what you know, or don't know."

"What the hell is going on?"

Someone was rattling the doorknob, trying to get in. Niobe started panicking, if you can call what had come before not panicking. She started talking very fast, in a desperate sort of whisper.

"I'm telling you this so that when you see these people you might get it, and have the sense to run, run like hell. Let me finish. Ryan, his nose has those big pores that people who drink get. He sweats a lot, too, and his clothes are always rumpled, but don't, don't underestimate him."

"And why not?"

"Just don't. But the worst one is Parks. Randy Parks, Ryan will just . . . I know you don't believe this . . . Ryan will just kill you. Parks will hurt you."

There was no more noise from the door. I figured whoever it was would go get Bill the butler, or somebody

else on the staff, and get the key. If any of this *was* true—
or if she was psycho and in some psycho game with her
husband, Jack, then this was the rattrap. Here we were,
ready to be found together.

I wanted to get out. I wanted to get out without
being seen with her. There were two doors: the one that
I'd just come in, the main door, from the hall, and the
side one, to the living room, packed with people,
including Jack Morgan. I knew the windows were never
opened; they were locked and hooked to an alarm
system.

"They think you know something," she said.

"What?" I said.

"They are doing something here, something to do
with the election. To win the election, steal the election,
something. And they figure you found it in Stowe's
papers or overheard it or something."

"Why would they think that?"

"I don't know, but they do."

"How do you know they do?"

"Because they want to kill you."

"I remember this, this is catch-twenty-two. OK."

"Why else would they want to kill you?"

"Niobe, this is America, twenty-first century, civilized place, lots of laws and law enforcement and all
of that."

"I'm trying to save your life."

"All right," I said, trying to calm her down. "If I
see any of these people, I will call the police. I promise."

"They are the police."

"Look," I sighed, trying to get away from her,
"time to let this go."

"Parks has a scar," she said. "From here . . ." she

touched me on the cheekbone and drew her fingernail down to my jaw. Why did I love her touch? Stupid. I loved her touch, ". . . to here. And his hair is almost white."

"Fine."

She took my hand and held it between both of hers. "They think you know something. The only way out of this is for you to find out what that is."

"What do you mean?"

"Find out what they are afraid for you to know. Then let the world know or your superiors know."

"My superiors?"

"They think maybe you're working for someone."

"Who? I work for the college, at the library. They're afraid of Dexter Hudley? I work for Stowe, in this library. I'm a librarian, not a spy or whatever. I'm a sane librarian."

"Listen to me, please listen, David, for when you find out, if you live, that I'm not crazy and I'm not lying, just listen. What you have to do is find out what they think you know. In the meantime, run and hide. It's only five days until the election. Whatever it is, it's about the election. Don't go home, don't go to work, don't use the phones. Buy a cell phone, the prepay kind. Buy it with cash. Here." She put a piece of paper in my hand. "When you find out what it is, or when the election is over, call this number."

She reached behind her and unlocked the library door.

She flipped the switch and the lights came on and they dazzled me because it had been so dark and she looked so beautiful, ethereal because everything looked too bright, and her eyes were shining and I stood there looking stupidly at her and at the piece of paper in my hand. She looked annoyed, took the paper out of my hand, and stuck it in my pocket, then she swung the door open and started to step outside. "An hour," she said, as she moved by me, "I figure you have an hour before they're here," and then she was out the door and gone.

Chapter

TWENTY-TWO

MY BREATH WAS caught in my chest. I had to force myself to breathe and I could feel the prickly sting of ugly perspiration. But I recalled what I could of yoga, concentrated on inhaling and exhaling and attempted to achieve calm. When I had something close to it, I decided to return to the party through the side door. I don't know why I didn't just get out of there.

When I did reenter the living room, nobody seemed to notice, nobody seemed to care. They were still flies, intent on their own business, making small leaps from place to place to feed, to drink, to buzz with one another. Niobe wasn't there. Neither was Jack. Nor Stowe, nor McClellan for that matter, nobody I really knew. McClellan's secretarial friend was there, avidly talking to an older man who looked like he had a lot of money.

The drapes were open and I went to the window and looked down and out. What was I looking for, Niobe?

The house was built on a small ridge. At the front

of the house, at the main entrance with the sweeping circular driveway, this was the ground floor; at the back it
was the second story. And it rose one more story above
us, bedrooms mostly. Directly below me there was a
stone patio, surrounded by a wall in a semicircle, and
three paths from there leading down to the fields, the
stables, the barns, and the breeding shed. The paths
were lined with lantern lights, smaller and smaller as
they wound down into the perspective painting of
country wealth, twinkling as hopefully as stars.

I tried to mingle in, but I couldn't really talk. I was
mouth dry and tongue-tied, confused. I heard buzz
words in the buzz, I heard oil and war, I heard money,
business, and anti-business, disaster for the nation, have
to hold on, ruin all we've gained, worse than the Clin-
tons. Then I saw someone I recognized, but didn't
know, the Senate majority leader, and I drifted toward
him. He was talking with a congressman from Texas
and someone in oil, who had a pipeline deal in Iraq, and
their eyeballs were popping and their faces were as fierce
as flies when you see them in a photography taken
through a microscope.

I wanted to go back where I belonged. Into the
peace of the library, surrounded by books, by considered
statements, exclamations that, no matter how impas-
sioned, would wait . . . quietly, for a considered response,
no matter how opinionated or biased, would wait quietly, for research into their proofs and into other points
of view.

So I did. I went back through the side door, into
the library. I was alone there. I touched some of the
books, I sighed, I pitied myself and my withdrawal from
life and wished, foolishly, that I could be a man of action,

of encounter, of wild face-to-face interactions, instead of a filer, a sorter, a reader, a keeper of the records of other people's deeds. I left the books, dry and dusty and so full of so many words, that so often didn't matter, that so often were ill-assembled, that were so often shrill and weak or sententious and pretentious, all those excesses of verbs and adverbs and adjectives and extravagances of metaphors and similes and the showings off of how smart and erudite and educated and arcane and esoteric and polylingual a writer could be, Ezra Pound with his "Δ _vas, your eyes are like clouds . . . plura diafana . . . Heliads lift the mist . . . the brightness of 'udor . . ."

So I sat down at the computer, and started browsing through those of Stowe's files that I had entered already. There were items that were mysterious. There were lists of names that meant nothing to me. It was part of his technique to research people before he did deals with them. So there were lots of names and financial profiles and sometimes one of those names would show up as "a deal" and frequently they were just lists.

I put in Scott's name. I found two letters of thanks, from the last election. One was clearly a form letter . . .

That's where I was when they came in. The one with the scar and the white hair came in the main door. The other one, the old guy, with the drinker's nose and a shoulder holster making a visible lump under his jacket and the thuggish presence of a cop, he came in the side door, with Jack behind him.

At that moment, from the faces of them, from the presence, the Gestapo assurance of them, at that moment I entered a state of belief. Whatever she said, yeah, I believed it now. The guy with the scar down from his eye to his jaw, he was happy to see me, in that scary way that people who like victims are happy to see someone they think they can hurt.

"Hey, hey, what's happening?" I said.

"You're going to have to come with us," Jack said.

"What, you have a warrant or something?" I asked.

"Just come on," Jack said.

"Look, I'm outta here, I don't know if Alan, Alan Stowe knows what you're doing." I had turned in my chair and I stood up and thought my chances were better against Mr. Evil over there with the white hair, after all, there was just one of him and the door was this big huge thing and I might be able to get around him, whereas there were two of them crowded by the side door and I'd have to push through Morgan and . . . and I tried to remember the name she'd told me and all that came to my faintly hysterical mind was spaghetti, and I knew it was wrong it was Spinnelli, but she'd said I'd never see Spinnelli, he was the electron man. No this was . . . Ryan? and he killed people?

A little assurance, a little bravado . . . I bet they could smell my fear, like Dobermans. But still, nobody moved but me, and I went forward, right toward scar-face Parks, and a little step around him and his hand came out of his pocket and I was zapped.

I turned into a cartoon character. I turned into a scream that could not be heard. My hair stood on end, my heart said, "Wah, wah, wah," my fingers and toes stood out and I hurt. I hurt and I fell to the floor. The guy with the scar loomed over me. I felt like a fish flopping on the floor of the fishing boat, except I wasn't moving. I couldn't move. He examined me, like he was looking for what would hurt. He pulled back his foot. I could see that from the periphery of my vision. He waited until I knew that he was going to kick me and he could see that I knew; we exchanged that information, building the intimacy of torture. He was going to hurt me until I belonged to him.

I wondered, if I burrowed deep, deep inside, could I find some strength to resist this? But why? What was I fighting for? What were they fighting for? That uncertainty was a place of tearful weakness, it was the residence of surrender, humiliation, and spiritual debasement, yet where else did I have to go?

He kicked. Into my ribs. Hard. It hurt, but they didn't crack, nor did he reach my organs.

Then he looked away from me. Behind him. I tried to lift my head and couldn't. I was still in that shocked mode. But I could hear the voice.

"Not here," Stowe said.

"We just incapacitated him," Morgan said.

"Not here," Stowe said. "Don't let the guests see either. You should have waited and picked him up away from here." There was no reply to the rebuke. "What are you going to do with him?"

I think that Stowe meant, How are you going to get him out of here? but Jack took it to mean, What were they ultimately going to do with me? and he didn't reply. My body was returning to some sort of normality now. I could tell that I had control of my limbs.

The silence kept going on and on and the longer it went on, the clearer my understanding was. If Jack had said, "We're just going to question him," or "Take him to HSHQ and run a check," or "Detain him until we're certain," of whatever, I would have surrendered into acquiescence as so many of my ancestors did when they said "Climb into these nice railroad cars, you're going to resettlement camps," but Jack's reluctance to lie directly to Stowe kept him from misleading me and kept me from deluding myself.

Tears ran down my cheeks. I could feel the obscene and humiliating trickle. I knew also that on my way to dying it would get a lot worse. My humiliation, I mean. When Stowe stepped out, I could see Parks turn away from me to watch the boss go.

It was my moment. I leapt up. Well, I tried to leap. It was pretty wobbly and lame. Parks turned back. He looked at me curiously as if I were a fish that could talk. There was a story, not so long ago, in the paper, about such a fish. It was a carp. A Latino worker in a Hasidic fish market in Brooklyn was about to cut its head off. The carp spoke in Hebrew. The Latino didn't recognize the language and ran screaming for the owner, who did. The strangest things go through my mind at times of stress and that's what went through my mind, so I screamed out in Hebrew, "Today I am bar mitzvah!" which is all the Hebrew I remember.

The three of them looked at me very curiously.

I ran. There were only two doors. The doors were closed and the doors were blocked. So I ran in the opposite direction, toward the windows, which were covered by the drapes. They were big windows.

Ryan made a move toward me. To get away from him, I scrambled up on a table, big library table, there were two of them in a line, so I went running along the first table and jumped to the next one.

They were laughing at me. They were coming after me, but in a casual stroll. Parks was waving his stun gun at me the way a mugger waves his knife.

There was the window in front of me. I knew that on the other side there was a one-and-a-half-story fall. Not two suburban stories, seven or eight feet each, no, rich man's stories, fourteen feet and another two feet thickness for the floor—you never heard the people upstairs at Stowe Stud Farm, no way. And the landing, solid stone.

I jumped.

I jumped as hard as I could into the drapes, hoping to go through them and out the window. I got tangled in them. But my forward momentum did carry me through, the heavy fabric wrapped around me. The crashing of the glass was muffled, so was the crying of the alarms that I set off. I went out past the window ledge. Of course, once I realized I was out and falling, fear prompted me to try not to fall and I clung onto the drapes. They didn't tear, but my weight and momentum pulled the rod off its hooks and, though I went down, I went down slowly ... again ... I had odd thoughts ... it was very quick in real time ... slow in subjective time ... there are all these crazy Jews, tough Jews, in Israel, in the Mossad and in the army and all of that, but the last time, the only time, I could think of a Jew like myself, a librarian Jew, a would-be poet Jew, pulling a stunt like this was Danny Kaye in *The Court Jester,* swinging outside the castle on a rope.

The drape got me to within a foot or two of the ground. I let go. I fell and I rolled. I looked back up. The old guy, with the fat nose, had a gun out. I ran. I pointed myself to the darkest darkness, ran, jumped up on the wall, and jumped down off it, onto the lawn, tumbled and rolled, heard them yelling. Heard the alarms, too. Started running, away from the lights. Then the alarms went silent. I was running, feet on the beautiful grass, hunting for the safety of the dark, and I knew they were coming behind me.

Chapter

Twenty-Three

STOWE SENT BILL to turn off the alarm and told him to call the security company to fix the alarm, fix it so it would work even with the windows smashed, and to call the glaziers to fix the window, "Now, tonight! of course."

He wanted the library cleaned up, too. But Jack said they needed forensics and they had to leave it until that was done.

Stowe didn't yell or shout, but fury shaped his face, that young and old face, and Morgan realized he was dealing with an eight-year-old about to have an implacable tantrum and that the eight-year-old was in possession of an old man who had the power to buy governments and lay waste the land.

"Forensics," Stowe said, like it was spit. He had been prepared to understand that sometimes things got out of control but he was not prepared to suffer the officiousness of fools. "Forensics? You saw what happened. You know who did what. Forensics, pah!"

"We'll catch him," Jack said.

"With no more damage," Stowe snapped.

Ryan and Parks had run down the stairs and out the back. The librarian had a lead on them. But where could he go? Spinnelli would hear it if he got into his car and he could track the car. Not that it was that complicated, there was only one road in and out of Stowe Stud and Whittaker had driven around to block it and they had Stowe's security people at the gate alerted, too.

Ryan moved out to the left, Parks to the right, circling. Ryan took his Glock out and had it in his hand. The unregistered piece. He'd been doing night patrols, it felt like, all his life. Starting when he was seventeen, in the jungle, looking for shadows of shadows, listening like a Sioux for the sighing that was not the wind, sniffing like a dog to catch the smell of rice and spice and fish sauce.

He couldn't smell like that anymore and his hearing was not what it had been and, he hated to admit it, his night vision was slipping, too. But what he had, what time hadn't blunted, were his instincts. The jaguar walks at midnight. Even if his nose couldn't smell his quarry, his being could smell the quarry.

The hunter needs to know what the hunted wants. That's the way to do it: enter the lands of fear and desire, habit and instincts, ah yes, into the darkness. Just follow the darkness, that's where he'll go.

Ryan moved with purpose, the dark guiding his route like an inverse lantern, following in David Goldberg's footsteps, and as his certainty grew the scales and encrustations of the sordid years fell from him and the soul of the soldier boy came back, though the belly was no longer tight and the knees creaked, and he could smell again, smell so well that he could tell that he was indeed walking where the librarian had walked, because he could smell the freshly broken grass where the librarian's running feet had torn it up.

Parks was surprised that the little guy had got up again. Tougher than he expected. And that escape, amazing. They hadn't even thought to block the windows, hadn't really noticed them, hidden behind the drapes, but even if they had, never would've expected the *librarian* to go out the window.

Parks figured that there might well be a shit storm of trouble for Colonel Morgan. His was the job of keeping messes from being made. But that was the colonel's problem. Not his. Parks was quite happy with the situation. He didn't doubt that they'd get Goldberg in the end, but this was like that story some English teacher had made him read in high school, it got made into a movie, too, somewhere along the line, and he'd seen it, but it wasn't much, not as good as the story, because what was great about the story was the *idea,* it was about this rich man, rich as Alan Carston Stowe, who had his own island, and he liked to hunt and he'd gotten bored with the stupidity of animals and he wanted to hunt something with smarts and cunning, so he hunted men.

Parks felt like Stowe Stud had just become his own private game park. Parks decided not to use the stun gun when he caught up with the librarian. It would be just hands and feet and balls and skills. For the sport of it.

Niobe saw that Stowe was ragging on Jack and came up beside them. "What happened?" she asked ingenuously.

Stowe assumed that Niobe was just another good wife, to be kept in the dark and bred with or whatever your fancy was. Oh, and nowadays they had jobs. Stowe gave jobs to the wives of people he wanted to influence, to own, but he thought of them as no-show jobs ways to get money to people that you couldn't legally give money to in an upfront, straightforward way. In addition to Niobe, he employed the wives of two Supreme Court justices, McClellan's and another, four or five other federal judges and the wife of the Speaker of the House, among others.

Old-fashioned gentlemen don't criticize husbands in front of their wives, so Stowe calmed himself down, he mumbled something about the librarian getting drunk or going mad or something and falling out the window. "Wandered off, afraid he's hurting, trying to find him."

"Oh, oh dear," she said, nodding along.

Then Stowe remembered that the librarian had been hot for Niobe, but then, who wasn't. Oh, hell, he didn't care about it, too confusing, too tiring. "Fix it," he mumbled to Jack and turned away.

Jack didn't say thanks to Niobe for getting Stowe off his back, but he didn't have to, a glance and a movement of the head, something less than a nod, did it. Then he asked her, "What did you tell him?" meaning Goldberg, and it was less a question than it was a request to report, though he should have asked before they moved on the librarian, and he knew, in his internal checklist, that he'd been wrong not to.

"I told him to run," she said.

"What? Why?"

"He wouldn't tell me anything. So I figured if I told him to run and he didn't run, he really is as innocent and stupid as he acts. But he went out the window?"

"Yes."

"Well, the other possibility is that he is some sort of super pro, and if that's what he is, he's probably got cover stories under his cover story and Parks will probably kill him trying to get at it."

"What do you know about Parks?" She really wasn't supposed to know about his Special Ops team.

"You told me," she said. "You told me you had this guy who was slipping out of control and you didn't know what to do about him, he was too valuable to lose."

"Yes, but I never told you it was Parks."

"But I know him. And you can see it. Sooner or later he'll slip over the edge."

Morgan nodded, he could accept that, that made sense, Niobe could read people, she really could.

"So," she said, explaining about Goldberg again, "the best bet was to get him running and see where he runs to. Then you know who he's working for."

"And if he slips away from us?"

"I thought our people were too good for that," she said, lightly.

"You know better," he said, harshly. It was the simple truth that once a man was on the run, if he didn't betray himself by running home to his mother, he could enter into the chaos of the world. It seems, to outsiders, that such a thing would be unlikely, improbable, impossible. That there are too many police, too many tracking systems, too many traitors and informers. Launch the FBI, the CIA, offer five million dollars, dead or alive, and you must, necessarily, catch anybody . . . and so where are Mullah Omar and Osama bin Ladin and the mystery man who sent anthrax through the mail and how did Abbie Hoffman hide in plain sight for twenty years and why was the Unibomber not found until his brother turned him in and how do a hundred thousand children or more go missing every year, forever.

Simple truth, man on the run enters into chaos.

"Besides," she said, finally, "warning him built trust. I gave him my phone number, and I told him, when he knows something, when he gets somewhere safe, to call me."

Chapter

TWENTY-FOUR

I KNEW THEY were coming after me. I didn't think any of them would jump out the window, so they'd have to run downstairs. I had a few steps on them. I'm not much of a runner, I hoped that fear and adrenaline would lend wings to my feet and keep my lungs from quitting.

Then the next thought came, the obvious one: Would they shoot? A bullet outruns any man.

Woods, there were woods, if I made it to the woods, I had a chance. Old man Stowe, who cut down forests and named the streets Oakwood and Maple Lane and Birch Road and Beech Tree Boulevard, with nothing but blacktop loops and pre-cut sod around the ticky-tacky houses, kept an entire forest of his own, surrounding his estate, a buffer between himself and the ugliness he'd built all around.

Here the grass was great, fabulous to run on, the horses must love it. Just a few minutes ago, not minutes, an hour or two, whatever, I'd been out here with Niobe.

Oh, yeah, so she wasn't a psychotic hiding her

madness behind mere neurosis. So I wasn't such a bad chooser after all. I felt better about that, have to pursue the relationship later, when I survived. What the hell was I going on about? I was so tired and my lungs were burning and my Achilles tendon, on my left ankle, hurt like hell and I was wearing actual shoes, fool, I should have come prepared. Right, sure, bring your running shoes to the party, you might have to escape in the middle of it.

I knew where I was. The down slope was going to end soon and flatten, it would even rise, and that was a desperate problem. Although I'd never been hunted prey before, I know that when you stand on top of a ridge you become a silhouette, one of the black outline cutouts, like popgun targets at the video arcade.

When? How soon? How many more steps and it would be, pop, pop, pow! Shot down!

This thing was crazy. Couldn't we sit down and talk it over and I would explain! No, definitely not, they had made it clear that was not considered an option.

Keep on running, although it hurt.

I looked back over my shoulder and I could see the lights of the house looming above. Figures in the window, some of them, I thought, looking out. Watching the sport on the lawn, eh?

I looked back over my shoulder again and saw a head bobbing between me and the house. Shit, one of them was right behind me. I hoped it was the old, fat, slow one. Yeah, right, he would just kill me. There's a wonderful Jack London story about that . . . oh hell, never mind. Think relevant thoughts, useful thoughts. Do not curse yourself for not taking that survival course. Do not curse yourself for not enlisting and becoming an

Airborne Ranger or whoever the toughest of the tough are. Useful thoughts. What was a useful thought? Then I stepped in a pile of horseshit and slid and skidded and fell to my knees.

I scrambled back up, having lost precious distance from my pursuer.

I knew I was going uphill now because gravity had struck, sucking at my feet, holding them to the earth, hands on my ankles, making it harder to lift my knees, grappling me at the shoulders, holding me downward. The useful thought was ... ah there ... it was darker than the darkness of the sky ... I'd lucked out, clouds up there, no moon, no stars . . . there was the ridge . . . the useful thought was, hit it low, with my body low, and then dive and roll, dive right over and down the other side, such as it was, and put the earth between my body and any bullet that might follow me. That was a good plan.

And I did. Running low, almost on all fours, and as soon as I felt that my head was over the highest point, making a silhouette, I dove, forward.

I'd guessed right. There was a blam! I'd always read about people feeling the bullet go by them, by the wind or the whistle or whatever. I didn't. But I did know that it didn't hit me.

The part I guessed wrong about was that I had this vision of myself sort of leaping over the high point of an actual ridge and rolling down the other side. But what I was doing was jumping into a low rise, which was still rising. It was almost flat, but still rising, and so I did what was essentially a belly flop on the ground and it was not pleasant. Better than being shot in the back with a 9mm, but not pleasant. And I still had to keep on moving.

I rolled. Sideways, roll, roll, roll, but now I could really hear that fucker coming up behind me. I wanted to cry. I really did. I was out of plans. But I was not interested in him catching up with me, either.

So I scrambled up on all fours, trying to . . . to move forward and not get shot . . . then . . . like a vision . . . it came to me . . . like a voice from the other side . . . it said, "Serpentine, serpentine." It was Peter Falk yelling at Alan Arkin while they were being shot at on a runway in South America. It worked for them and Alan was playing a *dentist*.

So I did, I ran serpentine, over the flat top of the rise and down the hill.

Blam! Blam! Two more misses.

Serpentine worked. I was overjoyed. It infected my legs, my being, my energy. I ran with excitement and pleasure, plus I had escaped the dreary, dragging grip of gravity. It was a liberation.

From the frying pan into the fire. In front of me, creating a wide arc, were the stables, the barn, and the breeding shed. And they were lit. And probably, there was security down there as well. You don't keep horses worth one, two, three, four million dollars apiece, without security. This was not good. That I-want-to-cry feeling came back.

"Serpentine, serpentine," the Peter Falk in my mind reminded me. I'd never known, until that moment, that I kept a Peter Falk in my mind for emergencies. It was pretty handy. I wondered who else was there and if they could help, too.

I tripped and fell, skidding on the grass. Oh shit, was this guy going to catch up with me? I looked back. He was now the silhouette on the high point. He was leaning forward, hands on his own knees, panting. Good. That'll teach you, whoever you are . . . Ryan . . . I guessed . . . to stay in shape. OK, I still have a chance. Run; run, down the hill to the stables, and then what? The last time I was on a horse it was a pony, I wore a cowboy hat and a plastic holster with a plastic gun and I had a plastic badge . . . that's how long ago that it was that I was on a horse, plus there was a guy holding the pony by his bridle thing, walking him and talking to me about what a great little cowboy I was and he was probably a pedophile and would have hit on me if my mother hadn't been watching him like a hawk.

Serpentine, serpentine, yes Peter, I'm going serpentine.

Oh shit. There was a security guard. At the stables. Staring at me. Hand on his holster. One armed man in front of me, one behind me.

"Help, help," I yelled.

"What! What!" he called.

"There was a break-in . . . home invaders . . . at the house . . . pant, pant, pant . . . they need you," I yelled. "I came for help," I yelled, proudly, what a great thing to come up with. "There's one behind *me,* after me, to stop me from warning you."

He was moving toward me. Then he stopped.

"Can't leave the horses," he said.

"I'll watch 'em," I said, stumbling forward, out of breath. I had to get him out of there, before Ryan caught up, flashed his badge or whatever he had, and said I was the real bad guy. Please, fella, buy it. "They need you!"

I got there. Got up to the security guard. Got around behind him. Another excellent idea. Put his body between me and whomever. And the security guard was buying it. Yes, sir, he was pulling out his rent-a-cop gun and it was a real gun with real bullets. A shoot-out at the Stowe Stud corral! Maybe the rent-a-cop would blow away Ryan! He wasn't winded, he was fresh, he could shoot clean and straight. He had his gun out, it was some sort of automatic, I'm not up on these things, but it had that square look and it didn't have a cylinder that went round and round like Marshall Dillon's.

"Don't shoot," a voice ordered. An authoritative voice. "Homeland Security," it announced. The guard and I both turned to look. It was the evil-looking Parks, the scar-face man with the white hair, and he was holding up his billfold, like the FBI agents do in the movies to show their ID.

The rent-a-cop all but went to attention.

"That's the man you want, behind you," Parks announced. He held that fucking stun gun in his hand. He was going to zap me again and make me flop like a fish on the floor. He was going to hurt me in all sorts of ways and humiliate and destroy me. "Detain him," Parks said.

No way. I gave the security guy a shove, as hard as I could. He went down. I flung open the stable door, got inside, and slammed it shut. There was a big old-fashioned iron bolt. I slammed it home. I heard a shot from outside. Then I heard the security guard yell, "Don't shoot, don't shoot, you fool, those horses are worth millions."

Ah hah! Yes, they were. I started opening stall doors, yeah, yeah, let 'em out, millions of dollars on the hoof. I bet Alan Stowe would want to save his horses more than he wanted to kill me. Holy shit, they were crazy. The horses were. They were starting to snort and rear. There were several studs and they were competitive and they had herd issues to settle, who was the stud of studs, keeper of the harem. And there were mares in there, too. I let them out. Oh yeah, one of them seemed like she was going into heat. She was doing that tail-swishing, arch-her-back thing. Oh, and the boys were getting excited.

Someone was banging on the door that I'd come in, trying to break it down. The guard was still yelling, "No shooting! No guns!" I was glad of that.

But just then the door at the other end of the stables swung open. A big block of a man, with white hair.

"Help!" I yelled, to the heavens, to God, to the spirit within, to inspiration. And it spooked the horses and they jumped and they ran and they headed for the open door and they knocked that prick Parks down, knocked him on his ass and went galloping right over him. Unfortunately they didn't trample him. They made great efforts to not do so. I had to admire their humanity in general, but regretted it in specific, but he was down and so was the stun gun, they'd knocked it away from him. I wanted it. Just so that he wouldn't get it. I moved toward it, and him, getting banged by horses as I went. It was a scene of divine madness and I had created it. I am usually a creature of order. What is a library if it is not order? Shelves, categories, neatness, record keeping. Let loose the chaos! Unleash the beasts. Let them gallop and run and I could escape while the rest of world tried to rescue Stowe's investment.

I opened up one more stall and it was Tommy. Poor old Tommy. He looked at me. He was not taking part in this excitement. He looked so calm. Like his groom had brought him relief. I left him as the stampede of horses all left the stable. Parks was still on the ground, filthy and unmoving. I picked up the stun gun.

Then someone touched me from behind.

"Oh, no!" I cried. I'd gotten so close to escaping. I'd fight back. I whirled, with the stun gun . . . no . . . it was Tommy. Kind of nuzzling at me. I looked around. Saw a stool. Dragged it over next to him. I climbed up on his back. The worst that could happen was he would throw me off. He seemed to accept me. He started to walk. "Come on, boy," I said. "Let's get out of here, but not too fast."

He made a whinny and started to move. I just clung on to his mane with my hands and clung onto his body with my legs, tight as I could, and we rode off. I hoped I could head him into the woods.

Chapter
TWENTY-FIVE

CALVIN HAGOPIAN HAD his own office at Murphy's campaign central. In stark contrast to the rest of the offices, indeed to campaign offices everywhere else throughout history, it was a clean, spare space. He didn't have a desk; he had a table, an antique Shaker piece. If he needed to handle papers his secretary, or someone else, brought them in, he dealt with them, then they were taken away. He had his own chair and two chairs for visitors. If more were needed, they were brought in, then taken away. He had his own interns, whom he never fucked or fondled or flirted with. Even when the campaign had seemed like a lost cause, a desert expedition that would end in dry choking thirst, when it seemed that the well where Hagopian was dipping his buckets was just a mirage and that if you went there for the promise of cool, clear water and date palms all around, you would eat nothing but sand, even then, even then there had been an endless supply of high-quality free labor, eager to work for media Zen master Hagopian.

His walls were clean and completely bare except for a single empty picture frame, three feet wide, two feet high, that hung around a graffiti scrawl, in fat black marker, that said the wall is real. If you looked at it very, very closely, you could see that the paint beneath the writing was fresher than the paint on the rest of the wall and, looking more carefully still, you could see that there had been something else written there before this statement, but you couldn't make out, short of some art restorer's peeling technique, what it had been.

If your style of observation was meticulous enough and painstaking enough to notice those details, you might reflect that of course he could have had the whole wall repainted, or the whole room, when he made the change, and being Hagopian, if that was what he had wanted, that was what would have been done. So if it wasn't done, since it was Hagopian, it had to be deliberate and there was a point to it.

Only three people had noticed the subtle discolorations and thought it through and then asked. To the first Hagopian had said, "Ahh," with a pleasant smile for the quite glamorous and very bright young woman from UCLA who, nonetheless, continued to struggle with his failure to hit on her. To the second, he said, "Change," obviously as a noun centered in a sentence that extended both sides of it like the slopes of a mountain seen in profile from a distance. But to the third, a print reporter who sometimes wrote for *Harper's* and sometimes for *The Atlantic Monthly* and sometimes for e-zines, he said, "I try to make what I'm doing clear and self-evident."

And the reporter had said, "Ahh," in a tone that was either simple acknowledgment or a very Zen way of saying that's not true, you tricky bastard you. Whichever it was, it made Hagopian laugh, a merry sound, and the reporter joined him and they laughed for a long time. The reporter, short of breath, said, "This is reality."

Hagopian clapped his hands, once, and said, "Yes, that's what it said before."

The reporter, suddenly sobered and curious and ready to take notes and you could see he was going to put it in a story, said, "Always?" meaning was there only one statement on the wall before this one, or had there been many?

Hagopian said, "You know, we're going to win this election."

Hagopian said it again, now, Thursday night, after the debate. He had a crowd of fifteen reporters—no video, just two still photographers, who had to pool their pix— and he said, "We're going to win this election." For the first time they didn't figure they'd find him, November third, the day after election day, dried up and desiccated in the dunes of disaster beside his dead camel and they jostled and pushed and shouted for his attention.

They kept shouting, as reporters do, "Was this planned?" "Did you know it was going to work?" "Aren't you afraid it will backfire?" "The latest polls have Murphy at forty-four, Scott at forty-three, that's a very slim lead, can you hold it?" "Do you think you'll hold that lead?" "The undecided vote is thirteen percent, that's huge, this could go either way. What's your comment?" "What are you doing about the undecideds?" "Who are the undecideds?" "What do you think the Scott campaign will do to fight back?" each thinking that his question, his own question, his own special question was really important.

"I'm not going to do this, if you behave like this," Hagopian said.

But of course that didn't silence them. They kept at it, each afraid that one of the others would get their special question answered, get more acknowledgment, get more credit.

Hagopian got up out of his chair, walked over to the corner, sat down facing it, cross-legged, which he didn't really like doing because he was not that flexible, and thought about his breathing. He pretended not to hear the shouts and pretended not to hear them say, *what are you doing, what is he doing, what the fuck is this, oh, come on, I thought this was a press conference, I got a story to file* and he thought to himself they should be used to this from him by now, they should have adverbed it by now, called it *doing a Hagopian,* or verbed it, *Hagopianing.*

"What I thought we'd do," he said, standing up, "is just talk, like we do on deep background but you can quote me, so long as the quotes convey my meaning, and if you don't understand what I mean, ask me about it. That way I can say some interesting things. If anybody's in a rush or has a deadline, Anne Lynn is giving a formal press conference and there are several people you can go to for quick sound bites." He rattled off a list, the press secretary, the East and West Coast managers, the central states coordinator, and four or five more.

"Now what a presidential campaign is about these days is what the candidate is like on TV. Some intellectuals and some pundits think there's something wrong with that. I don't. The problem, for most people, is too much information and too many issues. Also, most people understand that policy is not what it's about. It's too easy to lie about policy.

"Gus Scott calls himself the education president and cuts education programs and then still calls himself the education president. He calls himself 'the conservatives' conservationist,' nice sound, I like it, but you know that a more accurate description is radical anti-conservationist and we're all going to pay for it with bad air that causes cancer and who knows what else, global warming, rising seas, toxic dumping, but you know that and you either report it or you don't, depending on . . ." He shrugged. Who knew what made the media choose to report something or not?

"The other thing wrong with policy is that sometimes it's correct to change it. Roosevelt runs as a peace candidate, Pearl Harbor happens. Clinton runs on gays in the military; at a certain point he realizes if he sticks to that fight he loses everything else, so he makes an adjustment. Deregulation is a Scott policy, and he intended to let big media companies buy as many outlets as they could, that hit a roadblock, he backed off and I think that was the right thing to do. So did the voters.

"Voters know we live in the real world and the real world changes.

"So, how do they choose?

"What we really need in a president is someone who can handle overload, handle the unexpected, and handle chaos. Because that's what the job is. Through some cosmic process, some synchronicity, like Adam Smith's invisible hand, the modern campaign tests exactly that.

"Can the candidate go, go, go, sixteen hours a day, seven days a week, deal with you guys screaming at him with the most provocative questions you dare ask, handle being investigated, handle the opposition attacking every way they can? Can the candidate do that and stay healthy, calm, reasonable, good-humored, intelligent, balanced?

"When a voter says, or doesn't say, but our focus groups pull it out of them, that they voted for someone who they liked on TV, it seems like they're saying something really shallow and they would vote for any idiot with a high TVQ, but in fact what they're saying—at least to some degree—is that they know that this person has been down the long road, up against a thrashing, and they still have it, they're still as good on their feet as Phil Donohue, still as present and full of human vitality as Oprah. And that's a pretty good, intuitive way to make that judgment.

"You, if any of you is an intellectual . . ." that got a laugh, "you might ask, 'what about the candidate who is really good in all other ways, better than his opponent in all other ways, except as a TV performer?' I would say, in reply, that any politician who doesn't understand that how things appear on television is the beginning and the end of things, that politician is so out of touch that he shouldn't be president. There's no point in being right and not being able to convince other people of it. Save that for . . . poets.

"So all we did here, this campaign, was to invite President Scott to demonstrate for the American people who he really is . . ." Hagopian held his hands out, smiled ingenuously, then said, ". . . and the dumb fuck fell for it."

The reporters laughed, a bigger laugh this time, it was more fun to laugh at Scott than at themselves, but Hagopian held a hand up in a "hold it" gesture. "Hey guys," he said. "We did not trick him. How long have I been telling you, and him, and the world, that Anne Lynn was playing rope-a-dope.

"So he was warned that this was coming and he still couldn't cope and when he realized that he blew it, he didn't find his balance, and the nation can't afford to have a president who gets rattled and can't afford to have a president who can't remember when he's still 'on camera' and when he's genuinely off and can't afford a president who fails to find a quick and balanced response to the unexpected upset.

"So this was not a cheap trick, this is not just TV, this is a very real and accurate way to assess presidential character and Scott had the opportunity here to show that he has that character or that he doesn't. And he doesn't."

And that, Hagopian said to himself, smugly, is the zen of spin.

Chapter
TWENTY-SIX

FRIDAY MORNING. PRESIDENT Scott was in the air.

President Scott loved Air Force One. When he was in it, he knew he was president. He knew he had awesome powers. He knew he could kick ass. The polls, the damn numbers, who thought they could move so fast. Locked at seven points for two months. Every analyst and every projection said that there was a glass ceiling, that there was a solid block of the American people who simply would not elect a woman president and that Anne Lynn Murphy versus Any Male would lose by four points. So he'd had three points of his own plus a four-point guarantee. It was impossible for him to be behind. But here he was, behind.

He had a four-city tour, Tallahassee, Tampa, New Orleans, and Dallas, today. Fly in, touch down, into the limo, motorcade, get out, fifteen minutes of upbeat speechifying to the faithful, cheer on the troops, get out the vote, back in the limo, cops on their Electroglides leading the way, choppers overhead for security, secret service cars in front, secret service cars behind and out on the flanks, the President of America, Emperor of the World, is coming through, get out of the way.

It was supposed to be legs up, easy chatter, laughing and joking between the stops, the triumphant cruise to the finish line, and instead it was panic time. They couldn't cancel, change their plans, huddle in the White House to plot, plan, and regroup; that would look like they were off balance and they couldn't afford to look off balance because they were off balance.

The plane was packed, extra campaign staff stuffed in. In a crisis everyone wants to grab some face time, maybe some glory, to be heard and their idea noted and get their name mentioned in the instant histories of the campaign.

His campaign manager was an old pro named Roger Wallace. Wallace went at politics the way Colin Powell went at war. He believed in overwhelming force and crushing the enemy. In politics, overwhelming force consists of overwhelming money.

Wallace had run Scott's first campaign. They had gone into the primaries with at least three times the money of his nearest rivals. They bought up the air and they blasted and bombed and bombed and blasted and it worked.

The reelection campaign relied on the same tactic—no, it was more than a tactic, more than a strategy—it was perception of the nature of the world. Overwhelming force triumphs over all.

Scott had raised money, mountains of money, almost double the amount that anyone had ever raised for a presidential campaign before. The whole world had seemed to agree, fellow Republicans, intimidated Democrats, pundits, publishers, reporters, allies, and enemies, that Scott's fund-raising had settled the election before it began.

But Murphy had used the funerals after the plane crash and ridden the sympathy thing for all it was worth, and that tricky prick, Hagopian, some kind of Jew or Armenian or both, had made money a theme, "A Vote for Scott is a Vote for Money," implying the heresy that money was bad. And he played Murphy like she was Saint Joan out of Saint Teresa by Saint Frances.

Well, it hadn't mattered, and money had ruled, and the Scott campaign had rolled on like the Hummers and the Bradleys and the Abramses and the self-propelled long artillery, which is how Scott visualized his campaign. He did, after all, know how to drive a tank and he loved opening up the throttle and tearing up the countryside. That was real; that was more than just a photo op. So he hadn't driven one at the front, big deal, he'd been prepared to, he'd been ready to charge into battle, blasting away, spewing explosives, setting the jungle on fire. How was he to have known that some people would think of going into the guard as evading combat. Maybe the answer was to have a new war, quickly, only four days to the election and he could do it, this time he would lead the troops, personally, into combat, like Napoleon or William the Conqueror or somebody like that.

Fuck, it was Friday, and they were out over the Atlantic, heading for Tallahassee, and they had Saturday— five more cities—and they had Sunday—back to his hometown for church and a family photo op and to the stadium to be seen watching a football game—and then they had Monday, another five cities, and then it would be

Tuesday and the polls would be open. That's what they had, today, the next day, the day after, Monday, that's all that was left. He was behind and that's all that was left and if he stayed behind, that was the end.

So they were having a meeting, him and Wallace and the key members of the campaign staff. "We're going to win," Wallace said, his voice grim and determined, George C. Scott in *Patton,* and his growling brought Scott out of his thoughts. Wallace stood up. He didn't have a riding crop, but if he had, he would have slapped something with it, his own high-topped cavalry boots perhaps, if he'd been wearing them. "This is the Battle of the Bulge. The enemy has made one single, desperate attempt to break through our lines. But they have gotten only so far and will get no further. They have stalled.

"The skies will clear, then it will be clear that we rule the skies. We will counterattack their counterattack. They are outnumbered and outgunned. We have superior resources. And that is the abiding lesson of American military engagement: superior resources and the will to employ them are the key to victory, they are the certainty of victory."

This was, of course, self-serving. The more the campaign spent, the more Wallace made. Nobody objected. Not because they didn't notice or didn't realize, but because if they did, they approved. Making money was the moral thing to do.

"Let us commit all our resources," Wallace said, "for this last big push. Blanket the airwaves, bomb the shit out of them, sow dread and confusion. We will carry on to victory!"

The door opened, and Secretary of State Edward Hoagland—old, gray—came slowly in.

In the misty realms—out past Fog Facts—there
are things that Must Be So But Can't Be Stated. They
have happened as understandings, as nods and winks. If
at some point they had to be made explicit, none of the
parties will say that such agreements occurred because
they are, by nature, covert and are frequently crimes,
and must be protected by silence.

It's just that if there is fruit, somewhere there must
be a tree.

Here is one story, more or less the official one, and
it's the one that the media accept. Gus Scott was an
attractive, vigorous, young politician, elected to the
Senate on his first try. He was well connected and his
beliefs were in tune with America's rising tide of conser-
vatism and he had a knack for communicating that,
especially to people with money, who backed him enthu-
siastically and who encouraged him, with words and
dollars, to run for president, which he did, and once in
office he pursued the policies that he and they, synchro-
nistically, believed in.

Naturally he appointed people that he was sim-
patico with, like Edward Hoagland. Hoagland had virtually no formal foreign policy experience, but he was in
big oil, so he knew a lot of foreigners, especially in the
oil-producing countries.

Here is an alternative narrative using the same
characters and events.

Edward Hoagland, head of one of the great oil companies referred to as the seven sisters, decided, along with
his colleagues and peers in oil and coal and electricity, in
chemicals and petrochemicals and pharmaceuticals and
telecommunications and arms manufacturing—though
not with written agreements or even excessively explicit

conversations, but nonetheless decided in concord with one another—that they needed a president, they needed a man who was their man, in charge.

Scott had been a relatively undistinguished senator. When his record was examined closely, it turned out to be exaggerated and sometimes actually false. He misplaced words, like *is* instead of *are,* and sometimes *we* when he meant *them*. Still, Senator Scott was a cut above several of the others. He didn't bump his head on big words like *potato* or express glee upon finding an anatomically correct doll in South America. He had a certain swagger and energy and he was passable on TV.

Scott went to Hoagland or Hoagland picked him. Either way, it doesn't matter that much.

What matters is that once Edward Hoagland put the hand of blessing upon Scott and anointed him as their man, the floodgates of the world's big money opened and money poured into the Scott campaign.

Then, when candidate Scott became president, Ed Hoagland wanted a spot near to him, to keep an eye on things, and Hoagland selected State as a good place and Gus Scott cut all their taxes—that gave his backers their upfront investment back right away—and then he gave them deregulation and privatization, relaxed or eliminated environmental standards, and then, to top it off, he went and had three good quick wars and conquered three countries for them, one of which turned out to have less oil and gas than anticipated, and that country was more or less abandoned to fall back into its wild Islamic ways. But the other two were worth plenty, so Scott stationed semipermanent forces there, at great expense to those fools in America who couldn't get out of paying taxes, and gave the primary rights to exploit the oil to a consortium headed by the company that old, gray Ed Hoagland used to run. Before he ran Gus Scott.

As fruit must come from some tree, this is one of those stories That Must Be So.

This is not a story that the media will tell or that even the instant histories will tell because journalism is not about thinking things through, it's about cutting and pasting press releases and quotes and neither Hoagland nor Scott is about to tell it that way, so there are no recorded words, and probably never will be, that connect those particular fruits to that particular tree.

Unless . . . unless, perhaps, some Golden Elephant, getting old, and worrying absurdly about a place in history instead of his place in the present, had foolishly written something down in his diaries or notes and now wanted it enshrined in his privately endowed library in the hopes that some future scholar would ooh and ahh over that Elephant's contribution to the manipulation of the body politic.

Now this gray, old man, Edward Hoagland, nominally secretary of state, came into the central section of the plane, the one set up as a conference room. Conversation stopped and waited on him. The president stopped and waited on him and finally cleared his throat and said, "Glad you could join us, Ed. I'll bring you up to speed. Rog," he said to his campaign manager, "bring Ed up to speed, would you."

"It comes down to money," Roger said. "We'll blanket the airwaves. We'll double our spending. We'll roll with 'Let's roll!' "

Before the ground invasion of Iraq was launched, Wallace had set up giant video screens at the army's desert encampments—the diamond vision kind they use at rock concerts, sporting events, and on Times Square. President Scott, in Washington, was thus able to address the troops in a simulcast, moments before the troops went in. Scott had spoken, with well-rehearsed spontaneity, gravely and seriously, but briefly, of the risks and horrors of war and explained, briefly and pointedly, why it *had to be done,* and then said, in that optimistic, determined voice of film heroes from John Wayne to Ronald Reagan, "Let's roll."

The troops had cheered. Wallace had filmed them cheering.

Now, with artful editing, Wallace had produced commercials that showed the president's speech to the troops, but did not show that they were on video screens, and showed the enthusiastic responses, and made it seem, by that simple omission, that Gus Scott had been right there, with our men and women, in the desert and that he himself was rolling into combat with them.

Wallace had held back the "Let's Roll" spots. They were such an obvious manipulation that he feared a media backlash that would label them as what they were, misleading and deceptive, and if the media backlash was big enough, it might even effect the voters. But now, with just today, Saturday, Sunday, and Monday, and, to some degree, Tuesday, Election Day itself, remaining, they could broadcast and since the folks in the media were, in Wallace's opinion, pretty slow-witted, three days was not long enough for them to gear up for a backlash.

"Let's spend, spend big, rule the air," Wallace said, by which he meant buy up all the available time, at whatever price. "Let's roll with 'Let's Roll' and carpet bomb 'em."

Hoagland coughed. His cough was chastisement, calling the class to order, because they had erred.

"It's the way to go," Wallace said.

"Well . . . well," Ed said. Then he looked at them all. "Problem . . . There's damn little air time to buy."

There were various *what*'s and *how's that*'s around the table and taking notes, too, and Wallace's chief air time buyer got on a phone and started making frantic calls to confirm or deny the truth of Hoagland's announcement, though no one really doubted the secretary.

"Hagopian," Hoagland said, as if that were an explanation.

Scott, petulant at being thwarted, angry that he had not been served well, said, "How? How come we didn't know? And how come we didn't know what that bitch was going to pull? I was told we had their debate books. Weren't the books I was practicing with her debate books? Whose fucking debate books were they? Listen up, people, when you get the enemy's plans, you're supposed to get the *right* damn plans . . . and . . ."

Hoagland ignored the president's rants. It had become very clear in the last fourteen or so hours that Hagopian knew that there were Scott spies in his campaign and he'd laid low, he'd let them spy, and he'd let them steal good material—the books for the first two debates had been completely accurate—because Hagopian had been setting them up.

". . . and," Scott yelped, a yelp specifically directed at his secretary of state, "what do you mean, Hagopian?"

"Bought . . ."

"Bought? Bought what?"

"Every goddamn available advertising minute between now and when the polls close."

"How? How? That's impossible. They don't have the money!"

"They lied," the Gray Man said, in his bleak, gray way.

"They can't lie," Scott said. His anger made him sound astonishingly naive, considering his position and his career. "They filed, we've seen their filing."

"They've already refiled," Hoagland said. His hand made loose circular motions in the air. "Amended . . . accounting errors . . . oversights."

"There are rules about this. It's not fair," Scott said. "Let's hit them." He looked to his attorney general. "Shut them down, sue them."

"It's the FEC," the attorney general said, which was all he needed to say. They all understood that the Federal Elections Commission was a Lewis Carroll rabbit hole: things went in and disappeared for arbitrary lengths of time and encountered strange and curious events and came out, oh, years later, and sometimes someone was nominally fined, but nobody was ever stopped from doing anything and nobody had their office taken away because they violated the rules in winning it.

"Also," Hoagland said, "under cover of making some cockamamie documentary by some nobody filmmaker or videographer, up in New York . . . uh . . ." he consulted some notes in his mind, found the name, "Mitchell Wood, making a documentary, supposedly about nurses in Vietnam, they made a whole new slate of commercials. Ms.

Murphy as the warrior queen, the gun-toting nurse, whatever. Strong stuff, very strong stuff."

"How do you know? How come we didn't know about this earlier."

The Gray Man didn't bother to reply. He hadn't known before because his spies had failed. He knew now, because they got it right this time. He was certain they were right, because he cross-checked, called the networks personally. The reason they had gotten it right, now, he thought with contempt, was because Hagopian had let them.

Hagopian was good. He had told them, told the world, what he was doing. He had used Scott's strengths, money and position and certainty, and turned them into arrogance and liability and complacency. He had let Scott pound away, pound away, tire himself out, until he was a combination of overconfident, in a rush to get things over and done with, and overtired, so he overreacted.

Now, the thing to worry about was how much more they had underestimated Hagopian. Was this his final stroke, his big sucker punch? Or did he have more in store.

The other thing to worry about was how good Hagopian's spies were. If the Gray Man hadn't been sure before, just based on the nature of things, he was sure now that Hagopian had spies in the Scott campaign. He looked around. He wondered if anyone really close to Scott, on this plane, was helping out the enemy.

He wondered if anyone knew about one-one-three. He shook his head—the others in the room, watching him, took that to be one of his eternally mumbling mannerisms—he shook his head; the answer, he was sure, was that no one here knew. Not even Scott. It was a great knack the boy had, of having others do his dirty work, and not even "knowing" it was happening.

Scott had fucked up. Now Ed Hoagland was going to clean up.

The pilot's voice came over the speakers, just as it does on commercial craft, to announce they were coming into Tallahassee and to fasten their seat belts and all of that. Nobody paid much attention.

Wallace said, "There's gotta be time left. We'll buy what there is, everything there is, and run the hell out of our spots. They're strong, very strong."

"Sure," the secretary said.

He got up. He started back to his seat. "I'll be getting off at Tallahassee," he said, meaning he'd leave the four-city tour behind and go back to Washington and take care of business. Wallace was still pontificating, and now giving orders, too, ordering the time buyer to buy time. It was too late for mail, too late for phone banks. The Net geek started babbling about e-mail chain letters and spam with Murphy's name attached and porno pictures with Murphy's face pasted in. As Hoagland passed by President Scott, he put his hand on the younger man's shoulder and leaned over, mumbled, whispered, and only Scott could hear him and he said, "You're going to stay in office."

Chapter

TWENTY-SEVEN

FRIDAY MORNING. OCTOBER 30. Anne Lynn Murphy woke up happier than she had in months. And later, too. Hagopian had left her schedule light and loose. She argued with him about it. It seemed obvious, so obvious that you had to go all out, sprint for the finish line, hit every city, shake any hand, scrounge for every vote.

Hagopian said, "No, we go for broke Thursday night. If it doesn't work, you've lost and it's over. If it works, well then, we'll need to be flexible, the phone will be ringing off the hook."

But, she realized, that if she'd slept late, it hadn't rung. Something must be wrong. She'd been sure . . . Hagop . . . the polls . . . everyone told her she'd scored her twelfth-round knockdown last night. Now all she had to do was remain standing, the only knockdown of the fight . . . so it was hers . . . but the phones weren't ringing.

She flung on her robe and stumbled out of the bedroom, heart palpitating, a vertiginous sense of something wrong. There was her husband sitting with

Hagop. Her husband had his coffee and her adviser had his tea, looking so smugly Zen it made her want to pour it in his lap to see him yelp but it made her feel good, too. It was like having a wizard. It was scary because he operated in certainties that were beyond logic, no, not beyond logic, a product of his own special worldview, and once you saw the world that way, then he was logical. Like holding back, letting Scott have his lead, being patient until five days before the election and going for the one perfect shot. To do it, she had to believe that if she fought and clawed all the way through, all out, giving it her best and utmost every round, the way she had gone at everything her whole life, the thing that had worked for her in everything else she had done, she had to believe that wouldn't work. She had to be calm and sit and watch the time slip away, disappear, and do, seemingly, little about it, watch the lead never change, watch Scott appear more and more invincible, a very dangerous tactic, because the appearance of power brought him more actual power, money flowing to the front runner in ever-increasing amounts.

In order to bet it all on one shot, she had to believe that she'd lose every other way. She had to believe that Scott would respond like Hagopian predicted he would and not just laugh at her and say, hey, that's old news, hey, I volunteered, did my bit, and the army decided what to do with me, you've been in the army, you know that's how it works. If Scott had done that, he would have kept his ineradicable seven points.

What a gamble. And waiting three months to play it. With Hagopian telling everyone that they were imitating his hero, Muhammad Ali. So the enemy could have, should have, known.

So why weren't the phones ringing.

"We took the phones off the hook," her husband said. "Not literally," he said. "We forwarded everything to headquarters."

"But don't . . . aren't they . . ." She cupped her hand to her ear to mean wiretapped.

Hagopian nodded his head, agreeing, agreeable, yes, sure, they probably were. Then he said, "Everybody wants you."

She smiled. A girlish cute smile that she rarely showed anymore. They all knew that he meant that everyone from GMA to *Meet the Press* to Conan to Montel and Oprah, again, wanted her. But the phrase resonated with her girlhood, with any girl's girlhood, and the smile came from there. Hagopian was letting a scheduler and a handler work with the television and radio shows so that she would move from studio to studio, Washington most of today, New York for the evening and the following morning, then L.A. the next evening, and that worked because you were flying with the sun, making up three hours on a five-hour flight, and that was Saturday, fly back through Saturday night, sleeping on the plane, more shows in D.C. Sunday morning, then New York, again, Sunday night. Monday, however, was the campaign trail, Louisiana and Florida, swing states, and then Tuesday, home to Idaho, to vote. Idaho had gone big for Scott last election and was expected to again. It was a conservative stronghold and Murphy was considered an aberration. So, Idaho seemed like a waste of time. Maybe, fly in to vote, fly back out for all the last-minute campaigning.

Anne Lynn said, "No, win or lose, I want to be home. And besides, I think it's good luck."

"Hey, if it's good luck," Hagopian said, agreeing entirely.

Now, her husband got up and went to the kitchen and poured her some coffee. She drank it with no fat for her weight but hated the thin blue stuff. He put whole milk in, it was sort of saying I'd love you even if you were fat, or maybe here's a small celebration, or doing what you really like, at least sometimes, is the key to living, or some combination of all those things. It was a communication between them and when she tasted it, and she could taste the difference, instantly, with pleasure, slightly guilty pleasure, she smiled at her husband for doing it. She was grateful. She knew it had to be hard to be the husband of a woman running for president. He'd been playing his male consort role with Prince Albert dignity. Grace under pressure.

While she sipped, Hagopian went over to the preposterous music system he'd insisted that she have and put on some Gregorian chant. Anne Lynn had come to hate Gregorian chants, partly for their own sake and partly as a Pavlovian response. Gregorian chants meant that Hagopian was going to tell her things that he did not want overheard by the microphones that he believed were ubiquitous. Whether they were or were not, she couldn't be certain, but that was his belief and he was adamant in his belief. But why Gregorian chants? Because he believed that they vibrated in a special range that was not only healing; they also vibrated with his own voice and that made his speech unintelligible to electronic systems.

He wandered close to one of the speakers, drew her along, and said, "You know they're up to something."

"What?" she asked.

"I don't know," he said.

"Well?" she said, meaning, How can you say the one and not the other?

"They must be," he said, "because that's who they are."

"But we don't . . . ."

When Hagopian had first insisted on recruiting spies in the Scott campaign and in the White House as well, Anne Lynn had been resistant. He quoted Sun Tzu, Lao-tzu, and from a recent history of the Jesuits.

She replied that in all her years in politics she'd never used spies and gotten along without them just fine. He pointed out, in reply, that she came from a state so small that nobody ever did anything without everybody else instantly knowing. And it was true, as soon as somebody did something, someone else was on the phone to let her know, sometimes it had to go through two or three or four people before it got to her, but it did always get to her. Then he said, "If you get to be president, you have to use spies."

"But that's different," she said, and it even sounded naive to her own ears, like gentlemen don't open gentlemen's mail, naive, old-fashioned, and foolish.

"They are the enemy. And . . ." this had been before the convention, before the plane crash, ". . . and, if you get the nomination, or if they even realize you are a serious candidate, they will regard you as the enemy and they will subvert, buy, lie, whatever, to have people inside here."

"Isn't the point to be better than they are?" she said.

"Better *at*," he said. "Better *at* campaigning, better *at* getting votes, better *at* running a government."

"You are a most *a*moral man," she said.

"No, I'm not," he said, quite seriously. "I'm just different, consciously different."

"No," she said.

"If you're president you will use spies. You will rely on spies. You will wish you had more spies, more and more and more. To see into the hearts of your enemy before they act is efficient, economical, intelligent. You must be astute at listening to your spies. If this president had been astute at listening to his spies, the terrorist attacks on our own soil probably would not have happened. It is not easy because there is so much to listen to, *too* much to listen to, and the voices become a billion droplets of water joined together to make the waves on the beach, unless you know how to listen. So one of the great skills of being a president is learning how to listen through all the voices, shouting, begging, wheedling, demanding, hoping, conniving, manipulating, all that noise, and how do you listen, how do you listen to this great asset, your spies?

"A man who gets into the ring who has never sparred and practiced will, I guarantee you, fail. Even against a smaller, weaker, less fit opponent who has practiced and knows the ways of the ring. This is your chance to practice, your chance to learn, and if you don't take this opportunity, then you will not be fit to be president. But that won't matter because you won't get to be president."

"Back in Catholic school," she said, "they would have told me that men who reasoned like you were the snake in the garden."

"No, my dear, they would have recruited me for the Jesuits." Then, bored by trying to be cute and witty, he said, "If I regarded a political campaign as something other than a trial by fire, in which the voters get to see which candidate can stand the flames best, then I would, indeed, be immoral or amoral.

"*My* opponents," he said, "Wallace and Hoagland and some of the others, see it in roughly the same way, that anyone who doesn't win doesn't deserve the winnings. Are there differences between us, them and me? Yes. Their weapons of choice are righteousness and blunt force. These are good weapons and powerful ones. I like to think mine are intelligence and insight and intuition and that I can, at some point, find a way to redirect their forces and use them against them.

"Now, as to not using spies, that would be like fighting blindfolded. In order to fight blindfolded you must first decide that it is more important to you to do that, to fight blindfolded, than it is to win. Which is fine, and interesting, for a martial arts student or even for a candidate, but it is unacceptable in a president. A president, a leader of a country, a person responsible for the fate, the life and death of others, does not have the elegant, marvelously elegant luxury of saying it is more important that I fight blindfolded than that I win.

"This president, this Gus Scott, as I said, part of his strength is righteousness. He said to himself that his predecessor was unrighteous and therefore everything the predecessor had done had to be disrespected and disparaged. When his predecessor passed on warnings about Al-Qaeda and about airplanes being used as flying bombs, which he did, Scott indulged himself in his great righteousness and in that moment his strength became a blindfold, and more than three thousand people died terrible, frightening deaths. Of course, later on, many more died in his wars, which followed.

"Now you are telling me that you want to be able to indulge in the same luxury. A little different language perhaps, but you want to feel righteous about yourself and morally superior to your opponents and will even wear a blindfold to do so.

"And I am telling you that makes you unfit, in my morality, to be president. You're one of the game masters when you're president, except that when you fail, it's real people who die, not pieces on a board or computer-generated icons."

Anne Lynn Murphy said, angrily, "Follow that logic and anything can be justified."

"What I'm saying is that not being smart can never be justified. That when you're in a position of responsibility, being wrong, when you could have been right, is immoral. Being ignorant when you could have had clear sight is immoral. That's what I'm saying. And to use the tools of power, you must practice using the tools of power, just as with any other skill or craft."

So he had convinced her, reluctantly, to use spies and they did so. She worried that it might corrupt her, that she would come to like having inside knowledge, secret knowledge, foreknowledge. She did, indeed, come to like it. Especially in the long, dark days, when she had to appear weak so that Scott's arrogance could ripen and grow. To do that in the dark, simply having faith in Hagopian's assessments . . . no, faith was for God or perhaps for principles of science, but faith in a reality TV producer? The reports from their spies had become her secret comfort, and sometimes when the tension got to be too great and patience began to seem impossible, she would crave the reports and the feedback, and the right news would calm her just as if she'd taken a Valium.

So now, when Hagopian was telling her that he

believed that her opponents were planning some counterstroke, she expected that her spies had information
and that Hagopian had contacted them and could now
deliver that information to her.

But instead, he said, "Nobody knows anything."

"What do you mean?" she said. The choral of
monks with their liturgical Latin moaning kept moving
sound waves around them and it felt like they were
weaving some strange acoustic cloak.

"I mean," Hagopian said, "that none of my sources
has heard even a hint of what they're planning."

"Well, if they haven't heard anything . . ." Their
network had been quite good, better than she'd
expected, Hagopian, or somebody in his employ, had a
knack for finding pain and discontent and exploiting it
and they'd found informants very deep inside the Scott
campaign, ". . . then maybe there isn't anything."

Her adviser looked at her. He looked, in his
manner and demeanor and even in the papery quality of
his skin, like the old monk in that silly TV show that
used to be popular . . . when was it, before she went to
Vietnam or after she came back? . . . *Kung Fu.* There
were boyhood scenes when the hero as a youth was in
the Shao Lin Monastery and if the boy made a mistake
the old monk gave him a look that said, You are a child,
you know nothing, I have striven so hard to teach you
and yet you know nothing and only a blow across the
back of your head can communicate how blind you are.
Of course there was no blow from Hagopian, and the
look only lasted a moment. When you see something
that lasts a very short time, there is frequently an afterimage that somehow lingers after the event is gone and
you can see things defined in the afterimage that you

could not see in the actual moment. So, in the afterimage
of the Old Monk you could always see how much love
he had for the boy, that really, he was the father and this
was his special son and he was only harsh to prepare him
for his special destiny, which was likely to be a hard one,
a very hard one, and likely to come too soon. What Anne
Lynn saw, also, in the afterimage of this moment, in this
master's face, was the revelation that his skin had grown
papery and thin, that age or illness was stalking her
teacher, and a frisson of fear touched her, she needed
him, needed him and she truly loved him, not in a
romantic way, or a sexual way, whatsoever. He had not
just been running her campaign and playing his media
games and being a star in his own movie, his own reality
TV show, which was how she normally thought of him.
No, he had been teaching her, he had, all this time been
Merlin and he saw her as his Once and Future King, to
be raised, taught, matured, for the burdens, for the dif-
ficulties, for the tragedies of leadership.

The doctor in her raised its diagnostic voice and
opened her diagnostic eye. What was it? Had she underestimated his age? Did he lie about his age? Was he merely
tired? Was it cancer? Or AIDS or some other agent of mortality, one of the other deadly assassins out of the chaos?

But before the doctor could juggle preliminary
lines of inquiry, or even begin to take a closer look, the
moment was gone, his face was normal again, busi-
nesslike, calm, and thoughtful.

Yet neither of them resumed. Both of them stood
there, the chanting, she felt for the first time, moving her
spirit, she knew not where or how, but she felt the spiritual currents in her moving. There was fear where she
was going. Fear behind her and fear up ahead. For the

first time she truly understood that as much as she feared losing, feared losing at anything, and how that drove her, she now understood that she needed to fear winning just as much. Then, to the next level, that she had to accept that fear and overcome that fear, the warrior king, the Warrior Queen, dare not fear winning, could not afford to fear to win, because she was responsible to her tribe, she must take on the burdens of guilt and pain and failure, for the whole tribe. This made her understand some of Scott's popularity and success. He took on the responsibility of killing our enemies with blithe, football game cheer, without apparent guilt or trouble or worry over the blood of innocents or other such ambiguities and that made it easier for those who believed that these wars and killings needed doing. For if a thing needs doing, as with a medical procedure, you don't want the additional pain of feeling that the microbes you kill along the way are anything more than microbes.

"What," she said, finally, "do our spies say?"

"They say nothing," Hagopian said, staring at her, demanding that she understand.

Then she did. "They must be planning something, because that is their character. They will not let go of this government, will they? Not easily, no. And if we have no word of what they are planning it is because it is a very dark secret, so dark that only a very few can know. That's why we haven't heard and that's why silence is what you are worried about."

He nodded, almost imperceptibly, and almost imperceptibly, the old, old monk inside the reality TV producer twinkled out at her, secretly pleased by the young grasshopper. "All we can do, all you can do," he said, "is stay in balance, so that when the blow comes you flow with its force before you strike back."

Hagopian had heard one thing. A hint of something, an arrhythmia in the beat of his enemy's march, a tremble in the web. He'd heard of some wild to-do at Stowe Stud among the Golden Elephants and a man jumping out the window running from some real heavies, Homeland Security people, maybe, possibly private security, and horses run amok. But there hadn't been a police report. Or even a call to the police. At least as he'd been able to determine so far. A disturbance, but no call to the police. That meant there was something to keep quiet. But Homeland Security called in. That meant it was political. Not international terrorism. The Abduls and Mohammeds didn't have a clue who an Alan Carston Stowe was. They liked big, symbolic targets.

It was donkey and elephant politics. He was certain of it. And maybe it had to do with the big secret that he was certain must exist.

Chapter
TWENTY-EIGHT

DURING THE DEBATE and right afterward, The Gray Man had figured that Murphy had tried a Hail Mary pass at fourth and twenty, thirty seconds left on the clock, and got lucky.

If that had been the case, then it would have been up to the big guys to suck it up, buckle down, use their superior weight and experience and skills to drive back down the field, to field goal distance, kick, and score.

Now he understood that they had been suckered and it had been an ambush and that Hagopian had plans in place to exploit the success of the ambush and he had a defense-in-depth to stall a counterdrive.

So it was back to Stowe's to give that go ahead, to put one-one-three in place—even if it required some overt act—because it looked possible that without it, Murphy might actually take the presidency. And that would be the greater abomination.

Last night, he'd left the minute their brief meeting was over and was unaware of all that ensued afterward, the librarian jumping out the window, the shots in the night, and the full-on equine riot.

The first hint that he got that anything was even different than normal was when he arrived at the house and Bill told him that Mr. Stowe was down at the stables meeting with his bloodstock managers, some lawyers, and the owners of a mare named Kool Karine.

"I've been sitting too damn much. I'll walk down, thanks, Bill."

He enjoyed the stroll. He always marveled at what beautiful grounds Stowe had, didn't even want to speculate on the cost of the upkeep. He wondered what would happen when Stowe died. Would some developer get hold of it and turn it into an instant subdivision?

The first thing he saw as he entered the stables was a well-groomed woman in her fifties, wearing Englishy horse country clothes, running up to a chestnut mare. There was a huffing, puffing, jogging man, who was obviously her husband, following her and he, in turn, was being followed by several lawyers whose suits and ties and black leather courtroom shoes made no concession to horse country conditions, and they walked, albeit at a hurried pace, arguing every step of the way, and behind them was Alan Stowe.

She threw her arms around the horse's big glossy neck and cried, "Karine, Karine, my baby. What did they do to you? Those beasts, those horrid beasts."

The vet came out of the stall, pulling off rubber gloves and putting away a sample of some sort and said, "Someone got up on her."

"We paid one hundred and thirty-five thousand dollars," the woman with her arms around the animal yelled, the way she would at a Bloomingdale's customer service counter, yelling out the price to establish that she had a *right* "to have Kool Karine mated with Glorious Morning and you say that *someone* got up on her. We will sue, we will sue." Two of the lawyers were nodding in congress with her and the third lawyer was preparing to respond.

"Who got up on her?" the husband said.

"Well, it could have been Glorious Morning," the vet said. "We'll test for DNA." She tapped her pocket where she'd put the semen sample.

"There, Martha," the husband said. "Maybe all's well that ends well. Why don't we wait for the test?"

Martha paused. Maybe she would.

Then the vet went on. "That's if there's just one . . ."

"What do you mean just one?" Martha cried out.

"Well . . ."

"Gang raped!" Martha cried out, clutching Karine's big, hard head toward her bosom. "My baby was gang-raped. We'll sue. We'll sue for damages, emotional damages. What are your horses," she yelled at the vet and the grooms—most of whom were black—and at Alan Stowe, "a bunch of gangsta niggahs?"

"If your mare has a live foal by Glorious Morning," Stowe said, "we will keep the fee. If she does not, your fee is refunded. Those are the terms of the contract." He spoke with utter finality. "We will all adhere to them. Your mare is in good health and uninjured. As to rape, a mare cannot be raped. She is either in heat or not." He turned on his heel and stalked out. He saw Hoagland and gave him a wink.

Hoagland followed Stowe out of the barn, blinking in the brighter light. They moved slowly.

"What was all that?" Hoagland asked.

"Pah," Stowe waved it away, then he said, "So, you decided that we need to do it?"

Hoagland felt that Stowe was too eager and he needed to know that the brakes might still be applied, so he said, "I still have some tricks up my sleeve,"

"Do you?"

"Yes," Hoagland said. He had solved the problem with the time buys. Three of the major oil companies were, even now, reselling their TV time to the Scott campaign. It was in their best interests. They all knew damn well that just modernizing the electric grid and reclassifying SUVs as cars instead of trucks would cut American oil consumption by 20 percent. A shift of even a fraction of big oil's tax breaks to wind and solar power would make them genuinely competitive and Murphy had promised to support all of those things in the name of ending dependence on foreign oil, which it would.

Their friends in oil were doing it quietly, but if it did leak out and become an issue, each of them would make statements to the effect that they were doing it in the name of fairness. They had heard that in these final days the Murphy campaign had bought up all the available time and that was preventing Scott from getting his message out and it was important to the American people to have a chance to hear both sides. It was apparently irrelevant that Scott had outspent Murphy three-to-one on television in the previous three months.

He'd also gotten in touch with Milton Futter, the governor of Ohio, and Fred Arbusto, the governor of Florida, which were the key states if the election were close. He knew they both had presidential ambitions and were even now jostling to get in line for after-Scott. He let them know that if they didn't hold their states in this election they couldn't expect to be regarded as serious candidates in the next cycle. They knew what they had to do. And they both promised to get it done.

"But you're here," Stowe said.

"Yes."

"Well?"

"Yes, Alan, we'll go. Understand, we might call it off at the last moment."

"Of course," Stowe said, agreeably. He was clearly pleased.

Too pleased, the secretary thought, way too pleased. "You want to do this, don't you?" he said sharply.

"Well, if it weren't necessary . . ."

"You want to do this, don't you?"

Stowe, who had started out walking slowly and had then slowed down even more as they started uphill, pushed himself to take a few more steps to where this bit of a rise leveled out. Breathing hard, with a wheeze and a rattle, he stopped and looked around at his land, his grounds, their beauty, and their grooming, and knew that he would be dust to them and they would be nothing to him soon, very soon. Then he looked at the secretary of state, walking laboriously after him, not much sprier, though he was seventeen years younger, and he said, "Yes, I want to do this."

"Why is that?"

"Because I can," Stowe said.

"That's it?"

"Don't you feel that way? Look at some little town, some worn-out little town, with some scrub woods around it and you say to yourself, I could turn that into three million dollars' profit. I'm worth close to two billion dollars. I don't need another three million, not really, do I, but when I see one of those little towns, outside a major growth area . . ."

Hoagland looked at him. It was more than that. He could see the energy and vitality surging up in the older man, a lot more than would be created just by turning some village into profitable suburban sprawl.

"History," Stowe said into the silence and unasked question. "We'll be making history."

That was what Hoagland thought it was about and that was the answer that frightened him. After all, secret history was an oxymoron. History was not events; history was the description of events. "This can't be known," he said, sharply.

"Not in our lifetime, no," Stowe said.

Not in their lifetime? That was a bit like saying "not until next year" on December 31. He suddenly understood, that's what this business about the library and a librarian was for. Who would care about the Stowe Library or even the Collected Papers of Alan Carston Stowe unless he was the Man Who Stole the Presidency? Otherwise he was nothing, just another man who'd made lots and lots of money, not even the most money, in a time when lots of men had made lots and lots of money. For all the people who sucked up to him on a daily basis, there was hardly anybody who'd remember him a year after he died.

"Who else knows about one-one-three?" he said.

"Nobody," Stowe said, beyond those they were both aware of and who had to know to implement it.

"The librarian?" Hoagland said.

"He doesn't know," Stowe said.

"Then how are you going to get it into history?"

"I'm not trying to be in history," Stowe said. "Just make it."

Hoagland didn't believe him, but it was no time to be at each other's throats and they were both old-fashioned enough to think that calling a man a liar were fighting words. So he just noted it and realized he would have to make his own plans as to what to do about Stowe and his dreams of history and the librarian. He needed Alan to save the Republic, but only for a few more days.

He couldn't believe he was thinking that way. Damn Scott for putting him in this position. It wouldn't have to go that far. He'd find some way to divert Alan or make sure that his library was sealed for a hundred years. He'd do something. But in the meantime, there was that one dangling thread. "Where's the librarian?"

"With all that ruckus," Stowe said, "you would have thought they'd catch him."

Chapter
TWENTY-NINE

GARY J. HACKNEY, professor of law, is twinkly, in general, when you meet him by chance around the campus. But that is deceptive, I've been told. Students whine that he is brutally demanding in class and savage, it is said, in litigation on those few occasions when he climbs down the long, winding ivory tower stairs to the brawling screech of real-life courtrooms.

He has a mostly bald dome, shaped like an egg, with a fringe of gray hair, which starts, on the sides, just above his rather large ears. When it's dry it's quite wispy and stands out in the wind. Right now it was wet and it hung down like strands of rice noodles.

He has a slender frame, which I'd always known, and skinny shoulders. I'd known that too, but not how bony they are or that he has a small potbelly that looks like it's stuck on. He plays squash for exercise and I knew that he had a regular 10 a.m. game.

Here it was 11:07 and I was lurking around the men's locker room. His partner, an English grad student in organic chemistry, rushed off and as soon as he did, I stripped down, with some relief I must say, as I was stinking, filthy, and bruised, and my clothes were worse, and I sidled into the showers.

"Gary, Gary," I hissed.

"Huh, huh," he said, turning to the sound of my voice. He wiped the water from his eyes and peered in my direction, squinting, half blind without his glasses. "Who, who?"

"It's me, David Goldberg," I said. "The librarian."

"Ah David, I've never seen you so out of focus before."

"Yeah," I said, and stepped beneath the shower next to his. Gym showers are the best, high nozzles with tons of water. I sighed with pleasure.

"Good workout?" he asked.

"Oh God, I needed that," I said.

"Know what you mean," he said.

"Did you have a good game?" I asked, trying to be polite, make contact.

"Yes, indeed. Fucker is forty years my junior and I whipped his pasty English ass. It's good to kick ass, David, it's good."

"I need to talk to you, Gary," I said.

"Talk away, talk away," he said, scrubbing with enthusiasm at all the parts that rarely see the sun.

"I think I have some legal problems."

"Have you got money?"

"I don't know. I have twenty or thirty dollars on me," I said.

"David, my boy, when I step out of my role as befuddled academic and into the world of law, I charge four hundred and fifty dollars an hour, outrageous, I know, but I like it like that."

"Dammit, dammit, please, Gary, I need help."

"What, what kind of help?" he asked, and then sort of hummed to himself as he gave his genitals a thorough scrubbing.

How to begin? How to explain? What could I say? "I'm in the wrong movie," I blurted out. Then I babbled on about how I'd thought it was a Woody Allen film, a neurotic love story, but then it turned into a crazy thriller, with sadists chasing me. "Every time I see one of those movies, at some point I always think, 'Come on, you asshole, just call nine-one-one.' So I thought, hey, why don't I go to the police? But they are the police, or at least Homeland Security, which are, actually, some of them, police, federal police? And she told me they're the police. So I thought the next best thing to do was to go see a lawyer. Actually, a better thing, because you should never talk to the police without a lawyer. But the only lawyers I know are the real estate guys, who were at the closing when I sold my house and the divorce lawyer who took all the money from selling it and handed it over to the lawyer who represented my wife. Help me, please."

"Well, we can certainly talk about it," he said, with a certain squinty interest, and turned around under the spray, rinsing at last. "Come on up to the office."

"I can't," I said, desperately. "They're watching!" I was sure I sounded insane. "Or maybe they're watching, and you're right across from the library. I think they're watching the library."

"All right," he said. I knew that tone of voice. I'd used it myself with the professor of physics emeritus who had to sit underneath the steel girders in the library because they broke up the alien radio waves.

After we dried off and we started to dress, he

looked at my clothes and wrinkled his nose and I said, "I told you. They're watching. My house, too. Or maybe not, but I can't take a chance."

"Wait here," he said, pulling up his pants.

"How long?" I said, panic-stricken.

"A couple of minutes."

I hid in the toilet until he came back. He had a pair of sweatpants and a T-shirt and a hooded sweatshirt for me. The first two he had snatched from the lost and found. The sweatshirt was new, a college sweatshirt that he'd bought at the desk. I put them all on with gratitude.

I just threw out my torn pants and filthy shirt. "I've been afraid," I said, "to use my credit cards or my ATM. They can track by that."

"Probably, David, if they want to," he said, still quite patronizing. Then he said, in a much kinder tone, "Maybe we should get something to eat."

"Yes," I said, oh my God, the last thing I'd eaten had been vending machine peanuts at dawn, "Yes, yes, yes," going on like Molly Bloom in that last orgasmic scene in *Ulysses*.

"Pull up your hoodie," he said, conspiratorially.

We drove to a diner about fifteen miles down the road. Hungry as I was, my paranoia was worse and I suddenly said, "If this is as bad as . . . I mean if it's crazy it's crazy, but if it's not, you don't even want to be seen with me."

He said, "How about I go in get us a couple of sandwiches and we eat in the car."

"Good idea, that's fine, and a milk shake."

"Comfort food," he said.

• • •

We drove out onto the highway and parked in a scenic overlook, which I thought was a good idea, very natural; no cop was going to make a casual, what's wrong? what's up? what are you doing here? kind of stop. I told Gary everything as it had happened. The food brought me down and smoothed me better than any of the benzodiazepines could have done.

When we were done, he said, "Let's say it's all true. That's sort of the worst-case scenario. It seems to me that if you survive until Tuesday, which is not too far away, Tuesday night, Wednesday morning, say, when the election is over and someone has conceded, you're safe. That shouldn't be too hard to do."

"I don't have money and I'm afraid to get money."

"Hmm," he said. "I'm not going to give you money in case it turns out to be aiding and abetting . . . bank . . . no, you're probably on a list there . . . hey, you a member of the university credit union?"

"Yes."

"Go to the credit union. Cash a check, a couple of thousand even. They'll do that for you. Tell them a story if you feel you need to, a great deal on a boat or car or something, but you need cash, more than you can get at the ATM, whatever. It's Friday. It won't go into the system until at least Monday. And not to your bank until Tuesday, at the soonest, maybe Wednesday. I'll help you get on and off campus; that I can do. Get on a bus, cash, go somewhere; hang with a friend.

"What I will do, I will file a complaint. I'll put it on my desk for my secretary to mail, but she won't get to it until Monday. No mail moves on Tuesday, I don't think, so you have the virtue of having made your complaint immediately, gives credibility, went to an officer of the court, that's me, more credibility, not fleeing, blah, blah, blah, but it doesn't land anywhere until at least Wednesday. And, and you were so shaken up you said you wanted to get away for a couple of days at some vacation spot, you mentioned a lake, whatever, mention a lake, would you?"

"A lake," I said.

"There you go."

"Swimming," I said.

"It's late for that."

"A little sailing, fishing, too," I said.

"Very good," he said. "That's where you went and you told me you'd be back, which I have no reason to doubt and as far as I know you're not fleeing anything. You are the injured party."

"You know," I said, "this is a really good milk shake."

We gathered up the containers and the wrapping and stuffed them in the bag and I took them out to the waste bin. When I got back in the car, he started it up and we headed back to the campus. Gary looked thoughtful. Finally he said, "The other thing you better do is find out what this secret is. I have a feeling that in the end, that might be your only line of defense."

"Gary," I said, panicked all over again, "how the hell am I going to do that?"

"You're a librarian," he said. "Do research."

It was hard for me to take that much money out. It seemed like an act of excess. I dithered. Then I saw Parks walking down the path. He was giving some tender adolescent the evil eye. I never before saw a man look at a woman like he wanted to fuck her until she bled to death and it was the blood and the death that would be the sweetness in his heart. I saw it as clearly as a movie special effect, one of the ones where the flesh melts away and some grim skeleton is revealed. I took it to be a hallucination brought on by stress and fear and lack of sleep.

I ducked inside the credit union, quick before he looked from her to me. Once inside I walked up to the woman at the desk and said the first thing, the only thing, I could think of: "Short term loan, two thousand dollars." It was all moving too fast and too far off normality for me to be making many decisions of my own, so I just said what Gary J. Hackney had said. The woman who worked there, whose name I had known for years, whose name I could not, in that moment, remember at all, had me sign some papers and she gave me all that paper money in return.

Once I had the money, I was overwhelmed with confusion. Was it too much or too little? And where the hell was I going?

I couldn't stay, but I was terrified to leave, terrified both that he would be out there and that I would have to make decisions. Out that door were a hundred thousand choices, an infinity of choices, and how was I to make them?

Then I heard the voice of the credit union women—what was her name?—asking if I was all right. I said, "Yeah, sure . . . just . . ." something or other, and it seemed like I did have to go. So I opened the door, slowly, peering out, and I didn't see either Parks or Ryan, so I kept at it and made it out the door and pulled it shut behind me as she said, "Bye, David."

I pulled up my hoodie and headed for the bus stop. There were six or seven other people waiting.

Then the bus came and I hunched my way into the middle of the line, a few people in front of me, a couple behind me. The big step up and then two more small steps to the driver, then, as I looked toward the back of the bus, there was the big man with the white hair, looking square at me. There were three people on the steps behind me. I couldn't go forward or back. I was trapped.

I dropped my money so I could get down on my knees pretending to collect it, but really to hide from him, and then crawl backward between the legs of the people behind me. But then the damn people started helping me. Picking up the coins for me. Then some irritatingly strong undergraduate put steel hook fingers into my armpits and hoisted me like a crane and as I was coming up I was certain that this spook was coming forward and would be standing right there and we'd be nose to nose and I'd be hauled off with a USA PATRIOT Act warrant and disappear to Guantanamo, never to be heard from again. The power of the human crane was irresistible and the motion inexorable and he stood me up on my feet and I looked and, yes, there was a man with whitish hair and he was at least seventy-eight, more likely eighty-eight, and he was, indeed staring at me, but it was the vacant wonderment of Alzheimer's, the mind behind the eyes wondering, What am I looking at? and Have I seen it before?

I said, "Thanks."

"No problem, bud."

I paid my money. I walked back to an empty pair of seats and took one by the window. The bus started. I slouched down, but peered across the bottom of the window frame. We rolled, slowly, 15 mph limits on the university streets and speed bumps, too. I didn't see Parks or Ryan. I saw various other people I knew, quite a few of them, and I wanted to wave. I wanted to tell them what was happening to me. I wanted to say good-bye, just in case. We stopped a few more times. Someone took the seat next to me. As we left the campus I fell asleep.

"Hey, buddy, buddy." A hand was shaking me awake.

"Where are we?"

"End of the line, buddy."

I panicked until I realized that it was the driver and his words were a simple literalism, not a colloquialism or a metaphor.

"Thanks," I said.

It wasn't much of a station, a shabby old storefront and parking along the side and back for five, maybe six buses at a time and a yellow line on the curb with a NO PARKING CABSTAND sign, one lonesome driver hanging in. The first bus out, leaving in nine minutes, was an express to D.C. Next bus, which would have headed west, wasn't for over an hour. I wasn't in the mood to hang about. It was nineteen dollars one way and thirty-seven round-trip. Not much of a savings. I bought the one-way. A bus depot is the kind of place where there's nothing suspicious about a one-way ticket out of town. A lot of people who take the bus don't plan on ever coming back.

Chapter
THIRTY

MORGAN'S PAGER BEEPED. He read the phone number on the diodes and called it. An irritating electronic voice let him know that he had reached Pleasant Valley Mall. That was all he needed to know, so he had the pleasure of hanging up on it even before it launched into a recitation of his phone tree choices.

When he got to the mall he looked for a Footlocker. When he found the Footlocker, he glanced inside and didn't see anyone who looked remotely like the man he was looking for, so he went out and looked for the nearest place to sit, a wall, a bench, a food court, anything. About a hundred yards away, to his left, where the Footlocker's corridor met the next corridor to form a pentangle, there were some tables and chairs around a staircase, an escalator, and an elevator that went up three stories through a mini-atrium toward a glass roof. There was a candy store and a coffee shop and a pretzel vendor. Half a dozen people were sitting around and a security officer was telling some teenagers with attitudes not to loiter.

Morgan looked around with a practiced eye and spotted the surveillance cameras. He was certain they were running tape. But it would only matter if someone already knew about the meeting and knew where it took place and just needed proof of it. No one did except himself and the man who was waiting for him.

Nobody stared or even seemed to recognize the old man in the golf jacket and the baseball cap with a bag on the ground that draped itself over the square shape of a shoe box, even though he was the secretary of state, number three on People magazine's Ten Most Controversial People in America list just two months ago.

Still, Jack practiced the craft and went and bought himself a fancy coffee, a skim latté with unsweetened chocolate dusted across the foam, a double shot of espresso in it.

He looked around like he was searching for a place to sit and like he just spied the old man with a table to himself, looking tired and obscure under the bill of his baseball hat that had the name of some kind of company or other.

"Do you mind?" he said, with a gesture at one of the empty seats.

"Not at all, Jack, not at all," the Gray Man said, his voice unusually clear and easy to understand. "Sit down."

Jack sat and took the plastic lid off his cardboard cup.

"What did you get?"

"Trying some Asics," he said.

"The New Balance no good?"

"My feet were OK . . ." the secretary had problems with his feet. They hurt, a lot. His job and his station in life called for him to wear CEO footwear, not dot-com CEO, old-time CEO leather shoes with leather soles that looked correct with gray worsted suits. As soon as he decently could, he'd kick them off and stick his feet, covered in thin black or gray socks, usually with some odd little design, something to do with golf or barnyard animals on them, stick those properly stockinged, aching feet into jogging shoes. They were better, but still not exactly right, so he was on a constant search for the perfect sneakers for his personal feet and the only way to find them was to try them, not just try them on in the store, but buy them and try them for a week or two, because some of the problems surfaced slowly, like with the New Balance, ". . . but my knee blew up."

"Blew up?"

"Yes, it got all puffy. It didn't hurt a great deal, but it was unsightly . . ."

Morgan wondered who would look.

". . . unsightly and clearly a harbinger of worse to come."

"And you think it was the shoes?"

"Most definitely. I asked one of the young women . . ." he gestured vaguely in the direction of the Washington, so Morgan understood he was referring to someone in the State Department, not a shoe clerk, ". . . and she said that New Balance are comfortable but wobbly and that wobbliness is what affected my knee."

"Could be," Jack said.

"It's a go," the Gray Man said, no change of tone or emphasis or of anything, from his wobbly knee to stealing the election.

"All right," Jack said, eagerly.

"You all set?" the secretary of state asked.

"Yes, sir."

"I just came from Al's, Alan Stowe's."

"Oh."

"Quite a ruckus."

"Yes, sir."

"Have you found the librarian?"

"No," Morgan said. "Nobody expected . . ."

The Gray Man waved the explanation away, didn't care, didn't want to know. "Tell me what you're doing to find him."

Morgan told him that he'd written PATRIOT Act II warrants for any credit card, debit card, or bank transactions so that they'd be alerted the minute Goldberg tried to buy anything electronically or when he attempted to get cash. That they'd wired Goldberg's home and his office and they had people checking the campus for any sign of him. "I haven't put out an all points on him because I don't want him picked up by some town cop and Mirandized and let him show up with some ACLU type who starts babbling about Stowe and us and who knows what."

"Put out the all points," the Gray Man said, and the command in his voice meant now.

"Yes, sir," Jack said.

The Gray Man heard the unspoken "but" and replied to it. "Discredit him, Jack. Discredit him before he speaks." Hoagland had a talent for defamation that helped his rise in business and now in politics, a skill with slander that he'd honed through the years. Now he gave Jack a demonstration of how it could be done, extempore, on the spot, just grabbing things he'd come across during the day and reapplying them imaginatively. "Say that he's wanted for resisting arrest, for assault on a federal officer." Those were true, or almost true, but they wouldn't do the job. The secretary of state had learned long ago that truth didn't matter and once he'd overcome that hurdle, he'd discovered that even plausibility was unnecessary. What was actually important was a certain indefinable stickiness: the accusation should be both memorable and hard to refute so that the person accused would be forever on the defensive and anything he said would automatically sound suspect and self-serving. That's what he was searching for now. That ridiculous scene in the stables came to mind, and yes, with some substitutions, just in the pronouns, that would do very nicely. "Uh, yes, um attempted rape . . . oh why not . . . rape, uh, bestiality . . ." that made him smile and the librarian *had* done something or other with the horses, try to deny that one, ". . . cruelty to animals . . ." that would make him a pariah, ". . . sodomy and unnatural acts . . ." he said with a certain enthusiasm. "And say that he's armed and dangerous. Worst that happens is that someone shoots him. But if they don't, nobody will believe a word he says." Pleased with himself, he displayed a rare smile and huffed in a way that was a rheumatic cousin to a chuckle. Pleased with himself he repeated and savored the accusations: "Cruelty to animals, bestiality."

Chapter
THIRTY-ONE

IT HAD ALWAYS been my hope, my expectation, actually, that the Stowe collection would end up at our library. It wouldn't make us the Bodleian or the Library of Congress, but special collections of any kind give status and importance to a library. Naturally, and so as to prepare the way, and so as to make my life easier, and because the work has to be backed up somewhere, preferably, for obvious reasons, at a completely separate location, everything that went onto Stowe's computer had gone over the net to my computer, at the library, and from there to the library's main database. I hadn't mentioned it because technically, more than technically, in actuality, it was a breach of the confidentiality agreement I had signed and, were it discovered, and disapproved of, he could sue me. No matter how little I had, he could sue me. And probably win and my little would become nothing. He might also go after the deep pockets, my employer, the university, and win there, too. But even if he lost, I would lose my job and probably any chance of employment as a librarian anywhere else, "now and forever, on earth, within the solar system or anywhere in the universe" (the actual language of the agreement).

I guess I figured "no harm, no foul," and, moreover, that nobody would ever check and if they checked, they were unlikely to find anything without prior knowledge of the transgression.

Now, I had very mixed feelings because somebody might look, and now somebody might find it and that would put me out of a job, out of the entire job category, now and forever. But, it might also hold the key to my salvation.

Of course I had been reading, skimming really, the material right along. That was my job. And there had been discussions with the client, who had to explain, frequently, the meaning of what I had been reading. Much of it was notes, not narrative, and even when it was narrative, a lot of it had been written for an audience of one, and talking to yourself assumes the maximum level of common knowledge.

The sequences in which I loaded the material had been dictated partly by chronology, partly by physical location, and partly by format. Some of the more recent things were already on computer or in computer-friendly formats and a lot of that which was on old-fashioned paper was stacked in front of and on top of the older material.

But in terms of examining it, I had started with the oldest material first. Because life goes that way, physics may not, but life does. Presumably, whatever this great and terrible secret was, it would be in among the newest material, which I had not yet touched.

It was a forest, and in it I had to find a single tree, *the* tree.

Which could well be disguised as *a* tree.

To do that I would need someplace to sit down, safe and warm, in front of a computer with Internet access. Not a bus, not a motel room. I have, like I guess most of us do, friends all over the country, who I hadn't seen for a year, five years, ten years, and there had to be someone who had an extra bedroom and . . . I could go see Larry Berk, in upstate New York . . . Sandra Drew, in Pensacola last I heard . . . Eddie Gottlieb in Scranton. . . .

The Greyhound terminal backs up against the tracks behind Union Station, which is down the hill from the Capitol Building. I had my action plan. Get out of the terminal, find a drugstore, get a toothbrush, toothpaste, and a phone card, maybe even some Terminator sunglasses as a disguise, find a phone booth . . . Union Station had good phone booths, sit-down spots where people were expected to park themselves and make lots of calls. That would suit me very well . . . I might even take a train to . . . wherever it was that I was going to go. I like trains.

I got off the bus and went from the departure area into the main terminal. I saw, out of the corner of my eye, notices up by the ticket windows and stopped to take a closer look at one. It said that photo IDs were required to buy tickets. Well, so far . . . so far I didn't know if my name was on a list or if anyone besides Jack Morgan and his hearty buddies were looking for me. If they wanted IDs here, they would want them for Amtrak, which was, after all, a quasi government agency, and significantly more formal.

Well, first I had to figure out where I was going. One step at a time.

There were quite a few cops in the terminal. Some lolled and some strolled, but in either case they looked around warily.

Maybe, once you're an experienced fugitive, you can pass cops without checking them out, but as a newbie, it's impossible not to. So I stared at them.

Then I reminded myself: self, you are a white, middle-class, middle-aged male; you are quite accustomed to looking police square in the eye without fear or discomfort. They are, after all, *your* centurions, *your* thin blue line, standing firm between your orderly life—previously orderly life, soon to be orderly again—and the chaos of *the others*. In spite of this reminder, and what I believed to be my return to the easy nonchalance of a member of the ruling gender-ethno type, one of the cops looked at me with far too much interest.

What the hell should I do? Look away? Walk faster? Run? What would I do if I were in my normal life, my innocent and confident life? A nod and a wave, glad you're here defending the Homeland, yeah. So that's what I did, a nod and a wave, howdy cop. He nodded back, somewhat quizzical, and turned to his partner, a few feet away, and spoke, asking him, I assumed, from the response, to take a look at me.

By then I was already turning away, in, I hoped, a natural manner, as if I had business in another direction. It was taking me toward the buses, dumb and dumber; it was away from the exits. Ahead of me there was a line for the Peter Pan bus to Wilmington, then three empty slots and I was in Greyhound territory. Their next bus out was headed for a whole southern litany of towns, terminating in Atlanta.

My nervous system called out, *look, look back to see if the cops are following,* and every time I ignored it, it just changed its tone, from simple alarm to a panicky cry to a squeak and then a whine and then an irritating, insis tent whimper.

There was a food wagon, a hand-rolled roach coach, two or three feet past the queue for the Atlanta bus. I could pause there and look back with a natural air, as if all I wanted was some comfort food. I looked up from the food and there were the two cops, and they were coming in my direction. Not in a hurry, not in a rush, but they were coming.

I moved down the corridor and to the right. There were a couple of more queues farther down, so, hey, I could be going there. Don't panic. Middle-class, middle-aged white guy. Librarian. Works at a university. Reputable. Harmless. Librarians are harmless. I edged to the right, using the people on the Atlanta line to mask my movement. There were doors, lots of doors, going out to the buses. Were they locked? Unlocked?

I was up to a door. I pushed against it. It opened. I stepped through it. I was in a long narrow parking garage with bus-size slots. There was a bus going out, from my right. The air was thick from the diesel discharges of our petrochemical civilization. I dashed forward in front of the oncoming bus. No danger from that. It was moving slow, slow and lumbering.

I saw the driver. He saw me and frowned, with disapproval. And recognition. It was the bus I had just come in on. It had its destination written large across its elephantine forehead and was headed right back where it came from.

I heard a door bang open, the one I'd come through, and then a yell. It might have said, "Hey you,"

but I couldn't tell over the grumbling of the bus's bowels.
But when it got by me, the cops would see me and then
there would be no place left to go. So I reversed direction and began jogging beside the bus, keeping it
between them and me. But to where, to what end?
Could I keep that up until we were out of the terminal?

I was at midpoint alongside the behemoth, jogging, sucking up the hard, harsh air. This couldn't go on.
The luggage bins were beside me. No, couldn't be.
Worth a try. I grabbed the handle of the middle one,
lifted and pulled and it came up.

There was lots of space in there beside the suitcases
and badly taped cardboard boxes and duffel bags and I
dived inside and the door came down behind me.

Chapter
THIRTY-TWO

DEXTER HUDLEY WAS on his way out to "an important social function" when Jack Morgan flashed his HS credentials at Hudley's secretary, Taneesha, and bullied his way in. Hudley had his coat already half on, one sleeve up to the shoulder, the other coming up to the elbow, and he froze in that awkward position.

Morgan said, "One of your employees was involved in a disturbance at Stowe Stud Farm."

"Who? What?"

"David Goldberg."

"Our librarian? At Mr. *Stowe's* home?" University presidents are beggars in academic gowns and they're judged on the amount of the funds they raise. Stowe was not only one of the megarich, he was near death and he was in the neighborhood. "I've been trying to fire Goldberg for years," Hudley declared, with fervor. He'd never had a problem with David, but compared to the chance of a Stowe bequest, David was a disposable pen. "He's just been too sly. They have unions, you know.

That's one of the many areas in which I agree with Mr. Stowe. Unions are ruining this country. If you can't fire someone who needs firing, like Goldberg, you know things are out of control. Out of control. I wish you fellows had asked me. I would have warned you about Goldberg. What did he do?"

"He assaulted a Homeland Security officer."

"My God! What can *we* do?"

"If you could alert campus security . . ."

"Consider it done!" He pushed his intercom and spoke to his secretary. "Taneesha, get me the head of security. Now!" Then he said to Morgan, in his most ingratiating manner, "We're here to help." He shook his head in dismayed disbelief. "Homeland Security, my God, where is respect? Is there anything else I should know?"

"He appears to have gone berserk."

"Berserk?"

"Well, yes. As you know, Mr. Stowe has some very valuable thoroughbreds . . ."

"Of course. One of our country's great studs. One of the world's. My God, did he hurt a horse? Did he hurt an animal?"

"None of the animals suffered permanent injury."

"Thank God for small mercies."

"There was also a sexual incident."

"Taneesha," Hudley called through the door, not bothering with the intercom, and then louder, "Taneesha."

Taneesha came in. She was wide across the shoulders, wide across the hips, and had a wide smile; she was the color of chewy caramel candy.

Hudley said, "Let's fire Goldberg."

Taneesha looked confused. She was pretty sure that President Hudley couldn't fire a librarian, especially a senior librarian, by telling his secretary about it. Maybe this was one of his imitations, but if it was, it wasn't one she recognized. She decided to bide her time and see what was going on.

"Get the lawyers."

Oh, he was being serious.

"Malfeasance, inappropriate behavior." He turned to Morgan. "What was this sexual incident?"

"On a horse, too."

"He did it *on* a horse? Like a Cossack, like some Cossack? David . . ."

"No," Morgan said, "*to* a horse."

To a horse? Taneesha was incredulous. She would have figured Goldberg for a little dick. What was he doing with a horse? Goes to show, you can't judge a book by looking at the cover.

"Don't snicker," Hudley snapped at Taneesha. He was appalled, never having come across an incidence of bestiality among the faculty or staff before. And he felt that she should be appalled, too. Very appalled. "Get the lawyers. Get security. Keep him off the campus," he barked at Taneesha, then turned to Morgan. "We'll make sure he doesn't get a job anywhere else either. We don't want someone like that around our youth. These kids are the future of America. Goldberg will never work again, not in a library, that's for sure."

Chapter

THIRTY-THREE

THERE CAME A moment when two things coincided. My claustrophobia in the luggage bay reached a hysterical peak and the bus came to a stop. I kicked the door open and rolled out into the street. Some people looked at me curiously. Some ignored me.

The light changed, the bus rumbled, spewed evil diesel smoke—is Woody Harrelson right? Should all our diesels be converted to burn vegetable oil, most particularly hemp oil? Will that make a difference?—and lurched forward.

Nobody screamed or screeched or raised a hue and cry, though I was in one of the highest security zones in the world and just a few blocks from the headquarters of the FBI. I brushed off my hands on my pants. I had to move, get away from the people who'd seen my stowaway's dismount, and look purposeful and busy.

I looked around. This was a very familiar geography.

I'd bailed out on Third Street, NW, which is also IS 395, a couple of blocks from the Mall. If I went straight down Third, I'd be right in front of the Capitol.

If I stood facing the Capitol, the three House office buildings would be off to my right, lining Independence Avenue, and just after them, in the same line, would be the James Madison Building, one of the three buildings that house the Library of Congress.

The Thomas Jefferson Building is across the street from the James Madison, that is, behind the Capitol and next to the Supreme Court. The John Adams is catty-corner from the James Madison, behind the Thomas Jefferson.

Jefferson, built in 1897, is the oldest. Its design was based on the Paris Opera House; its dome is plated with twenty-three carat gold. The Madison was built in the 1930s. It was "modern" at the time. It has some Art Deco elements, but mostly it's simple and boxy, in a sort of muscular way, a lot like the new government buildings that Mussolini was putting up in Rome at the same time.

My feet took me toward the James Madison Building. I knew, without thinking about it, that the other two closed by 5:30, but that the newest and largest of them, the Madison, stayed open until 9:00.

The Madison strives to be a contemporary restatement of classical themes. Its façade is a row of columns, like the Parthenon, but stripped of all ornamentation and even of the softness of curves. It is all straight lines, all severe rectangles, and it does achieve elegance through the length and narrowness of those rectangles and by the purity of the materials with which it is constructed.

The only decorations are words, outside and in, quotations from James Madison. Those Virginians were very much in love with their own creation: "The happy union of these states is a wonder: their constitution a miracle: their example the hope of liberty throughout the world." And, in spite of the cognitive dissonance of living with slaves, they were great humanists, in love with those things that they saw to be the roots of their creation, in love with reason and knowledge and learning and books, with *libraries*. Thus, among the quotes is this: "The essence of government is power; and power, lodged as it must be in human hands, will ever be liable to abuse." Along with, "Learned institutions ought to be favorite objects with every free people. They throw that light over the public mind which is the best security against crafty & dangerous encroachments on the public liberty."

There was a guard at the door and I had to show ID. I still hadn't shaved. My clothes looked like second-hand clothes, which they were, on someone who'd been rolling around the inside of a luggage bay of a Greyhound bus and had fallen to the pavement besides. I'd been sweating the sweat of the stressed. There are some sweats that are almost sweet and some that are healthy, some that are enticing and sexy, but the sweat of stress is not among those; it has an evil odor that invites the attack of predators and creates dissension among lovers. Nonetheless, when I showed my Library of Congress library card he gave it a careless, lazy glance and let me stroll in.

I started to feel calm and comfortable, even as I rode up the elevator. I was back in familiar surroundings. The chase business seemed a silliness. There was, after all, no good reason for it. It was a mistake. It was based on someone's misassumption. Come Wednesday I would meet with my lawyer, my lawyer would contact the powers that be, and we would do whatever needed doing to allow me to slip back into my normal, old routine.

I went up to the fourth floor, which is the copyright area, and found an unoccupied space and a computer over in the southwest corner. I sat down, logged on, took a deep breath, and as I did so I wondered if there was some way to find out if I was a wanted man. I punched my own name into Google. I found lots of my namesakes, but nothing about myself. Then I tried Most Wanted and that search brought up several choices, private sites, a national site, and several sites for individual states and, as this had taken place in Virginia, I tried Virginia's Most Wanted.

It was a paltry collection. Just eight names and eight rectangular little headshots, driver's license style. There was Daniel Innsbrook, wanted for four counts of capital murder in the city of Norfolk, said to be a "hit man" from Brooklyn, New York, and there Hector Garcia-Gonzalez, wanted for murder and the use of a firearm in the commission of a felony and robbery. There, between them, in alphabetical order, was my face. From my college ID.

"David Goldberg," a voice called out. A woman's voice, a grating voice, an unfortunate voice. I would have found Susanne Cohen-Miller a lot more likeable if she had a different voice. I think it would have changed her whole life if she'd had a different voice. "What are you doing here?"

I'd known Susanne for years. And avoided her whenever possible. Her life, in the telling, was an opera of angst, her every relationship a tale told by an idiot full of sound and fury signifying nothing, said tales regaled over low-fat lattés, Healthy Choice entrées, and in women's restrooms for decades thereafter. Listening was bad enough, but I always felt as if she wanted more, she wanted me to sail off into the idiot wind with her and create a relationship full of tugging and tearing and weeping and terminating so that she would have another sound and fury to take into tomorrow's restroom with her.

So I looked up and she was approaching, full throttle, and I said her name in return.

Then I looked back at the screen. I had to shut it down or move to another window before she got to my station. But I also had to know what it was that I was wanted for. Just a quick peek. Assault. Cruelty to animals. And bestiality.

Bestiality? What the hell was that about?

I thought, in that moment, of a joke. It was not a utilitarian response. It came uncalled for and unbidden.

Maybe it's the nature of my people, my culture. Jews have jokes. Think in terms of jokes. If Freud had been a gentile he would never have wondered about the nature of jokes. Jung, that *mittel Europa* goy shrink, never wondered about jokes; he postulated universal archetypes, not one of which is intentionally funny.

This joke even has a title: "Pierre the Bridge Builder." Actually, there are two versions. One, in which Pierre is French and that variant is not applicable, and the other, in which he is Belgian, and that one is. Pierre says, "You see that bridge, I built that bridge, but am I called Pierre the bridge builder? No! You see that house, I built that house, but am I called Pierre the house builder? No! See that road, I made that road, but am I called Pierre the road builder? No! But you fuck one sheep . . ."

These people had made me something worse than a criminal. They'd turned me into an idiot, a fool, a most pathetic form of pervert. This was going to cost me my job, I knew it.

I hit Control and Q and the screen froze. The damn screen froze. I hit it and hit it and hit it. The curse of Microsoft was upon me.

Susanne was upon me.

I leapt up to meet her so as to keep her away from the screen. I knew it wasn't going to work. I know Susanne. Try to guide her east and she goes west. Try to outthink her and say go west, in the hope that her contrary streak will make her go east, and she'll go west. She knows, in her heart, where she's not wanted and heads right for it. This is the secret of her emotional life; this is the method by which she achieves her endless stream of soul-devouring encounters.

"What are you looking at, David?" she screeched, in that unfortunate and piercing voice. I wondered if she was aware that heads around the room swiveled toward her voice every time she spoke, especially in the hushed sanctuaries of libraries. Since she was within five feet of me, it meant that anyone who was looking at her was also looking at me.

I put my finger to my lips and said, "Shush." I felt like a self-parody.

She thought so too. "Ha-ha-ha," she laughed, her laugh ringing like an iron clapper on a cracked bell.

I moved toward her, right up to an intimate distance, in the hopes that it would prompt her to whisper.

She moved around me, saying, "Problem with the computer, David?"

I said, "No."

She said, "OhmiGawwwd!"

"Quiet, Suze, quiet, it's a library!"

Everybody in sight of us was staring as she yelped, "Bestiality, David?!"

At that point, all the eager listeners lost interest. There were snickers and smirks, but they lost interest, figuring, probably, that it was just another spinster librarian discovering another patron looking at porn.

"Listen to me, just be quiet, OK, can you be quiet, Suze?"

"Yes," she said and the monosyllable reverberated through the room.

"Can we go somewhere and talk? Don't answer," I whispered at her. "Just nod yes or no."

She nodded yes.

"Don't speak, lead me to it!"

She looked hesitant.

"I'm not a bestialist or whatever it's called, I don't have sex with animals." She looked doubtful, she actually looked doubtful. I had become Pierre the Bridge Builder without even having fucked a sheep. "I won't attack you or rape you. Let's find somewhere to talk, please, please. Just nod."

She understood that if we got off alone I would be willing to tell her more and she could get her emotions really churning. So she nodded and I nodded and we slunk off together to one of the rooms behind the books where the librarians lurk when they're alone.

Chapter
THIRTY-FOUR

THE PHONE RANG as Inga picked up her pocketbook.

What a thing it was to be old. Most of the time she accepted that age came creeping like cold from out of the ground, and had crawled up her legs and around her thighs and pubis and belly and breasts and neck and all around her face like some invisible vine, you couldn't see the vine itself, but you could see the lines it left and you could see how it pulled all the flesh downward into the ground.

She watched the students go by.

Once she had been so young and so wild and her flesh had been as firm as any of theirs. She could dance, dance all night long, making the boys hot and horny and grabbing at her, making them dance to try to keep up with her so that one of them would be the last one standing when she chose to go home, hoping she would choose to take that one home with her and sometimes, laughing, she did and tore at them as hungry for it as they could ever be, rode them as often as they rode her,

an old woman's memories wondering where the sap
went. A good thing, she told herself—imagine if she
came climbing across the library counter and jumped on
some eighteen-year-old.

There'd been love and she'd thrown herself into it,
broke up her professor's home and then won and kept
the prize for herself, but that had been, she now understood, the end of her, the beginning of the fade from
Viking girl to married Twentieth Century Western Civ
woman. Then he'd gone and ruined it all, ruined both
their lives, he'd committed suicide and she had never
recovered, never been young one day since, consumed
herself with wasted days of grief, regret, anger, and
guilt.

She picked up the phone and it was Taneesha, who
started to tell her all about David having sex with a
horse. Neither of them believed it. Well, Taneesha gave
it some credence. Maybe not credence, but she was
clearly getting the entertainment value out of the story.

Then Taneesha said that Homeland Security and
the FBI were coming to take all David's papers and
secure his computer and lock up his office or whatever
the hell they did and everyone was being alerted that if
David was seen, to call security instantly.

Inga felt her heart start to pound. She was angry.
She hated these police that came into libraries. Libraries
were freedom. They were the torches in the darkness,
bastions against the inherent power-mongering fascism
of all government.

"I have to go," she told Taneesha, much to the
other woman's disappointment. "I have to go."

She marched into David's office. Maybe he did
have sex with animals. If he did, there would probably

be pictures or stories about it on his computer. She hated the idea of thought crimes.

Even if that were all lies, there would be evidence of his *life* on his computer. There would be . . . who knows what and none of it was any of anybody's business.

She didn't know that much about computers. But she knew enough to unplug David's machine, disconnect it from the monitor and keyboard, pick it up, and carry it out. She put it underneath her own desk. Then she went back to David's office and put the monitor on a table in the corner, like it was a leftover, a thing being sent out for repair or some such. She took the keyboard and carried that away, too. That she placed in the store-room with the stationary supplies.

When the hotshot from Homeland Security came with his short-cropped hair and his police state stare, she looked him square in the eye and lied and lied and lied.

It felt good.

Chapter
THIRTY-FIVE

"**I'M IN A** mess," I said to Susanne.

"Well, I can see that," she said. "Tell me all about it," she said, eagerly. "You have to tell me."

So, behind a door that said DO NOT ENTER, STAFF USE ONLY, standing in a stairwell, I began to tell her, starting at the beginning with Elaina.

"I think I met her," she said. "She was sort of ethereal. Spoke softly, didn't speak much actually."

"That's her," I said, thinking, the exact opposite of you.

"Sort of the exact opposite of me," Susanne said, with a big heya-yah-yah laugh so loud that I was afraid it might be heard out in the reading rooms. "Now I remember, she was looking for a job. But she was almost afraid to ask for it. I wanted to help her. I wanted to get a job for her, but of course there are none."

So I went on from there. It took a long time, as every detail prompted her thoughts and feelings, her analysis and her anecdotes. There was a lot of blaming of the patriarchal, hierarchal system, legacy, theology, history of Western Civ. Intertwined with that, and along with the same theme, was the information that she was no longer Susanne Cohen-Miller. She was now Susie Bannockburn, having shortened the Susanne as too Hollywood or too suburban icky-pretentious and she had dumped the Cohen-Miller two marriages back—she was only thirty-three? Thirty-six? Something like that—gone through a couple of other names and finally taken what she claimed was her mother's maiden name because it was not enough to take her own maiden name, that would still be her father's name, the point was that the roots of patriarchism ran deep, generations deep. She hadn't liked her father particularly, still didn't like her father, and it made him crazy that she reached right on past him and took her mother's name, rejecting, flying in the face of, overturning the wrong he had done to her mother by forcing her to give up her own name.

With all that feminism flowing around I figured it would all be settled when I finally got to the part in the story where I explained that this whole thing seemed to be about electing Scott and stopping Murphy.

"Ah-hah!" she cried out. "Anne Lynn Murphy."

"Yes," I said.

"Worst thing that could happen."

"What?"

"Time to bring this country to a crisis, a real crisis. Now Scott, he'll bankrupt the country, I mean really, totally. Right now there's time, probably to reverse things, but if he stays in, whoa, the deck of cards collapses, blows away, plus he gets another Supreme Court justice, boom, end of *Roe v. Wade,* oh-hah-hah-hah, you want to see some angry women, oh-hah-hah-hah! And the repression, this attorney general, and the religious wackos. Do you really think that Scott himself thinks that it was Jesus who made him president?

"Two more years of Scott, the whole thing collapses, we'll have riots in the streets, looting, fires, really, the real thing, real revolution. Murphy, Murphy stops that from happening."

"Oh, Jesus," I said, sitting down on the steps. "Oh, fucking Jesus."

"What's the matter?" Susie Bannockburn said.

"Susie," I said. "They tried to kill me or mess me up at least, I got zapped with a stun gun, you wanna feel what that feels like?! Huh? Do you?"

"Don't you dare be violent with me! I've had it with violent men!"

"Don't scream!"

"I'm not screaming!"

"Yes, you are. Your normal tone of voice is a scream!"

"You hate me, don't you?"

"I don't hate you, Susan. I don't. I'm tired and scared and my picture is up on the Internet and I'm afraid to go outside. Every cop and security person and all these Homeland Security wackos, they're all after me! I'm scared, Suse, scared."

"You poor boy."

"Yes," I said.

"Don't worry, Momma Susie will take care of everything."

That went around the corner fast. I looked at her in astonishment. She must have thought it was relief, or pleasure, or helplessness, because she reached down and pulled my head toward her. Since I was sitting on a step and she was standing, that placed my forehead at the base of her belly and my mouth in such a position that if I spoke, it would be an act of clothed cunnilingus. "Don't worry, don't worry, Susie is here." She rocked slightly from side to side and rolled my head back and forth at the same time.

Once again, it was lost and found to the rescue. She found me a watch cap that would cover my curly hair. She found a rather spiffy leather jacket. It was too big for me, but that was better than too small.

Then she took me home with her. I took a shower and she gave me her guest toothbrush and guest razor. I used both with gratitude. She had an oversized T-shirt that she gave me to wear and a pair of men's boxers that had been left behind. She was uncharacteristically coy about who had left them, or she wasn't quite sure, but she assured me that they had been washed and were quite clean.

She made tea and we sent out for Chinese food. All of this done with constant talk that constantly flew off on tangents and threatened to fly off into the stratosphere. My hold on safety was only as long as her hold on sanity.

"I need a disguise," I said, over the tea.

"I could make you a blond," she said.

"Could you?" I said. It wasn't the brightest of queries as she had clearly made herself one.

She dragged me into the bathroom and had me take off my clothes. I hesitated and she gave me a come on, I'm a big girl, I've seen it all look. I take that back. She gave me an I'm a woman, I birth babies, I cut the nuts off of boars and turn them into swine, there's nothing I haven't seen, sort of look. So I stripped and got back in the shower and soaked my hair and then she gave me some stuff to put on it. "That's what I use," she said, with one of her guffaw sounds, a more gigglish one than usual, but still a guffaw. "I'm not a natural blonde."

I put the stuff on and then left it on, under a shower cap, while we ate our moo shu shrimp and Thai stuffed grape leaves in coconut milk curry sauce. She ate with gusto and licked her lips and sucked her fingers and looked at me while she did so. Which I didn't understand because I thought I looked remarkably unappetizing with that semiclear plastic thing on my head and a towel with a pattern of pink and lavender blobs wrapped around me.

By the time dinner was over, I was blond. I rinsed my hair and combed it. But I still looked like me. Then Susie said, "Buzz cut."

"I'm afraid to go out," I said.

"I can do it," she said. "I have scissors and clippers and all that."

Susie talked and talked as she chopped and chopped with the scissors and the hair fell in huge clumps all around us. She talked the whole time. Of her pain. Of the unfairness, unfaithfulness, and untrustworthiness of her first, second, and third husbands, respectively. The sex was good with the unfaithful one, inadequate with the unfair one, and spectacular but erratic with the untrustworthy one. She understood that she had unresolved issues with her father, his fault, as he wouldn't deal with her assaults as attempts to connect emotionally. Scott reminded her of her father, so it would be a good idea if we did something to destroy him. She explained that she had the clippers to use on herself and at the moment she was completely clean-shaven, and pierced; it was the look now.

"Do you have a computer here?" I said.

"Yes," she said, and turned on the clippers. She ran it, buzzing, up the back of my head. The top and front were all choppy yellow clumps. She ran her fingers through it and said, "Aiding and abetting a fugitive," she said it playfully, sexually, neurotically. She got out a comb and used the comb with the clippers so she could cut my hair to about half an inch. She pressed herself against me and asked about my romantic life.

"What I have to do," I said, "is get online and try to figure this out, before I get sent up for . . ." I couldn't bring myself to say bestiality, ". . . for whatever, or shot down by some trigger-happy cop." I thought I sounded insanely melodramatic.

She combed and cut and buzzed and I saw a new face emerging, the planes and lines becoming more distinct and my eyes more intense and staring, or maybe that was weariness and fear.

When she was done, I jumped back into the shower to wash the stray hairs off, Susie watching me the whole time and me not wanting to go there. Why not? Because she was just too neurotic? Because . . . because I was half in love with another woman, who was married to another man, and I was being faithful to a hope of being with Niobe?

Who knows? I dried myself and dressed as quickly as I could and asked to see her computer. She had Road-runner. I found my way into the university system and tried to log onto my personal machine. But I couldn't. It was either off or disconnected for some reason.

Had they come for it? Taken it? Were they examining it?

Would they find the names under which I'd hidden the Stowe files? And if they did, would they remove them? Set up traps if I tried to enter? How long did I have before they figured it out? Two days? One day?

Chapter

THIRTY-SIX

HOMELAND SECURITY HAD kept track of Elaina Whisthoven. She was up in the northwest corner of Massachusetts, about five hundred yards from the New Hampshire line. Live Free or Die. She had applied for work as a substitute teacher, but she'd only gotten two days' employment. She made a few dollars as a tutor in English, math, and French. She also did some work cleaning houses. She never went to the library.

It was one of those "can't get there from anywhere" places. All the flights had at least three legs and a three-hour layover in Podunk Aerodrome. Even after Parks arrived at Nearest to Nowhere Airport, he'd have to rent a car and drive an hour, hour and a half, showing ID and leaving paper tracks, as deep and as indelible as handprints in cement, at each stop along the way.

Simpler just to drive, pay everything in cash, tolls, gas, and meals. Stay off the grid.

Driving was quicker, too, if he drove straight through, drove through the night; he'd catch her in the dawn. A little more crystal and he could stay up all night, no problem, second night in a row, no problem, that's what the *Wehrmacht* made amphetamine for.

He went home, he showered, and snorted, took it off the crook where his forefinger met his hand when he made a fist. That felt good, made him feel like driving, lights on the blacktop burning through the night. Vanishing point, drive right into the vanishing point.

Parks got to Elaina's with the dawn.

There was frost across the lawns and fallen leaves and a mist among the branches and the sunlight was feeling its way through the gauzy layer of chill that the night had left behind. Elaina was down a country road and there'd been no traffic in the dark so the air had a chance to let its sediments fall and it had washed itself with the mist and gotten itself all clean and fresh and then perfumed itself with the living trees and the dying leaves.

The moment could not last, it would not last, and that temporal fragility gave it a special delicacy.

Parks was roaring inside, hoarse inside with all-night rock 'n' roll and DJs and hip-hop niggahs and talk show babble and ranters and complainers and a preacher named Howell, all calling loud and raucous through the automotive night. Vanishing point. Always up ahead, straight ahead, around a corner, vanishing point, high beams, those long bright best-money-could-buy BMW high beams reaching north on the interstate.

Three miles from Elaina's house he turned off his headlights; it was bright enough to drive without them by then, in fact and legally both. He rolled down the windows and felt the air, cool and moist and sweet. He forced himself to go slow, though he wanted to rush, the rhythm of the night, of night driving, of the relentless V6, seventy-eight miles an hour, was an incessant beat inside his veins and it would not stop. There was weariness and raggedness around all his edges and a foul and dry ridge along his teeth. He pulled off to the shoulder and rinsed his mouth with a bottle of water and spit it outside through a rolled-down window. Then he snorted some more of the meth and the rush came swift and sure, right down his spine and out the meridians, spider lines out across his back and around to his finger tips, and jolts of power and blood down to his groin, oh yes he could feel his cock swell and throb, felt like the engine under the shiny black hood.

The car moved so smoothly around the country corners, so smooth, so slick, just ate it up, windows open, sweet wind in his face, a little frost in it, a little bracing taste of winter times to come, cool, frozen dead times to come.

He was in front of her house in just three minutes. It seemed an instant. He just let the car roll up to her front door. It was a tiny place, a wonder that anyone lived in it at all, a dollhouse, surrounded by trees, a stream, a small stream, no wider than a young girl's hips at the widest, running in a small ravine and judging by its shape and depth, he imagined that when the winter snows melted or when there were big summer storms, the rain pelting down, relentless, for days, it would swell and rush, rush and swell, and tear on past, muddy and full of branches and twigs and anything loose that would float, swell, and rush the way the amphetamine was driving the detritus of a harsh and ugly life through his arteries and veins.

He stepped lightly. He could step remarkably lightly for a big man.

The door was around the far side of the house, which is probably why she hadn't heard his car come up. He knew she hadn't heard him because he saw her through the window and it was clear that she thought she was alone. She was wearing her nightgown, prim as old New England itself. But sexy, too, in its spinsterhood, not an eager, ripe young virgin, a waiting frail and frightened virgin. He was on the west, a good thing because it cast his shadow away from her, as he passed by her window, looking in.

The early light came in from the far windows, that early fragile light, that special light, cooled by the mist, holding the last clinging memories of night, as ephemeral as dreams.

He came around the house.

He kicked the door in. When she saw who it was, she froze in fright. She remembered him, vividly. As he knew she would. He guessed that she dreamt of him, and curdled herself with fear when she did, and now here he was and the roaring of crystal meth rose and rose and his cock got so hard in his pants that it hurt, it ached and throbbed and she didn't move at all and her fear fed his arousal and she could feel and smell his arousal and that increased her fear, which, in turn, took him right up to that line he had known all along that he'd been coming here to cross.

He stepped toward her. He stepped across the line.

Chapter

THIRTY-SEVEN

ALMOST EVERYTHING OF Stowe's that I'd put on my personal computer, except for maybe my last five days of work, I'd backed up to the library's computers. I got into my library's system and opened up the Stowe files. I didn't want to use my own name and password. There's half a dozen people who lose and forget their passwords so often that I've memorized them. So I started using theirs. I'd go in, browse, if there was something interesting, set it to "print," and as soon as there was a pile of stuff to read, I'd go off-line and then, when I went back in, I'd use one of the other names.

The hunter and the hunted invisible to each other, not knowing what the other knew, not knowing what the other could see and sense.

Not since college had I tried to run through a year's worth of reading in a weekend. I read all night. No. Most of the night. I fell asleep in the chair and when I woke up, blinking and gritty-eyed, Susie was there, telling me, "Go to bed, you need your rest." I said no, each time and the first time I asked, "Do you have any coffee?" she said, "It'll keep you up," and I said, "That's the point," and she said, "I'll make it for you," and I said, "Thanks," and was relieved when she walked away.

Of course what I wanted, what I needed, was what any serious librarian or biographer or scholar would have wanted, three to five years to familiarize myself with the material in its raw, bulk state, then another year, at least, to systematize what I'd found and then another year or so to relate it to external sources that would support or illuminate or contextualize the source material. I didn't have that. So I made very rough judgments of exclusion. For example, anything that had to do with his real estate deals, I ignored.

There were thousands of pages of begging letters. I wished he'd thrown them all out. It seemed as if every foundation and charity, every institution that thought they were doing good deeds, and every individual with a dream who could package his ideas as good deeds had written, e-mailed, and faxed Stowe asking for money. They'd also gotten their friends and relations to beg on their behalf.

Stowe, in turn, had raised massive amounts of money from others. He didn't beg, however. He bribed and browbeat. He wrote one developer that for a mere one hundred thousand dollars in contributions, the Chesapeake Bay real estate that he owned, which was currently worthless because the eco-Nazis said oysters were more important than people and jobs, could be declared to be not a wetland and that would make it a $27 million waterfront development, which was a hell of a deal by anyone's standards.

There was a lot of material about judges and the

judicial system. Stowe took a businessman's view of the law; liability should be limited, personal injury lawyers were agents of the devil, civil rights laws were the enemy of freedom because they violated an employer's right to hire and fire whomever he wanted, workman's compensation was a force of evil, all regulations were ungodly because God's will is expressed through free markets. Stowe had taken a visionary and missionary approach to the problem. He helped recruit bright young conservatives as early as law school and encouraged them to seek judicial careers and if they did he helped them financially through speaking engagements, investment opportunities, favorable terms on loans, and by employing their wives or other family members and he helped them politically through his network of contacts. He now had judges throughout the legal system who adhered to his political beliefs and with whom he had personal connections, right up to the Supreme Court. And he knew a lot about them, too, he kept tabs on their finances and personal lives. According to Stowe's files, for example, the sexual harassment charges against Supreme Court Justice McClellan were not only true, the incident was one of a series. He moderated his behavior for a time, but now that Viagra was available he'd become active again and was particularly fond of African-American women.

There was a lot of material from the Octavian Institute. It covered the whole spectrum of the American political system. Maybe because their papers appeared to be so very academic I put them aside. The word *academic* is taken to mean something merely theoretical and not of practical value. I should have known better. Ideas are more powerful than bullets.

• • •

Susie said that I could, that I should, sleep in her bed. I felt that would get more complicated than I was prepared to handle. But I also felt that saying no would risk losing my hideout. I stretched out on the couch, reading, and fell asleep with papers in my hand and others beside me on the floor. At some point she came and put covers on me and kissed me on the forehead.

Chapter
THIRTY-EIGHT

FLORIDA STATE TROOPERS made a series of drug raids in West Palm Beach.

Palm Beach is on the water. That's the famous place. That's where the rich people live. They're mostly white.

West Palm is inland, literally across the tracks. There are two parts to it. The new part is like so much of the new Florida, grids of bright, sunshine tributes to consumerism. But there is the old part and that's where the poor people live. Many of them work in Palm Beach. Maids, cleaners, busboys, bellhops, handymen, this and that. A lot of them are unemployed. They're mostly black.

It was Saturday night. A lot of people were drinking. A lot of people were high. The troopers were dramatic. They busted down doors. They crashed into parties. They used bright lights, big guns, screaming sirens, and loud PA systems.

Everybody in Florida has a gun. Gunshots were . . .

heard? fired? imagined? . . . the troopers fired . . . fired
back? started firing? An eight-year-old girl was killed.
The troopers insisted that she had been killed by a criminal, a crack dealer, somebody resisting arrest. Though
they couldn't name a name or actually find the gun.

step 1 The people claimed that the cops killed the kid.

Rioting ensued. Not just in West Palm, in Liberty
City, too, the dark town of Miami. Then it spread to the
Gulf Coast and rioting broke out in the low, sprawling
black districts of Tampa and St. Pete.

It was, Hagopian thought, very clever.

It would motivate the Latin vote. They were already
against the blacks and leaning toward the Republicans. It
would arouse fear in the Jews, make them waver in their
liberal instincts and maybe enough to be nervous and to
stay home, if not enough to actually change their votes.

But the topper, and he was willing to bet this was
going to happen . . . in the next few hours . . . by dawn,
certainly . . . Florida's very Republican governor would
call out the National Guard, if there were any left in
the country; if not, then all the state troopers in the
southeastern United States or the army or some damn
thing like that, and station them in the streets through
every African-American district in Florida. They'd
have curfews. Armored vehicles. Checkpoints. They'd
have lists of outstanding warrants and parking viola-
tions and every third African-American person who
stepped out on the street on Election Day would be
banged for something.

The question was whether his opponents were cynical
thieves and profiteers, or were they moral men on a

crusade. He greatly preferred the former, but suspected the latter.

They had two prophets. The first, of course, was Jesus Christ. Scott claimed to have been saved and the hard core of his support were Jesus people. Hagopian had never, even in childhood, fallen into salvation. He appreciated the power and utility of being saved, but was suspicious of the claims that it made to the truth and was wary of its misuse.

Their second prophet and, to Hagopian, their real prophet, was Adam Smith, the eighteenth-century economist and philosopher who had coined the phrase "invisible hand" to express the surprising, unplanned, and unlooked-for effects of each individual pursuing his own domestic plans for gain. To the intellectual mind, that was a simile, an "as if," but to the believer mind it was God and God wanted us each to pursue profit to our utmost and then His "invisible hand" would combine those efforts and guide them to the true good.

Adam Smith had also said, "Virtue is more to be feared than vice, because its excesses are not subject to the regulation of conscience."

Hagopian thought that was true.

If Scott's people were men of vice, merely greedy, there would be limits to what they might do. If they were men of virtue, there were no limits, no point at which they would stop. There was no lie they would not tell, no fraud they would not perpetrate. No murder they would not commit.

Was he ready to say that Scott was so ruthless in his pursuit of power that he had ordered the governor of Florida to unleash the troopers and given them orders to kill some child—even this particular child, this eight-year-old girl with nappy hair, tied in pigtails with pink ribbons, who loved swimming and was reading on a twelfth-grade level—the media had ferreted out photos and written the eulogies almost instantly—ordered the death of a child to create riots so as to manipulate an election?

If he was prepared to say that . . . think that . . . believe that . . . then . . . would he have to . . . do what? . . . see to it that the man was arrested and prosecuted and imprisoned? In the reality of reality, that was clearly impossible; then what? Assassinate?

He himself, Hagopian, was not a killer. He simply wasn't. Not even in defense of the world and of thousands of people, American soldiers and foreign soldiers and civilians of other countries, in wherever this imperialist sonofabitch was going to strike next. Not even to save all those lives.

Unfortunate, perhaps. But true. That was his limitation. One of many.

If he didn't come up with a counterstroke in the next forty-eight hours, Scott would win Florida and, with it, the election.

He turned off the telephones and locked the doors. He turned on all his television sets, all seventeen of them, all on different channels, the sound soft but audible from each and every set. Then he lay down on a thin mat on the floor, on his back, and closed his eyes. To listen, dream, meditate, to feel the forces at work in the imagistic world, to seek his balance in and among their unruly waves.

In the hours to come, while he thought and meditated, the machines informed him that Governor Fred Arbusto of Florida did, indeed, call out all the state troopers and put them on overtime. He declared a state of emergency and asked for federal assistance. He called President Scott, who took the call personally. Scott offered him the army.

It was, Scott said, important to have peace and security, what with the election three days away. Between the state troopers on their Harleys and the army in their Bradleys, the niggers weren't going to come out to vote. Scott didn't say that last point on the air, but Hagopian heard it nonetheless.

Chapter
THIRTY-NINE

To understand the Octavian Institute papers it was necessary to know about PNAC. This is their mission statement.

> **The Project for the New American Century** is a nonprofit educational organization dedicated to a few fundamental propositions: that American leadership is good both for America and for the world; that such leadership requires military strength, diplomatic energy, and commitment to moral principle; and that too few political leaders today are making the case for global leadership.
>
> The Project for the New American Century intends, through issue briefs, research papers, advocacy journalism, conferences, and seminars, to explain what American world leadership entails. It will also strive to rally support

for a vigorous and principled policy of American international involvement and to stimulate useful public debate on foreign and defense policy and America's role in the world.

In essence, it is a project to figure out how the United States will rule the world. It's not secret. It's available to all, friend and foe alike, at www.newamericancentury.org. One of the most significant papers on the site is "Rebuilding America's Defenses: Strategy, Forces, and Resources for a New Century."

(1) Now that America is the world's sole superpower, the paper says, we must do whatever is necessary to keep it that way. It means having larger, better-equipped military forces than any five other countries. Which we do.

(2) It means establishing a global military presence with our forces permanently placed at strategic points all around the world. Which we have done.

Part of the job of the military is to secure the resources necessary for that defense. Which turns out to mean oil. That means taking control of the Middle East, which, the paper suggests, may require a war or two or three. Which we have done.

These wars are to be short, sharp wars. Even if we didn't need the oil, it would be good to have the wars as a demonstration, a salutary lesson, to anyone who might think of challenging America's power. This, too, we have done.

The tone of the paper is not in the least bit cynical. It is idealistic. Whether that's sincere or not, I have no way of knowing, but it certainly sounds sincere.

A Pax Americana, like the Pax Britannia and the Pax Romano that came before it, are not really peaces, but they are forms of far-reaching international political order based on the military domination of technologically inferior peoples, so that all (or almost all) of the wars are, indeed, short and sharp and won by the legions.

These Paxes (while the plural of *pax* is *paces,* I believe that when it is used this way it becomes a proper noun and should be pluralized as an English word, but I am a librarian, not a lexicographer), these Paxes do have virtues, great virtues.

An empire with technological and bureaucratic talents brings stability and order, roads and judges, banking and trade, clean water and bathing, education and literacy. Those are great things, that much of the world lacked then, and lacks now, so a genuine case can be made for an empire as a beneficent operation. Also, it can be argued that being ruled by a well-run empire is truly an improvement over life under a miscellaneous assortment of despots and theocrats, corrupt warlords and colonels with torture chambers, that is to say, it is better to be ruled by the bureaucrats and legions of an American occupation than to be "free" and "independent" under Saddam Hussein or Charles Taylor or Slobodan Milosevic.

President Scott's secretary of state, his secretary of defense, his chief of staff, his national security adviser and the head of his Policy Initiatives Board were all signatories to this paper. That is a matter of public record.

The most provocative statement in it is:

> the process of transformation, even if it brings revolutionary change, is likely to be a long one, absent some catastrophic and catalyzing event—like a new Pearl Harbor.

• • •

That fragment of a sentence inspired several papers at the Octavian Institute, two of which seemed to me to be very important. They had multiple authors, from a variety of disciplines—history, anthropology, media studies, statistics, military studies, and so on. They were, for the most part, written in very academic language. They had charts and graphs and some quite complex mathematical projections. As far as I was able to determine, neither had been published.

The first was called "With or Without a Crisis?"

The authors cited thinkers, from Plato onward, to say that democracies are "dangerously unstable," subject to "a wide variety of events, beyond control," and "not to be trusted." Moments of power, in a democracy, have to be regarded as temporary and fleeting. Any significant change, therefore, should be instituted as quickly and as thoroughly as possible.

Under that theory, a slow "process of transformation" is the high-risk strategy. A "new Pearl Harbor" is the safe, sure way to go.

If that paper had been distributed and had found its way to the top ranks of the Scott administration and they had found it convincing, then, in that eleven months from Scott's election the United States had been a nation in search of a crisis, a nation that was waiting for "a new Pearl Harbor."

If you accept that paper, then the question asked in the second paper flows as naturally and inevitably as water flows down hill. It was called, "Hands On/Hands Off."

Part one speculated on the types of disaster we might face. These included natural disasters, environmental disasters, financial collapses, war, and terrorism.

The paper concluded that terrorism was both the most likely and the area that could "be best exploited."

So they had determined that a crisis was necessary and what kind would be the best. The question that remained was how to achieve one.

The possibilities, as the title said, fell into two groups, Hands On and Hands Off. In the first instance, the government would actually manufacture the crisis. A fed with a loose burnoose would go and blow an airplane and leave a Middle Eastern passport behind to be found by some other feds. "Hands Off" meant that the government would stand by and wait, prepared to exploit an event when it did happen.

The advantages of a "Hands On" event were that the timing and duration and levels of damage could be controlled. The disadvantages were that a manufactured event might not have the "raw authenticity" of a more real event and that it was likely to leave behind a "smoking gun"—some communiqué or e-mail or phone call or piece of turncoat testimony—that would link the government to the event it had created.

The big risk of a "Hands Off" policy was that the terrorists had to be trusted to act in a timely and dramatic fashion.

The largest part of the paper considered that question.

It gave a history of terrorist events, it cited then current raw intelligence and intelligence evaluations—presumably secret government material but the Octavians had access to it—and it made forecasts of what they might try to do in the future.

Then it suggested what steps could be taken to encourage terrorists and to enable their success.

    I jumped up and started stomping around Susan's living room, ranting out loud.

    Susan came out of the kitchen. "What is it? What is it?"

    "I'm crazy," I said.

    "What? What?"

    "I just read something, OK? I'm in Unabomber territory. Where all the crazy lines are connecting and there's a vast conspiracy and they're all in on it, they're *all* in on it, they're all *in on it*."

    "David, slow down, slow down, tell me."

    "Look at these papers," I said. I shoved them at her. "These guys," I said, pacing around, "the Scott people . . . they want a new Roman Empire. And they don't see anything wrong with the idea. The only problem, for them, is to sell it. Well, they figured the best way would be to have a new Pearl Harbor. OK?"

    "OK."

    "You don't get it." I took a breath. "So far, what I just said, that's public fucking knowledge. It's plastered up there on the Web, no more secret than *Mein Kampf* was."

    "But these guys"—I meant the Octavian Institute and poked my finger at the papers that she now held—"took it to the next level. They all agreed we *want* a new Pearl Harbor. Their only question is, like, do we bomb ourselves, or just get out of the way and let the terrorists . . . do their thing.

    "Look in there," I said, sounding hysterical, even to myself, "page goddamn seventeen. There are two statistical models. The first is: What are the odds of terrorists taking a second shot at the World Trade Center? The second . . . the second . . . is what are the odds that they

will succeed if the CIA and FBI . . . get out of the way,
just get out of the way and don't try to stop them?"

"But how would . . ." Susan said, then in a calming
way, for herself and for me, she went on. "Slow down,
all right, David, slow down. Listen, I mean, maybe we
don't believe that feds are like on TV, that they're like
super crime solvers. But there are some pretty serious
people, really there are. I mean, my brother is in Naval
Intelligence and I have to tell you he is, I mean, he's my
brother and I think he's an asshole a lot of the time, but
when it comes to protecting the United States"—she
put her hand over her heart in the Pledge of Allegiance position—"and all, he's damn serious, really,
really serious and he would never look the other way
and there are lots like him."

"Yeah, yeah, sure," I said. "But they have the
answers. One of the motherfucking *scholars* who wrote
this, is a motherfucking anthropologist who specializes
in 'contemporary bureaucratic cultures' and his
analysis—with these computer math models—is that if
the head of the organization says that yesterday's goal is
now a low priority and this and that new goal are now
the big priorities, middle management, the brown noses
and the gold-star seekers and the protect-my-pension
types, will just shove aside anything that comes up about
that old concern. The rank and file, like your brother,
might still go at it, but the middle managers, they'll bury
anything he finds, they won't ever show it to the big
boss, because that's how corporate cultures work."

"I don't get it, I don't really get it."

"The previous administration made terrorism a
priority. They stopped every attack on the domestic
United States. There were a whole bunch of them,

there's a list in there, take a look. They were going to blow up bridges and tunnels and steal airplanes. The terrorists had some success in Africa and the Middle East, but none here, none on American soil, OK?"

"Yeah, OK," she said. "And you're shouting."

"Yes, I'm fucking shouting. The paper says that all that Scott had to do was to get out of the way, just get out of the way, and some big terrorist event would happen. And when it did, they could use it to change this wimpy, old-fashioned, liberal democracy that believes in the rule of law, even international law, and they could send out the legions and launch the True American Empire!"

"So?"

"So that's what happened. That's what happened."

She looked at me. She finally got it. That it wasn't some academic paper. That it was a blueprint for the past three years of politics and war. And those were unthinkable, untenable, unacceptable thoughts. Impossible and frightening webs. But of course she was still Susie and part of her was enjoying it, too. This would be the greatest piece of Sturm und Drang of her whole life, this would be the tale of tales to regale the Gails and Wendys and Annes and whoever she lunched with, drank with, commiserated with. All it needed was a twisted little love affair to romanticize it and I was it, and my head was out of control, totally out of control.

I was at a loss for words.

Was that possible? It was one thing to imagine that the administration had simply made bad choices. It was another to imagine that the bad choices were deliberate. Had anyone in a position of power even seen these papers?

I looked down at what I was holding and the title

page was on top. I hadn't looked at it very closely, just glanced at it, 'cause I was skimming, racing to get to the essence, because there was so, so much to read. It's the natural thing to do. We tend to think of things like the date, the distribution list, the source material, or the names of the authors as pro forma. But sometimes those formal details are the most important details. In this case, I knew one of the seven people who had contributed to "Hands On/Hands Off." She had a knack for the language of mathematics and she had done the statistical tables. Niobe.

Chapter
FORTY

JACK CAME BACK from the gym all pumped. Hell, he wasn't a kid anymore. He wasn't some not- enough-to-do junior officer who could spend half his life in the gym, half at the track, and the other half chasing ass. He was a man with responsibilities, drowning in responsibilities, hardly time to hit the head sometimes, let alone keep fit. He took steroids. Not a lot. Just enough to help. A little help was justified. He loved the feel of his swollen biceps and the tautness in his belly after a workout.

Sunday night. There was a dinner party. It was a nervous time, the polls showing Murphy and Scott neck and neck, but everyone trying to project a calm and confidence that they barely felt. He felt it, because he knew, but the others had to force it. You could see that.

The secretary of state would be there. He'd shamble in, shamble out; you could tell who was climbing the ladders of power, who was sliding down, just by who the Gray Man nodded to, whose hands he shook. It was important to be at the event.

Still there was time. There was time for sex before the party. Even if Niobe already had her makeup on. He liked her lips all shiny, bright and red. Let it smear and muss; dishevelment suited her. And she could repair it. Even if she was already dressed for dinner. Let her undress and change. Or hike her dress up, bend her over, both of them dressed, only their genitalia naked. There was something animal and brutish in that. Elemental. A slender woman with a generous rump, riding her that way made him think of the stallions and the mares.

She was a good wife who never said no.

Sex. Party. Then he had to go up to New Jersey, straight from the party. He was already packed. He would stay up there until Wednesday. Yes, it was a good idea to have the sex now.

He thrust the door open and he took strong strides, his feet striking the floor, so that she would know that her man was virile and potent. He wanted to tell her just how potent he was. To tell her what he was going to do to ensure that Scott remained president. To ensure that America remained secure. To ensure dominance for the whole coming century, a dominance never seen before in the history of the world.

Here he was, Jack Morgan: "give me a lever long enough and a fulcrum on which to place it and I will move the world." He had his hand on the lever . . . if the world shaped up, all well and good, he'd leave it alone, but if the world slipped from the course it needed to be on . . . then Jack Morgan would put his back into it and pull that lever and he would move the world.

He grabbed his crotch, massaging to engorge himself,

to display his potency. He wanted to tell her, but knew he must not. Still, the explosiveness, the literal and figurative explosiveness of what he was going to do, pumped him up. He stomped through the house toward the bedroom, picturing his woman at his feet, a prize of war in a barbarian adventure, sprawled on top of jeweled loot and glittering spoils. Then rising, worshipfully, to her knees. Because she belonged to him. He was potent, potent beyond imagining.

He stamped through their home with a tread like that of a legion and he thrust the bedroom door open. There she was, as he'd hoped she'd be, in her black dress that left her shoulders bare. She had the smoothest, most perfect skin, stretched taut and glowing. Every time he looked at her shoulders he wanted to lower his mouth to them and place his devouring lips upon them and reach around and hold her firm breasts in his hands and squeeze them slowly until she moaned. He wanted to tear the dress off her, but of course he wouldn't, they weren't rich enough for that sort of extravagance, certainly not with the dress she was actually going to wear for a public evening out with influential shakers and movers, no he wouldn't rip some seven-, ten-, fourteen-hundred-dollar frippery. He didn't ask the prices. He was glad she looked so good, shone so bright, was his bauble, proof on his arm that he was a success and a stud as well. Yes, Niobe was a prize. Worth indulging. Worth debts for her dresses. Worth letting her work and run a little wild.

Now he was genuinely hot for her where she sat. His penis no longer needed a hand, it was growing by itself. Her makeup was done. She was in the midst of doing her hair. As if she was waiting to serve his fantasy.

He came up behind her, he put one hand on her

shoulder, the other on her hair, fine, soft hair. He pressed his swollen groin against her. She looked back at him in the mirror, her face cool, almost expressionless. He loved that look, proud, almost haughty. She was a prize worth ravishing. His thumb dug into her shoulder and he pushed forward with his turgid groin. His other hand almost trembled as he tried to be gentle with a caress, but he couldn't be and he wrapped his fingers into her hair and he pulled her head back and put his hungry mouth to her neck, teeth pressing so hard they threatened to bruise her. She would have to, she thought, cover it with makeup, if he bit any harder.

Now the hand that had been squeezing her shoulder so hard slid down into her dress, searching for a breast. Too hard, she wanted to say, but didn't. He did what he wanted. Once she had liked it that way, wanted it that way, been grateful for it that way. To have a ruler for her world. Order, she had desperately needed to follow orders, had needed whatever it took, in order to have order.

But, well, things change.

Meantime, if it were going to be done, best it were done quickly. If she stopped him or refused him he would think something was wrong and be cranky and unhappy. He'd worked himself up to this and all, it wasn't as if he did it every day. So she made some noises in her throat and from her chest. When she'd run away from home she'd made money, easy money, dancing, topless, so she knew about the noises as well as the moves and how easy it was to deal with men's ejaculatory needs.

He was really eager. He pulled her up out of the chair and she went along with it gracefully. He wanted, she guessed, to press up against her buttocks, fresh and round and resilient as new foam rubber. Fondle them, feel them, lift her dress and deal with her thong. Push it aside or pull it down, she wondered, idly, which? She reached down and touched herself. She got wet easily, which was fortunate; it made things convenient. She heard his zipper go down and felt him fumbling around, then she felt the heat of his erection pressing lengthwise between her buttocks, not seeking entry but first asking, in a way, just to be held, to feel welcome pressing against her. His hands ran all up and down, greedy and warm. She felt guilty that it didn't matter to her, but the least she could do was make some more encouraging noises and small wiggling movements. He squeezed her nipple. Once, long ago, she'd told him to go very lightly at the start and only later, near the end, to treat them roughly. No point in repeating it now. It was a pain that was negligible in the scale of things.

The rubbing between her cheeks had made him larger and hotter and harder and he grappled for her thong and he yanked it down and then he pulled back away from her to look at what was revealed. She turned so that when they went at it he couldn't see her face in the mirror. She was afraid she might cry. That wouldn't help anything. Or anybody.

Then there was a buzzing. A vibrator sound.

"What's that? What's that?" he said.

She knew exactly what it was. Her cell phone. Her other cell phone. The one that . . . she'd set it to vibrate, rather than ring, but it was out on the dresser, because she was changing pocketbooks, and it was vibrating against the wood and making that noise.

"Is that him?"

She wanted to pick it up. To answer it. But it had

to be Jack's decision. What did he want? To find David Goldberg, or have an orgasm?

"Pick it up," he said.

She nodded and straightened up. Her thong was dangling down by her knees. She didn't want to hop to the phone like someone in a sack race and her bare butt hanging out. She shook the bit of underwear loose and tried to kick it off. It came free of one leg, but stuck on the strap of her shoe, high on the other ankle. The phone had already rung for the third time when Jack had spoken, so now she only had a ring and a half, maybe two rings, to answer before the network kicked in and said the subscriber was unavailable. So she walked over with her thong dragging and she pulled her dress down over her cheeks and hips with one hand while the other reached for the phone. As she picked it up and pushed the button to speak and listen, she looked back, over her shoulder, at Jack. He was watching her intensely, but no longer erotically, his penis sticking out from the center of the floppy V made by his open pants and already softening. Funny, she thought, how when she was turned on, a penis could look attractive and interesting, when she had given herself to someone, their erections looked powerful and exciting, and when she was neither, they just looked like odd, awkward, misplaced handles, that you could grab men by and tow them around, wherever you wanted, like big suitcases, with feet instead of wheels.

"David," she said and his voice came on the other side, eager and urgent.

Chapter

FORTY-ONE

ELAINA WHISTHOVEN HAD been Parks's first killing that had been all his very own.

He'd killed before. But always in the line of duty or on assignment or as collateral damage or as one of those things that just went a little too far.

What it was, was that he never for a moment thought that Elaina had been anything but a poor butterfly of a librarian. The idea that this frightened, fragile, fluttery part-time book shelver could have been an undercover agent for anybody just seemed absurd to him. So there was no job there. Not really. Nothing to investigate or find out. So that left just her and him. Elaina was in the palm of his hand, and all he had to do was close his hand, curl his fingers tight, and he would crush her. The thought alone had roused him in a way that he could neither deny nor repress.

There was a great rolling explosion inside him when he killed her. It was like he was a huge empty hollow cave and the boom of it filled him up and echoed and echoed and stayed in there for the longest time.

That high—echoing around and ringing and rolling back and forth inside his skull—had stayed with him all through the aftertime that he'd had to spend resetting the stage so that it looked like she'd committed suicide.

He'd put her dead, naked body in a kneeling position with her head inside the oven. Then he turned on the gas. He lit a candle in the bedroom. It was a wooden house. An old wooden house. It was a pile of kindling. It would burn fast and burn hot and burn every trace that he might have left behind. It would burn away all her soft tissue and with it the marks that he'd made when he was making her cry and beg and plead and scream and moan; it would burn away the flesh of her vagina and anus and the semen he'd left inside her.

Parks had made a discovery. Something totally ordinary and extraordinary at the same time. He'd found out that he could do it. That he could kill for pleasure. Kill for pleasure, then walk away from it and feel good about it.

Now that he knew that he *could,* he knew that he *would,* that he would do it again.

What did they have up here, a volunteer fire department? A constabulary? A veterinarian for coroner? Whatever. They weren't going to be suspicious. Even if they were, they wouldn't have the wit or resources to act like an episode of some *CSI* show. It would pass, no question. But he had to have something to say to make it sound reasonable to Jack Morgan.

Parks needed a story for the colonel. A good story. Men like him had been lying to colonels since the day the military invented ranks. Could he say that Whisthoven had been tough?—he laughed to himself—yeah, tough, he could say that, say that she'd been tough, that she'd been a real pro and that he had to lean on her, lean hard. Yeah, that would fly and then he'd say that he had finally made her admit that she'd been working for—that one took some thought, who would she have been working for?—the Murphy campaign. Yeah, he would tell Morgan that she'd been working for the Murphy campaign. Then, when she thought her cover had been blown she'd cut and run and, and the Murphy people had slipped in this Goldberg in her place.

Yeah, Goldberg was a Murphy agent, too. Confirmed.

That's what Parks told Morgan. Morgan had no reason to doubt him. Also Morgan had other independent sources inside the Murphy team who had told him there was a Murphy spy in their camp, someone close to Stowe. So this fit, this was confirmation. Morgan didn't ask any further questions about why the Whisthoven woman had to die.

Jack had to admit it, Niobe had played Goldberg right. He hadn't really thought that the librarian would call and let himself be led into a trap. But now he had.

Time to zip it up and roll into action.

Goldberg had asked for a meet in one hour at a magazine and cigar store on the corner of M and Thirty-first NW. He'd been on and off the phone fast. He'd left no room for discussion or negotiation. So that's where and when it had to be.

What Jack wanted was a snatch and chat. He now knew that Goldberg was a spy, but he did not know if Goldberg had discovered one-one-three, and if, having discovered it, he had passed that information on to his masters. The optimum plan would be to whisk the wannabe poet away to a fortress of solitude, put him in a soundproof room with one alligator clip attached to his Jewish circumcision line and the other to his scrotum and let an electrical current complete a circuit between the two. That always brought forth frank and honest conversation.

They had an address and they could get to it, barely, before Niobe did. Morgan wanted to be present, himself, for the endgame. But how? Spinnelli's van. Him and Spinnelli in the van, across the street. Whittaker could cover it from one angle, Ryan from another. They could get to him. But could they snatch him?

M and Thirty-first NW was in the heart of Georgetown and Georgetown, even on a Sunday night, was date and drink central for D.C.'s poli-party people and it had tight, narrow streets that got crowded with pedestrians and the traffic was stop and go, stop and go, stop and go. A bad, bad place for a snatch.

They could hit him, but snatching him could turn into a mess. But before they took him out, he had to know what Goldberg knew.

It seemed like the only way to play it was let Niobe meet with him and let them talk, as Goldberg seemed so eager to do. Was there any danger to Niobe? Jack didn't think so. She could handle herself pretty well. Besides, why would the Jew want to hurt her? The only downside that Morgan could think of was that Niobe was not supposed to know about one-one-three.

But there was no other choice.

Once Niobe found out, she would walk away. Or signal them. They would work out a simple sign. Then they would move in and take him out. Pop him right on the street if they had to. Morgan could fix it so that it would go down as a mugging. He had plenty of contacts on the D.C. force. They were, for the most part, lazy and corrupt and they'd be happy to get it off the books quick and easy.

He visualized it. Niobe signals, they move, in a triangle. Goldberg sees him, Morgan, and turns to run. If he turns 180 degrees, bam, he runs right into Ryan. If he cuts sideways, trying to cross the street, Whittaker stops him, bangs into him, trips him, whatever. Then Ryan catches up. Ryan would get close enough for slow dancing, that's the way he liked to do it, to be certain, and put his gun right up in Goldberg's guts and pull the trigger.

Fuckin' Ryan, he'd want the ear.

Chapter

FORTY-TWO

THE OCTAVIAN INSTITUTE occupied a town house on Dumbarton Street between Wisconsin and Thirty-first. A very expensive piece of real estate. Close to Georgetown University, able to draw on all those scholars and a very trendy place to be.

I get over to Georgetown at least once a year. There's a bar and restaurant where I know the owner, Tom Roncich, on M, off of Thirtieth, two blocks south and two blocks east of the institute.

Tom is tall; he also wide and fleshy and sweaty. His face is flushed most of the time, as if blushing is his normal state. He belongs more to the end of the nineteenth century than to the start of the twenty-first. He belongs in saloons, he belongs around beer, he belongs among the sort of newsies who banged out their words on Underwoods and shouted into telephones that were made in two pieces.

I first met him when he was in the journalism department at the university and I taught him how to use a library. He was amazed at how much you could find out, on the record. He sent me some of his pieces over the years, with notes like, "You taught me how to find this stuff." I thought he was a good reporter. A minor-league Izzy Stone, which isn't bad at all, since Stone was in a league of his own. But Tom quit and went into PR and he also worked three card monte games as a shill. Then he came into some money and went into the restaurant business. It's a tough business. But he's had great success with it. He's got the whole building, three stories tall, a main bar downstairs, a quieter, more formal dining room on the second floor, and some private rooms and his offices up on the third.

Every time I went to Georgetown, and almost every time I went to D.C., I dropped in at Tom's Place, to say hello and have a drink. So that was my first thought. I mean, if I were just meeting Niobe, going for a drink, or a meal, or an assignation in contemplation of adultery, I would have said, "Hey, you know Tom's Place?"

I almost did.

The hardest thing about acting like some kind of spy, if you're not one, is believing that you have to do all those silly things. There is a constant impulse to say, Oh come on now, to the other people involved, and even more to yourself. Skulking around, sneaking around. It's weird and embarrassing. And yet, there I was, on Virginia's Most Wanted Web page for bestiality and I was considered armed and dangerous. Logic and reason had long ago gone out the window. So I knew I had to throw myself into James Bonding, embarrassment and hesitation be damned.

I stopped dialing abruptly, on the ninth digit, and put the phone down with a frown. Susie was staring at me. Full of feelings and questions. Even when she was silent she was noisy. I had to think. So I said that I had to go to the bathroom. I felt married. Married is when you have to perch in pretense upon the porcelain throne to find privacy enough to have a thought. There I sat and tried to visualize the streets of Georgetown and what would happen when I got there.

I was seated on the toilet seat with my pants up when I got the idea for the cigar store, which is a block west of Tom's Place, between the bar and the institute.

I was much closer to Georgetown than Niobe was. I got there early and went into the store and I said to the guy behind the counter, "Look, I'm supposed to meet someone here, but I can't. I have to leave. If I gave you a note and described her, could you give her the note?"

"I don't know," he said, "if I would recognize her."

"Well, if you doubted, you could say, 'Are you looking for a guy named Dave?' "

"I don't know. I'm not a dating service."

"Could you be a dating service for twenty dollars?"

"Yeah, I could, I could do that."

I gave him the money and the note.

"Good deal," he said.

"There's one more thing. Could you call me after you give her the note and she leaves."

"Why don't *she* call you?"

"I don't know," I said, "I didn't think of it. Could you do it? Would you? I don't know, it just would be better if you did it."

"The twenty bucks, that was for me giving her the note."

"What would you charge for making a phone call?"

"Twenty was good for the other. It would be good for this, too."

You never think of the expenses of being a spy. I guess because normally spies work for the government and they get to hand in padded expense accounts for their vodka martinis and their Aston Martins are issued to them by the Department of Exotic Transportation. "Yeah, sure," I said, and gave him another twenty, one of the new ones, that looks stained and mottled.

Then I went across the street to the Southern Clipper Coffee Trader and waited. About fifteen minutes later, my cell rang. "It's me," the cigar store guy said, "is that you?"

"That's me," I said.

"She's real pretty," he said.

"Yeah, she is."

"But stressed."

"Probably."

"Good luck," he said.

"Thanks," I said, touched and surprised.

"Yeah, you gonna need it. She's gonna mess you up."

She probably would.

I went outside to see her moving away from me toward the Octavian Institute, like it said to in the note. She didn't look around. Even at that distance, not even seeing her face, I felt . . . the things I felt toward her.

When we first glance at a scene, it's chaos. But look for even a moment longer and we begin to see the individual pieces as having trajectories and, from there, we detect patterns.

There was a van on M that lurched forward, to the corner—the windows had been darkened so they would be hard to see through and it had the name of some computer company on the door. It cut across traffic to make a turn before the light. Like it was following her and didn't want to get caught too far back. And there was one guy on foot who kind of kept half an eye on her and was keeping pace with her like they were tied together with a mental string about half a block long. He was also looking this way and that, probably looking for me. I recognized him. It was Ryan.

So she'd been followed, or she'd set me up. Bitch. I couldn't believe it. She got up to the corner and turned. I took out my cell phone and dialed her number. As I did so, I stepped back inside the coffee shop.

She answered and I said, "You have people following you."

"Oh . . ." she said.

"But I want to talk to you," I said. "If you want to talk to me, turn around, walk back the way you came, and tell them to fuck off. Tell them to disappear." I was whispering, but I was full of anger and the people in the shop were looking at me. "Ryan and the van and the other one, too." I hadn't seen another one and I wasn't sure of the van, but when you're playing spy you have to act like you know more than you do. "Tell them," I said, and turned off the phone before she had a chance to talk back, turned it completely off, so she couldn't call back.

I went out again, so I could see what happened. She came back around the corner. The van, moving up the street, slowed down. Ryan hesitated, then pretended like it meant nothing to him and kept going. During that moment of hesitation he touched himself, like people do when they're making sure that they have what they need with them, right hand going a little bit lower than if he were pledging allegiance. So, his gun was in a shoulder holster.

She stepped off the curb, toward the van. The van stopped, the window rolled down. I couldn't see inside from where I was. Somebody said something to Ryan and he stopped, too, and came to the van. I guess she told them that they'd been spotted. Ryan started looking around, looking for me. The van door opened. Morgan got out. Looking furious and athletic and tough. I was ruining his Sunday night, I could tell. They were looking around for me.

I went back into the coffee shop. I called again. "Don't bother looking around," I said. "I have someone else watching. They just called me and said your friends are jumping around looking for me. It's off, the hell with you."

"Wait," she said.

"Tell them to go away. I have another watcher," I said, making it up on the spot. "At Wisconsin and Whitehaven, all right? If the van shows up there, with Jack and Ryan and the driver in it, they'll call me, then I'll call you back." Would that actually work?

I went back outside. There were a couple of girls standing there smoking. I asked them if I could bum a cigarette or buy one from them. That was good, I thought, that was a reason to hang out on the street, to have a smoke. They gave me one and a light, too. I knew that if I really inhaled I'd end up coughing uncontrollably and exposing myself as a nonsmoker and they'd think I was hitting on them, cause a commotion, and draw attention to me. I had to do a sort of fake puffing. Meantime I was able to see Niobe and the van.

Morgan was out of the van, still looking furiously

around. His gaze swept across me without even a hitch of familiarity. Being a blond can do a lot for a guy. I recommend it. I chatted with the girls. They both worked at the bookstore. I told them I was a librarian. We chatted about books and the book business. All the time I kept looking past them.

I couldn't see expressions. I could see movement and, to some degree, body attitude.

Niobe seemed like she was informing Jack, but deferring to him. Ryan was waiting for orders.

Finally, Jack took a last searching look around, and Ryan did, too. I used my smoking hand, busily, in front of my face. Then he turned around and opened the van door. He said something to Ryan and Ryan got in and then Jack followed him. Then the van drove off, heading north. Niobe stood there, waiting. I thanked the girls for the cigarette and the conversation and walked down the block, heading east, to the next corner, where I turned. Then I called Niobe again. I told her to go back down to M and head toward the triangle, past Twenty-ninth, where Pennsylvania comes in at an angle. "Then we'll go talk in the park, or something," I said and hung up.

I put on a cap, one of those tweedy Irish things, to change my appearance again, and a pair of glasses that I'd bought at the Dollar Store. Then I called Paul. He wasn't at the phone and his hostess went to find him.

Niobe was walking, I assumed, on M, from Thirty-first, headed for Twenty-ninth. I was just down around the corner on Thirtieth. I would watch her walk by, then see if anyone came after her. Tom was supposed to come out of his place and flag her down and tell her to go in and meet me there. I wasn't sure how much sense doing all of that made, but it seemed very spylike. And paranoid. But now there was no Tom. If she got past him, I would have to run down to Pennsylvania Avenue to find her.

There she was, crossing Thirtieth, on M, directly in front of me. I slunk around behind a lamppost. I pretended to tie my shoe. With one hand, as I was holding the phone to my ear with the other. Where was Tom?

As she disappeared, Tom came on the line. "Quick," I said, "she's coming. She'll be in front of your place in two seconds. She's wearing jeans, and a short light brown leather jacket and black and green running shoes."

"Black and green?"

"Just go get her, will you?" I said, a little frantic.

"Relax, man, relax. I see her now. Bye."

I waited about three minutes, which is a huge long time when you're in a state of justifiable paranoia. It's forever. I didn't see anyone that I recognized or anyone that looked like they were trawling along behind her.

I went up to M, turned right, walked to Tom's Place, then on past it, and halfway down the block, then turned and retraced my footsteps. Everything still looked fine. I went in.

Tom came over wreathed in a faint cloud of fermented hops and tobacco smoke and greeted me with a smile and an arm around my shoulder. "Well, well, well, I always knew you had it in you. She's hot, David. Where'd you find her? Hiding from her husband? She's up on the third floor, past my office, two doors down on the right. I gave you a room with a bed," he giggled. For a large man he has a very small boy's giggle. "You can lock the door and you can get out the window, too. It opens on the fire escape, in case the husband comes, but don't worry, I won't let him pass."

"Thanks," I said. "Tom, listen, this is not just, it's not sex."

"Don't worry, don't worry, kid. Adulterers are welcome at Tom's Place hall of vice." He was hugely pleased with himself.

"It's not sex, it's politics."

"It's Washington," he said. It would pass for wit.

"Thanks," I said, in a hurry to get to her.

"Listen to me, librarian, you go do what you got to do. Do it large. You're a good man, David. How long have I known you, ten, fifteen years?"

"About that, listen, I got to . . ."

Walking and talking, he started leading me toward that stairs. "All that time, I said, 'This is a man who has to come out, come out from those dusty shelves.' "

"I like being a librarian," I said, trying to get past him. It was hard. He was large. I felt rude. But spies are entitled to be rude. Their lives are so much more urgent than regular people's.

"I know you do. And you made something out of it." There was an opening in the crowd; I sort of slithered past him. He didn't miss a beat and kept talking. "Most people just sleepwalk through their jobs." Nodding to him, I started up the stairs, quickly. He kept talking, following, but more slowly and huffing somewhat. "You made something out of it and you taught people. You really showed them how to find knowledge. You showed me. And I owe you."

I stopped at the second-floor landing. He was halfway down below. I said, "Debt paid."

"No," he said. Even as I turned and started for the next flight, he kept talking and I heard his voice receding behind me. "Certain debts can be paid, but some debt are never repaid, anything that you give that goes into the making of a man, that can never be repaid. Never. Go upstairs. She's waiting for you. Nobody will come up after you. I promise you."

It was an old building. The stairs were narrow and uneven and the walls were mottled and stained. I found the room easily enough and flung open the door. The light was on. A single bulb, naked in the ceiling. Seventy frosted watts. It was stark and romantic both.

I was in love. I was angry. Love was stupid. I was frightened. I was betrayed. "You bitch," I said. "You set me up."

"Tell me, tell me," she said. "Do you know?"

"I'll ask the questions," I snarled at her. "And you'll do the answers." I reached out and I grabbed her.

I don't have a clue what happened. I was on the floor. She was standing over me.

"Tell me, do you know?"

I got up on my hands and knees.

"Do I know what?"

I launched myself at her. She deftly stepped aside and did some elegant and invisible move that sent me flying halfway across the small room, toward the bed, which I hit, half on my side, half on my back, and the bed made a cracking sound and the bed groaned. I imagined Tom downstairs listening with avuncular lust and making up totally the wrong story to go with the sound effects.

Good as she was, I had managed to get one hand on her belt and I'd hung on to it for dear life and I had dragged her along after me and she fell, too. On top of me. Now she was off balance and had to struggle. I wrapped my arms around her. She twisted and she punched me in the back, near the kidney. It hurt like hell. To protect myself, I rolled over on top of her and we both fell to the floor, her under me, squirming and struggling. She got her leg between mine and tried to drive her knee up into my crotch, but my legs were too tight together and she had no leverage. She tried to hit me. I tightened my arms around her, holding her arms tight to her sides. I pressed down with my weight.

I pulled my head back to look at her. She looked at me. Our eyes locked. We kissed. As furiously and as randomly as we had been fighting. Nothing made sense. I didn't know if she was conning me or betraying me again or if she was loving me. She made mewing sounds in her throat and I have never felt such hunger.

Then we stopped.

"We don't have much time," she said.

"Tell me about the Octavian Institute," I said, my voice coming out in a croak from a dry throat. "Tell me about this paper," I said. I reached for my back pocket, but it wasn't there anymore, it was across the room, on the floor.

"It's a paper," she said, dismissing it.

"Just a paper, my ass," I said. Still lying on top of her. Still close enough for kissing, but I was barking. "It's a fucking instructional guide on how to kill three thousand innocent Americans so some sonuvabitch can use it as an excuse to conquer the world. And make money on oil."

"Did you find out what they're up to?" she said, as if what I had just said had been nothing, had been Good morning. How are you? Did you sleep well, dear?

"What do you mean did I find out? You tell me. You wrote the book on it. That makes you one of them."

"I'm not. I'm not," she said. "Get off me."

"No," I said, pinning her.

"Get off me or I'll hurt you. I can. Don't doubt it, I can."

I got off her. I stood up. "What the fuck do you mean you're not? Your name is on the paper. It's on the paper," I said, standing over her. "You're one of the authors of the paper that told the president of the United States how to commit mass murder." I didn't know if Scott or anyone high up had ever read it and it had become their instruction manual, or if it had just been the lunatic speculations inside a think tank run amok. In one case it was everything, in the other, it was nothing. She got up, not looking at me. I tried to get around her, in her face. "Mass murder. If I were a fucking federal prosecutor, right, I would charge you with murder and ask for the death penalty."

"Is this why you called me?"

"Yes, I want to know what's going on at the Octavian Institute."

"That's old news," she said.

"What do you mean, old news?"

"It's old. Past, done."

"What kind of monster are you?"

She looked at me with an expression I could only begin to unravel and even then I was sure I was getting it wrong, in detail and in essence. It was an attempt to be calm, to have some kind of control, over rage and hurt, but about what and at whom, I didn't know. "We don't have time for this," she said.

"How can we not have time to find out if you were part of the crime of the century?"

"David, just tell me, did you find out what they're planning to do about this election."

"Who, who's planning to do? Scott? The Republicans? Stowe? Jack, your husband? Who? Who?"

"So you don't know. You don't have a clue."

"No, I don't know. But I bet it has something to do with you and the Octavian Institute."

"Is that why Georgetown? So we can go around the corner and break in? It's just papers, papers and blather."

"Blather?" I snatched her paper, "Hands On/Hands Off," from the floor and shoved it at her. "Blueprint for betrayal. Instruction manual for murder."

"Now!" she snapped back at me. "We have to know what they're going to do now!"

There was banging and shouting and stomping on the stairs. I turned and opened the door. There was Tom, on the stairs, dragging at another man, who I didn't know. There was a uniformed D.C. cop. He had his department-issue automatic in one hand and his radio in the other and he was yelling some code numbers and the address into it. Then behind him came Morgan and Ryan. Morgan moving effortlessly and sure like a fitness brochure, holding up a badge in a billfold and announcing "Homeland Security," like the cameras were running. Lumbering in front of him, like a smoker's cough, was Ryan and Ryan had his gun drawn, too.

There were more people behind them, some running, some shoving to get ahead, lots of yelling and commotion and in the midst of all of them I thought I glimpsed Susie.

Just then there was a muffled thud and Tom jerked and his pale face turned even paler.

Tom kept his arms tight around the stranger and the two of them spun slowly on the stairs, a parody of love. As they came around, Tom's face turned toward me, his eyes met mine, and he said, "Run, run, David, run."

I could see, in a slow motion sort of way, that the stranger was struggling to break loose of Tom's bear hug. Tom had locked his hands together and he was going to hold on, like it was the last thing he was ever going to do.

There was a pause, a single moment of stasis, when the turning stopped, before the falling began. Then they went down, crashing against the wall and off the wall and against the rail. Then they fell. The stranger on his back and Tom on top, their heads pointing down and their feet pointing up, and Tom rode the other down, like he was a sled, or a lover, but no longer with his arms around him, grappling at the man's face instead. Both of them were moaning and screeching and swearing. The cop was calling on his radio and also yelling, "Freeze," and waving his gun. Ryan and Morgan were trying to get up the stairs, but they couldn't until Tom and the man he was riding bounced to a halt.

Either there was an echo, or Tom cried out one more time, "Run, run."

Chapter

FORTY-THREE

HAGOPIAN LAY ON his mat. The TV screens jabbered away at one another. It was pointless to protest that the raids had been a deliberate provocation and that the riots had been the intended result and that it had all been an election ploy. Unless there was a memo, an actual memo, from Scott to Governor Arbusto of Florida, that said so, in exactly that language, the media would treat it like Hillary Clinton's statement about "a vast right-wing conspiracy." Although it had been true, Hillary had come out of it sounding paranoid and like a whiner.

Hagopian lay on his mat, televisions buzzing all around him like cicadas on a summer night, and he breathed and he listened to his breath and all the video waves flowed through him and re-formed and he had, on the screens of his mind, a video vision: Sharpton and Jackson and Jesse, Jr., and black leaders and black preachers from all over the country converging on Florida, like nothing since the days of Martin Luther King in Alabama. Let them say they would not let these outrageous tactics disenfranchise black voters, let them say they would not let the abuse of police powers drive a wedge between black and brown and white, divide Christian and Jew and Moslem. Have them tell their people to be calm. Have them there to stare down the police with nonviolence and with video cameras, so if the police did act as provocateurs or if there was a police riot, the world would see it that way. The world is a media event. Bring in some rabbis and Catholic priests, too.

He would create a movement. An instant movement. Only a three-day movement, a Sunday-Monday-Tuesday movement, but a movement nonetheless. He rose up, as if from sleep, refreshed and invigorated.

He shut off all the televisions. Enjoyed the silence. Then he went to his desk, pulled out his laptop, and began to make a list.

He finished his list by eleven. Then he spent the day on the phone. It was working. The black leadership understood the riots as the deliberate work of government agent provocateurs and they were furious and eager to do something.

Then, at forty-seven minutes after nine on Sunday night, there was a knock on the door and one of his assistants came in with Monday morning's *New York Times*.

An unnamed source from an unnamed national security agency had heard rumors that a major terrorist group had plans to launch attacks on the United States if Anne Lynn Murphy was elected. The unnamed terrorists believed, the unsourced report stated, that a country run by a woman would be "weak" and unwilling to defend itself.

The headline could have been, "Desperate Scott Administration Leaks Fake Security Document to Scare Voters."

But it wasn't. The headline was "Terrorists Plan Attack If Woman Leads Nation." And it was on the front page.

Chapter

FORTY-FOUR

NIOBE HAD A gun.

It was a nice, neat, clean-looking smallish sort of gun. It was like herself: it had a nice finish, a sense of solid musculature, a functional elegance, a tight, sleek feeling of power, but not the monstrous phallic overkill of a Dirty Harry gun, and it was going to kill me.

"So kill me, fucking kill me and get it over with, you bitch," I said. I probably shouldn't have called her a bitch, but I found it all very confusing and irritating. I walked right up to her, right up to the gun, until the flesh of my stomach was pressing against it.

There was banging on the door, which I'd locked behind me, and yelling, too.

She seemed, for once, confused and indecisive. I reached down and put my hand on the gun and turned it to the side and, since she didn't seem to be resisting, I pulled it away from her. She looked at me, still vacant and at a loss, like she was looking to me to decide something. So I did. I turned the gun around and pointed it at her and said, "Out the fucking window. We're going out the fucking window."

She did what I told her to.

Surprised the hell out of me. She yanked the window up and put a foot on the sill and her body folded like a cat's as she went through. I followed, much more awkwardly, using my knee to get up on the sill and then crawling out to the fire escape.

She was already on her way down, swift and silent, like she'd been escaping out back windows all her life.

We went down the one flight and by the time I got to the landing she was already unlatching the metal straight ladder. It screeched when it was released and clanged when it stopped. "Go, go, go," I said and she went down as gracefully as she'd done everything else. There was noise above us now and as I followed her down, I looked up and saw several faces at the window and several guns, too. Somebody was trying to clamber out and he'd got in the way of everyone else and made it impossible for anyone to shoot at us and it bought us a couple of seconds.

Niobe had turned left when she landed. I followed, the gun in my hand. I wondered if, from above, it looked like I was kidnapping her or if we were escaping together. I wondered if, in fact, I was kidnapping her or we were escaping together. We were in an alley, narrow and dark, and I could see the street up ahead, bright with the street lamps. What the hell was I going to do when we got there? There were already sirens coming from different directions.

Chapter
FORTY-FIVE

ANNE LYNN'S HUSBAND, Mike, the local Idaho television producer, the first person who had a real sense of her talent and who had put her on the air, felt despair.

His instincts told him that this "leaked" report about terrorists attacking if a woman was president was going to tip the balance back to Scott. And Scott's people had chosen well, using the *New York Times* to stick the knife in her back.

Mike had become radicalized during the course of the campaign. Which was odd because the campaign itself was always striving to move toward the center. Positions were not necessarily changed, but they were continually being rephrased to find that place where they achieved maximum market share, bringing—or keeping—potential voters in, yet not driving any voters away. It was an arduous process and it was one in which it was difficult to stay true to any vision. He gave his wife high marks for negotiating the process and yet retaining her integrity.

It was also odd that having been a TV producer had kept him naive for a long time. He knew hundreds of news professionals personally and every single one of them thought of themselves as good people, honest, fair, objective, and idealistic. Sensibly idealistic, not self-destructively idealistic to be sure, call it realistically idealistic.

Now he thought of them all—including the self that he had been—as deluded. Self-deluded. Indeed, the capacity to survive and the ability to thrive in one of the big corporations that served up news as infotainment was in direct proportion to a journalist's capacity for self-delusion.

The Right had spent so many years castigating the *New York Times* as the flagship of the liberal media that everyone believed it, including the Left, including the people at the *Times* themselves. But the truth was that the *Times* was the house organ of the Establishment. It was committed, both editorially and in its presentation of the news, to the interests of an Establishment: continuity, security and legitimacy. Therefore they generally supported business and finance, the American version of empire, the government, and the president, until, and unless, some excess was so egregious that it posed a threat to continuity, security, or legitimacy. Then the *Times* would turn on the destabilizers, as they did, at last, on the Vietnam War, on Nixon, and on Enron, in the interests of restoring continuity, security, and legitimacy.

In its Establishment heart the *New York Times* had decided for Scott and they had, therefore, given him a great gift: they had dressed an underhanded campaign stratagem in the cloak of objectivity and bestowed upon it the authority of the newspaper of record and it would now play out through the whole media world as a real revelation to be taken at face value.

Mike looked at Hagopian, who had been so delighted with himself and his counter-stratagems for Florida, and he saw that Hagopian was tired, that he was ill, that he perhaps did not, probably did not, have the one last shot of genius that was needed to spin this one back and make it turn in upon itself.

The campaign was coming to an end with terrifying suddenness.

All that he thought in silence and only to himself.

Outwardly and in all communications he kept a smile on his face and projected an air of good cheer.

The plan was for them both, presidential candidate and husband, to go out to Idaho, together, Monday night, to vote on Tuesday. But now, on Sunday night, he said that he wanted to fly out ahead of her, set things up, which was true, so she'd have some quiet and rest and just the right friends around her and her favorite foods, too, when Tuesday came, when the end came.

Chapter
FORTY-SIX

THERE WAS A cab coming down Thirty-first as we stepped out of the alley. It jerked to a halt and the door swung open and I could hear Susie's incredibly annoying voice yelling at the driver, "Stop, stop! I told you to stop."

The cabby, in a syrup thick Southern black voice, was saying back to her, "I done stopped, I done stopped." Which he had.

But Susie was already on to the next thing, which was to jump out and yell at us, "Get in, get in."

Niobe, who arrived first, got in first. I jumped in after her and at the same time Susie climbed in on the front passenger side and slammed the door behind her.

"Drive, drive," I cried out.

"I'm sorry, so sorry," Susie said, turning around in the seat.

"I don' know who you peoples is, but I don' wan' no part of this no-how."

There was a gun in my hand. I've never been in a social setting with a gun in my hand, but I knew what to do because I've seen it so many times in the movies. I put it to his head and said, "Drive, drive."

"Shit," he said, drawing it out to at least three syllables, but he set us in motion. "Where to? Where you wanna go?"

"Can you ever forgive me?" Susie said.

What was she going on about? And where indeed? "The Octavian Institute," I said.

"No, they'll be all over," Niobe said.

"Whyn't you just take my money or something and walk."

"Please, please tell me you'll forgive me," Susie said.

"Drive! Drive," I said.

"I'm driving, I'm driving, but I don't know where."

"Where's your car?" I said to Niobe.

"At home."

"Bethesda," I told the driver.

"That's a long way, man," he said.

I reached into my pocket and pulled out three twenties. Twenties go fast in the espionage business. He snatched them out of the air with long dexterous fingers.

"I didn't mean to," Susie yawped. "I mean I did, in the moment, but not in my heart."

"What are you talking about?" I snapped at her.

"I called the police."

"Why? How? When? And what were you doing here?"

"I knew you were going to Tom's Place because I heard you on the phone. So I went there, directly and waited and then . . ."

"Then?"

"Then I saw her and I thought it was all lies and it

was about her and I got, I got a little crazy and called the police."

"What?" I cried out and looked over at her and I could see out of the corner of my eye that the driver thought I was distracted and he was going to try something, so I shoved the gun against the back of his skull and snarled.

"I'm married," Niobe said to Susie.

"Oh my," the driver said.

"Well, so what?" Susie said. "Is that who that man was? Is that why you were sneaking around? Her husband?"

"It's not about sex, it's about politics," I said.

"That's Washington," the driver said.

"What is that, D.C. wit?" I said.

"I'm just sayin'," the driver said.

"That's how they found us," Niobe said. "See, David, I didn't betray you, you see."

"If you put that gun away," the driver said, "I'll book you all on *Jerry Springer*. I got contacts, I do."

The cab dropped us off around the corner from Niobe's condo. Niobe said she needed to go up to get her car keys. Susie said she needed the bathroom. I told them to go ahead, I'd meet them in a minute. I counted out another hundred dollars.

"I'm new to this," I said to the cabdriver.

"Well, you're doing all right, boy."

"Thanks," I said. "What's bothering me is that, you know, it's obvious that we're in some kind of trouble here." I had the money in my left hand, the gun in my right hand.

"Oh, yeah."

"And I don't want you to go to the police."

"I hear you."

"I'm thinking that I should shoot you." I pointed the gun more specifically in his direction.

"No, no, you don wanna to go there, brother."

"Actually, I don't."

"All right, that's good thinkin'. That's good thinkin'."

"I'm trying to think of some kind of story to tell you, that would convince you that we're the good guys or confuse you so if you did go to the police you'd tell them all the wrong things, but, I couldn't. You understand what I'm saying?"

"No, not entirely, not entirely."

"I was thinking, a hundred dollars, over and above the fare, and your tip, would that buy your silence?"

"Oh, that would be very nice."

"But then I think, hey he could take the hundred and still rat on us and I think we said too much, in front of you, and I have to shoot you."

"I think the hundred dollars would do the trick just fine, just fine."

"Well, I'll take a chance," I said. "But if I find out I'm wrong, I know your name, I know where you work, I'll find you." I opened the door and got out.

"Excuse me," he said, as I started to walk away.

"What's that?"

"For a gentleman like yourself, with your high-stepping ways and two fine ladies, I was thinking you could actually do a little better than a hundred."

"Tell you the truth, a hundred is a lot for me."

"Really?"

"Yeah, my day job is I'm a librarian."

"That don't pay a lot, do it?"

"No."

"Damn. I like libraries, I do. We got a nice little library in our neighborhood, everybody is always welcome, they got free Internet and all and tell you the truth, I'm a reader."

"Really."

"I'm partial to Montaigne and I like Alexander Dumas."

"That's great," I said. "Look, if another twenty is gonna make the difference, I could do that."

"It would help, it would surely help."

Chapter
FORTY-SEVEN

WHAT A FUCKING mess.

Niobe kidnapped. Gone. The librarian gone. And Jack had two hours before he had to leave for New Jersey for a job that would not wait.

Hadn't realized that Goldberg had a team. Should have realized it. Still, they'd handled the switch in plans neatly enough. Goldberg's team hadn't been *perfect*. They'd missed Whittaker. And Whittaker had slid along very nicely behind Niobe, unnoticed. Kudos to Whittaker. Then he'd called Morgan back in. But then, when they charged in, there was that asshole in blue, radio and gun and 100 percent in the way. Just mucking up the works.

Niobe kidnapped. Where was she? In the hands of that . . .

It had to go out on the Com-Net. All law enforcement and security agencies alerted. But say what? Armed and dangerous? Approach with caution? Shoot on sight? How experienced was Goldberg? How trigger-happy? Didn't want to corner him and have him try to blast his way out and have Niobe go down in the crossfire. Morgan didn't kid himself that police operations went off with clockwork precision. Fog of war. That was the phrase for it in the military. Didn't have a phrase for it in the world, though they should, they sure as shit should; the world was even foggier than the battlefield. *Niobe.* He wanted to scream her name out. *Niobe.* Call and call and let his voice roll up and down the rivers, across the broad flats that had once been swamps, reaching out and out and out, until she heard and came back to him.

He had recruited her first. Married her second.

He felt in his heart that women had a place and men had a place. He knew many men who went out into the world and did dangerous and murderous and disturbing deeds and then came home and were good householders, taking out the trash, mowing the lawn, washing their cars, who were decent fathers, helping their daughters with the homework, tossing a ball with their sons, teaching the difference between right and wrong, who were good husbands, never a violent blow, hardly even a harsh word and faithful, too, good Christians who led good, normal church-on-Sunday lives.

Niobe had wanted to work and liked the excitement of life undercover, of flirtation for information, and she said that what was good for the goose was good for the gander, which sounded fair, but as far as Morgan was concerned, was not really true. It just wasn't. It was one of those leftist propaganda lies that was undermining the family and morality and was a whole lot more likely to bring about the downfall of America than any ragtag, rag head, terrorist troop of amateurs.

So he had compromised. He'd inserted her into the Octavian Institute as a statistician. It was a good cover; she did have a knack for math and had taken a couple of statistics courses in college. A very safe posting, mostly nine-to-five. Reporting back to Jack, and in turn to Hoagland and his rarely named associates, through GIAP, General Intelligence Applications Program, Inc., an outsourced intelligence organization. Strange that the government has more restrictions on its domestic spying than private companies do. The future of intelligence is privatization.

Then this librarian thing had come up and the level of secrecy around Stowe was so high that he really hadn't wanted to bring in anyone that he couldn't keep a constant eye on, and Niobe being so good at interrogation by temptation, none better, that he'd brought her in.

Now, now he knew how wrong he'd been.

Notify all the agencies. Considered to be armed and dangerous. Do not approach under any circumstance. Notify Homeland Security only. *Notify only*.

Add a new, updated description of Goldberg now. Short, blond hair. Fucker *was* a pro. It had totally changed his appearance and Morgan now realized that he had seen Goldberg earlier that night. He'd been standing on the corner, smoking a cigarette with two girls, and Morgan hadn't even had a flicker of recognition.

The big fat fuck who owned the bar had to be taken to a hospital. The EMS guys grunting and groaning and almost dropping the stretcher, carrying him like a whale down the stairs. Morgan wished they could have let him bleed to death on the landing. Riding Whittaker down the steps like a human bobsled. Poor Whittaker, cracked pelvis, in the hospital, no humpety-hump for him for a while; he'd better hope that his dick was longer than the plaster was thick.

Morgan had to make more calls, take jurisdiction, make it a formal terrorist inquiry. He really wanted to be out there, getting Niobe back.

Witnesses, all sorts of witnesses, though they didn't know what they were witnesses to. Maybe Roncich knew something. Well, as soon as the doctors patched him up, Morgan would start questioning him. Without a lawyer. Terrorist inquiry. Morgan was in a mood foul enough to name him an enemy combatant and disappear him; that would teach him to interfere with one of his operations. Yeah, Roncich would talk.

It was an hour until Roncich came out of the emergency room. And when he did Morgan was there waiting. The nurse said he had to get permission from the doctor. The doctor started making noises about questioning a man in Roncich's condition, drugged and in pain and all that liberal doctor bleeding-heart bullshit that the guy probably got from watching too much TV. And, Morgan saw from his name tag, he was another fucking berg, a Ginsberg. Frazzled and stretched thin as he was, Morgan was ready to put the 'berg up against the wall and teach him a little terrorist alerting, when the PA system came on and paged, "Dr. Ginsberg to ER, Dr. Ginsberg to ER," and Ginsberg slid on out.

Morgan glared the nurse out of his way and started questioning Roncich who, in Morgan's estimation, was pretending to be in too much pain to reply, when his cell phone rang. He only answered because he was desperate to find Niobe.

"It's me," she said, like the voice of a miracle.

"Where are you?" he said urgently.

"I only have a couple of seconds," she said, whispering and urgent also. "I let him take me. Otherwise he would have disappeared on you. Your people really blew it. He doesn't seem to know."

Morgan sighed with relief.

"It would help," she continued in her whisper, "if I knew what it was that he's . . ."

"You can't," Morgan said, "Wuh . . ."—There was breakup on the line—". . . ree is need to know but believe me, if he stumbles across it, you'll know, know beyond a doubt. Listen, listen to me. I want you to come in."

"I can handle him," Niobe said. "This way, you know for sure, someone's got an eye on him and . . ."

"It's gone on too long. Come in," he ordered her. "Let us handle it."

"Gotta go," she said, hanging up, and Morgan could imagine from her tone how close to being discovered she must be.

But still, but still he was relieved. Both for Niobe and for the project. And a good thing, too. He didn't have any more time to mess around chasing after Goldberg. They had to go and get in position and be ready to act. He had a flight to catch.

Chapter
FORTY-EIGHT

"COME ON," I called, as I went in the condo door. I didn't really trust the cabdriver and wanted to get the hell out of there.

Susie shushed me and dragged me in and led me to an interior door and made me put my ear to it just in time to hear Niobe say, ". . . handle him. . . ."—then she spoke too softly for me to hear except ". . . someone's got . . ."—then she must have heard us because she said, "Gotta go."

I pushed the door open and she was standing in her bedroom, by the dresser, a drawer open as if she was rummaging through it, but caught in the act of putting her cell phone in it.

"What's going on?" I said.

"I'm just looking for my car keys."

"Don't," I said.

"David . . ."

"You can handle him," Susie said, "but you can't handle me."

"What's that supposed to mean?"

"That means I overheard you," Susie said.

"Who were you talking to?" I said.

"Jack, I was talking to Jack."

"I knew it," Susie said.

"I had to tell him something," Niobe said. "To keep him away. To save you."

"Don't trust her," Susie said.

"You're the one who called the cops on him," Niobe said to Susie.

"You're the one," I said to Niobe, "who showed up with Jack, plus Ryan and who else? Spaghetti, Spinnelli, whatever his name is, and the other guy, the one on the steps."

"Whittaker."

"When you came to meet me you brought your whole army with you."

"What the hell else was I going to do? Jack was right there. We were getting dressed for dinner when you called. I'm trying to ignore the phone and he's saying pick it up, pick it up, so I had to pick it up. So I figured, I figured I'd play it by ear and figure some way out of it when I got there. David, if I wanted Jack to catch you, I would have used my home phone. It's right there and it would show up on his caller ID and he would know where I am and the cops would be surrounding the place right now. I want to be with you. That's why I came with you."

"I had a gun on you."

"Do you think that I think you would shoot me? You wouldn't shoot me. I came with you because I wanted to."

"I would love to believe that you want to be with

me. I really would. But that's not what's going on.
You've been playing some game, some game that I don't
know about since we met and if you don't tell me what
it is, I'm gonna walk out that door and disappear or, or
I'm going to give Susie the gun . . . in fact . . ." I took it
out of my jacket pocket and handed it to Susie. It was
obvious, from the instant she got her hands on it, that
she knew what she was doing with a gun. She flicked
something—it had to be the safety, I knew enough to
figure that out—and now I realized I'd had the safety on
the whole time. Then she pulled the top back and there
were smart, solid, clicking noises. Ah, a round into the
chamber. So it was clear that Niobe had not felt threatened when I held the gun, and for very good reasons.

Susie spread her feet into a balanced stance, held
the gun in two hands, and pointed it at Niobe. She said,
"At the range, from this distance, I put nine out of ten in
a target the size of your heart."

"There's some kind of plot to steal the election for
Scott, and I'm trying to find out what it is," Niobe said.

"You told me that, but why? Why are you doing it?"

"I'm working for Anne Lynn Murphy."

Chapter
FORTY-NINE

IF WE WERE going to look for more information, there were three places to go to: Stowe Stud Farm, to my personal computer at the university—unless Homeland Security had already confiscated it—and to the Octavian Institute.

The farm had very high security. I was sure that the library was under surveillance. The institute was the softest target of the three.

We took Niobe's car. The cabbie hadn't seen it, didn't know the license plate or even what kind it was. I figured it would do to get us back to D.C. Then we'd ditch it and . . . do something else. Niobe drove. I sat beside her and asked her questions. Susie sat in back and made comments.

Niobe had been attractive from the moment she hit puberty. She immediately felt the power it gave her, intuitively understood how to use that power, but was too young to understand when she shouldn't use it and began to play with it.

She got very wild and then she got saved. An ex-FBI guy at the church she was going to got her a job at the security company where he worked. Privatization was coming in and the company was doing outsourced intelligence work. It was like the NSA or the CIA, except that they had greater freedom, little accountability, and no civil service protection. Most of her training, however, had taken place at government facilities.

That's where she met Jack Morgan.

He was impressive. He knew people in the CIA, in the State Department, in Military Intelligence, and later, when the Republicans got back in, in the White House itself. He believed in family values, the flag, the marines, and when he went to church, it was for real, not just what you had to do on Sunday. When he asked her to marry him, she was happy to fold her life into his. It brought her a certainty and contentment second only to having been saved. Indeed, it seemed to be the completion of that process, part of what she had been saved for, and having him say how the world was supposed to be and making the rules made her feel secure and safe.

Susie was appalled by a woman's embrace of such a subordinate role and it was very difficult to have the conversation with her present. She and I had something of an argument over not arguing and allowing Niobe to tell her story.

Niobe had never been political. Didn't read the papers, didn't watch the news on TV. But Jack was out there saving the country from feminists and homosexuals who wanted to destroy families, from atheists who wanted to destroy our God, from Marxists who wanted to destroy freedom by taking all our property away, and they were all disguised as Democrats, and that meant saving the world, because America was the world's last hope and had been designated to be the world's salvation. Those beliefs, and sharing in those beliefs with others, made her feel certain and safe and secure.

Susie found it impossible, in the literal sense, to sit still for all of that. She was coughing and rolling her eyes and twitching in her seat. I begged her to be patient. I told her to pretend she was watching a movie.

None of the people who Jack and Niobe knew thought any differently. Some were more extreme.

Where and how it started to go off, she wasn't sure. Jack began to change. She thought it was after he got close to Hoagland and to Alan Stowe. They offered short-cuts. Instead of taking the long slog around, if you stepped on the right square you could jump up, one, two, three, four levels in a single move like a game of Chutes and Ladders. Stowe had put him next to Hoagland and Hoagland could lift him right into the White House where Jack saw himself becoming another Oliver North. Ollie had only been a colonel and he had been right there, next to Ronald Reagan, jetting around the world, handling millions, carrying out secret missions.

It was also around that time that people like Parks, Ryan, Whittaker, and Spinnelli started showing up. They were different than Jack's earlier friends, acquaintances, and coworkers. There was darkness around them. When any of them was in the room, even when they themselves were perfectly decent and polite it was as if there were shadows that lounged against the wall, sneering and ogling. She overheard things from them directly, but also Jack started coming home with stories about them that he seemed to find admirable and exciting, like about Ryan's two necklaces of ears.

A few days after Swenson's plane had crashed with Davidson on board as well, Niobe had gone to see Jack at his office. Parks and Ryan were there and a couple of others and they were talking about it. Someone said, "I'm sure it was pilot error."

Parks laughed and said, "Yeah."

Ryan said, "Anne Lynn Murphy sure got lucky."

Parks said something that she wasn't quite sure of, and then said, "The thing is to know how to *make* your luck."

Niobe took that to mean that Murphy had somehow been involved in the plane crash. Bearing in mind that she heard every day, both from people she knew and on talk radio, that Murphy was a feminist and the feminist agenda was not about equal rights for women, it was about a socialist, anti-family political movement that encouraged women to leave their husbands, kill their children, practice witchcraft, destroy capitalism, and become lesbians, she now figured that Murphy had to be some kind of monster.

Driven by curiosity, she started watching the news for Anne Lynn Murphy stories and even went to her Web site and Murphy didn't sound like a monster. She sounded reasonable and sensible. Niobe knew that if she asked Jack about it, Jack would talk about the devil in disguise, and Murphy trying to pass herself off as a "responsible liberal," or some such garbage, but if she ever got in office her true colors would appear, with a vengeance.

Niobe trusted in her intuitive assessment of people more than she trusted in their position papers and press releases. She got herself invited to a Murphy fund-raiser and slipped past the secret service agents and followed the candidate into the ladies' room and went up to her and said, "I just want to meet you and look you in the eye."

Something happened in that meeting. It wasn't about the words that Anne Lynn spoke. It was about her demeanor, her balance, and how she listened. In any case Niobe walked away convinced, utterly convinced, that Anne Lynn Murphy was the sort of person who would never have been involved in making Swenson's plane crash. Only someone for whom pain and violent death were distant fictions could have done it. "She's had her hands in blood," Niobe said, trying to explain her certainty. "She's healed the wounded and closed the eyes of the dead."

Yet Parks and Ryan had seemed so certain that the accident had been no accident. More certain than barrack room braggadocio. Now she rethought the conversation and realized that they were talking about Murphy being surprised to get that lucky and that someone else, who had also gotten lucky, was the sort of person who did know how to "make their luck."

That, that was impossible, that was all wrong. And yet. . . .

Niobe went home and suddenly everything seemed different. Her husband's certainty now sounded like arrogance. His high-mindedness like narrow-mindedness. His patriotism like permission to commit acts that were otherwise amoral. His rules stopped making her feel secure. They made her feel oppressed and they made her irritated. He kept dropping hints about doing things to undermine the Murphy campaign and being certain that Murphy could never get elected "even if she pulled the wool over the eyes of the voters."

She checked Murphy's schedule and managed to approach the candidate again. Anne Lynn, remarkably, remembered her and was willing to talk to her.

This time, even more than the last, Niobe found something incredibly magnetic and inspiring in Anne Lynn Murphy's being.

When Niobe spoke about Murphy, she spoke about her with a fervor that Susie found disturbing and Susie blurted from the backseat, "She's not a saint."

But I think to Niobe she was. Or perhaps she was a cause, a new order, to replace the one that Jack had supplied, now that she had become suspicious and dissatisfied. And as Niobe had been an agent in the service of Jack's various missions, she would now be a soldier-saint in Anne Lynn Murphy's vision of a better world.

That would seem to be, at first glance, hyperbole. But to live a conscious lie, making love to at least two men—in different ways and to different degrees—to be comfortable with those dishonesties, a woman must either be a whore or in service to a higher cause. Susie would disagree with me and say that women do that all the time; that's how marriages survive and that cheating and lies are simply the necessary and natural garments of hypocrisy in exactly the same way that we wear clothing to cover our physical shame.

In the manner of a convert renouncing previous sins, Niobe told Anne Lynn that her husband was plotting against her. Anne Lynn had Niobe come up to their hotel and meet with Calvin Hagopian, who had Gregorian chants playing the whole time they talked, and he tried to recruit her as a spy. Anne Lynn stepped in and said, "No, don't push her to spy on her husband." Afterward, on the way out, in the hall, when they were alone, Anne Lynn asked her if she did want to help and get information and Niobe said that she did.

"Good," Anne Lynn said. "I need the help. If you find out anything I need to know, call me, me personally," and gave her a phone number and an e-mail address.

Niobe had picked up enough to know that Jack and Stowe had a plan to make sure that Scott would win the election, even if he didn't win. Since then, it had been her mission to find out what, exactly, that plan was.

"What? A coup?" I asked her. America was becoming Paraguay, but not that fast. Gore Vidal said that, a long time ago, back when he was explaining why Ronald Reagan could never be elected president.

Niobe had keys and the codes and we got into the institute easily enough. It was a converted four-story town house.

I figured we had seven, maybe eight hours. There were at least eighteen separate offices, plus a conference room, an AV room, waiting rooms, storage space, bathrooms, and a kitchen. Everybody had their own computers. Computers, computers, computers—the quantity of information stored, created, connected, and re-created has been raised by some unknown and still growing exponential factor. It was overwhelming.

We each took different rooms. Two hours later we met in the kitchen.

Niobe said, "I checked, like you asked me to, if there was a distribution list for the two papers, 'With or Without a Crisis' and 'Hands On/Hands Off'. There were four copies made. They all went to Alan Stowe."

"And I only found one of each," I said. "So that

probably means he passed them on. But by hand. Unless somewhere there's a note of who he gave it to."

"You guys did a lot of weird stuff," Susie said. "Did you know they did a whole research project on curses? I'm not kidding. Somebody did a serious study of the Curse of the Bambino. And there's a Voodoo and Santeria thing. OK, OK, it's not relevant, it's just so off topic for everything else this place is about."

"If it's about the election," I said, thinking out loud, "which is now, and Stowe is an important part of it, important enough that the mere idea of a librarian poking around in his papers made Jack crazy, then the best odds of finding something relevant is in Stowe's most recent papers, which are at the farm, which we can't go to, and on my computer, which I can't seem to access. Now, it would be nice to know if it's just turned off or disconnected or if Homeland Security grabbed it.

"The obvious way to find out is to go to the library. Which I can't do. I could check with Inga, who's the head librarian. I trust her. But I don't dare call her. They have everything wired, don't they?"

"Yes," Niobe said.

"Susie," I said, "you could go. You could go and talk to her. Don't use the phone. Do it in person. And it would be even better if you went to her house."

She nodded.

"And you should go by yourself. Without us. Because I'm wanted and Niobe must be on some kind of watch list by now, too."

Susie accepted that also.

"And you should probably go now. She leaves for work at seven. And we have to be out of here, by what, six? So you should go there and then come back and get us."

Susie hesitated. She looked back and forth, like she was looking at a riddle, something like the one about the farmer with a cabbage, a goat, and a wolf, and a river to cross in a small boat that will hold only him and one other thing at a time. But the goat can never be left alone with the cabbage and the wolf can never be left alone with the goat.

It's a fairly simple riddle, but we weren't, so she dithered and tried to find some way out of going. But the necessity and the logic of the situation left her little choice.

At last she left. At last Niobe and I were alone.

I turned back to the files, but my eyes inevitably flicked back toward Niobe until I caught her looking at me and then looking quickly away. It happened again a minute or two later and I said, "Don't look away."

She said, "We have work to do."

"I know, we have to save the world."

"It's not a joke," she told me, and indeed, there was no trace of humor in her voice, her expression, or her demeanor.

"No," I said, getting up and going toward her, "it's not a joke, but there's no reason we can't make jokes about it."

"There's no time," she said, so serious, so determined, so beautiful.

"I want to know," I said. "Was all of it a setup? Was all of it about using me?"

"Yes," she said, bluntly, "it was."

"From the first day, when we met?"

"Yes, I was there to help Jack figure out if you were dangerous."

"Kennedy Center?"

"I was told you would be there. They wanted to be sure."

"They own the president of my university? They can call him up and say, hey, we want you to give away a ticket to a concert for us and he'll go do it. Do they own everybody? . . . And then you decided to use me?"

"They seemed to think you knew something or could find it out, so . . ."

"So you used me and I went for it."

"I warned you."

"Yes, yes you did. Good for you. And the kisses and the touches and whatever, did you feel anything, anything for me?"

"Yes," she said. "I felt something for you."

"And us, is there an us?"

"What there is, is a plot to steal the election and that's important. It just is."

"Well, that's all of a day and a half away. And afterward, what are you going to do? Go back to Jack?"

"I don't think I can."

"You're going to break up with him?"

"Yes," she said, painfully. "I have to do that."

"And after you do that, then what about us? How would you feel about kissing me then?"

"I think I would like that," she said.

"All right. I'll ask again, after the election," I said. And we went back to searching through an unsearchable volume of papers.

Chapter

FIFTY

MONDAY MORNING. THE boy with the rifle heard the jeep coming from miles and miles away. It was early and the light was low across the Sawtooth Mountains. You could hide for a hundred years just in the shadows alone.

Maybe the car was just some damn tourist. Probably. Money had begun to discover Idaho. There'd always been rich folk come to the mountains, over in Sun Valley and up the rivers for the fishing, sporting types, been coming for years and years. But lately, with cell phones and the Net and staying in touch with everywhere from anywhere, they'd started buying the state up and building homes and claiming land, acres and acres, thousands of acres of land. Coming close, too close to people like himself and his family.

America was coming to an end, just like his dad said. His America, the real America, where self-reliant people built their own homes with their own hands and drew their own water and chopped their own wood and shot the wild game, slaughtered it and smoked it or put it in snow packs to freeze it through the winter.

Soon there'd be nothing left, no place a man could roam, call his own, them California people, movie and computer millionaires, coming in, dragging government in behind them. Vaccinating. Forcing schooling. Forcing the races to mix. Telling you what to think, what to say, how to live, crowding in.

The boy hated all that. Hated them. He wondered if this was one of the new outsiders. His rifle was loaded. He didn't figure it would come to that. Not today. But someday, maybe.

Whoever it was coming, it wasn't somebody he knew. The vehicle was too far off to make out in detail, but the boy was a young huntsman, a backwoodsman. In an earlier day he would have walked with Crockett through the Cumberland Gap, and he had the knack of recognizing even the things that he couldn't quite see. He knew all the vehicles that ought to be coming up this way, which were very few, and this was not one of them.

He loped through the trees, an easy and tireless run, something you didn't see much anymore, with all the sitting and TV watching and fear of living outdoors, but the boy didn't know that he was so unusual, because he didn't live down there, didn't see the kids at the mall too wide to sit in a normal chair, too used to going from car to car to video game, to ever run eight or nine miles just because it was the only way to get from here to there.

This was just half a mile or so, through meadows and tall, wide-apart trees. There was time, time to warn his father; his father would know what to do, to fight or to run. His father always knew. A bearded man, iron-hard, hickory brown, lean and streaked with gray, not quick-tempered but with a long slow burn in his belly, like some underground coal seam that had a fire that would never go out.

His father was splitting logs. Hard enough work that he had his shirt off and the boy could see the twisted old scars from the bullet wounds from where the feds had shot him up. Bastards. Motherfucking bastards. Hated government and government men. Tried to kill his daddy. Shot him down like a dog.

But like some cunning old wolf his old man had crept off into the trees, into the deep dark woods, wrapping himself around his wounds, clutching straw and moss against his belly to stanch the flow of the blood, and he survived the shock and fought the fever and he'd lived. The scar was puckered and tight and white.

"Car coming," the boy called.

His father put down the ax. He didn't rush. Just put down the ax. He stretched and took a sip of water from the bottle he had sitting on a stump beside him. "Get the binoculars, boy."

The boy went past his father and into the cabin. It was all hand built, mostly by his dad, himself, and his older brother, now doing twelve years' federal time, built by the three of them, every board, every nail, every beam and shingle and the pipes and plumbing, too. The indoor plumbing was practically new, just finished it eight, nine months back. There was a cellar, underneath; they'd dug that out, with shovels. Storage for fruit and vegetables and ammo.

Damn arsenal down there. They could stand off whoever came for them. Well, that's what the boy liked to say, said it the way boys do, full of pleasant bravado, but thinking, in his heart and in his head, too, that it might not be true. The government had all sorts of things, helicopters and missiles and lasers and all kinds of things. Maybe he and his pa couldn't stand them off if they came in force, but the two of them could fade into the trees, head for the deep scarred passes made of stone, go for the caves. If the goddamn government couldn't find no goddamn Osama bin damn A-rab, they must be pretty damn dumb, too dumb to catch up with an honest-to-God Idaho mountain man and his son.

The boy brought out the long-range sniper rifle with the scope and the hand loads along with the binoculars. His father gestured to him that he didn't want the rifle, but he took the glasses and climbed up onto the big rock outcropping that gave him some extra height and a pretty clear field of vision, clear field of fire, too.

About forty minutes later, with an eagle flying overhead, by coincidence, but beautiful all the same, Neil Carllson came up to the house with the stranger, the stranger driving Neil's car, Neil with a shotgun across his lap. At a word, the stranger stopped and turned off the engine, put the parking brake on. At a gesture, he got out, Neil covering him.

The stranger was a city type. He was wearing boots and jeans and a plaid shirt and wool-lined denim jacket that had seen a few years, but you could tell he was a city type. The boy had never seen him before, but his father clearly had, the two of them recognizing each other without saying much.

There was some uncertainty there, in his father, which the boy rarely saw. For the most part his father showed no more vacillation than the forests and the bears and the elements themselves. Not that a bear couldn't start one way, then go another, not that sunshine couldn't turn to a raging storm in a matter of moments, but that such changes weren't full of confusion and bafflement and conflicted selves as humans were.

"You want something?" his father said.

"I want to talk to you," the city man said.

The boy's father seemed to study on that, consider it, like looking at the horizon for weather signs. Finally he said, "All right, Michael, you come on in then," and he turned and walked toward the cabin, stopped after a couple of steps, and looked back and said, "Thank you, Neil, I'll get him on down."

"Right enough," Neil said, holding his shotgun like he was born with one in his hand. He headed back to his old Cherokee and pulled himself in, released the brake, stepped on the clutch, spun the wheel, and let it roll in a half circle backward. Then he spun the wheels the other way and moved off down the hill.

The city man, Michael, followed the boy's father into the cabin. Then the boy followed after, not having been told not to, and being curious.

It was dim inside, shadowy, and smelled of smoke: wood smoke and tobacco and the smoke from kerosene lamps. The boy had a knack for shadows, indoors and out, and he found one now, because he didn't want to be sent away, not that his father often did send him away, but he sensed there was something unusual here.

"You want a drink?" his father asked the stranger.

"Sure."

His father opened a cupboard. They'd built that and the boy was proud of it. It was clean and square and it swung smooth on its hinges and closed just right. He took out a bottle and then found a couple of glasses and set everything on the table. Only then did either of them sit. His father poured, a couple of fingers in each glass, clear liquid.

The stranger raised his glass, offering it.

There was that odd hesitation, a reservation—his father never did anything with reservation—but then they touched glasses. The stranger lifted his to his mouth, took a small sip, tasting it like a curious man seeking understanding, then lifted the glass and swallowed it all down. His father did the same.

The stranger shuddered, though not too, too hard, then said, "Smooth," in a drawn-out, comic way.

His father smiled, not that it was funny, but more like it was funny once, long ago. "Kinda vodka," he said. "Learned it from the Russkies, from potatoes."

"Hey, it's Idaho."

"Yeah, it's Idaho."

Then they sat, looking. His father poured another, into the silence, poured it into the silence. They raised their glasses to each other, but did not touch, and they drank.

"You want something?"

"Yes. Yes I do."

His father nodded his head, not that it would be given, whatever it was, but that he would listen.

"I don't know how this election is going to turn out," Mike said. "Anne Lynn's done a hell of a job."

The boy's father shrugged. It was none of his never mind.

"I thought she might make it. Now I think she might get beat. But I don't want her humiliated. I don't want her to lose Idaho. I want her to at least win her home state. You understand what I'm saying."

The boy's father looked stern and angry even.

"Damn it," the stranger said.

"I don't hold with it."

"I want you to tell your people and the people who listen to your people to come out for Anne Lynn. I'm asking you, Kevin."

"You go to hell, Michael. I tol' you, I don' hold with it. Don' hold with nothin' to do with this government. It's an illegal government as far as I'm concerned, it's tax collectin', rights stealin', coercive thing and I do not hold with it and will have nothing to do with it."

"I am asking you."

"You got no right, no call, to come here asking me for any damn thing."

"I don't?"

"'Cause we're brothers?" the boy's father said derisively. If that was the stranger's excuse for asking, it wouldn't hold.

Brothers? The boy was astounded. He didn't know anything about a brother. This man was his uncle?

"I've never asked anything before."

"Your wife, running for president, well, I don't know, I don't know if I hold with that either. Bible says the place of a woman is beneath that of the man. That would make you the first lady, and that's all wrong. I don't hold with it."

The boy wanted to speak but was afraid to. He was kin to Anne Lynn Murphy, first woman to ever run for president?

"The hell with what you hold with," the stranger snapped back.

The boy was surprised. He looked soft, this man, his newfound Uncle Michael, too soft to be talking that way to his father, hard, hard as an ax handle.

"You got no right to talk that way to me," his father said, face set in stone, even his beard looking like granite. "Our father traveling around from town to town planting his seed may make us kin but we didn't grow up as brothers. There's blood but no bond."

"That's not what I'm calling on."

"Don't matter what you're calling on."

The stranger suddenly lunged up from his seat, his right hand driving toward his father's chest. His father rose up too and his left hand came sweeping down and around and grabbed the other man, swift and hard as a third-time felony count, and grabbed him and turned, flinging the city man toward the floor, but the city man had grabbed on to Kevin's shirt and he clutched the fabric tight in his fist and the shirt ripped open even as he went and landed on his side, Kevin following, looming over him, looking like he was about to give his brother, half brother, a stomping.

But they stopped. Both of them frozen there, the mountain man's scar seeming to glow in the dimness.

The stranger pushed himself up.

"You don't owe me shit," he said. "You owe her, and you damn well know it."

Kevin McCullough touched his hand to his scar. He'd been shot in a botched bank robbery up in Coeur d'Leon. Three men dead. Two of his, one of theirs, a cop. A long time ago. He was still wanted for the things that happened that night. For murder. Bank robbery. Terrorism. Conspiracy. Lot of things, a whole lot of things. He'd been gut shot. He'd been close to death. His wife, Esther, a good Bible name, Esther, had done her best, tried to nurse him, knew she was failing, knew he was going to die. She knew a lady doctor, down in Ketchum, and went to see her, this Anne Lynn Murphy. Took a chance, had to take a chance, though Kevin would have told her not to, would've rather died than spend a life in prison. Live free or goddamn die. Still would. Still would, if they came for him now—he'd fight to the death. Send the boy away and go down dying.

But Esther brought this lady doctor. And the lady doctor had cleaned the wound. Hadn't flinched, Esther told him later, done it like she'd seen lots of wounds, seen worse even. So she'd gone in and cleaned it, pulled out bullet fragments and bits of cloth and chips of bone and washed away the pus and put topical antibiotics on the flesh and gave him antibiotics to take internally and painkillers, too. She'd never reported it. She never said nothin', not to nobody.

So Kevin owed her. Of course, she wasn't asking.

Strange twists of fate, that it was his own blood kin, though they were raised separately, raised differently, never knew each other until Kevin was almost thirty and Mike just turned twenty-one.

Esther was dead. Oh, twelve years now. Died two years after her second son was born. Kevin missed her. Her second son, the boy in the corner, watching, his name was Andrew. Closest Esther could get to Anne for a boy. Andy. That was how grateful Esther had been.

Kevin didn't hold with government. He was a bank robber and a terrorist. But he did hold with paying his debts and he knew that this was a debt that was owed. Didn't matter what her politics were. Could be a goddamn Communist and a Taliban besides. Didn't matter a good goddamn. Kevin McCullough paid his debts.

Chapter
FIFTY-ONE

SUSIE RENTED A Buick from Budget and drove out to Inga's house.

Although it was late, when Susie told Inga that she'd come from me and that she herself was a librarian at the Library of Congress, Inga welcomed her in and made her tea. Susie asked her about my computer.

After the man from Homeland Security came to the library, and Inga had lied to him with so much pleasure, she decided someone more thorough and intelligent might show up and actually search for my computer, so she'd lugged it home with her. And it was still there.

Susie drove back into Washington and picked us up just before dawn and we all went to Inga's house.

At last, I was finally going to get to these final pieces from the Stowe papers. But would they be the final pieces of the puzzle?

You would think that a man who was very near to death, who was richer than God, though not quite as

rich as Bill Gates or Warren Buffet, who could be moved
to tears by boys' adventure heroism and tragic ends as
they were told of in old-fashioned rhymed and metered
verse, who worried about curses and that he had no heirs
and who wondered if anyone would remember, fifteen
minutes after his passing, that he had ever been more
than dust, you would think a man like that would want
to spend his final days creating something epic and
memorable.

The fact that he wanted to create a library at least
hinted that he had that impulse.

But, no. Instead, he seemed to be recapitulating, in
frantic miniature, what he had been doing his whole life.
He had immersed himself in an extraordinarily large
number of new business deals of, as far as I could tell,
astonishingly little importance. Many of them seemed to
be downright trivial, like buying up some guy's mortgage in Missouri—through a mortgage company that
was co-owned by a consortium of three banks, two of
which were controlled by Stowe—and becoming a silent
partner in a gardening supply store in Ellis, Ohio.

He went at it each of these twenty-, fifty-, hun-
dred-thousand dollar deals with the same thoroughness
and attention to detail that he had, in the past, put into
twenty-, fifty- and hundred-*million*-dollar deals,
including complete financial reports and personal
dossiers on everyone that he did business with. The style
was no surprise. It's what he'd been doing for almost
seventy years, from way before computers and credit
agencies and credit cards and credit reports, when it was
much harder to dig up all that information. It was only
the small size of the prizes that seemed different from
anything else he had done through the years.

A prototypical example was Ward Martucci of Hiawatha, Iowa, a packing plant supervisor with a gross annual income of $64,500 against monthly obligations of $998 on his mortgage, $493 on his supplemental medical insurance, and car payments of $326.

His wife, Greta Martucci (maiden name Gunter), worked part-time at a day care center. Her job had no benefits. They had three children, one in fourth grade, two in middle school. One of the middle schoolers was special ed.

Their credit history was mixed. He'd always made his mortgage but he'd been late on his car payments six times and his credit cards were up there where he was paying mostly interest and not a lot of principle. He was having a sexual relationship with Oswald Finelli, a long-haul trucker who was a distant relation, specifically Ward's father's cousin's son.

Ward wanted to start his own business selling used cars. He'd gone to the bank with a business plan; he'd been turned down. He was in negotiation with a small business capitalization fund and was scheduled to go to contract with them on November 10 of this year. The SBC fund was run by an investment group that was controlled by Fiduciary Trust Management, a privately held company owned by Alan Stowe.

It was clear that this was not just one of a group of investments that the management of FTM was doing on its own, with Stowe checking only their bottom line, because it was all by itself, not in a folder with all of FTM's deals or even a sampling of FTM's deals, and, in addition, Stowe's initials were on the hard copy of the original papers.

Over the course of the last one to six months, Stowe

had gotten involved in about sixty transactions in that approximate range. I thought, perhaps, that he was assembling properties for malls or subdivisions, so I looked at the geography of them. There were six more like Martucci in Iowa, but when I checked the locations on Internet maps, they were too far apart for that. The same for the five in New Mexico and eleven in Ohio. So I couldn't figure them at all. Except that he was compulsively doing deals.

We worked until 7:00 A.M., EST, Tuesday morning, November 2. The polls were open. People were starting to vote. We hadn't found a damn thing.

We had failed.

Chapter

FIFTY-TWO

I SLEPT A little bit on Tuesday morning. It was a caffeinated, nervous sort of lying-on-the-couch-under-a-blanket-that-itched type of sleep. My limbs twitched and there was no position that felt comfortable. Susie came by and said something. Niobe didn't.

I got up around two or three in the afternoon and Inga let me use her shower. It was an old woman's bathroom, with lots of powders and prescription pills. But I was grateful. I shaved then wiped the litter of stubble out of the sink.

Well, I told myself, another half a day or so and I could try, try to go back to my normal life. Of course, now I would be the librarian who fucked a horse and that would be a legend throughout library land and a blot that would never disappear from the Internet. Did I even want to go back? Had these few action-filled days changed me forever, da-dum, da-dum?

Well, if they had, too damn bad. There weren't a hell of a lot of jobs with benefits that fit the description of librarian on the run or fugitive researcher trying to stop the reelection of a sitting president.

Niobe had gone out. For a walk, Inga told me. I cooked up some eggs and toast and tea. While we were eating, Inga asked me if everything on my computer, all the Stowe material, was word searchable. I told her that it was. She asked how far back it went. Almost thirty years, I said, on my machine, which overlapped with the library's data storage, which went back about sixty years, and a few things were even older.

She asked if she could take a look. I said yes and started to show her, but of course she knew how and I let her be. Susie put on the television to listen for election news. I went out to look for Niobe.

I found her and we walked together for a while.

"Tomorrow," she said, "I'll tell Jack that I'm leaving him."

I nodded.

"Then," she said, "we can try. But not until I've done that. I want it to be honest, completely honest."

When we got back to the house, Inga was sitting at the kitchen table. There were tears rolling out of her eyes and down her cheeks and she was ignoring them and letting them spill, unchecked, and she had Niobe's gun in her hands.

"All those years ago," she said, "I cursed Alan Stowe, but I should have killed him."

"Yes," Susie said. She pulled up a chair and sat down next to Inga and reached to take the gun away. There was the slight moment of resistance, but then Inga let it go. "Tell me."

"Forty-two years," Inga said. "Forty-two years ago."

"What?"

"You know Monument Mall?"

"Yes," I said. It was a few miles from the campus.

"There was once a monument there. From the Civil War. You know Wilson's Pond Estates?" It was a subdivision. There were thousands like them. Indistinguishable, for the most part, from one another.

"There was once a real pond there, in a real forest, that people would hike to, and go swimming in the summertime." Inga looked at me. "Did you see how that horrible man does research on people? With spies and everything? He wanted those properties." Why was she bemoaning two forty-two-year-old real estate developments, however aesthetically and socially reprehensible they might have been? "And he tried, but people didn't want to sell to him, partly because he wanted to pay next to nothing.

"But then, then there was a rumor that some big corporation was going to come and build a factory. It was going to make plastic furniture. For all the new malls and schools. Everything was going to be plastic. We even saw surveyors and site managers come around and measure the land.

"So Stowe tried again to put together a package. This time everybody was very suspicious. They'd all seen or heard of the surveys, so they 'knew' he was trying to pull a fast one.

"Then somehow, people started talking about putting together the land, without Stowe, and then everybody would make money and it would be a good thing. Then some men, a lawyer and a man who owned a dairy farm and two others, came to a college professor, a very dignified man whom everyone trusted, and asked him to be the head of things. He wouldn't have to do anything, and they would all make four or five times what they put in, plus the whole town would then make more money on selling things to the factory and building the roads for it and the other construction and all of those things that make people stupid with greed.

"My husband, they got my husband to do this.

"Then, then it all collapsed, because the factory didn't come. And the thing that my husband organized, his land consortium, it went bankrupt. Then Alan Stowe came and he bought the land cheap from the bankruptcy and he put up his mall and his subdivisions.

"People were very, very angry, very upset. Many had lost everything and my husband was despondent. Then, to make it worse, there were accusations of fraud. And he was going to be charged. I knew him and I knew he would not commit fraud. I knew, without knowing the details, because no one knew, that somehow Alan Stowe was behind all of it, and also Stowe owned all the judges and the prosecuting attorneys around, just like he does now.

"So I went to him, I went to him to plead with him to ask him to stop my husband from being branded a criminal, charged with fraud.

"He said that he would help me if I would have sex with him. He talked and talked and said he knew I had had sex with many people, which was true, before I was married, I was only married three years then, and he said one more wouldn't hurt. So I let myself be persuaded. One more wouldn't hurt, who would know, it was just sex. Never in my life had I had sex for any reason but for myself, for love or fun or curiosity. Never to buy something or through coercion. Except that one time.

"Afterward I went home, and its always like that, isn't it, things happen at the same time, they come together in particularly awful ways, I went home and he was dead. My husband was dead, he had committed suicide, with pills.

"All of this, of course," Inga said, "I have known for all these forty-two years.

"Now, now I look in your computer and Stowe's own history of himself and it's in there. Except now I know that he owned the company that was supposed to build the factory, but that they never intended to build it, never, never. He started the rumor, sent the surveyors. But never intended. The lawyer and the dairyman were both working for Stowe. It was all planned. All intended."

Inga looked around at all of us. One at a time. "And now I know, even one more thing, and that is the reason they picked my husband. That is in Alan Stowe's note. It was because my husband was an older man with a young wife and he was afraid of losing her and they convinced him that having money and big success would help him keep me.

"I should have killed him," she said, again.

Instead of cursing him? I asked myself, and by cursing, I wondered if she meant swearing at him or ruing the day we met or actually putting a curse on him, like in the Dylan song that Stowe seemed to know:

> *These be seven curses on a judge so cruel:*
> *That one doctor will not save him,*
> *That two healers will not heal him,*
> *That three eyes will not see him.*

That four ears will not hear him,
That five walls will not hide him,
That six diggers will not bury him
And that seven deaths shall never kill him.

I wondered if it was possible to curse someone. It should be. But I don't think it is.

Chapter

FIFTY-THREE

HAGOPIAN HAD HIS black ministers and they were going door to door, preaching, singing, clapping, carrying signs, handing out leaflets, getting out the vote. And he had his cameras to protect them, or, better yet, to record an incident of abuse that would backfire and explode out of one of the Florida ghettos across the state and across the nation and mobilize Murphy voters and potential Murphy voters and the undecideds and pull the fence sitters down on her side, too.

Scott had the Florida state police and the U.S. Army and they had roadblocks and checkpoints and inspection stations and everyone who wanted to cross them had to show ID and the authorities checked the names against lists of fugitive warrants and the lists had been collected with deliberate latitude so that if a certain William Jones was a wanted man—and there was a William Jones who was wanted—then Bill, Billy, Will, Willy, and William

with-any-middle-initial-at-all Jones were all, all on the
list, and the police detained Bill, Billy, Will, Willy,
William A., William B., and all the Williams through ·
William X. Jones, and then placed the burden on the
Bills and Wills, the Willies and the Williamses to
somehow prove that they were not the dreaded William
Jones who was wanted on the fugitive warrant for
failure to show in Matecumbe Key town court two years
previous for doing 65 in a 40 mph zone.

Then, at a checkpoint in Miami's Liberty City, the police
grabbed a William S. Jones. They were pretty casual and
careless about it, as he was the ninth Willy or Billy Jones
they'd detained that day, all on that single warrant for
failure to pay a speeding ticket. But this Jones, according
to a police spokesman, sometime later, was actually a
Santiago Jonez and he was, at that moment, strapped,
cracked, and dirty, which is one dumb-ass way to pass
through a police checkpoint, but that's the way it was, so
he made a break for it and when they started hollering,
he pulled out his nine, did more than pull it out, he
turned and pointed it and seemed to pull the trigger,
though it misfired or it was empty or the safety was on,
and then someone else started shooting and three people
got shot, though not Santiago and not any of the police.
When the shooting stopped and the wail of sirens began,
heralds that more cops were coming and the EMS, too,
people poured out of their houses and what was already
an ugly disarray began to grow with a sort of throbbing
aspiration toward a riot.

• • •

The police called for reenforcements. Only the army was available. So segments of the 101st Airborne, on stateside rotation from Afghanistan, were called in to place their bodies and body armor and arms between the natives of Liberty City and a moment of genuine insurgency. They came in Bradley fighting vehicles and they came in trucks and they disembarked and they came marching through the streets with their helmets and their vests and the big boots that made them seem like the troops of some alien empire here in the flop-flop, shorts and Haitian shirt heat of South Florida. And the dark people started shouting at them and razzing them and doing the dozens and some kids, probably some kids, but it would be hard to prove it, started to throw things. Squashy fruit at first, then whatever they could find out of overturned trash bins, used, fat, heavy diapers, fast-food remnants and containers, things that went splat and stank and made the soldiers feel assaulted with filth and filled them with disgust and resentment. Then some harder things got into the mix, cans and bottles and the bottles smashed and glass splattered and that made them feel threatened and angry though it was better, in most ways, than the stink. And then someone in the crowd pushed someone else in the crowd into the neatly drawn-up and formed line of the 101st Airborne. A soldier pushed back. A punch was thrown. One of the soldiers swung out with the butt of his rifle and caught a fat woman under the jaw and sent her reeling and screaming back into the crowd and now more things were being thrown and people were trying to attack the soldier who had rammed the butt of his rifle into a grandmother of three and his buddies began to defend him as they'd been taught and trained to do.

They were, by chance, mostly white, five or six of them in that segment of the line. So there they were, white soldiers of the United States Army, battling with black civilians of the state of Florida.

And it was being taped.

Then a black sergeant started screaming at the men and put himself between the civilians and the soldiers who were fighting, they felt, for their lives, or their buddies, or their dignity, or from the heat and exhaustion, or from the burnout of a nine-month tour in a hostile land—a different hostile land, not this hostile land, this was supposed to be the land of rest and recreation and regrouping and beaches and wives and get to know the kids again and drink in public and walk where there were no snipers or roadside explosives or suicide bombers. The sergeant got hit by one of his own men. Four of his other men rushed to the sergeant's support. And, as it happened, three were black, and although there was one white private on the black side, it sure as hell looked like a race riot inside the military itself.

A lieutenant called for help and MPs came from somewhere and choppers came from all directions and the lieutenant ordered one of the Bradleys forward and made it drive slowly into the crowd and they had to disperse or be crushed and they got lucky and nobody was caught under the treads of the fifty-thousand-pound vehicle and most of the civilians ended up on one side and most of the soldiers ended up on the other. The few civilians caught on the wrong side were quickly knocked to the ground, stomped, and subdued. There were only two soldiers caught on the wrong side and with the help of their comrades in arms they were yanked up on board and out of the crowd.

It was taped. All of it was taped. There were at least four camcorders going.

The footage was raced to Democratic headquarters on Miami Beach and it was beamed up in digital bursts to satellites and it went around the world. Hagopian was overjoyed. He was certain that this was a historic set of images—like the water cannons and the dogs of Selma—epic images that would change history. It was seen in England on the BBC. It was seen on French and German TV. *Al-Jazeera* loved it and played it again and again and again. Russians saw it. The Scandinavians and Finns saw it. Everybody saw it.

Except the majority of Americans. The networks and major cable news stations decided to hold it back as too "confusing" and "incendiary."

Hagopian worked the phones and called all his old friends but he couldn't get the story pulled out of the fog. He should have known better. He'd seen it happen before. Like when Jon Alpert risked his life to bring back footage of what happened to Iraqi civilians in Gulf War One and no one in America would broadcast it.

Even more to the point was the brilliant disappearance of the true story of the last election.

Scott, back then, appeared to have taken Florida by a few hundred votes. Or possibly a few thousand. The law in Florida was actually quite simple and direct

> (4) If the returns for any office reflect that a candidate was defeated or eliminated by one-half of a percent or less of the votes cast for such office . . . the board responsible for certifying the results of the vote on such race or measure shall order a recount of the votes cast with respect to such office or measure.

That seemed like a no-brainer. The state court ordered a recount.

Then the legal maneuvering began—there were local suits and federal suits and state pleadings—until the Supreme Court stepped in and shut the recounts down. None of the possible recounts ever took place, not the full statewide one or any of the local ones that the Democratic candidate was asking for, at least not to completion. Scott had been left the victor.

But, presumably, the whole world wanted to know who actually did get the most votes. It would make a great and important story. So the *New York Times,* the *Washington Post,* the Tribune Co., the *Wall Street Journal,* Associated Press, CNN, and several others formed a consortium to share the expense and count the votes.

It cost over a million dollars and took almost a year.

But when they got the results they decided they really didn't like the results and they decided to bury them. *Decided* is a strange word here because there is no record of the decision, no description of the process of decision, no explanation of how so many parties collaborated in the same decision.

All there are, are the facts and the acts.

The facts were these: If all the votes had been recounted Scott would have lost. That was what was required by Florida law. There were several possible standards that could have been used to evaluate the ballots. But no matter which standard was used to evaluate the ballots, the bottom line was the same: Scott lost.

The acts were these headlines:

The *New York Times:* "Study of Disputed Florida Ballots Finds Justices Did Not Cast the Deciding Vote"

The *Wall Street Journal:* "In Election Review, Scott Wins Without Supreme Court Help"

Los Angeles Times: "Scott Still Had Votes to Win in a Recount, Study Finds"

The *Washington Post:* "Florida Recounts Would Have Favored Scott"

CNN.com: "Florida Recount Study: Scott Still Wins"

The *St. Petersburg Times:* "Recount: Scott

Did they lie?

The *New York Times* spent the first three paragraphs of the story supporting the headline and explicitly stated that Scott would have won even with a statewide recount. But then, in the fourth paragraph, in a very convoluted sentence, it said that Scott would have lost in a statewide recount. Then the story spent five more paragraphs explaining that a statewide recount was never a realistic possibility and then listed a clutter of partial recount scenarios under which Scott could have won.

Most of the lawsuits had only asked for partial recounts—this county or that county or three counties or five. If any of those had been carried to term, then Scott would have won. So the *Times* could presumably say to the world and to itself that it was only a matter of interpretation.

So, now, when the news director at CNN told Hagopian that the footage was fabulous but that it would be "irresponsible" to run it without "contextualizing" it and the same exact words cropped up in his approaches to the news directors at CBS, NBC, and Fox, Hagopian cursed at himself for being naive.

Hagopian figured they had lost. He kept smiling. Another however many hours. Then Anne Lynn would make her concession speech. It would be gracious and dignified and memorable, as she herself was.

Then, in the morning, it would be off to New York, to check himself into Sloan-Kettering and let the doctors start playing with his body until the pain and the humiliation were so intense that he would prefer death itself and, at the point, he would have the pleasure of testing the true efficacy of his meditations and his practice of Zen.

Chapter

FIFTY-FOUR

LIKE SO MANY others did, we watched the election on television. Television, I think, trivializes everything. We made popcorn and the four of us sat around and chatted. We were subdued. The idea that we could have affected the outcome of the election now seemed far-fetched, to say the least.

Rush Limbaugh had loudly and at great length declared that the only states that Murphy would take would be Massachusetts and San Francisco, the only states with gay marriage, hah-hah, ditto, so, at 8:00 P.M. when she was also holding Vermont, Rhode Island, Delaware, and Maryland, it seemed to be remarkably good news.

Then, when they called New Jersey for her, it looked for the first time like a real race.

At one point I got on the Net and found stories about riots in Florida and U.S. Army units battling one another. Which was extraordinary, unbelievable. But there was no mention of it on U.S. television. I went back and forth. I even got streaming video from *Al-Jazeera* and I got stills from the BBC Web site. They looked real enough. I couldn't believe that the foreign press had suddenly become more informative—more free—than America's famous free press. It wasn't possible and I tried to say as much to the women, only to discover that they were all, in this area at least, far more cynical than I was.

Scott had originally scheduled his victory speech for 9:00 P.M., which seemed to me to be arrogantly optimistic, but with Rush telling you that you were going to take all the marbles but that one wacky one with Harvard built in, it was understandable. 9:00 P.M. passed.

At 10:00 Fox News said they were standing by their prediction that Scott would win, though not, as God had told the Reverend Tod Puttersback, in a landslide.

At 11:00 P.M. CBS was the first to call California for Murphy. ABC followed suit and then CNN. Fox had it as too close to call, but leaning for Scott.

It was also at that point that a real pattern became apparent. Divisions had become deeper. Scott's margins were higher where he had won before. He was also losing by larger margins in the states he'd lost before.

Fewer states were falling into the maybe and too-close-to-call categories. Except at Fox, which, after all, was Fox and had President Scott's former press secretary as coanchor on the election desk.

At midnight, Fox called Florida for Scott.

Within the hour everyone else had followed suit. I didn't know if it was real or just the media doing what the media seems to do now, all following the loudest noise. But whatever it was, it took the wind out of my sails and I fell asleep.

Chapter

FIFTY-FIVE

By two o'clock in the morning, Hagopian really wanted to give it up. He was just too, too tired. But Anne Lynn deserved for this day to have as much hope as she could squeeze out of it, to last as long as possible, so he forced the mouth on his weary body not to speak. Then somebody said Idaho, what if she pulled Idaho? After all, it was her home state.

"Who said that?" Hagopian asked, with almost a smile.

Mike, Anne Lynn's husband, said, "I did."

Hagopian looked at the polls and the projections and shrugged, not likely, not damn likely.

Mike looked, for a moment, as if he was going to say something, but stopped. They all had the same basic information.

It was true that Anne Lynn had won in Idaho on the Democratic line before, as a congressperson and then a senator. Neither the pundits nor the pollsters had disregarded that. The theory was that she'd been lucky in her first shot at Congress. Her opponent, Conrad "Connie" McCorkle, had been charged in mid-September with soliciting a forest ranger in a public restroom at Massacre Rocks State Park. In addition, at the time of his arrest, he was found in possession of three prescriptions for Percocet, one for Percodan, and four for Vicodin, all from different physicians. He wasn't charged for this last, but the information found its way out of the park police office. Connie cried, "Foul!" He cried that the liberal, Democratic, tree-hugger media were out to get him because he was pro-logging, pro-industry, and pro-*jobs*!

Still, he lost.

Then she was the incumbent. Over the past fifty years, congressional incumbents who have run for reelection have been successful 92 percent of the time. So her success at getting reelected was also discounted.

It was harder to dismiss her win in her first, and only, Senate race. But it had been by a razor-thin margin, against a weak and badly funded opponent who had made the mistake, as so many had, of underestimating her.

Still, the theorists said, none of that meant that Idaho would go for a Democrat in a presidential race. It had only happened once since Truman in '48. In 1964 Johnson beat Goldwater. But it was only by one point and it was a long time ago. Since then the Republican presidential candidates in Idaho had done better than 60 percent. Reagan got 72 percent and 73 percent. Scott had pulled 67 percent in the last election.

Murphy was expected to get a significant home court advantage. But even eleven points off of Scott's last run, and that's what the tracking polls had been showing, would still make it fifty-six for Scott and just forty-four for Murphy.

The exit polls were showing that Anne Lynn was doing better than predicted. They were giving her close to 47 percent of the major party vote, but they still weren't saying that she would get a win.

Mind you, a few of the pollsters working Idaho were reporting anomalies. Most notably, one Jerry Hogarty, a native of Boise, majoring in poli-sci at UC Berkeley, reported back that he didn't trust his numbers, that he had an unusual number of people who refused to be interviewed, who were, in fact, downright hostile to him when he tried to ask.

Curious, he'd gone into a couple of polling places and chatted with those nice older men and women who keep the registration books in which voters sign in and he was told that they were seeing people that they hadn't seen in years; they were seeing some voters that they'd *never* seen before.

Idaho is a small state, with only 750,000 registered voters. In the previous presidential cycle 71 percent of those actually voted, approximately 532,000 people.

This time the turnout was running closer to 79 percent, 592,534 people by actual count. Of them, 297,779 of them voted Anne Lynn Murphy.

Later on, when all those commentators and prognosticators and pundits tried to understand it, to humanize it, to make it a narrative, they talked about how small the state was and how personal things were, how everyone in the whole state was connected by no more than three degrees of separation.

Every baby that Dr. Murphy had birthed had a mother and a father and every mother and every father had parents of their own and sisters and brothers and cousins and uncles and aunts. For every emergency call, for every kind word, for every time she'd come out at night, in the snow, there was someone who was grateful, and every one of those people had memories and families and friends.

There was also talk of mountain men coming down from the hills. And their wives and their friends. Those were the folks, Jerry Hogarty said, who refused to be interviewed for the exit polls. So nobody could even guess how many like them there had actually been. There was even a story that the outlaw Kevin McCullough had appeared like a ghost at some polling place or other, a public school it was said, strolled on in, big as life, and in spite of the fact that he was the most wanted white man in the West since Jesse James, the poll watchers let him in the booth and let him vote.

The story was widely dismissed. Nobody actually could find a sign-in book with his signature on it. And it made no sense that he would risk his life—if he was still alive—in order to vote. Either for Augustus Winthrop Scott or Anne Lynn Murphy. Didn't make any sense.

Andy McCullough listened to the election returns on the radio. So that was the running-for-president lady he had been named for. He walked off into the woods alone, which was what he did when he started thinking about his mother. Waves of loss and sadness came over him and sometimes he cried about her and he didn't like to do that in front of his father, not that his old man would hit him for it or anything or even laugh at him, but his father was like an old lion, a mountain lion—an American lion, not one of those

African Lion King lions with a mane—a mountain lion and you didn't want to go around girlishly weeping in front of no damn mountain lion. What it was, he thought, was like that story his mother had told him—his father only told him Bible stories and stories about real things that happened now—his mother told him stories of long ago and sometimes they were about made-up things. It was Androcles, that was name of the story, *Androcles and the Lion*. It was one of those African lions, the kind with the big mane, king of the jungle, and everybody was afraid of lions as well they should be, especially as that was from long-ago days when they didn't have firearms of any kind whatsoever. But this lion had a thorn in his paw and he couldn't get it out. And Androcles saw that the lion was in pain and, even though he was afraid of the lion, as everybody was, he went to the lion and he pulled the thorn out. He was afraid, right then, that the lion would turn and jump on him and kill him, but the lion didn't, the lion just turned and ran off to do the things that lions do.

Androcles was a Christian. And this was in the bad old days when it was illegal to be a Christian, the Roman times, and it came to pass that he was captured and they took him to the Coliseum where gladiators fought and where there were chariot races and where Christians were thrown barehanded into the arena to fight against wild beasts for the amusement of horrible people who enjoyed seeing defenseless people torn apart and eaten.

There was Androcles, thrown into the ring, thousands looking down on him, waiting for him to be torn limb from limb and devoured. And they opened the door at the other side and this giant lion came running out. This lion had not been fed for ten days and he was starving. He was ravenous. He was primed for some ripe, raw Christian to turn into meat to eat and he came racing toward Androcles, the saliva dripping from his huge fangs, his monstrous claws outstretched and he skidded to a stop. Just stopped dead there in front of all those thousands of people and Androcles didn't even realize it because he had his eyes closed and he was praying as hard as he could pray. Not to escape, but to meet his death with dignity and to keep his faith and to go to heaven.

The first moment that Androcles knew that things were not going as scheduled, that he was not going to be devoured, was when a big, wet, sloppy tongue licked him up the side of his face, splat! He opened one eye. But he couldn't see too well because it was kind of covered with lion slime. Then he opened his other eye and there was the lion standing there, tongue hanging out of his big mouth with his giant scary teeth and then he looked twice and the lion was looking back at him, with intelligence in his eyes, with recognition, and Androcles realized that this was the very same lion.

For even the beasts in the field may be touched by love and duty and justice.

A total of 294,755 people voted for Augustus Winthrop Scott. That was 3,024 less than voted for Anne Lynn Murphy. It was a margin of only .005 percent. But it could have been two votes and it would have given Anne Lynn all of Idaho's electoral votes, all four. And from there the math was even simpler. That gave Scott 267 electoral votes. Anne Lynn had 270.

That was going to make Anne Lynn Murphy the next president of the United States.

Chapter

FIFTY-SIX

AT THREE-FIFTEEN in the morning Niobe woke me up with kisses. "She won," Niobe said. "She won."

"You're kidding," I said.

"No. She won."

"I love you," I said.

"I know," she said.

"And you're happy now?" I asked her.

She nodded her head up and down, so pleased she could barely speak.

"And us? We're really going to give it a shot?"

She kept nodding. "Take a look," she said, pointing me at the television. I sat up and watched. It was CNN and they'd called it for Murphy.

"Fox won't call it for her," Inga said. "They say it's too close to call. They say they have to have recounts in three states. Complete recounts."

"But everybody else called it for her," Susie said. Her voice was calm and sounded pleased. Her face looked strained and starched and her eyes switched back and forth across the narrow distance between Niobe and me.

"Scott won't make a concession speech," Inga said. "He has his spokesperson, you know, the righteous one, the one who said Scott was chosen by God to be president, you know who I mean, he's short and bald and talks down to everyone, even the dog."

"Yeah, him," I said.

"Yes, him," Inga said. "He said the president has gone to bed. That he will examine the situation in the morning, that it's too close to call, more information is needed."

"Is it?" I asked.

"No," Inga, with certainty, "no."

"Not really," Susie said, still using reason, but looking very, very sad.

"She's won," Niobe said. "They can't steal it now. They can't, they can't, the whole world knows. She's won."

Chapter

FIFTY-SEVEN

AT 5:13 A.M. Eastern Standard Time, it was still dark. Solid dark. No hint of the dawn lit the sky. Though in the big cities, it was never completely dark.

In New York, for example, if you stood at the southern tip of Manhattan, you'd see that sweet, low arc of light from the Verrazano Bridge crossing the harbor. To the left you'd see the ribbon of lights from the Belt Parkway, sliding around the wide belly of Brooklyn. You'd see the lights from the Statue of Liberty. You'd see the harbor lights over on Staten Island from the ferry slip. And beyond that you'd see a sort of haze of light coming from the New Jersey Turnpike and the cars and trucks that drove through the night, all night long. And you'd see light coming from the planes in the sky, mostly cargo planes this time of the early morning, the express mail companies bringing in all those urgent papers for the coming business day.

If you were looking, on this day, November third, a Wednesday, the day after Election Day, from that very

spot, and you didn't blink or look away to light a cigarette or over at some footsteps behind you, if you were
looking out at the harbor, in the general direction of
the bridge and more toward the Jersey side than the
Brooklyn side, you might have seen the first, hugely
bright ignition flare of a Javelin missile.

The Javelin is a medium-range, man-portable,
shoulder-launched missile that utilizes fire and forget
technology. The gunner can lock on the target, fire, and
immediately take cover. If you saw that first bright flare,
then you probably would not have looked away and you
would have followed the Javelin's flight. You would not
have seen the dark shape of the boat from which it was
launched, nor the man who fired it. Your eye would
have followed the bright light from west to east and then
you would have seen it strike the Statue of Liberty and
you would have seen the explosion and then heard it a
moment later and known that war once again had come
to New York.

You would have seen the statue seem to break
beneath her breasts and the top half slowly begin to
topple.

Anyway, that was the way it was re-created for
the morning news utilizing computer animation, since,
amazingly enough, nobody had a video camera on it,
nobody actually recorded it, not the launch of the missile, not the explosion upon impact, not even the
statue's fall.

Shortly thereafter there was a dull thud in the
harbor and it was thought to have been an explosion
inside the hull and below the waterline of the boat from
which the missile had been launched. Water rushed in
and dragged the boat down to the bottom of the harbor.

. . .

An hour and ten minutes later a mortar—of all things—
fired a shell at the Duane Arnold nuclear power facility,
in Palo, Iowa.

Alarms were sounded. Emergency procedures
were launched. Fire and police were called out. People
scrambled to evacuate. Nobody knew if there had been
a nuclear event.

Order was restored fairly quickly. The damage
had been slight. A parking lot had been hit, a Ford
Escort was destroyed, two Nissans and a Chevrolet were
seriously damaged, and fifteen other cars were somewhat damaged. One person died; two were hospitalized.

Both events received intensive, round-the-clock, team
coverage.

The weapons employed in both incidents were
identified. They were American weapons said to have
been stolen from U.S. installations in Afghanistan. Terrorists and, more specifically, the *Al-Qaeda* network
were quickly named. *Al-Jazeera* reported those reports
derisively and suggested that it was probably home-
grown Americans. But nobody listened to *Al-Jazeera;*
they were Arabs, after all.

As if to erase the memory of his dithering when the
World Trade Center had been hit and that he'd taken
three days to get to ground zero, this time President
Scott jumped aboard Air Force One and raced to
Newark Airport and from there jumped aboard a

waiting helicopter and was in New York by seven in the morning and he caught magic hour, that early morning light that any cinematographer will tell you is gold, literally gold, but better.

He looked great in that morning light. He looked decisive and active. He gave a quick and gut-stirring speech. He redeclared war on terror. He rededicated himself, personally, to destroying America's enemies. He announced that the armed forces were now on high alert and that he was prepared to strike at the last remaining redoubts of terrorism worldwide and that any nation that still harbored terrorists had best turn them over instantly or face his wrath. And the Lord's wrath.

Scott didn't say anything about it, but Fox News quickly drew the connection to the leaked report that had come out just three days earlier that spoke of some shadowy terrorist group who would strike in the event that America elected a woman. Fox explained that this showed how ignorant the terrorists really were of the American system, they didn't even understand that just because the people had voted for Anne Lynn Murphy, that didn't make her president. There was lots to go through first. She wasn't even the president-elect yet. She was still just a candidate. Those terrorists were really stupid. A *man* was still president of these United States, a man who was sure as hell going to strike back. They all praised Scott as a man who would see to it that it would be the terrorists who felt the pain this time.

Anne Lynn Murphy flew to New York on a private jet offered by one of her supporters. She didn't get there until almost noon. She was kept away from this new ground zero as if she were some grandstanding civilian intruder.

This was Scott's show, Scott's show all the way, and he was making the most of it.

Nobody paid nearly as much attention to the second incident, the essentially failed attack on the Iowa nuclear facility, though the people out there experienced terrible fear. The local media was full of reassurances, but also produced instant maps of the distances various degrees of nuclear disaster might be expected to travel.

Chapter

FIFTY-EIGHT

CAL CARLYLE CALLED Ward Martucci first thing in the morning.

"Hey, buddy, buddy, you OK?"

"Oh yeah, fine," Ward said. "Fine, no problem."

"Well, hell, buddy, I was worried about you."

"Nothing to worry about with me."

"I got to look after my investments," Cal said, warm and chuckling. Cal was "the man" in the small business capitalization department of White Star Investment Group, one of several limited partnerships in which Fiduciary Trust Management was the managing partner. Technically, Cal had not yet invested, but it was good to go, just seven calendar days, five business days, away. "I heard Palo got hit and I said to myself, oh my, I better check in on my buddy."

"All they got was the parking lot."

"Hey, buddy," Cal said. "We're talking nuclear, and Hiawatha is how far from Palo? Ten miles? Twelve?"

"Fuckin' A-rabs," Ward said. "Totally incompetent, that's our salvation right there."

"No siree," Cal said. "Our salvation is Gus Scott! Did you see him this morning, on the news, he went right up there to that Statue of Liberty and he's gonna fix it, just you wait and see. And in the meantime, he is gonna kick some serious ass. You watch, there is gonna be some ser-i-ous butt whupping."

"I bet there will be," Ward said, cheering right along.

"We need Scott. Now more than ever," Cal said.

"Well," Ward said. He wasn't going to argue with the man who held the purse strings, but on the other hand he could hardly give his whole-hearted agreement, seeing as how he was a life-long Democrat and an active member of the party, organizing and fund-raising and everything.

"We do, we need him."

"Well, he didn't stop them this time."

"You fool! Don't you listen to the news! It's all over the damn news! The A-rabs struck because they think we got a woman president. You got to remember they are primitive people, desert dwellers and such, and to them this is an outrage. See, their pride will never allow them to kow-tow to a female. Their pride, their whole way of life, will now force them to come at us twice as hard and they will never ever surrender."

"You're probably right, you're probably right," Ward said, bobbing his head, though Cal couldn't see it. It was a conciliatory mannerism that went with his conciliatory noises.

"We *got* to do something about it," Cal said, winding himself up tighter and tighter.

"Well, there's not much we can . . ."

"Damn, damn, damn. In the name of the Lord Jesus Christ, we *got* to do something."

"How can we?" Ward said, a verbal shrug.

"You! You're one of those electors, aren't you!" Cal cried out, as if it suddenly occurred to him.

"Yeah, well, so . . ."

"You could change your vote!"

"No. No. I really can't."

"Yes, yes you can, I remember it from high school. That's the way it works, that's the way it's supposed to work. The people are supposed to elect electors, valued for their knowledge and judgment, and then the electors are supposed to do the electing. You can do it, and you're *supposed* to do it."

"Yeah, well, maybe once upon a time, but now, now we're pledged. You know, it's just a matter of form."

"It is not just a matter of form. Electors change their minds all the time."

"They do not."

"Oh they do. They've done it more than a hundred times."

"That's not true."

"Oh, yes it is," Cal said, forcefully, as if he were standing right there and jabbing Ward with his poking finger. "I'm online. I'll look it up for you right now, while we speak, here it is, here it is, it was way more than a hundred, it was a hundred and fifty-six times, that electors spoke their conscience and voted their conscience and did what they thought was best for their country."

"It's against the law."

"Nope," Cal declared. Correctly. "It is not against the law. There is no law about it, not here in Iowa."

"Hey, you know what I'll do," Ward said. He was still trying to be calm and conciliatory, "I'll tell you what I'll do, I'll talk to my committeeman and, and I'll, uhm I'll even check with a lawyer . . ."

"What are you, stupid?"

"Cal, Cal, calm down."

"No, no I mean it. Where do you live?"

"You know were I live, 33148 Eastern Drive."

"You live in the Plano fucking blast area, that's where you live!" Cal was yelling at him now. Flinging exclamation points like darts at the end of every phrase. "You live next to a nuclear facility! That a terrorist just attacked! He missed this time. But with Murphy in and Scott gone, he will be back! Next time he'll get lucky! You and your wife and your kids will be microwaved! You understand!? You will be fried! Down to your very molecules! You will be atomized! and you want to go check with your committeeman!? How stupid are you!?"

"Look, Cal, I understand that you're upset."

"Upset? I'll tell you what's upset me, I'm about to invest in a used-car dealership in Hiawatha."

"The dealership is not in Hiawatha," Ward protested. "It's practically in Cedar Rapids."

Which didn't slow Cal down at all, ". . . when the whole town is going to go ka-bomb! Ka-bomb! Before I get my money back! because the idiot I'm loaning it to is too stupid to save his own life and his family's life!"

"We don't need to go there, Cal, we really don't."

"I do," Cal said and slammed the phone down.

Ward could feel his heart start galloping. His

breath was coming in short little gasps and acid was spraying out from the center of his stomach, shooting up in nasty little vomit-flavored geysers. If Cal pulled out he was totally fucked, he was ruined. It had all been going so smoothly, with such unimpeded certainty, and it was Cal—damn him, it was Cal—who had encouraged him to commit, to buy the four Mercedes, the Porsche, and that crazy Lamborghini with only twenty-eight thousand miles on it, hit the ground running, Cal had said, hit the ground running and you'll take off at high speed, pay us back in no time, and really be raking it in for yourself, and that Lamborghini, that's visibility, that's what Cal said, you can't afford not to grab a deal like that. Vroom, crossing the open plains with that Diablo V-12, grab it for only $62,500, that'll bring the gawkers in the door. Awesome. And there was the option on the lot and the signs he'd ordered, ordered them so that they'd be ready on Day One, the day the loan was signed, but even if he didn't take delivery—due to not having a business—he was still on the hook for the signs, the lot and the cars.

Was he just hyperventilating? Or having a heart attack?

Chapter

FIFTY-NINE

I CALLED MY lawyer, Gary J. Hackney. He wasn't in. I left a message, but not a number at which he could call me back.

Niobe called Jack. He was relieved to hear from her, relieved that she was safe. He said it was all he'd been thinking of. She said they needed to talk, the sooner the better.

Susie and Inga had claimed that when men break up with women they always take them to fancy restaurants so they can't make a scene. I'd never done that. I didn't know anybody who'd ever done that. I think it's a movie and TV convention. Why waste the money on a high-priced meal that you know nobody will enjoy? But they were sure and they said that was the way Niobe should do it. She agreed and set up a meeting with Jack at a posh Washington place near the State Department, which was where Jack was going for some major, major meeting and a big, big announcement.

When she got off the phone she kissed me, as if to say, all right, see, I'm keeping my word.

We started to make plans about what each of us would do.

"I want to go in alone," Niobe said. "I operate best alone. If any of you are there, I'll be aware of you, thinking of you, worrying about you, watching out for you. I need to concentrate on Jack."

None of us wanted her to go alone. We all said it was for her protection, but I think all our motives were mixed.

Niobe pointed out the obvious, that I couldn't go into the restaurant; Jack would go ballistic if he saw me. If he claimed I was a terrorist, he could probably hold me for life in a secret locale without even letting me see a lawyer, let alone giving me a trial and where he could torture unto his heart's content, and take souvenir photos to remember how fun it was. Or he might shoot me.

I agreed that I would wait somewhere outside. Then Susie wavered. She wanted to be where I was.

Still, the three of us didn't want her to face Jack completely alone. So it was decided that Niobe would go in by herself and then five or ten minutes later, Inga would go in, sit at a far table or at the bar, and if things went really wrong she could call us or 911.

Niobe accepted that, reluctantly.

She and Jack had settled on Ristorante Puccini. I looked up its location on the map. I knew the block and figured we could wait around the corner. But just to leave the house, I needed a new disguise. This time we shaved my head and then they made me a paste-on mustache.

Chapter
SIXTY

JACK GOT TO Ristorante Puccini first. It was after two, very late for lunch by Washington standards, and the place was almost empty. He picked out a small, romantic-looking corner table.

He was feeling larger than life. He decided to order a bottle of champagne. He looked at the wine list. The prices ran up into the astronomically bizarre.

He had just flown back from New York to brief the secretary of state on the investigation of the bombing of the Statue of Liberty. The secretary had held a press conference and named Jack to head the task force that would take charge of the investigation.

It was a marvelous piece of political engineering. To put the man who had committed this—this extravagant and operatic act of patriotism—in charge of its investigation was like dropping the keystone into an arch. It was Ed Hoagland at his best. And, of course, it served Jack Morgan's needs. It gave him the public role and the credibility that would let him make his next big jump, to become the go-to guy in the White House for special operations.

And Niobe was safe and eager, so very eager to see him again.

"I'll take that one," he said. It was French, the real thing, and it had a lovely name, Veuve Clicquot La Grande Dame. Six hundred and forty-eight dollars. It was an absurd, extravagant—operatic—gesture.

La Bohème played softly over the restaurant's sound system.

He wished he had more time to just glory in the moment and share it with Niobe. But he had to get his new office up and running and get all the various investigators and agencies working through that office before someone ran off on their own and followed something too far up the wrong trail. No, he was not going to let that happen. He had to stay on top of things.

He was so immensely relieved and happy that Niobe was all right and free again. His feelings for her were—downright operatic.

There were going to have to be some changes there.

He was going to see to it that she was withdrawn from ops after this one, for sure, stay home and have some damn babies. Withdrawn from active duty, entirely. You never saw the president's wife out on her own. Or the veep's wife or the wives of any of the top people in this administration. In an unspoken, but in a clear and definitive way, that was part of what this regime was about. Reining in the excess, restoring order. Wives back in the home, not in the *House* and definitely not in the *White House* with a househusband in an apron, playing *First Lady-man,* which was how Jack's peers routinely referred to Murphy's spouse.

Thank God, Goldberg hadn't found anything out. Niobe would tell him where to find the librarian. To that end, Jack had arranged to have Parks and Spinnelli standing by. Right outside the restaurant, in Spinnelli's van, and the instant he got the information he needed from Niobe, he would set them in motion.

But something about his conversation with Niobe was nagging at him.

After she'd told him that she was fine and all of that, she'd asked where he was and he'd said he was in New York, that he'd flown up to take part in the investigation of the terrorist attack on the statue. That was fine. It was public knowledge. He'd even given a terse but determined statement to the cameras.

Ah, it was the phrase "just flown up." She knew he'd actually gone up on Sunday night and been up there—well, next door in New Jersey—since then.

Would she notice the slip? She would—she didn't miss anything.

Hell, what was he thinking about? Niobe was his wife. A beauty fit to be seen on the arm of a hero, such as himself, a man on the fast track to recognition and rewards.

Niobe was certain, in her own mind, that she was leaving Jack because he was not what he promised her he was. He was not a servant of the Good. He was like the Devil that they talked about in Jack's church, a cunning, persistent, and seductive liar.

No, she decided, that did not sound right.

No, her intuition about those things was too reliable. He hadn't fooled her. He had been a good man, a very good man, who later changed.

Tempted by power and ego and greed, he had gone over to the dark side. His goodness, actually, had been his ultimate weakness. He had been so certain of himself that he had become self-righteous. The self-righteous believe that all that they themselves do must be right, for they are Good, and that which issues from the Good must also be good.

Once that happens, the self-righteous man has blinded himself and all sorts of sins can walk right in—envy, greed, anger, and pride—and, once in, they can take possession of the man as they now possessed Jack, and they had led him to believe that he was above the law, that he could subvert a nation, that he could kill people, and that, because he was among the Good, those acts must be good.

She still felt she could handle him and find some way to break up with him.

She wasn't sure how, exactly, yet. Niobe was an improviser, not a plotter. She sensed some parameters. She couldn't say it was because she thought he had become evil and corrupt. She certainly couldn't make it about David—if Jack once thought it was about David, then it would be man against man, strength against strength, and Jack would not be able to help himself, he would attack, attack whatever he saw, whatever was in his path, fight to prove he was the stronger, no matter what the cost.

It had to be about her weakness: he could suffer the weak to crawl away and live.

She got out of the car without saying anything, without letting them say anything to her, concentrating. She walked up the block, then stepped around the corner. Then she disappeared from their sight.

As soon as she did, the minute she was all alone on E Street, she saw the van with CompSys.Org painted on the side. Well, good thing she had forced the others to stay behind. Just a few feet from having everyone's cover blown. The van meant Spinnelli. And who else? Parks? Ryan? And what the hell was Jack doing, bringing backup to a meeting with her? Was he suspicious, directly suspicious of her? Did he suspect she was with David, *with* David?

Then a kind of calm came over her. There are people who think better than they act, who train better than they perform, who practice better than they play. Niobe was one of those people who was at her best in the game.

She began to slump and drag.

Usually when a woman breaks up with a man she wants to look her best, so as to hurt him—see, this is what you'll be missing, this is what other men will have now. No, not this time. This time she wanted to look her least, so he wouldn't mind letting her go, so he might think, well, time to trade her in for a newer, fresher ride. Yes, that was how to play it.

He was there when she walked in. Even sitting, he was proud as a peacock and she could see his tail feathers all fanned out behind him.

He rose. Eagerly. She walked slowly. Indeed, she almost shuffled. Anybody familiar with her normal, confident, long-legged stride, buttocks flexing with every step and her normal posture, proud, sometimes provocative, would hardly have recognized her. He picked up on it, but he was already in gear with his own elation and his own news. "This new post," he said. "It puts me in position, it puts me in position . . . well, for something close to the president."

"With Murphy?" she said. That made no sense.

"With Scott, of course," he said.

"But . . ."

"Niobe, trust me on this. This Murphy thing is not going to stand," he said, to reassure and let her know that she could still trust that he had the world under control. Then he said, "Listen, I just briefed Ed Hoagland and he held a press conference. It's probably on the news already. I'm heading up Task Force One One Three. We were thinking of calling it eleven-three, the date, but it was too much like nine-eleven, so it wouldn't have the impact. One One Three, that has a ring to it."

She wasn't entirely listening. She was remembering. When she'd called him and the sound had broken up, at the time all she could make out was "wuh—static—ree." Now, hearing the full phrase in the clear, she realized that this was actually what he had said back then, "one-one three."

He had also said he could not tell her what it was, it was "need to know," but if she came across it, she would recognize it. Well, he'd been right about that. Bells of alarm were ringing up and down her spine.

Jack had known the name of the task force that would investigate the bombing of the Statue of Liberty and of the Duane Arnold nuclear facility at least two days, two and half days, before the attacks took place. And here and now, Jack seemed so casually, almost thoughtlessly, certain that Murphy would not become president and that Scott would serve a second term.

The plot to defeat Murphy hadn't gone into play before the election. It had come into play after the election. It was in play *now*. So this was not the time to leave

Jack. This was the time to get as close to him as possible. Smile. Look adoring. Sexy. Flirtatious. Make him trust her and want her so much his brain went to sleep.

Niobe was doing it already. Before the thoughts had articulated into words up in her frontal lobes, she was already giving him that look, that girlish, "Oh my, what a big, important man you are" look. Her attitude already said, "I can't believe how lucky I am to be with someone like you." And her posture had changed, she'd sat up a little straighter, she was leaning in toward him, she was arching her back—buttocks out, breasts up—and her breathing, she was breathing a little deeper. Oh my, a little sigh.

Jack was eating it up, and that too was happening before thought took place, as if their inner doppelgängers were out in front of their bodies and doing doppelgänger dirty dancing, dragging their lagging regular selves along from where they were, some split seconds back in time. Jack thought he had just seen, right before his eyes, the Viagra of power, transforming the scene to the obscene, on the tail of his news, his big news. Working the way it had always worked since the caveman's day.

Inga came in. She was trying to be cool, but she stared at Jack and Niobe.

Niobe noticed, out of the corner of her eye, and saw that Inga was peering at them, almost bug-eyed.

Niobe had always thought she had been wrong to let Inga come along. Now she knew why. The situation had changed, so the plan had to change. Inga wouldn't know it. She would see Niobe flirting with Jack, seducing Jack—Inga didn't have to be close enough to hear them, you didn't have to hear words to know if a couple is working themselves up to getting a room or to getting a divorce. And Inga might react in some way that would ruin it all.

The maître d' intercepted the old, lined woman who was staring at the vibrant young Washington power couple and told her that it was too late for lunch.

Thank God, Niobe thought, deducing words from the distant body language, throw her out.

"Could I just have a drink, at the bar?" Inga said. But she felt quite strange saying that, as she was not the sort of person who drank in the afternoon. Rarely enough in the evening, but certainly not at two o'clock. "Probably just a soft drink," she added.

"Of course," the host said, and showed her to the bar as Niobe cried out inside, No, no, no.

Chapter
SIXTY-ONE

"I BET," SUSIE said, "that she doesn't go through with it."

"Well, we'll find out soon enough," I said.

I pressed my fake mustache down against my upper lip. The radio was on. Between the election, which Scott had still not conceded, and the bombing of the Statue of Liberty and the mortar shell fired in Iowa—the plant supposed to be one of the best, built by Bechtel and run by GE—it was a big news day and they were going on and on and on about all of it and knowing very little, it seemed, about any of it. But it was big news, so they had to keep on going.

"I dated some married men and I have to tell you, just like everybody told me, and I should have listened, they never tell their wives, never ever, and they never leave them. If their wives find out, then their wives dump them and when it's all over they don't go to the girlfriend that got found out about, uh-uh, they go find some entirely new third party, some totally undeserving third party, so, so, if you're counting chickens, don't, that chicken has not hatched yet."

"Susie, why do you even care?"

"Come on, David, you're like, like James Bond or something, only you're Jewish and you're literate. OK, you're not really highbrow, but I mean if I quoted Milton or Keats or Sylvia Plath, you wouldn't say, 'huh?' 'wah?' And yet you race down alleys and jump out windows and outrun bad guys with guns. I have a theory about you, David. I do. You have a self-esteem problem."

"Please . . ."

"No, really. You think you don't really deserve love."

"Please don't."

"That's why, that's why when you have a clear choice, totally clear, Choice A is a woman who admires you and wants to give you love, Choice B is a woman who doesn't love you, who manipulates you, uses you, even when it risks your life, who is actually married to another man and probably won't leave him—and yet you're choosing Choice B. You are actually *turned on* by Choice B. That's virtually masochistic, David."

"Genuck es genuck," I said, enough is enough.

"If you said that to her, she wouldn't understand it."

"Let's leave it alone, all right?" I said and turned up the radio. The news was on, big blather about where all those votes in Idaho came from and if there would be any recounts.

Suddenly, on the radio, there was real excitement. They had breaking news. A group of Iowa electors had changed their votes. All seven of them had changed their electoral votes from Murphy to Scott and that would make Scott president for a second term.

"What?" I said out loud and turned the radio up. The electors, in a joint statement, claimed that their understanding of their constitutional role was that they were elected to cast their votes as they saw fit. They also felt, according to the statement, that this was a national emergency and that it was in the interests of the United States and of the people of the United States, in their war on terrorism, to have Augustus Winthrop Scott as president.

I said what the fuck and holy fuck and several other variations of fuck. I was swearing away as they started naming the electors—Morton Safer, Quentin Carlyle, Dennis Linn—and I only began to pay attention in the middle—Leslie Bender, April Harrigan, Wilkie Johnson—and then the last name snapped me back in my seat—Ward Martucci.

Ward Martucci? I remembered Martucci. Alan Stowe was in the process of making him a loan. And he was having an affair with his second cousin or some damn thing like that, a guy cousin. Linn, Safer, Harrigan, Carlyle, Bender, and Johnson. Stowe was doing business with each of them, with all of them. Bender was a farmer with complicated financing based on land values. Stowe had bought up his loans. Carlyle had some kind of investment in one of Stowe's real estate packages. Johnson had something to do with refinancing and gambling debts. I didn't remember the details of Harrigan or Linn or Safer, but Stowe definitely had business with them, too.

Could electors change their votes? Was that possible? Would that stand?

If they could and if it stood, that was it, that was how you could steal an American presidential election, buying, or leaning on, or blackmailing, just seven people. Just seven people.

Chapter
SIXTY-TWO

INGA COULDN'T UNDERSTAND it. Niobe was supposed to be there to break up with this horrible man, who had been working for President Scott to deny the election to Anne Lynn Murphy, who was also working for the man she hated most in the world, Alan Stowe. But she wasn't. She was acting like some hormone-saturated sophomore, squiggling around in her chair.

Then, for some reason or other, the husband, this Jack Morgan, a colonel no less, obviously full of himself, preening himself as if he were enthroned, turned slightly and, for the first time, Inga saw his face. And recognized him. He was the one who had come to the library looking for David. She might have actually gasped. She wasn't sure. Certainly her mouth was gaping open when—maybe because she had gasped, maybe out of some sixth sense, maybe following Niobe's eyes—Jack turned and saw her, an old woman with a lined face, not dressed quite well enough for a restaurant with these prices, sitting at the bar with a pineapple juice on ice.

He recognized her. Woman from the library. The librarian's library. The woman who worked directly for David Goldberg. What the hell was she doing here?

Now it was Jack's alarm system that went off. It was not chimes ringing lightly along his spine. He had a waa-waa air raid siren that bounced against the insides of his skull and filled the whole space inside with its high-pitched howling. He looked from the old lady to his wife and he sketched it out like the coach used to sketch out the plays back when he was playing high school football, a circle around the old woman, an arrow to Niobe, a circle around her, and another line going out through the wall to some unknown point where David Goldberg had to be, then another line back into Puccini, from David to the old woman, and the play was complete.

They were playing him. He was the one being played, he, Jack Morgan was being played by his own wife, by his own wife and an old lady and a librarian who was actually a spy for Anne Lynn Murphy.

Suddenly, he was looking at the immediate past—and the present as well—from a new point of view. Suddenly, all the awkward bits, hesitations, unanswered questions, missed connections, apparent failures fell right into place. Every inconsistency was actually consistent, except with a different story.

He didn't understand how or why it had happened. He couldn't believe that the librarian, *a librarian,* had seduced Niobe away from him. It didn't matter, it didn't fucking matter. All that mattered was that she had betrayed him, that she was on the other side, that his wife was really the enemy.

His elbow was on the table. His hand swung from that fulcrum point as if his forearm were an iron bar. His hand fell upon her wrist with the weight of a cast-iron shackle and his fingers closed around her tight, manacles snapping shut.

He squeezed, pulled, and twisted and he said, "What is this?"

"Jack, what? What do you mean?"

"She's with you . . ."

"Jack, let go."

"Why is she with you? What are you up to? Tell me, I want to know."

"Nothing, Jack, nothing at all."

"This whole last month, nothing made sense. But now it all falls in place. You've been playing a double game. You've been lying to my face. What did you do, fall in love with him? That sneaking, dirty Jew? I can't believe it. You were married to me, and I was in love with you."

"Jack, you've got it wrong. Jack, that isn't true." She tried not to wince or to show pain as thick fingers pincered her wrist, crushing the tender veins.

"Where is he? Where the fuck is he? Tell me, or I'll put you in a world of pain."

Inga was rising now. Jack saw the motion and as he looked in her direction he saw the maître d', too. His free hand went to the inner pocket of the jacket of his suit. He pulled his wallet out with a flip, held it up, straight-armed, like a Fascist salute, held it out for the maître d', the bartender, and all to see, here take a look, official ID, and he said, out loud, "Homeland Security." He stood up, hauling his wife along, and called out to stop Inga. "Don't let that woman leave," and he sounded in charge, authoritative and strong.

He needed his right hand free, so he released

Niobe, who tried to go, but she wasn't ready and moved too slow. He took her hand with a delicate stroke, then bent her wrist until it almost broke, then added some twist and she was back under control. With his right hand he pulled out his cell phone, hit a quick dial number, and got the van. "I'm coming out, there's an old lady and Niobe, too." He almost spat her name. "You'll take them both and then you'll find the Jew."

Niobe started fighting back, she tried to kick, to butt, to bite, but it was all too late, way too late, she'd already lost the fight. Now both of his hands were free, and now he could use his right. He led her around with pain as a guide, brought her like a dance step, right by his side. He grasped her at the base of her skull and clamped down on the pressure points. Niobe knew that at least for now, and maybe forever, he'd won. It was all she could do to call to Inga to run.

Inga moved for the door. The maître d' came across the floor and made some effort to try to stop her. He blocked her way and he said, "Please, signora," but he was hardly going to hit her with a right cross and drop her. She stumbled against him, stayed on her feet, pushed herself off of him, and clawed her way out to the street.

The first thing she saw when she got outside was a man who looked like a giant. He was six foot three, more than a head taller than she was, a scar on his face, the strange white hair, and as wide as the sidewalk. He looked at her with casual contempt and then, with one finger, he touched her—it seemed like all he did was touch her, though in fact it was a jab, with the power of his arm and his weight deftly behind it, right in the spot in the center between her low hanging breasts—and all the breath left her body and she was gasping, gasping like she didn't know if she would ever breathe again. She would have fallen, but he didn't let her fall. He grabbed her, with great ease, beneath one arm and held her up and swiveled her around and then in three steps dragged her across the sidewalk to a van. The back doors were open. The monster half flung her, half swung her inside. There was another man there who looked bewildered. Then the monster was gone, but Inga couldn't do anything about it because she had no air and was certain she would die if she could not, somehow, get her lungs started again.

As Jack frog-marched his wife out the door, she thought she would try to yell, but she was already half paralyzed from the fingers pressing hard and precisely into the back of her neck and immobilized by the way her hand was bent at the wrist. Then she saw Parks in front of her. He was so happy to see her. And Niobe knew more fear than she had ever known in her life.

Jack wouldn't give her to Parks, surely not. Surely he loved her still, surely he still had the need to own her, surely he still had the need to end his doubts, surely he had the need to be sure that he had been betrayed, that this was not paranoia, that it was fact, not mere suspicion. Surely he would need to be sure.

Jack's heart had broken into a rage and the rage was a flood that surged in waves of blood out through his arteries and back up his veins. It pulsed and pounded, it rose and fell and crashed on every thought. It washed out his memories and drowned all tenderness. He put his hand on her mouth to silence her pleading lips. Any word she could speak would be a lie, just another Judas kiss. She tried to catch his eye, to say what her voice couldn't say, oh mercy, mercy me, but he kept her head twisted away so he would not have to look at her face.

Parks stood like the lion waiting for Daniel to be tossed in the den. "Find out what we need," Jack said. "And then . . ."

"And then?"

"Then I never want to see her again."

Niobe saw that Parks was wearing a single glove. It looked perversely comic, some strange eighties, Michael Jackson thing. It was rubber or vinyl. It fit him badly, not at all snugly. It was blocky and crude, like a mismatched part that Dr. Frankenstein would have used to complete his ungainly golem. Then like a ballroom dancer, passing his partner on, a clumsy one who bumbled, Jack pushed her so that she stumbled. Parks, the new partner, caught her, like he was doing his part, his bare hand on her hand, the glove on her rib cage, just below her heart.

The glove was Park's new toy. There were electrodes in his palm; a cable ran up his wrist to the batteries strapped to his arm. The advantages, the salesman said, was that it couldn't be dropped and it couldn't be taken and they'd never know what was coming. Three hundred thousand volts but just nine amps. The amperage is so low that it's guaranteed, more or less, not to kill, except perhaps where there is a preexisting predisposition.

The first jolt hurts, though that's not the point. The point is to incapacitate. The nervous system, which gives control over the body, is a fine-tuned microelectrical system. A stun gun, or a stun glove, sends an irresistible flood of electricity that blows out all the normal signals. So the person is frozen and the muscles just twitch until the connection is broken.

Parks held Niobe, his hand pressed close to her heart, and the jolts kept coming and coming. She wanted to scream, her throat tore at itself as it tried, but no sound emerged; every cry stuck deep inside. She went weak at the knees. Still Parks reached for her heart and held her close until she fainted.

Jack held up his ID card again, flashing the street if anyone cared. "Homeland Security. Terrorist threat. This is an arrest."

That's what Susie saw when she came around the corner.

Chapter

SIXTY-THREE

WHEN I SAW Susie come running back toward the car, I turned the engine on and started to maneuver out of the parking space. She looked hysterical and ran out into the street around to the passenger side and pulled the door open. She yelled, "They took them, they took them."

"Who took who?"

"I don't know, some guys in a van took Inga and Niobe. Come on. Chase them."

I said, "Where? Where?" Though I knew that it had to be from in front of the restaurant, around the corner. That's where I went. As we turned onto E, I saw the van moving off into the distance, not moving in any great hurry, just driving away. Susie said, "That one, that one, there's the one."

We drove past Jack. But his glance failed to see through my mustache and slid right off my newly polished dome. Then we were past him.

Up ahead the van turned. I accelerated. I was afraid to go too fast and get stopped. I was afraid to lose them. I didn't know how we could keep following, but we got lucky. They didn't seem to have a clue that someone might be after them and they made directly for I395 and once they were on the highway, it was easy as could be to keep them in sight.

The next question was what we would do when we caught them. I imagined they were taking the women to some secure location, a safe house, or whatever the hell they called such places.

Chapter
SIXTY-FOUR

SPINNELLI DROVE.

He really didn't like this. This was his van. It was his workspace, an office on wheels, everything in order and in place. It was a custom setup that he'd built himself.

He'd personally welded the stanchions, floor to ceiling, for the shelves and the tabletop desk that ran along the side of the van behind the driver. The other wall had been made into a giant tool chest with every variety of gear he might ever need, plus replacement parts and tools for repairs and even the capacity to make up new gadgets on the spot, right out there in the field.

A perfect example of just how well thought through it all was, in terms of Spinnelli's own genius: lots of times he had supervisors or colleagues, or whomever, who wanted to participate in surveillance and those look-over-your-shoulder people needed something to sit on, so he'd gotten hold of two of those fold-down seats that they put on airplanes for flight attendants when all the regular seats are full and he'd built them into the side with the tool chests. The genius part was that they seemed like they were perfect—convenient and comfortable—but actually they were just a little too far away from the screens and read-outs so that the supervisors, or whomever, always had to perch on the edges of their seats and sort of peer forward and if they were farsighted and needed glasses for reading, they were always at the wrong distance, and the discomfort subtly discouraged them.

Spinnelli was proud of that because he didn't like other people messing around in his space and yet circumstances—and face it, his nature—didn't allow him, really, to say, hey, get the hell out of here.

It was a surveillance van, the perfect surveillance van, and now Parks was turning it into, what? an action vehicle? a kidnap truck? Parks was going to create a mess back there, Spinnelli was certain of it. What if one of those ladies really lost it and threw up or pissed themselves or shit themselves back there? Who was going to clean it up? Not Parks. He, Spinnelli, would have to do it. He'd probably have to rip out the carpeting, throw it away, and replace it.

Spinnelli really didn't like it.

Parks, on the other hand, seemed happy. He had a too wide, too tight grin pasted on his face. Spinnelli realized that Parks was flying coast to coast and he'd handed over the controls to his copilot, Mr. Crystal.

Inga got her breath back and, after a tryout moan, she started in with her scolding, grandmother motor-mouth. "What are you doing? Where are you taking me?" Parks held up his hand with the glove. She didn't know why he was doing that and she kept on yapping, "Let me go! I insist, right now." So Parks put his hand upon her.

She hadn't felt anything like it since she was a little girl and she'd touched a standing metal lamp with a frayed cord inside. The shock had literally knocked her over. Now she was already on the floor and there was nowhere to fall and when the electrical shock made her spasm, her head banged against a metal closet.

Parks waited a moment for her to recover. Then he held the glove up, once again, for her to see. She looked at him with horror and tried to wiggle away in fear. Ahh, instant conditioning. Doctor Pavlov would be proud.

Niobe was coming around and Parks realized that two of them moaning and yapping and struggling and trying to do all those things that women try to do would be more than he wanted to handle. It would interfere with the fun he foresaw himself having.

So he zapped Niobe again and held the electrodes on her until she passed out again. He needed a few minutes of peace and quiet in order to get it all organized and under control.

Spinnelli was trying to ignore what was happening in back. He did not want to witness whatever it was that Parks was doing. But when he heard Parks clanging around, opening the cupboards, Spinnelli got annoyed and said, over his shoulder, "What do you want? What are you doing? Don't mess that stuff up."

"Rope. You got some rope? Or some wire, some shit like that? You got duct tape?"

"Bottom row, second one in from the rear, and put it back where you found it," Spinnelli said.

Spinnelli looked away. He concentrated on driving. Parks got the tape. He turned Inga over and taped her hands behind her back. She pleaded, "Why? What for? What are you going to do to me?" and all of that. Parks shut his ears. He wasn't going to have to listen to it too long. He knelt on top of her and taped her ankles together. When he was done, he turned her back over and slapped a piece of tape over her mouth. "Shhh," he put his forefinger to his lips, "like in the library."

She tried to move away from him, kind of flopping like a fish. There was nowhere to go. Parks laughed.

Niobe was starting to come around. Parks went to her quickly, grabbed her wrists, and taped them, too. He'd wanted Niobe a long time. Since the first time he ever saw her. He knew her for what she was, a jumped-up lap dancer, looking down at him when he should have been able to have her for a two-Jackson tip and he bet she could have lifted the tip with her lips. Now he would have her like she'd never been had. He was going to have her until she could never be had again. Poor dear, Parks was gonna be her last ever.

He put her hands up over her head and taped them to one of the stanchions holding up Spinnelli's custom shelves.

Spinnelli glanced back. This was bullshit. Parks wasn't going to strip the tape off when he was done, let alone clean off the residue of the sticky stuff. Real bullshit.

Niobe was starting to try to move around. Parks put his knees on her stomach to hold her down. Somehow she found the will to try to resist and tried to get some leverage with her legs. Parks rose up and came down on her with one knee and his full 220 pounds behind it. It blew the wind right out of her and made her think she was going to vomit. "Don't fight," he said. "Not yet. Not until we start with the fun."

Her hands were tied to a stanchion right behind Spinnelli. Now Parks took her right leg and taped it to the stanchion nearest the rear door, on her right, driver's left. He took her other leg and spreading it wide, looked for something to attach it to. Spinnelli's flight attendant seats hung from angle braces when they were in the down position. Parks picked the one farthest from Niobe and that worked for him just fine. That spread her legs, and the one up, one down thing was kind of interesting, better, Parks thought, than both of the them flat down on the floor, yeah, actually much better. He was happy with his improvised handiwork and getting happier.

Spinnelli heard Parks say, "Maybe you'll get to like it." Then he heard Niobe's body jerking and he heard her moan.

"Hey, hey come on," Spinnelli said.

"Shut the fuck up," Parks said. He took out some more crystal meth and tapped it out on the back of his glove. "Anybody want some?" he called out, and sort of hummed, "Come fly with me," before he snorted. "You know what this does, this makes me like a hammer, like one of those . . ." he put his hands up in front of him and moved them up and down and said, ". . . bam-bam-bam-bam . . . *Jack*-hammers."

Inga started coming around. She was having trouble breathing with the tape on her mouth and she made choking and whimpering noises.

"Jesus, man," Spinnelli said, "she's choking."

"So?"

"Hey, man."

"Don't worry, I won't let her choke." He stepped over Niobe and reached down and ripped the tape off Inga's mouth. "They're not as much fun after they're dead."

Inga gasped for breath. That's all she wanted to do, was to breath.

"How about," Parks said, "I do the bitch, you do the witch, then we take a break and then we switch." He laughed. When Spinnelli didn't answer, he said, "Spinner, hey Spinner, you got a knife back here?"

Spinnelli didn't like to be called Spinner or Spin or Spinster or Spinny or any of the many variations that people made of his name, but now he was more distraught over what might happen than what names were being used, "Parks, no! No! Parks, you're not going to cut people up in the back of my van, dammit, no."

"Shut your face, Spinner, I'll do what I want, exactly what I want, but I don't happen to want to cut anybody up, so don't shit yourself. I just want to rearrange some clothing here. Come on, you fuckhead, where's your knife? I know with all your shit, you got some kind of knife in here."

"Matte knife," Spinnelli mumbled.

"Matte knife?"

"Yeah."

"Where?"

Spinnelli told him which drawer. But when Parks looked, he found a box of the blades that went in it, and they were little and gleaming and sharp and they looked to him like more fun. They were all the same, but he carefully picked out one.

What was he going to do with that razor? It was bad enough what he'd been doing with that stun glove. Spinnelli didn't want to know, didn't know how not to look. He wished he was seeing this on his monitors, not in person. He was afraid of Parks and didn't know how to stop him.

Parks was opening his pants, being careful to use his naked hand. "Wouldn't it be funny," he said, "if I zapped myself. Don't worry, I'll be careful."

Spinnelli didn't want any part of this. He didn't want it happening in his van. He blurted out, "You're going crazy, Parks, you're going crazy."

"I'm having fun," Parks said.

One of Spinnelli's nightmares—one that kept him at home in the hopes that somehow he could prevent it— was of his daughters falling in with some monster like this. And they were stupid enough and drug addled enough and TV hyped enough to end up with a crank head gone over the edge, they really were. Now Parks was doing it to the old woman, too, zapping her just to feel how she spasmed. He was crazy. He was totally insane.

"Hey, listen to me, listen to me," Spinnelli said. "I don't know what you think you're doing, but Morgan, Morgan is not going to appreciate it if you rape his old lady."

"She won't be alive to tell him," Parks said, dismissing the issue out of hand.

No, no, no. Parks was going to kill them? Kill them right here? In his van? The bodies would be in his van and who would fry for it? Who would end up holding the bag?

The man in back was insane, a monster, and Spinnelli couldn't stop him. All he could do was get out of there, get the hell away from whatever was going to happen. He started slowing down and pulling over onto the shoulder.

"What are you doing?" Parks asked him.

He had to get out of there. Would Parks stop him? Make him stay? Make him keep driving, driving around while he did unspeakable things in the back? Make him participate? What could he say so Parks wouldn't stop him from getting away.

"I gotta piss," Spinnelli said, as the van lurched onto the shoulder.

Parks mocked him. "Jesus, fuck, Spinner, didn't your mommy ever tell you to make pee-pee before you went on a trip," but otherwise didn't seem to care when the van came to a stop and the door opened and Spinnelli jumped out. He had his crystal meth, his razor, and his stun glove. He had two women in bondage and no limits. It was a dream come true.

Chapter
SIXTY-FIVE

THEN THE VAN drifted over to the outside lane, the slow lane. I followed. It kept slowing down and it was going to be difficult for me to keep my distance. Then the van began to pull off onto the shoulder. If I did the same, then they were certain to spot me. People were already pulling out around me with glares and gestures and honks. What would I do? Pass them, then lurk somewhere up ahead? Someplace I could hide? Where could I hide on an interstate? And when you pull up on a major road, helpful drivers call the cops on their cell phones and helpful troopers pull up and say, "What's the problem, sir?" And then they say, "Oh, I've seen you on Virginia's Most Wanted, you're practically a celebrity in our station, come on down and meet the rest of the troop . . ."

As we came up beside the van, Susie said, "The driver's gone. Someone's getting out."

I glanced over. She was right. There was no one in the driver's seat. I figured he was getting out for an emergency piss stop. I kept watching, using the mirrors, as we went past. There was the driver—it wasn't Parks—and he jumped over the fence. There's a certain way that men will move if they're looking for a convenient tree to get behind and that's not what this man was doing. He was running and he wasn't stopping. He was running, into the woods, stumbling, tripping, and scared.

I pulled over abruptly. A tractor-trailer on my ass let out a blast from his horn. He hit the brakes and slowed himself before he climbed over our back and then he blew on past. As soon as I was out of the lane and on the shoulder, I turned and looked back. I went in reverse as fast as I could without hitting the rail or veering back into the road.

Almost bumper to bumper with the van, I braked and jumped out and Susie did the same. The door was still hanging open and she went for the passenger side. I grabbed the driver's door and yanked it open wide. I pulled myself up and here was Inga, on the floor, silver tape around her wrists and also around her feet, she was screaming, and there was horror on her face. As my head turned, Parks came into view and Niobe, too. Niobe practically naked, her clothes in tattered shreds, welts and some blood and what looked like a bite mark and Parks had his pants down.

It was a narrow space. I charged between the seats into the rear section. It was only then that Parks became aware of me at all. Even on his knees with his pants half down he looked twice my size and he had clearly gone mad. I tackled him and banged him back against the rear doors. He yelled, "I'll fuck you, too." Then he grabbed me and it was the damn stun gun again and I had no control over my own body. I was flopping and if he kept it up I was going to pass out. Then he let me go and tried to throw me aside. There was a gigantic noise. A gunshot. Inside the tiny space. It seemed the loudest thing I'd ever heard. Inga was yelling. Niobe was moaning. Susie was yelling. It was Susie who had shot, but she'd missed Parks and now he was going after her. He lunged. She fired. The gun went off right beside his head, the bullet taking a piece from his ear. He whacked her arm and the gun went flying.

Blood was streaming down the side of his face. He looked surprised and pained. And he put his hand with that strange black rubbery glove up to the pain, in a reflex action. And suddenly he was twitching. I didn't know what it was, exactly, but obviously that glove did something. I grabbed his wrist and shoved his hand, hard, hard as I could, against his head, and he twitched and spasmed, and I was so glad. He had no control and he fell to the floor and I grabbed his head and pushed it down, down onto his own glove and I put all my weight on his head and pushed it down and down and held it there and he was twitching and twitching. For a long time. I don't know how long. I think the batteries ran out.

There was a sort of calm, a sort of endless resonating echo and a sort of calm.

Chapter

SIXTY-SIX

INGA WAS SHAKEN, practically in shock. "Stop him," she said, "stop him," as Susie peeled the tape from her wrists and then from her ankles.

"It's going to be all right, it is all right," Susie said.

"Stop him," Inga said.

"He's dead," I said to Inga. I asked Niobe, "Are you all right?" She nodded. I'd seen the glint of the razor blade on the floor when I got up from Parks. I had it now and was slicing through the tape that held her.

"You shot him?" Inga said, to Susie.

"I think the shock, that glove thing, that killed him," I said.

"Are you sure he's dead?"

"Yes," I said.

"Good," Inga said. "Good. Get me out of here."

As soon as her hand was free, Niobe reached up and grabbed the tape and tore it off her mouth. She seemed remarkably self-possessed and the first thing out of her mouth was, "They're trying to overturn the election."

"Yes," I said, cutting her other hand free.

"I don't know how," Niobe said, "but Jack let it slip."

As I started slicing the tape from around her ankles she pulled the pieces of her skirt down to cover herself. "They've already half done it," I said. "It's on the radio. They got the electors in Iowa to change their votes."

"Can they do that?" She tried to pull the tatters of her blouse over her breasts.

"Can you give her your jacket?" I said to Susie.

Susie said, "Sure," shrugged out of it, and passed it over.

"Are you hurt?" I said to Niobe, looking at where she'd been cut and at the abrasions on her ankles and wrists where she'd struggled against her bonds.

"No, not a lot. Can they do that?" she asked again, insistently, about the electors.

"Yes, maybe, maybe not. No one knows for sure." Susie passed me her jacket and I gave it to Niobe. I told her, "We've been listening, on the radio."

"I want to leave. I want to leave here," Inga said.

"Yes," Susie said to the older woman. "Come on, I'll help you."

"Tell me," Niobe said to me.

"There are twenty-four states where there's no law that says electors have to vote, you know, the way they're supposed to vote. Iowa is one of them. That's why they picked it."

"What do you mean, picked it? How do you know they picked it?"

"Because I recognized all the names. They're all people Stowe has his hooks into, one way or another. He's either financing their business or can take their businesses or he has some dirt on them or both, all seven of the electors."

"Why Iowa?" she asked.

"I'm guessing," I said. She was moving with difficulty. "Are you OK?"

"I'm just cramped. I just have cramps in my leg."

I reached for her and she snapped, "Don't, don't touch me."

"All right," I said.

"I don't want to be touched," she said, harsher than I'd ever heard her.

I figured that was good. It was a sign that she was human. If she were totally indifferent it would have been even more disturbing. I offered my hands to help her get up and she took them, guardedly, and got up in one of the seats and started to massage her calf and said again, "Why Iowa?"

"Small state," I said. "One of the very few small states that went for Murphy. There's New Mexico, with five votes, but there's a law against it in New Mexico. It's actually a felony. The felony thing might not hold up in court, but it makes it more complicated. Then there's Rhode Island, no law, only four votes, but it went for Murphy by seven points. In Iowa, the margin was only about half a percentage point."

"She hasn't conceded, has she?" Niobe said, sounding more anxious about that than about what had happened to her.

"No, no. She's gonna fight."

"Good. Then there's time."

"Yeah, who knows how long, I guess it's got to go to court out in Iowa first and then it'll go federal."

"What we need, what we need is proof, David, that

this was Stowe's doing. That he bribed and black-mailed."

"What we need is to get out of here and figure out what to do with him," I said. "Before some trooper pulls up and notices the bullet hole in the rear door and the dead man with his pants down."

"I want to burn it," she said. "Burn it."

"Well, that's going to attract a lot of attention," I said. "Sitting here by the side of the road, setting a truck on fire, there's a big, constant audience driving by."

"I'll do it," she said. "You don't have to do it."

"Look, I just want to do what makes sense."

"I'll do it," she said, again.

"All right," I said. Our fingerprints were all over and fibers and who knows what else. And Parks was some kind of something in Homeland Security, some kind of cop, and proving that he was Mr. Evil and that Niobe and Inga had been his victims and that Susie and I had been the Lone Ranger and Tonto was going to be a whole additional nightmare. So it did make some sense to destroy as much of the evidence as we could. I couldn't see how it would make things worse, though it might. That wasn't what it was about for Niobe anyway, I don't think, it was about literally destroying the monster, and if I had time to consult a psychologist, he or she would surely tell me it would be a very healthy thing to do.

"All right," I said, because it was what she wanted. "We'll burn it, but first we drive it somewhere where we won't be seen doing it."

● ● ●

It's hard to find a private spot anymore in the sprawl that spreads outward from our capital. From every major center, I guess. You'd think somewhere they'd keep some sections a little bit like countryside. But I guess not. The value is a patch of lawn, four decorative trees, one a Japanese maple, for that touch of nature's red, one magnolia to bloom in the spring, for the songs about the Southland. If that makes me a snob, an elitist, to look down upon other people's plastic tastes, then I am, but when you're trying to rid yourself of a corpse in a van, it's a huge source of irritation.

I drove the van. Niobe stayed with me. Susie and Inga were in the Buick behind. We listened to the news as we drove. The multitude of legal experts all agreed that this was ultimately a case for the Supreme Court. It was a constitutional time bomb that had been waiting to go off for over two hundred years. We were treated to a complete and detailed history of all the "Faithless Electors." There had been 156 of them since 1796.

Almost half, 71 of them, didn't really count, because the candidates they were pledged to—Horace Greeley, Democrat for president in 1872 and James S. Sherman, Republican for vice president in 1912—had died before the electors got to vote. In Greeley's case, all 63 electors changed their votes. In Sherman's case, only 8 bothered to change their votes and all of them still voted faithfully for their presidential candidate, William Howard Taft.

That left 82, of which 67—like the 8 in the Sherman case—were just about vice presidents.

Only 15 electors had actually changed their votes for a live presidential candidate. On the one hand, none of those changes had actually affected the final outcome of an election. Which was also true of the faithless votes in the vice-presidential races. On the other hand, not one of the faithless votes had ever been overturned or overruled or changed back. Nor had any elector ever been prosecuted, removed, or replaced for their dereliction of duty.

Still, it seemed to me that we had quite enough material for a few well-paid lawyers on Murphy's side, or some zealous local prosecutor looking to make his name, to blow the whole thing open. And even if the Supreme Court said it was legal for the electors to change their votes, surely there had to be some quirk in the law that said it was illegal for them to change their votes as a result of bribery or coercion.

Surely there had to be.

Quite a few pundits opined that the Supremes should step in immediately, so as to put the matter to rest. This was a time of crisis. Terrorists attacking the homeland.

Maybe back in 1789 the country could wait a couple of months to know who would be president because our enemies had to cross an ocean at sailboat speed or walk on up from Mexico, nothing anyone could do in a great big hurry.

But this is the twenty-first century. The enemy uses jets—our jets—and missiles—our missiles—and computers—over our Internet. Warp speed. Matters needed to be settled now. Instant gratification was required. The Court should announce today that they would take the case tomorrow.

This became a trope and a meme, a viral event infecting the collective media minds, and was repeated, on radio, television, and online. Settle it now, settle it fast, settle it before we run out of gas. Faster is better. Resolution is what counts. Get it over, get it done, then let it be. We need unity in the land of the free. Resolution, solution, declaration, decree.

Endless damn suburbia and a corpse in the back and cops everywhere.

After an hour of driving around, I saw an old stand-alone Grand Union, bankrupt and empty, a forlorn FOR LEASE sign out front. I turned in, the Buick following us. We got out. I borrowed Susie's gun. I lay down on the ground ten yards away and fired into the gas tank. It did not ignite, but there was a hole and gas began to pour out. Then we had to search around for a match. Nobody carries matches or lighters anymore. It used to be that you could turn around and say, "Got a light?" and someone would say, "Sure."

We decided to use the lighter in the rental car. Fortunately it had one and it worked. We found a piece of windblown newspaper up against the old loading dock. It was nice and dry and by putting it in the lighter and blowing on it, we managed to get a flame going. Holding it cupped in my hands to keep the wind from extinguishing it, I touched it to the flowing gas and it caught in a rush and whoosh and scared the hell out of me and I tumbled away from it and we all ran for the car and the flames went zipping up under the van and we took off and about twenty seconds later, when we were driving on the road again, we heard the explosion behind us.

Chapter
SIXTY-SEVEN

EDWARD HOAGLAND had the television on. It was four
o'clock. There was supposed to be an announcement.
There was supposed to be a goddamn announcement. It
was all orchestrated. They'd had all the information
available, they'd fed it to the networks, they'd floated the
stories with their pundits and favorite commentators,
the whole world knew that there was a crisis, that the crisis
had to be ended as soon as possible and that the only
way to end the crisis was for the Supreme Court to step
in and that the best time for the Supreme Court to step in
was immediately, right away, end it now.

Now that all that groundwork had been done, and
it had been done very well, it was amazing how fast you
could blitz the media and how they were a pack that all
bayed the same song, and now that that was done, the
Supremes were supposed to step up to the microphone
for their little number—resolution, solution, declaration, decree.

Scott's people would say, primly, that we wish to

abide by the wishes of the Court in the greater interests of the nation. Of course Scott's team was ready, prepped, prepared, good to go, and the other side was surprised, taken aback. Murphy would howl, her lawyers complain, the Court would graciously permit them to speak, give them one more day, even a week. It wouldn't be enough, they couldn't win. Lambs to slaughter. A beautiful plan.

And only four people in the whole world really knew. The four completely essential people. He himself, to connect them and keep them under control. Stowe to provide the money and the research to bribe and to blackmail the electors. Morgan to provide security and the crisis.

And McClellan to deliver the court.

It was critical to keep this damn thing moving, moving so fast that no one ever caught up, then close it and shut it down and declare it over and settled and if they did that fast enough and with the proper pomp and ritual, all the questions would go away in the interests of stability and continuity and getting on with things and making money, just like it had after the Kennedy assassination and after the last election.

Sure, people still asked questions, but they were dismissed as conspiracy nuts. Not because they were wrong, but because nothing was going to change if they were right, so they were obsessing themselves with meaningless trivia, because truth upon which you cannot act is what trivia is.

He had made it completely clear to McClellan that he wanted that announcement today. The court was shutting down at four and it was damn near four and he had yet to see the Supremes step out, in their matching robes, doing their song and dance, as they were supposed to be doing, on those gleaming marble steps.

And the big hand ticked over and it was after four and Hoagland felt the fury rise and took his blood pressure medication and managed to contain himself for over half an hour but by 4:40 he'd had it and knew he had to track the justice down, find out what the problem was, and fix it. Delay was death.

Reluctantly, because he did not want any damn telephone traces, any damn record that the secretary had called the associate justice—those were the hairs that special prosecutors grabbed you by, pulled you down, and dragged you through the mud with—Hoagland reluctantly called McClellan.

"What happened?"

"We didn't have the votes. Give me a couple of days."

"No."

"There's not much choice, the mood around here is, is that this is a serious issue and it needs serious consideration. . . ."

Hoagland cut him off, he wanted to keep this short—visualizing himself at some future date looking back to explain the phone call, "it was to invite him to some damn anniversary or something, believe me nothing of substance could be discussed in fifteen seconds" something like that—so he said, "Let's meet . . ."

"I . . ."

". . . dinner."

". . . don't know about being seen . . ."

It couldn't be his own place, or McClellan's, it couldn't be a public place, not at this juncture, it had to be somewhere private. "Stowe's," Hoagland said.

Besides, if they needed something, some point of influence or persuasion to motivate one of the other justices
to vote as was needed, it was Stowe who had stockpiled
judicial connections and secret files of the lives that
judges keep in their closets. Hoagland thought he could
guess, pretty accurately, what Stowe had on McClellan.
The difference was that he could only guess at it, Stowe
had it. Yes, best to meet at Alan Stowe's.

"I couldn't get there before . . . nine-thirty . . . ."

"Fine."

". . . more likely ten."

"Ten it is," Hoagland said and hung up the phone.
Close things off. Don't leave them any room. Get it settled and move on.

Chapter
SIXTY-EIGHT

THERE WAS AN unfamiliar car outside Inga's house. It was a late-model Crown Victoria with a government plate and it sat there and said, in its quiet way, police, police, police.

This time we had been slow and Jack had been quick. We should have expected it. He'd recognized Inga. If he hadn't already known her name, it was easy enough to discover, and from her name, her phone and address would effortlessly flow, especially with the powers of Homeland Security to call on, then either of those could be put up on the Net, by a civilian as easily as by a policeman, and a road map would come right back that would direct him door to door, from wherever he was, by the quickest route, to the very spot.

Then, warrant or not, he would have it searched and, having searched it, he would have found my computer, which I'd left out in plain sight on her dining room table.

Now that Jack had the computer, he also had all of our critical evidence.

In addition, my computer would deliver him a handy record of every place I had searched over the Net, including all the material that I had transferred, in contravention of my contract, to the university's system. Now that they knew it was there and exactly where there was, file name by file name, they could proceed to erase it and make it disappear, for all time.

Having come and searched and confiscated, the logical thing, the traditional cop thing, to do would be to leave a team behind to wait for my return. Not for Inga's return. He had to think that she was . . . gone.

And there sat their car.

Jack would have learned from his search that Niobe had been at the house, too. But he wouldn't expect her back either. Had he begun to wonder about her yet? To regret the fate he'd consigned her to? To maybe even want her back? To at least have a few moments to ask the questions that he hadn't asked? Or did he know it was better never to hear those answers.

Had Susan left anything behind, in Inga's house, that would let Colonel Morgan know that there had been a fourth person in our group, and would that lead him to identify her? If she'd been identified, he would try to trace her. If he was tracing her, he would follow her credit cards and they would lead to the car we were in.

We drove on by. We drove away. We wondered where we could possibly go.

We went to a shopping center and Susie went in and bought some clothes for Niobe and some aspirin and some gauze and tape for the abrasions that both Niobe and Inga had from fighting against the tape. Niobe wanted to buy a cell phone and a phone card and we bought that, too.

Then we found a big truck-stop diner, where we could at least sit down and get some food and try to figure out what to do next. We took a table in the back as far from other people as we could.

Niobe called Anne Lynn Murphy.

The woman who had won the presidential election in both the popular and electoral vote, who might one day be commander in chief of an army, an air force, and a fleet greater than any ten other militaries in the world put together, now had only one soldier to command and she told that soldier that there was a mission for her and that mission was to get the originals of all those contracts that Stowe had with the electors and of any other plans that tied the plot together. Nothing less than originals would do and she suggested it be done fast, since the conspirators, if they had any sense, would rapidly destroy them.

Niobe, being Niobe, was going to go, alone and on foot if she had to, naked and on her hands and knees if they tried to beat her down, but she would certainly go, and we knew it. Therefore, we were going, too.

I pointed out, halting as the waitress brought us coffee, that this was not the place to plot. They all agreed, but no one moved. As we ate, we somehow couldn't keep from talking, whispering as if it were gossip too urgent not to share.

"The hard part is getting in," Niobe said. Stowe's entire 237 acres were walled like an English estate, walls ten feet high of stone. There were cameras mounted at regular intervals. There was broken glass cemented into the top of the wall. There were two wires, one that would sound the alarm if it were touched or cut, the other, old-fashioned, with barbs. There were three gates. Two were normally locked and were only used, by pre-arrangement, for horse trucks, farm equipment, and construction gear. The third, the main entrance, had armed guards as well as cameras and a system wired into the local police.

"No," I said, "the hard part is once you're inside. There's the butler and the maid, plus security people in the house. I mean, what does he have, a full-time staff of ten, fifteen people?"

"If I got in, I would be all right," Niobe said.

"How?"

"Everybody knows me," Niobe said. "Alan adores me, everyone knows that. So if someone sees me, they'll figure I should be there."

"But what if Jack warned them?" Inga asked.

"He wouldn't. First of all, he won't imagine that I got away from Parks. So why would he have to warn anyone about someone who's . . ." She didn't quite finish the sentence.

But Susie did. "Who's dead."

Niobe didn't comment. She took a breath and sort of swiveled her head around it. "He won't say anything. Because it would make him look bad. If you can't keep your own woman under control, what can you control? That's how they think. The only place I would be asked anything is at the gate, where they always call up to the house or check their list. If I could get past the gate . . ."

"I want to go with you," Inga said.

"No," Niobe said. "No, I'm going in alone."

"You can't," I said.

"Why not?"

"Two reasons," I said. "You don't know what to look for, and if you did, you wouldn't know where it is and it would take you too long to find it."

"Is that one or two?" Niobe said.

"The second thing," I said, "is that I know how to get in."

"You do?" Niobe said.

"I got out, didn't I?"

"How?"

"It's not easy," I said. "From this side, we'd need a ladder."

"You can't just put a ladder up against that wall. There are sensors and wires."

"There's a branch, from a tree, on the Pearl Hollow Road side. We need a fifteen-foot ladder, maybe twenty. Then we can scramble across and on the other side, it's a pretty easy climb down."

"But Pearl Hollow Road is way away from the house."

"Probably two miles," I said.

"Through the woods at night."

"It's a way in," I said.

"All right," Niobe said. "I can do that."

"*We* can do that."

"No," she insisted. "Inga would never make it."

"I can. Indeed I can," Inga said. "I am hiking all the time. I do rock climbs. Old is not dead. There are many young people a lot more feeble than I am, I assure you."

"No," Niobe said, adamantly. "And David can't go in." Inga was fuming, but Niobe ignored her and went on. "The minute anyone at Stowe's sees him the alarms will go off, they'll call the police and Homeland Security, and they'll shoot on sight."

Inga reached over and grabbed Niobe's cell phone, which was sitting out on the table. She closed her eyes in concentration and then punched in a number. We all shut up and were watching her. "Alan, please," she said, then, "tell him it is Inga Lokisborg . . . he'll know . . . yes, hello, Alan. . . . Yes, yes it is me. . . . I'm returning your call. . . . If you did not expect me to return your call, why did you keep calling? . . . Yes, I am accepting your invitation to come and see you. . . . Tonight. . . . Because tonight I feel like it. Tomorrow I won't. . . . You can wait until after you're dead before I call you back again. . . . Good, I will see you then at 10:00. . . . I don't know if I can make it as early as 9:30 . . . but I will try." She closed the phone and looked at us. "There," she said. "I am in the house."

"I don't understand," I said. "I'm speaking for all of us, I think, when I say I don't understand."

"He has been calling me ever since. For forty-two years. He always leaves his number, since there have been answering machines. This is the first time I have had a reason to return his calls."

"Why? Why has he been calling you?"

"You should ask him that."

"Well, what does he tell you his reason is?"

"Well, you know, he says many things."

"What, what does he say?"

She sighed. "He used to say he loved me, many years ago, of course. Sometimes he said he wanted to give me money to make things up to me. He offered money for the library.

"I think, perhaps he hired poor Elaina, even, as a way to talk to me—no, I know he did—because he told me so."

"He told you?"

"I didn't speak to him, he left it on a message on my answering machine—to let me know that he had a library, of his own, and oh, so much money, as if I give a damn about him and all his money. Even you, David, I expect he took you as the next librarian because that way I would hear of it, and I warned you, did I not? Because he is evil. And because he is cursed. Which is really why he calls, I think. He thinks that I have cursed him."

"Sure," I said, with a touch of modernist irony.

"Of course," Niobe said, as if now it all made sense.

"Yes," Susie said, agreeing.

"You don't believe," Inga said, to me, specifically. "Well, I am not sure that I do, either, you know. Curses, they are strange things to believe in. Here we are in this century. But I certainly did pronounce curses upon him, so he may think his troubles come from me."

"For a cursed guy, he's done pretty well," I said. "He's worth more money than God, he's lived to a ripe old age, he's still kicking, pulling strings, turning the world upside down."

"He lives on pills and doctors. There is no peace in his body. He has no rest at night." Inga half chanted these things, as if these were things she had sworn upon him, forty-two years ago. "And worse than that, he has no wife." The other two women nodded, yes, that was a curse indeed. "He will never know, until the end of time, if anyone would care for him if he were without his money. He has no true friend. He has no love. Worse than that, far worse than that, he has not a single child.

When he dies, his line will end. There's no one there, for all that money. When he dies he will be forgotten and it will be as if he had never been."

"Well," I said, "well. That would explain some things."

She nodded.

"So, you can get in. Do you think if I told you what we were looking for and where to look, you could get it?"

"No," Inga said. "If you want me to, I will try. But I don't think I can do that. What I can do is provide a diversion and I can help. Leave a door open, maybe, or a window, something like that, and you, since you are such great hikers, hikers and woodsmen, you can climb the wall and walk through the forest. Also, I must tell you, he has a meeting, an important meeting, at ten o'clock, so that should keep him busy."

"As long as it's not in the library," I said.

"Well, if I must, I can say I will stay and wait for his meeting to end, and I can say I want to stay in the library, after all, I'm a librarian."

"You think he'll do what you want him to?"

"He believes in the curse," Inga said.

"Do you believe in it? Do you actually believe that you cursed him?"

"It doesn't matter what I believe. What matters is what Alan Stowe believes and he believes in money, he believes in money so much that when he comes to those things that money doesn't buy, love and trust and health and happiness, he thinks that there must be some reason, like when he can't buy a property because some other developer got there first or was willing to pay more, he thinks there must be someone or something working against him. Like a curse.

"And he will want to at least try to fix it, to force it, to trick it, to buy it. Because that's what he does."

We needed to get some more clothes, makeup, toiletries, a wig, and a ladder. Wal-Mart again and Lowe's. We argued about Wal-Mart. None of the women wanted to buy their clothes at Wal-Mart. I pointed out that whatever clothes we had would only have to pass inspection one time, briefly, hopefully in the dark, and if we were smart, with the light behind us. Plus, we didn't dare use credit cards or checks or bank cards. We could only use the cash on hand, which was my cash, and although I was prepared to be generous with it, in fact to use it all—there was nothing to do about it except say, what the hell, today is a good day to die and what difference does it make if I die middle class broke or truly destitute?—still, there wasn't all that much left.

Riding Tommy, I'd seen a tree, a huge old spreading oak, easy to climb from inside, with a branch that went over the wall. Had I seen it from the outside, I never would have tried it, it would have looked too far to fall. But once I was over and once I was out there, it seemed too far to go back. Its very height would have been the reason that it had not been cut.

We drove with Susie at the wheel and Niobe and I looking up. It took awhile but we found it. It was easy to get up with the ladder, and crawling across wasn't bad, and then it was a pretty easy climb down.

I went last and hauled the ladder up behind me, so it wouldn't be seen. That was difficult and frightening. Once I almost lost my balance and fell and twice I barely missed touching the wires that would have set off the alarms.

Inga took the car. She would kill some time, then drive around to the gate and waltz in the front entrance.

It was a quarter to eight and we had about a two-hour walk. Thank God, Stowe didn't have dogs. I think once upon a time he did, but there had been a stallion who was spooked by dogs or a dog that bit a horse right on his delicate ankle or something like that and now Stowe relied on technology and men.

We bushwhacked for a while. It was strange and even frightening in the dark. I mean in and of itself, irrespective of the circumstance. But in about twenty minutes we came across a riding path.

It got darker and lighter as the clouds sailed, blocking the moon, and then getting out of its way. When it was too dark to see ahead or even down to our feet, we discovered that we could navigate by looking straight up because the sky above the path was always lighter than the dark beneath the trees.

At about nine-twenty we started getting glimpses—twinkles really—of light, coming from the house, the barns, and the stables. We went on, another five minutes or so and then we were out of the woods. There were still trees to the right of us, but on our left side there was a rail fence and past the fence there was a meadow where the horses could run and there were three great trees in that meadow, standing proud and alone. Allowed to flourish without competition, they had each grown wide, hugely wide, and symmetrical as well. Beyond those trees, up a long, gentle slope, Stowe's house stood waiting. The stables and barns were more or less straight ahead.

We had decided that it was unlikely that we would be able to creep past the working parts of the farm, across the lawns, up to the house, and then into the house without once being seen. It seemed that our best chance was Niobe's idea, to act as if we had arrived at some earlier hour, quite openly and by invitation, and we were now guests of the owner, casually enjoying a postprandial stroll.

We had leaves in our hair, twigs on our clothes, and in general we looked like we'd just climbed trees and bushwhacked through the woods. The sort of guests Alan Stowe had didn't do those sorts of things.

We had to clean ourselves up. We turned around and went back into the woods where we could use a flashlight and keep it shielded. The women brushed each other off and helped each other with their makeup. Then they started on me and with great awkwardness and great reluctance, I put on a wig, a blouse, and a brassiere and stuffed the brassiere with socks to make fake breasts. Over that, I put on a baggy jacket thing, like a woman concerned with her weight, to hide the facts that I was full at the waist and insufficiently wide at the hips. I also used a stick and walked with a limp to disguise the fact that I did not walk at all like a woman.

When we were all satisfied with our appearance we strolled up the lane arm in arm, Niobe with Susie like sisters and me, some older, dowdier dame. We chatted about the moonlight and how sweet the air was at night, we talked of horses and racing and said they were a great delight. Then from out of the barns and darkness, like a ghost from out of the past, there stepped the same security guard who had seen me when I'd been there last. "Hello. How are you, Billy?" Niobe said with a smile. "We've been out for a stroll in the evening, we must have walked more than a mile."

"Mrs. Morgan, how good to see you. Haven't seen you for a while." He practically tipped his hat and he returned her smile.

"This is my good friend Susan," Niobe said. "The wife of Senator Brill."

"It's so good to be in the country," Susie said. "I love to get away from the Hill."

"And very nice to meet you," Bill very politely said.

Niobe introduced me as her Aunt Cecelia and I mumbled and nodded my head.

"She twisted her ankle," Niobe said, "so I think we'll head back up inside."

"I could fetch you one of the golf carts," Bill offered, "if she would rather ride."

"That's so kind of you, Bill," said Niobe. "But it's best that she walk it off."

"I think that's right," said Susie.

And good old Bill said, "Of course, of course."

So they strolled, and I limped, on past, and we went up the hill, the colonel's lady, Aunt Cecelia, and the wife of Senator Brill.

Chapter
SIXTY-NINE

"YOU LOOK OLD," Alan said to Inga, sounding more surprised than he should have.

"Of course I do," Inga said. "And you look like death."

"Everyone tells me I look twenty years younger than my actual age."

"Money makes people into liars."

"Money is the greatest force for good that there has ever been on this planet," Alan said. "The invisible hand, each man pursues his own profit and out of that comes the greater good."

"You were always a fool. Now you are a doddering old fool."

"I was in love with you."

"Nonsense. You wanted me like you wanted some pretty piece of woodland, so you could tear it down and make something ugly out of it."

"Well, well, time did it anyway."

"Of course it did," Inga said, with her head held

up. "You think I am ashamed because I have lines on my face, I have lines and sags all over, like you. There is no shame in that, except in America."

"I was in love with you and you were in love with me."

"Pah, such foolishness."

"Why won't you admit it?"

"Because it is false. I do not admit to false things."

"That night we had, you enjoyed it. More than enjoyed it. You would have come back for more. You would have left him for me."

"Evil," she said, dismissively. "You are an evil man."

"You could have changed that."

"Nothing could have changed that."

"I would have been a better man with you."

"What you did was blackmail. What I did was betrayal. It stained me then and forever."

"You did it to help him."

"I did it because I was a fool and young and I thought I was invulnerable, but I was not. I was old enough to be mortal, to be damaged."

"Your husband was weak and he killed himself and that's not your fault and it's not mine. By killing himself he not only took his own life, he ruined what we had. You would have come to me, come to me freely in the end."

"You are surrounded by money and money tells you lies and you don't know what the truth is now or probably forever."

"You cried out for more. Yes, you did. 'More, more, more.'"

Inga turned on her heel and began to walk out.

"Where are you going?" Alan called after her. "Don't run away. Forty-two years I waited for this. You can't run away."

"I am just going to get some fresh air," Inga said. "I need to breathe fresh air and then I will come back."

"You better come back."

"Why is that?" she asked him, pausing.

"I've made you one of my heirs."

"Of course you have."

"Ten million dollars. How about that?"

She walked away, toward the back of the house. "There's a door here that goes outside?"

"Yes," he said, and he followed along behind her.

When she got to the door, he said, "Stop."

"Why?"

"There's an alarm," he said. "I have to put in the code. Otherwise they'll come with guns."

"So do it," she said. "I need some air. So do you. You see how stupid this is. You are rich, so you have alarms, and what do they do? They lock you in. I have a little house, you probably think it is an insignificant, stupid little house, but for me it is enough, and I can walk in and out. My guests can walk in and out. We have the air. You have alarms."

By then he had put in the code and she pushed the door open and stepped outside.

"The reason I put you in my will," Stowe said, "is so that for the last few years of your life you can live any way you want, have anything you want, do anything . . . and then you will realize that you could have had that all along, every day for these forty-two years. You could have been rich your whole life long. I want you to know, in your insides, in your every waking moment, what you said no to."

They were on a stone patio. The house was stone and wood. And it was all quite beautiful. More beautiful than she remembered. It occurred to her that when she'd been young, she'd been so enamored of the beauty of her own body and hair and face and the bodies of her lovers and of the young people she danced with and the beauty of their movements and actions and lovemakings, that she had been less responsive to the beauty in things, in objects, in structures, even in the land and in nature.

The patio had been here. In fact, they'd come out on the patio and . . . and they had danced . . . and they had fucked, too. The shame of it. The disgust of it. Though, he was right, she had enjoyed it then. Enjoyed it inordinately. He hadn't been a particularly good lover as those things are generally rated, but he had been vigorous and ravenous, too, as if he hadn't eaten at the table of love in a terribly long time, and her ego had taken his extravagant greed as a personal compliment and her ego had been flattered and pleased.

Now she saw, the patio was really quite beautiful.

"Lovely, isn't it?" he said, wanting some admission of how well he lived.

She shrugged, denying him the satisfaction. "Where's the library?" she asked. He pointed at the windows above them, one floor up from where they stood. "And your famous stables?" she asked.

Alan pointed down the slope. She could see the lights below. Ah, that's where David and Niobe and Susan would be coming from. Were her eyes playing tricks? Did she see people coming, walking up the hill?

"You can show me the library," she said, turning back toward the house. He was going to stand by the door and wait for her to pass, as good manners dictated. "Go on, go on," she said, ushering him in, being sure she went second and pulling the door not quite shut behind her. When she was inside, she took his arm, surprising him, distracting him, leading him from the unlocked door. "Tell me, why a library?"

"That's the record," he said. "That's how things are remembered. I *will* be remembered," like he was arguing with her about it, like he was swearing an oath.

Chapter
SEVENTY

WE SAW THEM. Inga and Stowe on the patio. Below the window I had jumped out of, just six days ago. It looked to have been perfectly repaired.

We did our best to stay casual and natural, hiding in plain sight.

A few minutes later, the curtain on the library window was pushed aside and we could see that the lights were on and Inga peered out the window, staring out at the night. She made a gesture.

"What's that?"

"It looks like she's pointing."

"Yeah, it docs, doesn't it."

"Downstairs."

"Yeah."

"You think she managed to leave the door open?"

"Maybe, we have to check it out. That's the library she's in now," I said to Susie.

"So we have to get in there and she has to get Stowe out of there."

"Yeah."

"Then we have to find the documents and get back out with them."

"That's the idea."

"I don't think we're gonna make it," Susie said.

"But the fate of the nation depends on it," I said.

Susie laughed, but softly, controlling her usual bray.

"It does," Niobe said, quite seriously. Not that she was wrong.

We got in through the open patio door. It seemed to me better luck than we deserved. But nonetheless we took it. Then we made our way up the back stairs.

We made it through the house without being seen and went to the living room, which was next to the library. The big screen on which Stowe's guests had watched Gus Scott make his critical mistake had been removed, taken back, I presumed, to the media room. But the ghosts of the event had returned. For that's who we were, we were ghoulies and haunts trying to prevent him from stealing back the gold that he'd squandered.

My wig was irritating me no end. I rarely even wear a hat and having that thing on my newly bald skull was a source of constant discomfort. Now, I crept over to the door between the living room and library and tried to look underneath and tried to listen through. The craftsmanship and quality of the materials was very high and all I could discern was there were lights on, on the other side. Which is something I already knew. And we presumed that Inga was in there with Stowe. Niobe was doing the same at the door that opened to the hall. We were also watching the clock. At ten he was supposed to have guests, which would take him, we hoped, away.

At 9:56 there was a knock on the library door. I didn't hear it, but Niobe faintly did, as sound waves traveled laterally through the wall.

We gave it a few more minutes. Which was hard. It was also hard to believe that we were right. We opened the door. I let Niobe go in first, just in case Stowe, or someone else besides Inga, was there—she might be able to talk her way out of trouble.

We all three held our breath when she swung the door open.

Chapter
SEVENTY-ONE

MCCLELLAN WAS THE last to arrive, because he was the one to be pressured and chastised and he didn't particularly want to face it, but even he was there by ten after ten.

Stowe, the host, offered drinks.

"Yes, I think I will," the justice said. "I'll have some Scotch, straight up."

Jack Morgan, whose glass had been full and was now empty, moved to the bar, indicating that he would get it for the judge.

Ed Hoagland said to McClellan, "Maybe you've had enough."

Who was he to say such a thing? Sure, he'd had a few, one after work. Or two. And he'd had a few sips in the car coming over. He thought of himself as man who held his liquor very well and he was sure that it didn't show. "What difference does it make?" McClellan said. "I'm not driving."

"You should have driven yourself," was the secretary's reply. A goddamn driver, another potential witness. But, but hopefully it would never come to that.

"You're really starting in, Ed. Back off," McClellan said. A lot of people were afraid of Hoagland. Well, he didn't have to be. He was on the Court, for life. Hoagland didn't understand what it was to have the position he had. He stepped past Morgan, who had paused when Hoagland spoke, and looked over the bottles and picked one that he liked and poured himself a generous measure into a heavy glass. "How about you?" he said to the colonel, as if to continue the point.

"Thanks, I'll have the same," Morgan said.

McClellan poured a second and noticed that Jack's eyes seemed a little bloodshot and that his face seemed a little strained. He almost wanted to say, hey, this man's drunker than me.

"Thanks," said Morgan, sounding truly grateful when the judge passed him the glass, and he immediately raised it to his lips and took a drink. He licked his lips. He wanted to speak but the things he had to say were unspeakable.

They were in Stowe's den.

Den, like a lion's den. Except the lion was old and desiccated.

"Damn it," McClellan said. "Why so glum? We should be celebrating. I think we've done it."

Jack wanted to say, we're not celebrating because I lost her. And what I've done to her . . . is unspeakable. But he could not say that, ever, anywhere. For the rest of his life. Suck it up. Live it with. Just himself.

"We haven't done anything yet," Hoagland said. No mumbling tonight. "It's not over until we shut the door. We set it up, Andy. It's up to you to close it."

"You don't understand," the justice said. "What a difficult situation this is."

"I don't care how difficult it is. Get it done."

"You don't push Supreme Court justices, Ed," McClellan said and since he was one, he was also saying, you don't push me.

"Why's that?"

"Because that's the point of it, Ed. The point of the Supreme Court is that we're supposed to be above push and pull. Appointed for life. No one to reverse us." Hoagland looked as if he was about to say something, but McClellan held up a finger to forestall him and he had the habit of judicial authority, nobody interrupts judges, judges interrupt others. "Each and every one of the nine of us believes that, each of us is invested in that. So if you push, the resistance is automatic. If you push harder, it grows greater."

Hoagland again tried to speak.

"Of course I have lobbied them all. Especially my conservative colleagues. We do lobby one another. Observing, of course, appropriate limits and courtesies. It's pretty damn obvious that if Murphy gets in she'll try to put flaming liberals on the bench, feminist, socialist, big-government types. And with Scott things are going along quite nicely and if he gets the next two appointments, well then, it would be 'our' court for almost a full generation." He didn't run down the list. They all knew it. Strike down *Roe v. Wade*. Finally get rid of Miranda. End affirmative action. Make it clear that free speech was not absolute, especially during times of war, including the war on terrorism. Put prayer back into the schools. Indeed all of American life could stand for a good dose of prayer. "We all understand what's at stake."

"To hell with theories," Hoagland said. "Let's do the numbers, Andy. How many do you have to sway?"

"Two. I need two," McClellan said.

Hoagland turned to Stowe. "Are there two justices we can lean on? Or lead on? Or whatever we have to do."

"Yes," Stowe said. "Yes . . ." he hesitated. He was fairly certain there were. His damn short-term memory was . . . unreliable . . . just today he'd gone over that. . . . Now . . . now he could remember the night with Inga with perfect vividness, like it was a movie playing on the private screening room of the smooth white inside of his skull, but he could not remember even the names of the other eight justices. She had not just danced on the patio, she had danced naked, and he could remember the shape of her breasts and color of her nipples as they had been forty-two years ago, but not, not these damn judges.

"In the library," he said. Was he speaking of Inga, who was in the library, or of the files, which were in the library? He concentrated and sorted it out. "But I have a friend waiting there for me . . ."

"A friend," McClellan said, a little drunkenly, not a lot, but a little. "Glad to see you still have it in you. A toast," he winked, "to Viagra."

"She shouldn't see us together," Hoagland said.

"No," Alan said.

"Women," Jack said. "Never trust women."

"I'll have her move."

"Send her away," Hoagland said.

"Yeah, send her away," Jack said.

"No," Stowe said, shaking his head. There was still business there, unfinished. In the cold light of day he could keep superstition away, but in the restless nights he wondered. He bought judges and land, he looted freely and plundered, yet for all of his gold, he still had grown old, for all he owned, he was still alone, and it could only be explained as curses. And that woman was here after all of these years, so he had to find out and change it. "Just give me a few minutes and then come along."

Chapter

SEVENTY-TWO

I WAS ON the computer, figuring out what we needed. Susie and Inga were going through Stowe's papers. We were, after all, trained librarians and that's what we do.

Niobe was at the door.

She didn't hear Alan approach. His feet made no sound as he shuffled along on the thick carpets in the hall, so she was surprised when the door swung open.

"Niobe?" he said when he saw her. "My dear, what are you doing here? Did Jack bring you?" By then he saw Inga and two more strange women at his papers and at his computer. He knew we didn't belong, he knew it was all wrong, and said, in a plaintive way, "Inga?"

She stood up with his files stacked thick in her hands.

He said, "You betrayed me."

"Who betrayed whom?" Inga asked him with polite precision.

"You don't belong here. I'll have you all arrested."

"No, Alan, no you won't. It's all over, Alan. We have the evidence," Niobe said. "We're going to walk out of here, with the evidence, and we're going to give it to Anne Lynn Murphy and the faithless electors will have their votes overturned . . ."

Stowe looked at me. "Do I know you?" he asked. "You look familiar." He shook his head.

Then the door swung open again.

Andrew McClellan and Jack Morgan entered the room. The judge looked drunk. The colonel had been drinking, too. He was red-eyed and weary. The two of them carried glasses of whiskey. Secretary of State Edward Hoagland came behind like their shepherd.

When Jack saw Niobe he cried out, "You!"

"Yes, it's me."

"You betrayed me," he said.

"No," she said. "You betrayed yourself, Jack. You betrayed who you used to be and you betrayed your country, and then, then you betrayed me."

Jack dropped his glass and it splashed on the floor.

He recognized Inga and said, "What's she doing here?"

"She's my friend," Alan said.

"You fool," Jack said to Stowe. "Who are you?" he barked at Susie. "And you?" he said to me, squinting at the made-up face framed by the wig as recognition slowly came. "You?" he asked, disgusted and revolted. "You," he said again, now that he was certain. He said it with a cop's contempt and with an action to match his tone. He reached around to the small of his back and drew out an automatic.

I stepped in front of Susie. No reason for her to die

if Jack started shooting. I took off the damn wig with
great relief. "Calm down, Jack," I said.

"Shut up," he barked. "I don't want to hear anything from you."

"Calm down," Hoagland said. "Calm down, Jack.
Let's figure out what's happening."

Jack stared at me and from me to Niobe. "You left
me for him?"

"I didn't get a chance to leave you," she said. "You
gave me to Parks who was going to torture and rape me
and you knew that's what he was going to do, didn't you,
because he's done it before."

"No, no, I didn't know that."

"But David and his friend, they rescued me."

"And now you're with him?" he yelled at her,
drunken and hoarse. "I want to know, I want to know. Is
it about him?"

Niobe stared at him, defying him.

"Are you with him, now?" he demanded to know.

Now she looked at me. I must have looked ridiculous with my wig in my hand, my bald head and my lipstick, my bra and sock breasts. I dropped the wig and
wiped the lipstick with the back of my hand.

"I'll tell you the truth, Jack. I promised him that when
this was over, we'd go off together and we'd see. But I told
him I would tell you first. Now I have and now I can."

She turned from him and she looked at me.

Jack looked at Hoagland and he looked at Stowe to
see if they were seeing what he was seeing, that she was
leaving the warrior to join the circus and run off with
the clown.

The look she gave me was an extraordinary thing.
I saw myself reflected in her eyes, a better man than I

would ever have dared to see if I was looking at my face alone in a mirror made of glass. To be looked at that way was to be a hero.

To be looked away from, as she had looked away from Jack, was to be stripped of rank and standing.

The way she looked at me said, See what we've done together. There's no braver or better man than you. They underestimated you. And I did, too. I'm free now, free to come to you.

And that's what she began to do. She took a step.

He yelled, "No!" and grabbed her.

She spun around and faced him. She said, "Yes," in defiance and in his face.

He had walked in the room a hero. Now he was in disgrace. He was the one who had blown it. Those were the facts of the case. He'd brought Niobe in and he failed to get me out. Stowe and Hoagland would never want him again, but there was worse to come. This would never be seen, he understood now, as he had seen it, as a patriot's act. He would be sliced and diced and slandered by a prosecutor's recitation of fact upon remorseless fact. He would be damned for a fool and a traitor and no one would want him back.

He looked to his wife who once loved and adored him and saw the reflection in her eyes of what he made himself into. If he'd employed Parks, he was Parks. If he'd sanctioned the torture and rape of women, then he, too, was a sadist and rapist. He wanted to explain, but there was no explanation. What was true, to her, was implacably and remorselessly true.

"How? Why?" he cried. First he turned white like smoke, then he flushed from his neck on up, and you could see the blood pumping from deep inside. He blamed her and he blamed himself and he didn't know, any longer, which was which. In one continuous set of motions he flicked the safety off and he chambered a round and held it pointing at her.

"No," he shouted.

"Yes," she said once again and he knew she would never back down.

I said, "No, no, don't do it."

So did Hoagland, I think. Susie cried out, too, and her hand clutched my shoulder.

Jack fired three times. Niobe was hit, then spun, then she was hit again and then she fell. Blood spurted from the holes, blood drenched her clothes. He shot her again, before I could reach her, shot her where she fell on the floor.

I held her in my arms so I didn't see it when he backed into the corner, put the gun in his mouth, and fired just once more.

Chapter
SEVENTY-THREE

NOW IT IS up to the courts to decide.

The police came. As was inevitable with a murder-suicide.

Susie and I were arrested for breaking and entering and attempted burglary, in addition to the charges already outstanding against me.

Inga was not charged as she was there by invitation. And what had she done? Sort documents stored in a library? Also, I think Stowe had some feelings toward her, a mix of love and fear and a sense that he still owed her some sort of reparations.

The three of us—the librarians—insisted that the police take the documents we were after into evidence. That if we were being charged with attempted burglary, the goods we were attempting to burgle needed to be in evidence. Alan Stowe, the richest man in the state, and the secretary of state argued against it, citing privacy rights and property rights and that they could have the cops' jobs if they were so inclined. There was a Supreme Court justice standing there and they demanded that he advise the police, as the ultimate authority on American law, that they could not do so. McClellan was drunk and he was shocked and he knew he was in over his head.

I was not about to let Niobe have died in vain if I could help it. At that point, I committed the last bold and outrageous action I had in me. I blackmailed him. "Andy," I called out from behind the cop who was keeping me sequestered in the corner. "I'm the librarian. I've seen what's in Alan's papers."

"What? What?"

"Tell them to let me talk to you."

"Officer, officer, let me talk to this man," he said, shoving Hoagland's hand off when the Gray Man tried to keep him from coming to me.

He came close to me and leaned in and I whispered to him what it was that Alan had on him and I said, "Advise the police they can take the papers, that they must take the papers, as evidence. By the way, they don't implicate you, not at all."

"Really?"

"I guarantee it," I said. "What it does is connect Stowe to the faithless electors in Iowa and to Morgan and the bombings."

He was stuck between two threats of exposure, mine and Stowe's. Stowe didn't need to speak his; his was understood and permanently in place. You could see the stress shake the man, like quick changes in the wind hitting a sailing vessel. Eventually he said, with an incomprehensibility worthy of Hoagland's famous mumblings, "This is, matter of police judgment . . . local . . . not the sort of thing . . . until it's been adjudicated . . ."

and put the weight back on the police, which was as good as I thought I could get out of him and I let it go.

The police did take the papers.

Gary J. Hackney took my call and has taken the case pro bono. He thinks it's fascinating.

I have a job, roots in the community, never been arrested, and so forth. Susie's credentials are even more reputable than mine. Gary got us out on our own recognizance. We are awaiting trial.

The one thing we clearly did achieve was to stop the Supreme Court from stepping in immediately and immediately certifying that the votes of the faithless electors would be allowed to stand.

Also it is anticipated that Justice McClellan will recuse himself from most of the proceedings, since he is a witness, a participant, and a party to many of the suits and trials that are currently under way and those that are expected to commence shortly. He may not. A certain shamelessness has entered that Court in recent years.

What will the ultimate outcome be?

That depends. On how hard Anne Lynn Murphy fights. On how good her lawyers are and how good Scott's lawyers are. On what the courts do. Will they permit into evidence the papers that were taken when Susie and I were arrested? Will those papers become public?

If they become public, will the mainstream media make the effort to read them and connect the dots and, having understood them, will they decide to make a story out of them, or leave them to dissipate in the mist, even do their bit to obscure the truth that they imply, as they did, for example, with the vote count stories in the previous election.

It depends on the people as well. Will they just want to get it over within twenty-six minutes, solved like the conflict in a sitcom? Or will they demand to get the facts clearly and in detail and sort the wheat from the chaff and the flash and the trash?

It depends on you. Sorry about that. But it does.

The story I will tell in court, to the degree that I get to tell my story in court, will not be this one. It will be the one that Gary J. Hackney guides me to. It will be limited to what I have firsthand knowledge of, what is relevant to the case, what must be kept out as a matter of national security, what the prosecution contests, and what the judge permits.

So why have I written this? I can't show it if it's going to contradict or undermine my case.

There are a number of reasons. First, and simplest, is because I am a librarian. I live for records and documents.

For Niobe. There are women who turn men into heroes. Turn people into heroes. It's crazy. I've never met it before in my life. My father and mother made me feel like I had to live up to something, but not like that. The closest thing to it is that stirring you get when you're a kid and you read something like "Invictus" . . .

Out of the night that covers me,
Black as the Pit from pole to pole,
I thank whatever gods may be
For my unconquerable soul.

In the fell clutch of circumstance
I have not winced nor cried aloud.
Under the bludgeonings of chance
My head is bloody, but unbowed. . . .

It matters not how strait the gate,
How charged with punishments the scroll,
I am the master of my fate:
I am the captain of my soul.

. . . or stare up at the flag at Gettysburg on a school field trip and recite the Pledge of Allegiance surrounded by those who "gave the last full measure of devotion." She was someone who could draw you into her cause and let you know this is what she expected of you and you'd want to do it just so that you could live up to her vision.

And for myself. This time, this time, I was not just the keeper of the flame.

About
LARRY BEINHART

Larry Beinhart is the author of *American Hero*, which became the critically acclaimed film *Wag the Dog*. He has won an Edgar, a Gold Dagger, a Gold Medal at the Virgin Islands International Film Festival, and a couple of local Emmys in Miami. He was a Fulbright recipient of the the Raymond Chandler Award. His other books include *No One Rides for Free, You Get What You Pay For,* and *Foreign Exchange*. His *How to Write a Mystery* has been called the best genre specific book on writing there is and he has also written screenplays, short stories, journalism, and worked in commercial film production and as a political consultant. He's been a motion picture grip and a gaffer and he's taught skiing in upstate New York, in Killington, Vermont, and in Les Trois Vallees, France. Sometimes he yearns for legitimate employment. He has a wife and two children and they're all very interesting people. If you want to see him, he is the host of a homemade (public access, zero budget) television show now syndicated on Free Speech TV. If you like the book and want to tell him so, his email is beinhart@earthlink.net.